Beauty for Ashes

Also by Win Blevins

Stone Song
The Rock Child
RavenShadow
So Wild a Dream

Beauty for Ashes

WIN BLEVINS

A Tom Doherty Associates Book

New York

BEAUTY FOR ASHES

This book is printed on acid-free paper.

Map by Mark Stein Studios

A Forge Book
Published by Tom Doherty Associates, LLC
175 Fifth Avenue
New York, NY 10010

www.tor.com

Forge® is a registered trademark of Tom Doherty Associates, LLC.

Library of Congress Cataloging-in-Publication Data

Blevins, Winfred.
    Beauty for ashes / Win Blevins.—1st ed.
        p.   cm.
    Sequel to: So wild a dream.
    ISBN 0-765-30574-7 (acid-free paper)
    EAN 978-0765-30574-9
    1. Trappers—Fiction.   2. Indian captivities—Fiction.   3. Rocky   Mountains—Fiction.
4. Mountain life—Fiction.   5. Crow women—Fiction.   6. Fur trade—Fiction.   I. Title.

    PS3552.L45B43   2004
    813'.54—dc22

                                                                                        2004047160

First Edition: October 2004

Printed in the United States of America

0   9   8   7   6   5   4   3   2   1

This book is for Meredith—
wife, partner, friend, all.

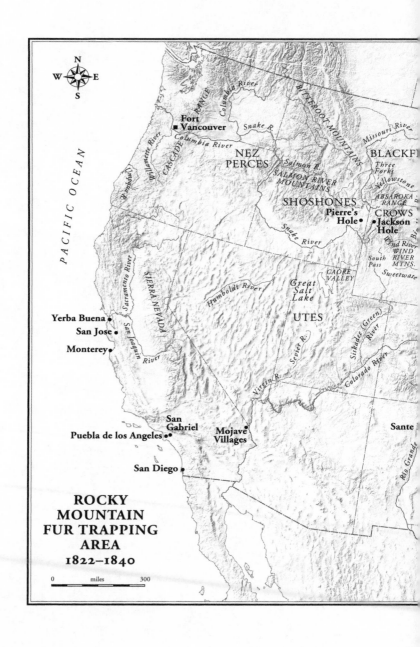

ROCKY
MOUNTAIN
FUR TRAPPING
AREA
1822–1840

0   miles   300

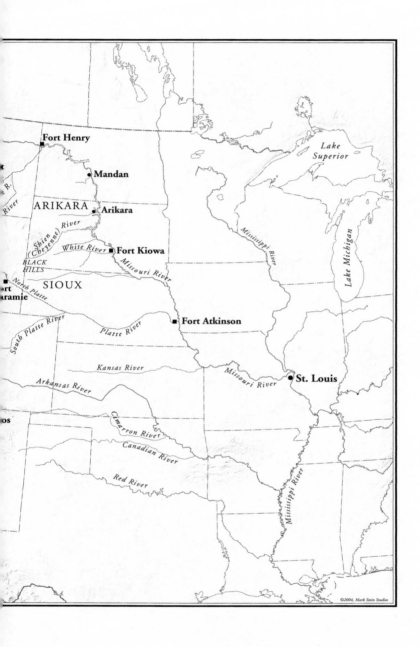

Fort Henry

Mandan

ARIKARA • Arikara

Shien (Cheyenne) River

White River • Fort Kiowa

BLACK HILLS

North Platte

SIOUX

ort aramie

South Platte River

Platte River

Fort Atkinson

Kansas River

Arkansas River

Cimarron River

Canadian River

Red River

Lake Superior

Mississippi River

Lake Michigan

Missouri River

Missouri River • St. Louis

Mississippi River

©2004, Mark Stein Studios

The spirit of the Lord . . . hath sent me to bind up the broken-hearted . . . to comfort all that mourn . . . to give unto them beauty for ashes, the oil of joy for mourning, the garment of praise for the spirit of heaviness.

—Isaiah 61:1–3

Part One

STALKING LOVE

Chapter One

SAM PICTURED HIMSELF as a hollow bone, stripped of the marrow that made him alive.

A hollow man notices little. He barely registered his fellow passengers, the captain, and crew. He barely knew the name of the steamboat, or the ports they stopped in, Cincinnati, Louisville, Evansville . . .

He did feel the force of the current, the urge of the river, westward, westward, down the Ohio River. As much as he could experience any emotion, he was glad.

At night he dreamt of emptiness. He slept outside on the bow of the steamer, wrapped in the moon's misty light and curled up with his pet coyote. Sometimes he dreamt that he was a feather, drifting on the wind alone. He had heard Crow men, his friends, make a piping music with the hollow bone from the wing of an eagle. But Sam's flight made no music. The air passed through him, sterile, and no song filled his emptiness.

For the past two years he had wandered as a beaver hunter through the Rocky Mountains and the huge plains that stretched from them to the Missouri River. Two weeks ago he had started home, drawn by a force he could not name. After traveling a thousand miles he found a world and a family he no longer knew. He felled his older brother with a fist. He said a hurried goodbye to his mother and his sisters, a last goodbye. In effect, he had tipped his life upside down and poured out his past, his family, his home.

Now he was empty.

It was Sam's nature to be curious, especially curious about people. Yet these days he wanted to talk only to his coyote, Coy. Why? He didn't know. He didn't always know himself.

He paid attention mostly to the motion of the currents, downriver. He didn't see the passing woodlands of Ohio, Kentucky, Indiana, Illinois, though he knew they were beautiful. He used mostly his mind's eye. He saw stretches of plain so vast they must embrace the whole world. He saw mountains rolling sensuously against a lilac sky. He tasted the water in clear mountain creeks, so cold it hurt the gullet. He saw huge herds of buffalo running across the grasslands, so thick a man could dance across an entire herd and never touch the ground. He saw friends, both trappers and Indians. He saw his best friend, Blue Medicine Horse, and the woman he loved, Meadowlark.

When he looked at his fellow passengers, and only then, he thought of what was behind him. Home, yes, maybe that was the word for it, which was closed to him now. He said the word in his mind only—homeless.

He set his feet on the bow of the steamboat, which now rode the turbulent waters of the Ohio and would soon churn up the great

Mississippi to St. Louis, the river town. There he would set off for the Rocky Mountains, alone. Home? He didn't know. He only wanted to be there, now.

Sometimes, wrapped in his blankets on the bow, he had another dream. In this dream he was not a hollow feather floating on the wind. He was a buffalo, a buffalo not of the earthly world, but of another dimension, maybe the spirit world. There something happened to him and the buffalo, something that could not happen in the ordinary world.

This realm seemed to him more real than the ordinary world, and more alive. In his dream he held his arms out toward the Spirit Buffalo, but it was always too far away, elusive, and mysterious. In the West, when he got there, he would feel the buffalo close again, and vital.

He was aware that his companions on the boat had no thought of buffalo, and certainly not Spirit Buffalo. They cared nothing about the tow-headed youth who was obviously the expedition's poorest, least-educated, least-decorous passenger. They showed distaste for the dog that hung near him. (Sam had been obliged to lie to the captain that his coyote was a common dog.) Sam overheard the captain dismissing him curtly to Mrs. Goodwill as "a backwoodsman of the roughest sort." He noticed how they avoided him.

They felt equally alien to him. He rolled into the rhythm of the waters.

AFTER THE BOAT turned up the Mississippi, closer to buffalo country, Sam saw the Spirit Buffalo more often, saw it with his inner eyes.

The Spirit Buffalo taunted him every night. Sometimes he pictured it exactly as it first came to him. On these nights he once again performed the miracle. He entered into the body of the Spirit Buffalo, knitted himself into it, mingled his blood with its blood, its heart with his own, and they breathed with one breath. Then he and the Buffalo rose as one man-beast, surveyed all, and set forth.

"Samalo." That one word sounded, though he didn't know who

spoke it. It was his own name and the name Buffalo joined. One creature—Samalo.

Some nights he got just pieces of the dream, and some nights the pieces were mad, like a painting on glass—but the glass had been dropped, the paintings turned to shards, glinting hints of a beauty that once had been, and might or might not be again.

Sam would put the painting back together—once he was in the West, once he got up the Missouri River to the country where the buffalo lived, the buffalo that were physical and fed the belly, and the Buffalo that fed the spirit.

And once he was in the West, he would make his way to the Wind River Mountains, where her village lived, and seek out Meadowlark.

Passengers embarked, passengers disembarked, and Sam spoke to few. Port after port passed. Sam learned the rhythm of his travel.

In St. Louis the clerk asked his name. Sam nearly said "Samalo," but managed to announce clearly, "Sam Morgan." The clerk informed him that General Ashley expected him to join the outfit at Fort Atkinson. Four hundred miles of country to ride alone, but that didn't bother Sam—it was to the west.

He went about his business, tied up loose ends. He visited with dear friends from his first trip to St. Louis, Abby and Grumble, and said goodbye to them with indecent haste. "When I get to the West," he kept saying to himself, "I will come alive."

Chapter Two

FORT ATKINSON WAS a damned funny place to feel like home. It was home to the U.S. Army, an organization no mountain man wanted much to do with. On the other hand, right now it was full of Sam's mountain man friends. And this spot, not far upstream from where the Platte River flowed into the Missouri, was the beginning of the West. Here was the demarcation between the upper and lower Missouri Rivers, and between the prairies to the east and the arid plains of the West. It was also, effectively, the last bit of the U.S. The wilds beyond were marked *unknown* on the maps. Sam couldn't wait to get there.

He clucked his problematic mare up to the fort. She'd been problematic, and he was tired of her, tired of pushing hard, ready to rest, and ready for some company. This wasn't a bit like when he got to Fort Atkinson a couple of months ago. Then he'd walked, come all the way from the Rocky Mountains on foot and alone, half-starved to death. Then Fort Atkinson felt like survival. Now it felt like a beginning.

Out of a sense of propriety, he checked in first with the man who owned and ran the company, General William Ashley. But Ashley gave Coy a wary look. "I have to talk to this man about horses," he said. "I'll see you later."

A cold greeting, it seemed to Sam, when you've ridden more than four hundred miles alone through dangerous country to catch up with a man at his request.

Later, though, turned out to be a very good time. Supper. Sam was chewing and jawing around a fire with his old partner Gideon Poor Boy, a French-Canadian whose father was a French Jew and mother a Cree. Chesty as a bear and friendly as a St. Bernard, Gideon was relating his adventures. He'd gone back up the Platte to raise a cache of peltries and brought them to Fort Atkinson, all to earn a few dollars for their employer the general.

"Hey, Sam."

Sam was so glad to hear this voice he jumped up and clapped Tom Fitzpatrick on the shoulder. He shook hands with another old friend behind Fitzpatrick, James Clyman.

"See your brother didn't take your scalp," said Clyman.

Sam smiled wryly. Most of the fur men probably thought it was funny to take some weeks off to go home. Probably most of them didn't have homes, or weren't welcome there. *Now I don't have a home either.* That picture jumped into his mind—his older brother Owen, head of the Morgan clan, on the end of Sam's fist.

"How you doing, Towhead?"

"Don't call me Towhead." Fitz was always joshing Sam about his white hair. "Sit down and have some coffee."

They did, and traded news of the day. New men sidled by too, green hands, some even younger than Sam. They wanted to become mountain men—Sam wondered if he looked as green a year and a half ago.

One new man sat, Jim Beckwourth he called himself. He was black. "I'm a mulatto," Beckwourth explained. "You might say I'm a confusion of black and white." He grinned ironically. "What else could I be, mother a slave, father *Sir* Jennings Beckwourth?"

That grin was fine, but Sam knew a brag when he heard one.

"Who's your friend?" asked Jim, nodding his head at Coy.

"Coyote pup. Found him when I walked down the Platte last summer. That's a big story, I'll tell you some time."

"Sam is greatly attached to his canine companion," said Clyman.

"Oh, *mi coyote*." This was Fitz. He pronounced it the Spanish way, *koy-oh-tay*.

Ashley stepped up, and the men fell quiet. The general stayed a few minutes but stood the whole time and spoke of nothing but business. "Can't get enough horses," he said. "We're leaving in a few days, with or without them."

The old hands—Sam was an old hand, though not quite twenty—eyed each other. They knew how bad it was, traveling and trapping without enough mounts. Ashley had been told, but he didn't *know*.

Later, in the full dark, when the group was down to Sam, Gideon, Beckwourth, Clyman, and Fitzpatrick, the Irishman said, "Sam, you went off quick in September. Did you hear the big story about Glass?"

Sam gave him a quizzical look. "I remember Hugh Glass from the fight at the Arickaree villages, but . . ."

"Didn't think so."

"You know you're a story yourself," said Gideon. "Walking down the Platte maybe seven hundred miles alone, coming in half-starved."

"Gideon and I are stories too," said Fitzpatrick. They'd done almost the same thing, arriving a little later. "But Glass is a story unto himself."

Several men reached for their white clay pipes, looking forward to the tale.

Stories were getting to be a big part of this Rocky Mountain fur trade, new as it was. John Colter, for example—men still told about how he ran from the Blackfeet naked, escaped from them, and made his way back to the fort. Of the men now in the mountains, Sam's captain of last year, Jedediah Smith, was a story: Diah traveled alone down the Missouri River from Henry's Fort to below the Arickaree villages, where he delivered an urgent message to General Ashley, who was coming up the river—"Bring horses, lots of them. Trapping doesn't work without horses." Then, more daringly, Diah found a land route back to Henry with an express pleading for help. This was not to mention the time he got mauled by a grizzly, was sewn up by Clyman, yet stayed cool enough to give instructions about his care.

"You remember, Glass went with Major Henry after the Arickaree fight."

"And that was fine wit' us," put in Gideon. Everyone chuckled. Glass was an ornery fellow.

"Undisciplined as always, he was going through a thicket along a creek by himself, out in front, when he ran into a grizzly. The brigade came fast when they heard Glass screaming, and a dozen rifles did away with Old Ephraim. Well, anyone could see, Glass, he was a goner. The brigade waited to give him a decent burial.

"A few minutes, then a few hours—amazing, Glass was still holding on. Every man admired his grit."

"Wagh!" exclaimed Gideon.

"Henry, though, was worried. The Arickarees were still around somewhere. The major had an obligation to keep the whole brigade safe. So he asked for volunteers to stay with Glass until he died and then bury him. Henry offered a reward for taking this risk.

"Do you remember Jim Bridger?"

"No."

"New to the mountains, young, practically a boy, like you."

"I'm not any newer than you," Sam reminded Fitz. Though Fitz was five years older, they'd come to the mountains the same year.

"True enough. Bridger, anyway, he volunteered. So did an older man named John Fitzgerald. They stayed while Henry took the trail.

"That cursed Glass, though, he just kept breathing. Bridger and Fitzgerald watched and fidgeted. One day, two, three. Why didn't Glass get down to business and die?

"Now Fitzgerald began to work on Bridger's mind, how the money wasn't enough, the risk bigger than the major figured, how they were going to die out here.

"On the fifth day Bridger caved in.

"Fitzgerald made Bridger take Glass's possibles—his rifle, his knife, his shot pouch, his flint and steel for making fire—everything needed to survive out here in this blasted wilderness. Otherwise, argued Fitzgerald, everyone would know. Know, that is, what Bridger was so ashamed to do, abandon Glass while he lived.

"Bridger hated it, but he was rattled. They took all, and away they went."

"Bastards," murmured Sam.

"But boyo, when Glass came to, he remembered. 'Henry paid Bridger and Fitzgerald to stay with me. They abandoned me. And robbed me.'

"This lit the fire in Glass's belly. Soon he was inching over to the little creek to drink, and nibbling on the chokecherries hanging nearby.

"When he felt strong enough to go after his betrayers, he headed back to Fort Kiowa, where they'd started out. But Hugh Glass couldn't walk." Fitz made a dramatic pause. "So he crawled."

"That child is some!" said Gideon.

Fitz plunged on. "He crawled down White River, his wounds bleeding every time he moved. He ate roots, berries, and the like. Once, it's told, he came on a buffalo felled by wolves, chased them off and fed on the raw meat."

"Wagh!" grunted Gideon.

"At Kiowa, instead of recuperating, he insisted on going after Fitzgerald and Bridger. He started upriver with a boat of a half-dozen men. The trip went bad. His companions got killed by Arickarees, but Hugh survived. Lads, he had grit, but he also had luck, mountain luck. And he must have been hell bent on revenge. On upriver he went, alone.

"On the last day of 1823, Hugh found the new fort on the Yellowstone. Right while the crew was celebrating drunkenly, a ghost appeared. A battered, scarred, emaciated figure. No one could believe it was Hugh Glass, believed dead for three months."

"Wagh!"

"The man most shocked by the appearance of this ghost was Jim Bridger.

"Glass went straight at his betrayer. But the fire in his belly, maybe after several months the coals had begun to cool.

"Anyhow, face to face with Bridger at last, Glass says, 'Yes, it is Glass that is before you, the man who gives you nightmares. The man you left to a cruel death on the prairie. And worse, you robbed me when I was helpless. You took my rifle, my knife, everything I might use to save myself. I swore I'd take revenge on you, and that other ass, Fitzgerald. I crawled back to the Missouri, and came this long way upriver, aiming to drink your blood.' "

Fitz's listeners held their breath.

"Glass glared at Bridger now, but his eyes lost their flame. 'I can't do it. You have nothing to fear from me. You're free. On account of your youth, I forgive you.' "

Whew! Sam felt damn glad he wasn't Jim Bridger. Bridger was trapping with Captain Weber now, somewhere in the Siskadee country. And every man he traveled with, or ever would, knew he was a fellow who'd walk out on you when things got rough.

"Still, there was that damned Fitzgerald, plenty old enough to know better. Fitzgerald had quit and had gone down to Fort Atkinson, and took Glass's rifle with him. Quick as it began to thaw, Glass headed out. When he got to the fort, he found Fitzgerald had become a soldier, and the commander told him shooting up U.S. soldiers wasn't permitted. Glass got his rifle back, turned Fitzgerald over to God and his own conscience, and headed for Santa Fe.

"Now, lads, what do you think of that?"

"Grit," said Gideon.

"Will to survive," said Sam.

"Mountain luck," said Clyman.

They regarded each other. The Irishman who left County Cavan to get away from the priests. The Virginian, the group's elder. The French-Canadian, who knew death companionably. The mulatto, young and vigorously alive.

The white-haired young man from Pennsylvania, far from home, was constantly learning, and it wasn't comfortable.

Chapter Three

SAM FELT EDGY. A cold, restless wind flicked at his face. The mare fidgeted, pawed around like she wanted to get down off this sandstone outcropping, out of the wind. Coy mewled. Sam couldn't tell what the coyote pup wanted.

Sam looked around, west, north to the hills, east. Nothing. He'd come up from the south and seen nothing. His cheeks were getting leathery from the cold. The wind brought dust to his nose, plus alkali, sage, and the musky smell of buffalo.

The alkali and sage reminded him, and he thought how glad he was to be back in the real West, where the plains began to break and jumble and lift toward the mountains, and where the buffalo lived. He decided to look a little harder for buffalo, and maybe ride a little further, on that faint hope.

The brigade was hungry. They'd left Fort Atkinson on the Missouri River on the first day of November, headed for the Rocky Mountains on faith—had to be faith, because they didn't have enough food or horses. General Ashley hoped to trade with the Pawnee Loups. Word at the fort was, these Pawnees were in an uproar. The general issued his orders anyway.

Sam did his duty—went to Ashley and told about his run-in with the Loup Pawnees three months ago, how they caught him and intended to torture him, but a good fellow named Third Wing sneaked him out of camp. Sam had to add that, in stealing his rifle back, he killed a Pawnee guard. He didn't say that the guard was the first man he ever killed. He told how the Pawnees searched the whole country for him, but he got away. How they probably still hated him.

Ashley brushed the information aside. He was a man of firm purpose. He led the way west into the plains winter, counting on the Pawnee Loups.

Now, nine days out, they were on starving times. On the second day a blizzard staggered them. On the fifth day another one blitzed them, a foot of Rocky Mountain snow.

The Pawnees were not where Ashley expected, at the Loup River. A day went by while two of the leaders, Fitzpatrick and Clyman, searched for sign of them up the tributary. They saw nothing, no Indians and no buffalo.

So some flour stirred into water was the daily ration of each of the twenty-five men. Half rations of food, or quarter, and double rations of cold and snow. In bitter weather a man needed more meat, and they had none. Which was why Sam was out here a couple of miles north of the river toward some hills, hunting.

From the breakfast fire this morning, he thought he'd seen a lone beast. The brigade had no breakfast, just the warmth of some flames and coffee. No one else could see the buffalo. Odd, how men get down at the mouth and mutter in their beards when they're cold and hungry, and say or do as little as possible.

"Hunt it if you want to," Fitzpatrick said, "and catch up tonight."

An hour later Sam couldn't tell whether he'd seen a buffalo or mistaken these two scrubby trees for one. They stood behind each other on the rim of the sandstone in the right shape, if you stood at a certain angle. Maybe his hope shaped his eyesight. At night he was dreaming about food, sumptuous banquets of beef, chicken, ham, turkey, potatoes, garden vegetables, cheeses, bread, and butter, all spread out on a table before him. Not even buffalo and elk, which he preferred.

From above Sam studied the earth of the plain. There were lots of buffalo pies and would be lots of hoofprints—this was buffalo country. But he feared he wouldn't find any that looked fresh. He spoke to Coy. "Want to go a little further? Or turn around and catch up? A little further, and maybe . . ."

A shot roared. The mare crow-hopped sideways, and Sam nearly lost his seat. Coy arched his back and bristled. *Godamighty*. Shots— Indians!

Time to cache.

The mare crow-hopped again, and this time came to a stop teetering on the rim. "Idjit," he spat at her. She gave a whicker of protest.

Damned animal. Sam wheeled her and let the critter pussy-foot down the outcropping, muttering curses at her slowness. This mare was no favorite of Sam's. He wanted a horse that felt like a partner, the way Coy did. Gideon told him, though, "Don't ever get attached to any horse, because that's ze one ze Indians will run off."

Sam kicked her to a gallop and scurried down into a brushy draw. Whew. Now he was cached. Unless they saw him, he could sit this one out right here.

An hour later Sam rode out of the draw on the south and started a wide circle to the west. *Damn, I can never believe trouble is really trouble.* "Coy, it has to be a buffalo—what else would anyone shoot at out here?"

He put some words into the coyote pup's mouth. "What if it's a brigade member who's followed to help us hunt?"

Sam answered, "What if it's a lone Indian I could take? Buffalo meat's worth a risk, isn't it?"

He wanted to get a look into the next valley to the west, where the shot sounded like it came from. He made his way up another draw. At the last of the scrawny cedars, a hundred yards short of the lip of the hill, he tied his mount and walked on with Coy. The little coyote walked quieter than Sam anyway. He crawled to the summit and looked out from behind a rock.

A fine sight! A cow lay crumpled in the middle of the little valley—

Sam's hair crinkled and his toenails curled backward.

No one was gutting her out. Which meant . . .

He jumped up and sprinted for his mare.

Just before he got to the cedars—

"*Hi-ya-ya, hi-ya-ya!*" Out of the draw came the cry and the Indian.

Sam cursed out loud. The bastard was on Sam's mare.

I'm gonna be stuck on foot a long way out.

Stuck, hell, once I'm on foot, these Indians will kill me.

He dropped to sitting, propped his father's rifle on one knee, and steadied. The riding figure bobbed up and down in front of Sam's sight. *I'll shoot the damn mare*, he thought with satisfaction. He held on the mare's big hindquarters and fired.

The Indian pitched to the ground roaring. The mare skittered off. *Why doesn't she act hurt?*

Sam drew his pistol and ran forward.

The man scurried on hands and knees for his bow.

Sam caught up and held his pistol two-handed, straight at the bastard's face. The fellow was young, younger even than Sam's nineteen.

From hands and knees the Indian threw a sneer of hatred at him and lunged forward with a knife.

Coy skittered away, barking.

Sam shot the Indian in the thigh.

First he reloaded the rifle, which he called The Celt, as fast as he could. This Indian had no rifle. Which meant he had a partner close by, the shooter. Sam looked around carefully.

Coy snapped and snapped, keeping the Indian busy. The Indian swiped at Coy with the knife. Sam jumped forward and clubbed the man with the butt of his pistol. He sagged to the ground.

Sam breathed relief, and dragged him into the cedars. *Where's your damn partner?*

As the Indian regained consciousness, Sam checked him over. Pawnee, from the moccasins. Then he saw the blood on back of one leg. *Hell, I shot you in the butt.* He grinned.

Sound of hoofs. Along the ridge of the hill, in the distance, a rider.

Sam's mare was standing in the open twenty yards away, grazing.

Coy ran at the mare and herded her back to the cedars. Sam reloaded the pistol.

The wounded man looked daggers at Sam again.

Sam signed to him, 'I come in friendship. I do not want to hurt you or your friend. I do not want your buffalo.' Not that Sam had a chance at the meat with Pawnees around. 'Signal your friend to get off his horse and I won't shoot you or him.'

The rider had stopped on top of the hill. Certainly he had seen the saddled mare. The rider had the high ground, but Sam had the cover.

'Signal him to come closer,' Sam signed.

The Indian spat at Sam.

Sam leapt on him and pricked the bastard's throat with the tip of his butcher knife. "Now," he shouted in English, though the Pawnee couldn't understand him.

Sam backed away, knife held forward, and signed awkwardly, 'Tell him what I said now!'

The Indian spat at him. Coy bit the Indian on the forearm, and the man howled. He tried to get to his knees.

From six feet Sam lifted his pistol and shot the man's ear off.

The Indian screamed.

The rider galloped down the hill.

Sam jumped behind his hostage, lifted him, and catapulted him into a low cedar branch. The man crumpled across the branch.

The rider charged.

Sam lifted The Celt and shot the pony out from under him.

The rider hurtled across the bunch grass, tumbling over and over.

Sam reloaded The Celt.

The rider didn't move.

Sam reloaded the pistol.

The rider got to his feet woozily.

Sam walked into the clear. Coy growled and kept the wounded Indian in the tree.

The rider sank to one knee.

Sam yelled, *"Hau!"* Most Indians would understand the greeting.

The rider looked at him dizzily.

Sam signed, 'I do not want to kill you or your friend. Come closer.'

The rider sank into the grass.

Sam wondered how many Pawnees were around. If the young men had come out hunting, there could be two or a dozen.

He didn't intend to wait around to find out. He stepped into the cedars and took the mare's reins. "At least you don't run off," he said to her. He was half tempted to take an Indian pony instead.

Leading the mare, he walked toward the rider. Behind, he could hear Coy growling at the draped man. Sam picked up the dizzy one's rifle, an old fusil. "Spoils of war," he said with a grin.

He swung up on the mare and clucked at Coy. "Let's go. It's a hell of a ride to camp."

Chapter Four

"BREAKFAST," SAID GIDEON in Frenchy style, "the best idea ze general has yet."

Sam and Beckwourth grinned around hump ribs. Sam was enjoying two of his favorite smells, broiled buffalo and burning sagebrush. It was enough to make him forget the campfire smoke that sometimes blew into his eyes.

"I thought white folks never went hungry," said Beckwourth.

"Even I look like a cub," said Gideon, who definitely was bear-sized.

Sam looked at Beckwourth with a half smile. Compared with Gideon and Sam, who'd marched down this same river last summer, eating only occasionally, the mulatto didn't know anything about hunger. And Gideon had a lot more dramatic hunger stories to tell, like the time he ate grasshoppers for a week.

Sam threw his half-gnawed rib to Coy. The coyote had learned to wait patiently during meals, knowing Sam would feed him.

"If your pup stay wit' us, Towhead," said Gideon mildly, "he maybe starve to death."

Sam frowned at the word "towhead."

"Hell," put in Beckwourth, "when we was starvin', he was feeding on deer mice and other little critters. He'll live long enough to chew our bones."

They might have chuckled if they weren't busy feeding.

After a minute Sam said, "I told you to stop that Towhead bull."

"Oh, I forget," said Gideon with a big smile.

The brigade was done missing breakfasts, at least for a while. Maybe they were done with dying horses, too, and eating horseflesh.

Three weeks out from Fort Atkinson the weather turned mild. One day they stumbled into a place on the river that was full of buffalo to hunt. Rushes lined the river, good feed for the gaunt horses. Paradise, Sam learned, depended on how painful your hell had been. The men spent several days gorging themselves.

Further up river they came upon the Grand Pawnees, who were headed south to warmer climates. At least these Pawnees weren't Sam's personal enemies. He wondered whether the two young men he'd wounded back yonder were Grand or Loup Pawnees. The Grands didn't say anything about the incident.

'Stop here,' the Indians signed, 'or you will all die. On toward the mountains there's not enough wood for fires ahead, and not enough feed for the horses.'

Ashley ignored them and followed the westward compass in his mind.

Finally, yesterday they came on the Pawnee Loups. That's why Sam was nervous at breakfast this morning.

Right then Ashley strode up, with Fitzpatrick and Clyman in file behind him. "Let's go, Sam. We need to palaver with the Loups."

Sam looked wildly at Ashley. "These are the ones . . ."

"Who are out for your hair, I know. Let's go."

Since Sam had learned a good deal of Crow tongue last winter, and was quick and accurate with sign talk, the general had decided he had an aptitude for languages and appointed him interpreter.

The argument was short, its conclusion predetermined.

Beckwourth and Gideon asked to go along, and Ashley agreed. As they rode out, he called to Zacharias Ham, "No Indians in camp, for any reason."

They rode. Frosty horse breath swirled around Sam's head. He began to think of what these Pawnees had once planned for him. The slowest possible torture until he died.

"Sam, stop maundering."

Sam threw Ashley a look. *You and your big words. You and your fancy ideas. You and your fixed notions.*

"You don't hesitate with Indians, you don't mollycoddle, you put everything right in front and show you're not afraid."

But what if I am?

Six horses jingle-jangled. Sam was taking the fusil, just in case.

"Get your head clear for your job," said Ashley. "Responsibility for the outcome is mine."

Sam bit his tongue and turned his head away. *Yeah, if I lose my scalp, you'll admit it was your fault.*

THERE WAS RAVEN, who still gave Sam nightmares. The chief had come to the edge of the village to greet the beaver men with the traditional sign for welcome. He was surrounded by Big Bellies. Third Wing wasn't there.

Raven was a short, chunky man with very dark skin, huge shoulders, and a beak nose. His head even seemed to have wings, for the hair pulled back above his ears flashed silver, like a raven's wings struck by light. His eyes glittered with a blackness that brought up the word "evil."

Sam gave Raven the sign of friendship.

The trappers dismounted and left Beckwourth with the mounts.

Ashley treats Jim like a servant, thought Sam.

"Holler if there's trouble," Ashley told Beckwourth.

And Jim pretends not to notice.

"I'll stay wit' him," said Gideon.

The big mulatto nodded. The whites had quickly learned that the Indians interpreted his black skin as a sign of being warlike all the time. Which was handy.

"Not that there'll be anything you can do except holler," muttered Sam.

Ashley scalded him with a look, and Sam shut his mouth.

The other four beaver men walked toward the council lodge with Raven, Sam and Ashley in front, Fitzpatrick and Clyman behind. No one needed to tell these old hands to keep their wits about them. The council lodge, at least, would be safe.

The ceremonial pipe seemed to last forever, but there was no rushing it. The smoke wafting toward the top hole in the tipi, Sam understood, declared everyone's friendly intentions. Sam would have felt more friendly had he not noticed a nasty glint of recognition in Raven's eyes.

When it was over, Sam made his way impatiently through the necessaries, translating into English as he signed. He greeted the respected Raven once more. The beaver men were passing through the country on the way to the mountains, and would like to make a gesture of thanks to the Pawnee people. Clyman stuck out the beautiful blanket in chief's blue he carried and opened it to reveal half a dozen big twists of tobacco.

Raven nodded his approval. Several of the Big Bellies smiled.

Sam put the fusil next to the blanket. He signed, 'I took this rifle from a young Pawnee who attacked me. I hope he and his friend got back to the village safely. I want him to have his rifle.'

Raven looked at the Big Bellies. One of them nodded yes, said one word, and took the fusil.

'Badger's rifle,' signed Raven. Then he added with an enigmatic smile, 'You again.'

Ashley gave Sam a nod of approval. Sam knew his policy, Be straight up front with Indians.

'The beaver hunters would also like to trade with their friends the Pawnees,' Sam signed. 'We want horses and dried meat, and offer blankets, hatchets, knives, and cooking utensils in return.'

'Whiskey?' asked Raven with his fingers.

'And whiskey as a gift of friendship,' confirmed Sam. Last night they'd cached all the kegs of whiskey but two, which they would share with the Pawnees. It would lubricate the trading.

Raven talked with the Big Bellies in Pawnee. After a while he said, 'Tomorrow we move camp to the forks of the river, where we stay for the winter. Come there and we will trade with you.'

Ashley looked at Fitzpatrick. "Forks of the Platte are a couple of days upstream. Fine camping place, plenty of feed."

"Tell him," Ashley said to Sam, "we will be glad to join him at the forks." Sam did.

Raven nodded his acceptance, and Sam could see he was ready to rise and close the meeting.

Impetuously, Sam signed, 'Where is Third Wing?'

It was a risk. Changes that Sam didn't like registered in Raven's eyes. He glared at Sam.

'A foolish young white man with white hair,' Raven signed, staring blackly at Sam, 'was captured by my young men at the time when berries get ripe. Third Wing, even more foolishly, helped him escape. Since then he has not been well.'

'I want to see him.'

Lightning flashed in Raven's eyes.

Ashley butted in. "Tell him you regret what happened last summer. You regret killing that sentry. It was all a misunderstanding. You had to get your rifle back or die."

Sam signed that much. Raven paid close attention, but did not look mollified.

Ashley said, "Remind him you let his young warriors live when most men would have killed them."

Sam signed it. Letting those Indians live, in fact, had been controversial among his own friends.

Now Fitzpatrick jumped in with words to Ashley. "Have Sam tell Raven that Sam is important to you. You will give tobacco to the family of the sentry killed, and blankets, and a horse to express your sorrow at their loss."

Ashley nodded to Sam, and Sam signed it.

Raven said with his fingers, 'I cannot speak for the family. You must talk to them.'

Sam knew that meant it would be all right. He ventured again, 'May I see Third Wing?'

Raven stared at Sam, then signed, 'When you have spoken to the family of the fine young man Two Stones, Third Wing maybe will come to your camp.'

Sam and Fitz glanced at each other. "The line we're walking with these Pawnees is narrow," said Fitz, "and would be easy to fall off."

TWO STONES' FATHER and mother, waiting in front of their lodge, wore their mourning on the outside. The father had chopped off his hair crudely, and the mother bore scars on her forearms where she had hacked herself in her grief. They said nothing but seemed pleased by the gifts. Sam guessed that the kind and amount of the gifts meant nothing to them, but the fact of Ashley making this gesture did. They seemed willing enough for Sam to stay on the planet.

But the teenage brother half-hid inside the tipi, his face bristling with hatred. Sam knew he better check his back trail against that one.

The parents never did speak, which gave Sam the willies. Ashley handed over the gifts and ended things.

On the way out of the village Ashley said unnecessarily, "Don't get to feeling complacent, not for an instant."

No chance, thought Sam.

*   *   *

BACK AT CAMP the men were gathered around fires for a noon meal. Food and company were Sam's great yearnings. On his long walk from the Sweetwater River to Fort Atkinson, nearly three months alone, he'd missed people as much as food.

Ashley's twenty-five beaver hunters grouped themselves loosely into units of six or seven around the four leaders, the general, Fitzpatrick, Clyman, and Ham. And they ate heartily when the eating was good—next week might be starving times. Sam had lost thirty pounds on his long walk alone, regained it, and lost fifteen more on the way up the river this month. Feast or famine, for sure. Men wandered from fire to fire as the spirit moved them. Some didn't like Coy, claiming a coyote would sooner or later turn vicious, and they stayed away from the fire where Sam and Coy usually sat, Fitzpatrick's.

Through this meal Sam barely noticed the buffalo meat. He was thinking about Two Stones and his parents. Odd how knowing a name made the killing feel different. Back then Two Stones was just an obstacle between Sam and his rifle, The Celt, his only hope for survival on the plains. The creeping approach and swift knife to the throat had been a primitive exultation.

Now Sam's head jumped with pictures of blood spurting between his own hands, vital life bursting out, ended forever. Sometimes his mind's eye rotated the faces of Two Stones' father and mother, bleak and forlorn. The holes in their hearts had been ripped by Sam's hands.

"Black life we live, no?" Gideon usually saw Sam's moods, in the way of friends.

"Yeah. Black."

They were still eating, Beckwourth too, after the other men had finished. "You people use 'black' like it means evil, forces of darkness," said Jim. "I don't care for that."

Sam cocked an eyebrow at his friend. Beckwourth concentrated on the buffalo meat on the tip of his knife. All three were quiet for a moment, preoccupied.

"What you think it means," Beckwourth asked, "when Raven says he's friendly and wants to trade?"

"Nothing," said a voice behind them. It was Tom Fitzpatrick. He squatted and sliced a hunk off the spitted buffalo roast above the fire.

"Nothing?" This was Beckwourth.

"The Arickarees traded with us and then attacked us," Fitz said. Sam and Gideon had been there.

Beckwourth looked at Sam.

"Nothing," Sam agreed.

"Treacherous bastard." Beckwourth pushed the words out over the meat in his mouth.

"I don't think so," said Sam.

Everyone looked at Sam. Raven had tried to torture and kill him.

"I agree," said Gideon.

Sam threw Coy a rib with some meat on it. "Looks to me like every tribe has pretty much the same name for themselves—the people, the true people, something like that. And pretty much the same name for everybody else—others, outsiders, enemies. That's how the tribes see the whole world. To Raven there are Pawnees, who are like him, and there's everybody else. His job is to protect the good people, his, against everything and everybody who's not Pawnee."

"So he don't hate us while he kills us?" Beckwourth gave an ironic grin.

"No," said Sam. "He doesn't hate us, period. Maybe he hates the Sioux and the Cheyennes—hostility there goes back generations. But he doesn't hate anybody else. We're just the others. To him we don't count."

"All Indians be like zis," put in Gideon.

Sam looked at his friends. Funny conversation this was, between a Pennsylvania backwoodsman like himself, an Irishman, a colored man, and a French-Canadian whose father was a Jew and mother an Indian.

Fitz pitched in. "Everybody's like this. Your father's people do it too. They're Jews and everyone else is a gentile."

Gideon shrugged. "My mother's people, the Crees, ze same."

"You white people are that way to us colored," said Beckwourth.

Sam looked into his friend's face. Sometimes he couldn't tell Jim's moods.

Sam said, "It's crazy. Look here. I like Hannibal." They'd all heard about the combination Delaware Indian and classical scholar more than once. "I like the Shawnees I've known, and despise General Harrison, who destroyed them for no reason. I love Meadowlark, a Crow, and like her brother. I didn't hate Two Stones, the Pawnee I killed, nor the ones I let go. But I'm damn mad at the Arickarees—they killed my friends." He looked Beckwourth candidly in the face. "I would fight for you against any white man, or red man, or black man." He turned his eyes to Gideon. "You too."

Said Fitz, "Next you'll be wanting us to love prairie wolves." He grinned and threw Coy his bone, too.

"Mine's different."

"He probably thinks you're not bad either, *mi coyote*," teased Fitz. "For a two-legged."

"Sometimes we have to kill," said Sam, "sometimes we choose to kill." His head still hurt with the memory of Two Stones.

"Hmpf," grunted Beckwourth loudly. "My pappy taught me something about that. Everything that lives, it kills and is killed."

"I rode to St. Louis on the steamboat with a scientific Frenchman," said Fitz. "He studies plants that grow in water. He had a microscope, showed me some Mississippi River water in it. Water's full of living creatures, little fellas, way too small to see with the naked eye. Every time you take a drink you kill a hundred or a thousand of them."

"Every time I take a drink," Sam pondered that.

"Every time, *mi coyote*," repeated Fitz.

Sam broke the silence. "When I kill, I don't like me much."

"Do it anyhow," said Beckwourth.

"If you want to partner me," said Gideon.

"But don't get to liking it," added Fitz.

THIRD WING DIDN'T show up that afternoon, or the evening either. Sam looked for him the next day as the Crows formed a long line of horse-drawn travois and rode upriver. The young men policed the line and kept lookout, but Third Wing wasn't among them. The

mountain men, riding behind, said they'd seen no sign of any straggler. It was the same story the next day, and the third day, when they
reached the forks and made camp. Sam walked over and over from the
beaver men's camp above the north fork and the tipis of Raven's people. No Third Wing.

For a week they rested and fed their horses and themselves. Every
day they traded with the Indians. Each Pawnee who came to camp
kept his eyes open, but none acted hostile. The trading went well.
Ashley got fifteen horses and a lot of pemmican. Some of the men
even got squaws for the night. But no sign of Third Wing, and Sam
did not dare to ask Raven.

Still Raven managed, talking to Ashley, to roll a stone into the
garden of Sam's hopes. The chief and two Big Bellies said the route up
the south fork toward the mountains had plenty of feed for the
horses and plenty of wood for fires. But the north fork, they claimed,
did not.

Ashley sent Sam for Clyman and Fitzpatrick. None of them had
been up the south fork. On his long walk Sam came down the north
fork, never saw the south fork until he got right here.

The whites squatted and scratched rivers and mountains in the dirt
until it looked like what they'd seen. The Pawnees added the south
fork and showed how it ran straight at some other mountains to the
south. The north fork looped around the end of the same range.

Coy whined to come forward and show the two-leggeds how to
dig in the earth, but Sam staked him several steps away.

They looked hopefully at Raven and the Big Bellies. 'On the north
fork,' signed the Indians, 'little for the horses to eat, little wood for
the men to burn.'

'Seemed like enough to me,' signed Sam.

'No. Too many men, too many horses for winter on the north fork.
Must use south fork.'

Then the Big Bellies showed them where to cross the mountains
when the snow melted, a line from the south fork to the northwest.

"It's the long way around to the Siskadee," Sam told Ashley.

The general looked at Clyman and Fitz.

"True enough," said Clyman.

"But it's only way now," said Fitz.

Sam made a face.

"What's wrong?" asked Ashley.

Sam just shook his head.

"Sam's counting on seeing Meadowlark this winter," said Fitz in a kindly tone. To Ashley's questioning face he added, "Look at his *gage d'amour.*" Which meant the beautiful beaded pouch that hung inside his shirt. "Our coyote keeper has a Crow woman."

Ashley gave the briefest glance at the pouch, normally a gift an Indian woman used to signal her affection. He said, "I'm sure these Indians are telling us the truth. It's the south fork for us." He turned back to Raven and the Big Bellies. "Thank you."

Sam hung his head while he made the signs.

Then he flashed his eyes into Raven's face. He signed, 'Where's Third Wing?'

'He has not been well,' Raven signed back. His smile was superior, his eyes amused. 'Maybe he does not want to see you.'

SAM KICKED A snow-covered stone into the stream, the main river below the forks. Since it hurt, he kicked another one. "Very satisfying," he told Coy, "but I'm damned if I know why."

He looked through the graying evening at the western sky. It was the color of the mustard Katherine's mother made back home, and the lavender his mother grew to keep under your pillow for a calm mind and good sleep. Which seemed far away to Sam. His spirits felt the way the sky looked, battered and bruised.

He was well rid of Katherine—his brother Owen was welcome to her. And he didn't think he'd see his mother again. Pennsylvania was a long ways off, and he wanted to be in the mountains. Among the peaks and valleys that still lay to the west of these flat plains. He wished he could see the mountains from here.

Coy splashed into the river and lapped up the cold water. The sunset colors rippled with the colors of Sam's pain. He gazed at the western horizon. The lavender was a thin line of clouds hiding the last of the sun, not her mountains.

He seldom said the name Meadowlark, even in his thoughts. The picture of her, the touch of her, these came to his mind familiar as campfire smells, but he didn't let himself think her name.

"No Crow camp this winter," he said to the pup bitterly. "Let her down again. 'The white man can't be trusted,' her parents will tell her. She'll make a tipi for another man."

That one hurt him sharply, right in the groin.

He stared at the horizon blankly. The sun was down, the light fading, like his chance with . . . her.

"*Hnnn.*"

He spun around. A voice. Whose? Where?

His hair prickled. If it wasn't a friendly voice, he would already be dead. Still . . .

"*Hnnn.*"

Then he saw. A man figure moved out of the grove of cottonwoods into the open. A scrawny, haggard Pawnee.

He gaped. He could hardly believe this was Third Wing.

Chapter Five

SAM BUILT THE fire for the two of them on the riverbank, well away from camp. His companions might get grumpy about having both a coyote and Pawnee as dinner companions. He made the fire roar. Normally, he'd have built a smaller one, but he kept looking at Third Wing and wondering what had happened to . . . his friend?

Was "friend" the word for a man you'd only been around a few hours? But if he saved your life, what else could you call him?

Coy thought he was a friend too. Though the pup stayed clear of most people, he went to Third Wing right away and lay down against his foot like it was a corner of blanket, or a warm rock.

Third Wing flaunted Sam's hair at the world, two big hanks of white draping down his gleaming sheet of black onto his shoulders. That had been the price of Sam's life. Sam had never understood what Third Wing wanted with the hair. But there was a lot he didn't understand about Third Wing, or any Pawnee, or any Indian. Maybe any person.

Coy licked Third Wing's hand and accepted a few pats.

Mountain life was strange, and Third Wing was Sam's strangest experience. Last summer he'd been walking down the Platte alone, the river the Indians called Shell River. A hard time—Sam had gotten separated from his brigade, and very lost. Then Arapahos took his horse. He had only eleven rifle balls left, so couldn't get much food. And he guessed—only *guessed*—that the settlements were a seven-hundred-mile walk down river.

After maybe six weeks of walking, he was training Coy one afternoon, teaching him to jump up and take a stick from the hand. Some young men of the Loup Pawnees sneaked up on him, captured him, and took him back to camp.

The people were very curious about Coy and his tricks, so they wanted to keep the pup. The council of Big Bellies decided, though, that Sam would be given a choice for tomorrow—die quickly, or show brave as you die. Showing brave meant demonstrating how much pain you could stand without complaint. Never moan, never ask for water, never beg for death. The women did the torturing, because they gave a man a chance to be very, very brave.

Third Wing rescued him. Third Wing spoke English, so he promised to watch the captive overnight. At his tipi Third Wing fed Sam and offered him a deal—give me your beautiful white hair and I'll help you escape. Sam wondered if the Indian was out of his mind. But that didn't matter. Sam let the Pawnee cut his hair off right down to the nubs. He also held out for taking Coy with him. In the darkest hours, a shorn Sam followed Third Wing out of camp and to the river.

But he couldn't keep going. Without his rifle he would starve. One of his young captors had stolen it. So the next night Sam crept back into camp, killed a sentry—dammit, Two Stones, not just a sentry—and stole his rifle back.

Then he had to spend several days running and hiding from the angry Pawnees.

At that time Third Wing was a stocky man in his mid-twenties. Four months later he looked like a half-starved, half-frozen relic.

They sliced meat off a spitted roast and ate in silence. Third Wing attacked food the way Coy did, like this was the last bite he'd ever get. Sam waited for him to say something. Maybe the fellow had gone the rest of the way crazy.

After a while, observing Sam feeding Coy fatty or gristly pieces, Third Wing did the same. He tossed the scraps with an odd smile, like he savored the irony of a half-starved man feeding a well-fatted coyote.

He ate for a long time after Sam quit, which was a good sign, but still said nothing.

When Third Wing let Coy lick the grease off his fingers and wiped his hands thoroughly on his hide leggings, Sam said, "I'm glad to see you. I thank you again for saving my life."

Third Wing flashed that same crazy grin at him. "Dumbest goddam thing I ever did."

Sam swallowed hard. To cover his feelings, he reached for the small white clay pipe in his *gage d'amour*, filled it with tobacco, and used sticks to get an ember and drop it onto the tobacco. When Sam had the pipe going, he handed it to Third Wing. The Pawnee took it shakily, overeager.

"What do you mean?"

"I mean my wife put my goddam moccasins outside the tipi."

Sam supposed Third Wing used the English he heard, without a sense that some of it was profane. He raised an eyebrow quizzically at Third Wing.

The Pawnee gave him a friendly smile. "When your woman puts your moccasins outside, that means you're through. Take your weapons and go. Your kids aren't even yours anymore." There was an edge of bitterness in Third Wing's voice.

He drew deep on the pipe and let the smoke wander upward from his lips. "She went to live with her sister's husband." His eyes lit up wildly. "He likes having two women to jump on top of."

"Where have you been living?"

Third Wing pretended to shrug lightly. "In a brush hut with the other young, single men." The word *single* bristled with sarcasm.

"What have you been eating?"

Third Wing took a while to answer. "I've been feeling kind of off, haven't hunted much."

Sam could see that. Coy whined like he also knew what it was like to be hungry.

"Why haven't you come around until now?"

"I was off on a vision quest."

"Starving yourself?"

"Yes."

Godawmighty, starving a starved man. Sam wanted to ask what Third Wing saw, but he didn't dare.

"Your wife, she leave you because of me?"

"The whole tribe thinks I'm strange about whites. I like white people, and I've been waiting for you." He looked into the night sky. Sam wondered what he saw there, among the pulsing stars, where some people saw stories. Third Wing was giving him the willies.

"Maybe some day I'll tell you why. Why I like you."

The guy was sweet. It was hard to be suspicious about him. "Tell me how you got such good English, too."

"Yip-YIP!" cried Coy, as though seconding the motion.

Third Wing grunted, took his belt knife, and sliced at the roast again. "Maybe I better eat while I can."

When he had devoured another half pound of meat, Third Wing went on, "I speak English good because traders raised me."

So Sam poked at that conversationally. "What traders? How long were you among them?"

Third Wing just waited until he'd finished eating and then said,

"The traders out of Fort Osage found me alone on the river trail, near where Atkinson is now, it wasn't then. I was maybe five years old. I didn't remember anything about my family or my tribe, but the words I spoke were Pawnee. One of the traders, Gannett, he raised me, maybe, ten years. Not that he was much of a father. I more or less hung around Fort Osage like a stray dog. Seems Gannett didn't think a whole lot of me, either. When I was about fifteen, I had some trouble getting a bridle on a horse, and Gannett said, 'That boy's as much use as a third wing.' I figured a third wing would mess a bird up completely. Anyway, the name stuck."

"Why aren't you working at one of the trading posts?"

"Oh, not long after I got my name, Gannett took an outfit out to trade with the Loup Pawnees. Raven was curious about me, a redskinned boy. When Gannett told him I spoke Pawnee, Raven checked but couldn't find anyone who remembered me. Maybe I came from the other big Pawnee tribe. Anyhow, Raven got one of the families to trade a horse for me." He laughed. "Hell, once I was worth a horse."

Sam didn't know what to say to this outburst of information and feeling.

Third Wing said, "Let's make camp together here."

Sam looked at the sky. Swept clear by the winds, no rain or snow tonight. "I'll get my blankets," said Sam.

When he got back, Third Wing had cleared an area for sleeping—the pebbles and little sticks were tossed away. He was bringing willows, their finger-shaped yellow leaves still on, and fashioning a hut from them. Sam cut the willows while Third Wing made them into a house. Sam had the teasing thought. *Just like a good little woman.*

He ended up lending most of his blankets to Third Wing. The Pawnee slept like a baby. Coy spooned up close to him on the belly side. Sam sat up most of the night, feeling bad about Third Wing, and wondering.

OVER THE NEXT few days Sam sometimes felt like he had two dogs tagging around with him, except that neither Coy nor Third Wing was a dog. Sam's job was to help Ashley with the trading. The general set his trade goods out—beads, vermilion, kettles, knives, cotton cloth, wool strouding, tobacco, and lots of other items, including the blankets they sat on. The Indians surveyed all, trying to keep their faces impassive and prevent their eyes from lighting up. At length they made offers.

The process was long, sometimes tedious and sometimes fun. The Pawnees treated the trading as a form of play. Back-and-forth banter wasn't easy in signs.

"Why don't you let me do the translating?" asked Third Wing. He was lounging on the edge of a trade blanket in the noonday sun, which was weak, this near the solstice.

Sam looked at Ashley. "Yes," said the general to Sam, "but you stay and help too."

"Goddam," said Third Wing, "my own people don't trust me, and neither do you whites." But he chuckled when he said it.

Always the disciplinarian, Ashley frowned at the "goddam," and the trading got started again. It went a lot faster with Third Wing making English out of Pawnee and then telling the people what Sam's answer was. Sam was sure Third Wing spiced the answers up with humor, and sometimes a mocking edge. Now and then the women giggled like the banter was bawdy.

At first they got a lot of buffalo robes, which would help the men stay warm at night. Then came jerked meat, which was welcome, because the winter was looking longer and hungrier to everyone. Trading for horseflesh, though, was slow and difficult. Only one animal the first day, three the second, two the third. Ashley wanted a pack horse for every man, twenty-five altogether.

ON THE SECOND night Jim Beckwourth and Gideon made a change in everyone's living arrangements. They dropped their bedrolls on the far side of Sam and Third Wing's fire. "We want to be over here," said the French-Canadian.

"Where there's some skin that ain't white," added Jim. He threw a shiny, big-toothed smile at Third Wing.

"I'm kinda mixed up between white and red," said Third Wing.

"Me too," said Gideon. "Born that way."

"I figure that makes us blood brothers," said Jim. They all chortled at that.

Jim told his story about what a gentleman his father, Sir Jennings Beckwourth, had been, a kind of aristocrat to hear Jim tell it. He didn't know how Sir Jennings came to be with his mother, a slave, "But I can guess." Sir Jennings even brought the family to St. Louis to get away from color prejudice and give the half-and-half children a decent chance in life.

"How'd that work?"

"Not a bit."

"May be better in the mountains," put in Sam.

"He's an optimist," said Gideon with a smile.

"I think white people is white people wherever you go," Jim said.

Third Wing hopped back into the conversation. "What do you mean," he asked Gideon, "born that way?"

"My father was a French Jew, my mother a Cree," said Gideon.

"You aren't much dark," said Third Wing.

"One of my sisters be light as cream," said Jim, who was dark. One of the odd things about Jim, Sam had noticed, was that he could talk good English to the general, better English than Sam's, and rough English to his fellow trappers. He also noticed that Jim wore a mustard seed in a drop of glass around his neck, an old way of warding off illness. Sam approved. Black folks, Indians, and country whites, he thought, knew some things fancy white people didn't.

"Here's what my father told me," said Jim, "and this child thinks it speaks to red as well as black. My father pointed at the piano where we gathered round to sing church songs, you know, hymns, and my father he says, 'There are twelve tones on the piano. Some of them are white, and some of them are black. Each one strikes a pure and beautiful tone, and music is made equally of both.' "

Third Wing cackled like that was one truly funny-peculiar story.

Gideon said, "Except people don't see it that way, do they?"

TWO MORE DAYS work and they had nine horses. It was slow. Fortunately, the winter weather was fine, the hunting was good, and the men were happy here.

Third Wing asked for a robe from Ashley for all the translating he was doing. He got a robe and a blanket.

Sam wanted to sit around with Gideon and Jim and Fitz and Clyman and tell stories. He wanted to hunt. Mostly he wanted this boring work to be over. As long as they were trading, though, Ashley would pack up and ride the south fork toward that big range of mountains. Then they would be moving away from the camp of the girl whose name he wouldn't speak, even to himself.

That night across the fire—still plenty of buffalo meat to eat and all four friends were doing their best on it—Third Wing asked Sam, "Why do you act so glum?"

Sam didn't answer.

"It's that Crow woman," Jim said. "Look at him fingering that *gage d'amour*, don't even know he's doing it."

Third Wing laughed.

"If you don't tell him," said Gideon, "I will."

So Sam did, told Third Wing how he got to know her when the brigade lived at the Crow village led by Rides Twice last winter, how enchanting she was, how beautifully she moved.

"Her name, it's Meadowlark," put in Gideon.

"Yeah. She's a virgin," Sam went on, "because she wants to lead that ceremony reserved for virgins."

"You hope she hasn't led it yet," said Jim with a chuckle.

"I didn't know where I stood with her until she gave me this *gage d'amour*. Then I promised to come back last summer."

"Which you didn't," said Gideon.

"Life got in the way," said Sam. To Third Wing he added, "That's when I got lost."

"And came wandering down the river, half-addled and half-starved, and I saved your silly ass," said Third Wing.

"Yeah."

"So now you're worried," Third Wing went on. "You didn't show up last summer. If you don't go back to her this winter, it will be no more kootchy-coo." Sometimes Third Wing acted like his friend, sometimes his mother, and sometimes like a little kid.

"Yeah."

"Where is her village?"

"Wind River," said Gideon. "Up the north fork here a long way, up the Sweetwater, over a divide, follow Wind River upstream."

"So why don't we just go see her? Leave straight from here. Right away. What are we waiting for?"

Sam gawked at Third Wing.

"Young love is supposed to be keen," said Jim.

Third Wing held out his arms in a what-are-you-waiting-for gesture.

"You want to go?" Sam asked Third Wing, half-believing.

"What would I sit around here for?"

"You?" Sam asked Gideon.

"I like Crow women."

Sam looked at Jim.

"I like all women."

"Let's go!" Sam shouted.

Chapter Six

THEY TOOK A week to get ready. Ashley insisted that Sam and Third Wing help him finish trading for those horses, and the general ended up with twenty-three new ones. Beckwourth shot a buffalo cow and a deer. Third Wing kept a low fire going all day, every day to dry the meat. Figuring the journey would take three weeks, they were taking a month's worth of food. All four men knew that could be a recipe for starvation—anything could happen in the mountains.

Third Wing contributed two pack horses.

Fitzpatrick came to their fire by the river the night before they left. He settled on his haunches and looked one by one at the four of them. His mouth had an ironic set, but his Irish eyes were full of merriment. "You *compañeros* following *mi coyote's* yen for poontang, you are lucky fellows. The general will not fire your arses. He will not even change your financial arrangements. You may chase skirts wherever you want to this winter, and make the same money—that's *if* you turn up next spring for the hunt."

"Being generous, is he, the general?" Beckwourth said.

"Why certainly," said Fitz with mock melody.

Coy crawled over between Third Wing's feet and turned onto his back. The Pawnee rubbed the belly obligingly. He said, "Ashley wants you to bring your beaver to him. He don't want you selling it to nobody else."

"He doesn't mind if we shine up his relationship wit' ze Crows either," said Gideon.

To Sam, Fitz added, "Meet us the day of the spring equinox, he says, on the Siskadee."

Third Wing gave Coy's belly a playful pinch. The dog yipped and mouthed the fingers. The Pawnee made a loud flutter with his lips and tongue. The pup yipped.

"Too early," said Sam.

"We'll frostbite our tails in the Southern Pass in March," said Gideon.

"So will you," said Sam.

Sam, Gideon, and Fitzpatrick remembered well the howling winds and choking blizzards on the pass last March, right before they had mountain luck and stumbled on beaver paradise in the valley of the Siskadee. Along with Bill Sublette and James Clyman, Sam had nearly frozen to death one night on the pass because the wind kept scattering their pathetic attempts at a fire. Only the next morning's discovery of a single live coal the size of a kernel of corn had saved them.

Coy slithered to the fire and put his head on his paws like he remembered and was trying to get warm. "You weren't even born when that happened," Sam told him. The pup mewled a little and didn't move.

"Diah and Sublette be on the Siskadee?" asked Sam.

"Yeah," said Fitz. "And I already told the general March is a hell-freezer-till-your-short-hairs-get-stiff. Make it the middle of April."

"Good," said Sam. He was eager to show cooperation with the general. Having an employer seemed proper.

"Now the general has a surprise for you." He walked off into the dark and came back leading a horse bearing big panniers, sacks that hung heavy on each side. "*Mi coyote*, you aren't thinking of how you should treat the Crows." He opened a pannier to show them. "This is tobacco, blankets, beads, strouding, all kind of foofuraw. You tell them these presents are from General Ashley."

"Dammit," said Sam, "we didn't think of presents."

"Gideon did," said Fitz, "that's how come you get all these nice things."

Gideon managed a half bow. "I have a word with Ashley private," he said. "I also have two jugs. One is for us on New Year's Eve, the ozzer for the Crows."

"I'll pretend I didn't hear that," said Fitz. The government forbade the use of whiskey in the Indian trade, but most traders disregarded this ban.

"You can take the pack horse too," said Fitz, "but remember, it's the general's."

Third Wing got up, took the panniers off, led the pack horse a dozen steps, and staked it with their other horses.

"Now *mi coyote*, how are you going to know when the first week of April comes?" asked Fitz. "You can't go by the Indian way, the moon when the grass greens up."

Sam just looked at him, stuck.

Fitzpatrick took out a stick stripped of bark, painted blue on one end, red on the other, and bare wood in the middle, which had lots of knife cuts on it, in lines. "This is my counting stick." He held it out to Sam.

The moment Sam grasped it, Coy snatched the stick and scooted away. He sat with his back to the fire, looking straight at Sam, stick in his mouth. Though his tail didn't wag, his legs trembled.

Sam patted the ground.

Coy bounded forward and laid the stick on the ground. Then he leapt into Sam's lap. At six or seven months, he was getting big for the lap.

Fitz grabbed the stick and looked to see whether his cuts were spoiled by tooth marks. Apparently not. "I keep the time for the brigade in the ledger. But a man who doesn't read or write"—like Sam—"can do it like this. See here, make seven notches for each day in a week, then make one of these big rings all the way around the stick. Those are weeks, or quarters of the moon. Every four quarters, make a ring and paint it with vermilion—that's a month." Sam nodded—he saw what the system was. "Today is December 21, the shortest day and longest night of the year. Tomorrow night's camp, make your own counting stick. When the rings say it's April, put your minds on moving out. Be on the Siskadee four moon from now."

"Only white men count their days," Beckwourth said with broad mockery.

"This should be long enough for even you boys to dip your wicks a lot of places," answered Fitz.

Sam blushed.

"Middle of April we'll be looking for you. When you get to where the Sandy comes into the Siskadee, if you don't see lots of sign we've been there, wait. If we've come and gone, I'll leave a cairn. One rock on the side of the cairn, that points whether I went upriver or downriver."

He looked all four of them in the eyes.

"Zis is easy," said Gideon. "I find your outfit anywhere in the Rocky Mountains, maybe by the smell of your feet."

Fitz grinned. "Don't end up walking back to civilization, boys."

Sam, Gideon, and Fitzpatrick all grinned. That wasn't on the agenda again.

Suddenly, wraithlike, Fitz was gone.

Sam laid awake all night, thinking of Meadowlark. He was up

before the sun the next morning making coffee. The party rode off earlier than his companions wanted to, and they were grumbling.

MOUNTAIN LUCK SWINGS big each way. Easy—alive—hard—dead. Gone under, as the trappers called it, in the lingo they were developing. One winter trip goes lickety-split, the next one is inch by inch, leading the horse through thigh-deep snow, pulling your leg out of one deep hole, pushing it across the snow in front of you, and shifting your weight awkwardly forward so you can plunge a foot down again. Naturally, if you have a dog with you, or in Sam's case, a coyote, the critter will trot blithely over the surface of the snow, look back at you, and give you a superior smile.

That December their luck was variable, but mostly good. Where the Sweetwater River flowed into the Platte, they spent a day and a half sitting out a snowstorm. A tent gets close when you're in it all day—Sam spent the evening outside, watching the big flakes sift silently through the branches of cottonwood trees. Where they left the Sweetwater to cross over to Wind River, they got into deep snow in spots, and they huddled one afternoon and night below a cut bank, trying to get out of the screaming wind. Holding Coy to his front, Sam was not as shivery as his companions.

The country was mostly open, though. Beckwourth said it was because the damn wind blew the snow all the way to the Missouri River.

When wood failed them, they made fires of sagebrush and buffalo pies. The flames kept them warm, more or less, through the long nights. Thoughts of Meadowlark kept Sam nearly hot.

When you ride day after day through Indian country, your mind should never wander. There are always ridges to be scoured with the eyes, brushy flats to be inspected. You watch for anything that's out of place, a silhouette moving on a hilltop or a duck quacking up off the river for no reason.

Sam was inexperienced, though, and young, and hot-blooded. His mind ran from Meadowlark walking to Meadowlark smiling to Meadowlark snuggled up . . . He had no promises from her, only this one gift, the *gage d'amour* he always wore around his neck. He thought again of the reason she'd given for declining his courting, that she wanted to be one of the girls who led the dancers in the goose egg dance. The leaders had to be virgins, others explained to Sam, completely above suspicion. Meadowlark spent time with no young man.

But Sam couldn't keep from wondering. *Was she sincere? Was she stalling him to let someone else into her arms? Did she have that ceremony last summer?* Some summers they visited the River Crows, and that's when they did the ceremony. *If she did, did she go berry-picking afterwards with some good-looking stranger and take the pleasures of the flesh? Is she being courted? Is she already married?*

These thoughts bounced off Elk Mountain and back into Sam's mind, off the waters of the Sweetwater River and back to him, from the snowy world of the Wind River Mountains on the southwest to the red hills and gray, stony peaks of the steep Absarokas on the northeast and back, always, into Sam's mind. When he woke in the middle of the night, these thoughts haunted him.

On the day of Christmas Eve Sam rode with his mind in the past. It was his twentieth birthday, and the fourth anniversary of his father's death. He didn't call up many words about Lew Morgan, and none of the kinds of words people said at a burying. He just let pictures float into his mind. He and Lew playing cat's cradle. The father teaching the child to milk the cow, shooting the warm milk into his boy's face, and the sweet taste of that milk right out of the tit. Learning to measure his powder with care, both kinds of powder, for the pan and for the barrel. Easing through the Pennsylvania woods behind Lew, trying not to make a sound, and failing. Then finding a spot and spending the whole day watching to see what was there—what birds lived in these trees and when they sang and when they were silent; the deer, grazing quietly because they didn't know human beings were around; the fish, and how you could build a dam and catch them with your hands and scoop them onto the bank. He stroked the stock of his rifle, where he'd had a brass plate put on and CELC engraved in a fancy script, surrounded by a circle of Celtic love knots, like the ones in a belt Sam's mother had given his father. But the name and the circle had been scorched by the prairie fire, and were only half legible. Still, his memories of his father gleamed.

That night, as they sat around the fire in the early dark, Third Wing said, "I have a treat for you." The two great whacks of Sam's hair, tied into Third Wing's, glinted dramatically white in the firelight. "First this." He disappeared into the darkness and brought back a tin cup filled with grease. Sam had noticed him rendering buffalo fat the last couple of days. Out of the grease hung a piece of patch cloth like a wick. Third Wing put the whole affair on the cold ground and used an ember to get the wick burning. It burned nicely because it was soaked in oil.

"This is your birthday candle. We couldn't make twenty of them," said Third Wing. "Blow it out for good luck."

Sam made an immense gust and out went the candle. Gideon and Beckwourth applauded.

"Now your very special surprise," said Third Wing.

He stepped into the dark again and brought back a tin bowl of . . . It looked sort of like . . . "Cherry ice cream," said Third Wing proudly.

"Well, ice cream Athabascan style," said Gideon.

Third Wing thrust the bowl forward. "Everyone help yourself."

The four spooned the goop into their coffee cups.

Sam scooped some up with his tongue, then kept himself from making a face.

"*Pas mal* when you get used to it," said Gideon. "I learned way north, when I spent the winter at Slave Lake."

Beckwourth did make a face.

Sam tried again, and didn't exactly dislike it. It was sweet.

"I put lots of sugar in it," Third Wing said, "to improve the taste."

"What is it?" Beckwourth asked.

"Liquid buffalo fat," said Gideon, "mushed up with snow."

"With lots of sugar," repeated Third Wing, "and all the chokecherries we had left."

"Thanks," said Sam.

"Happy birthday," said Third Wing.

"Happy birthday," the others chorused.

"Oh to be twenty again," chanted Gideon like he was in church.

"Thanks, everyone!" said Sam. He meant it.

Sneakily, later, he would give his cherry ice cream to Coy.

"Now I'm going to give you a special birthday present," said Third Wing.

Everyone fell silent. Sam could tell Gideon and Beckwourth didn't know about this.

"I'm going to tell you why I like you so much."

This was strange.

"I saw you in a dream before you ever came."

Sam felt weird. "What do you mean?"

"I saw a white man with white hair in a dream. So I was expecting you. Some time."

"What happened in the dream?"

"You came walking in the shape of buffalo, a red buffalo. Then you stopped, turned all the way around, and came walking as a yellow buffalo. Then you stopped, turned around, and came walking in a sacred way as a black buffalo. Then you stopped, turned around, and came toward us as a white buffalo."

Third Wing looked at his listeners as though expecting some reaction they didn't give, maybe awe.

"Just a minute," said Sam. "If it was a buffalo, why do you think it was me?"

"Your medicine, is it buffalo?"

Sam thought of his own dream, and the cow he joined beings with. Still, he said, "I don't know what you mean."

"I think it is buffalo, but . . . it was you that stood on the hill above the village." Then he explained, as though to children, "You in your human shape and your beautiful white hair. You carried a deer skin tanned beautifully white, and in it was some gift for the people. You opened it, and it shone. You set it down on the crest of the hill and walked away in a sacred manner."

He stopped awkwardly. "But I never saw what it was. Others rushed up the hill to see the gift, but I woke up. I don't know what you brought us."

The four men looked at each other, uncertain.

"But I knew you had a gift. That's why I saved you. You bore a gift."

"Third Wing, I honestly don't have anything for the Pawnee."

The Pawnee shrugged. "Maybe you don't know what it is, but you have it. The gift, that's why I want to be with you."

Sam considered, and then knew what he wanted to do. He scooted over to Third Wing, made his eyes big as a demon's, gave him a big smooch on the cheek, and said in a honeyed voice, "I like you, too."

Everyone laughed.

Sam fell asleep thinking, *He's a strange friend, but I like him.*

SAM'S COUNTING STICK told him when New Year's Eve was, and they broke open one of the two whiskey jugs and got uproariously drunk. Only Third Wing stayed mostly sober, so he could take care of the fools who overindulged, he said.

That night Gideon and Beckwourth got into a storytelling contest Sam would never forget. His favorite was one Gideon told. "Me, ze first winter I am on Saskatchewan River, I walk sometimes from trading post to village, maybe one hour walk. I need, you know, a woman warm against ze long, long winter. Very cold, Saskatchewan, very much snow. I am lonesome on the walk, so I whistle along the way. This was my favorite song,

As I strolled by,
At the clear fountain,
noticed the water was exquisite,
And dipped myself in it.
I've loved you so long—
I will never forget you.

"A young man in on ze far plains, during the long winter, he *naturalement* t'ink of his lady love back home, no?

"Remember, I whistle this song as I walk, no did sing it, just whistle.

"One winter day it is so cold. I remember my breath frosted my beard. The hairs in my nose, they crust with ice. My lungs hurt from drawing in ze air. But I whistle, always I whistle.

"I mean I try. Zis time it is for nothing, it . . . Nothing comes out. My whistles, ze cold freezes ze sound. I keep whistling, I am superstitious. If I don't send my song to my love, maybe she is, you know, *infidel* with another man."

"*Infidel* like you are, huh?" asked Sam, taking pleasure in catching on to a new word.

"Yes, *naturalement*, I am a man. Two weeks later, maybe three, comes ze wind we call chinook. You know? Warm winter wind, melts ze snow, bares ze ground, makes you feel good. After three days of chinook I must walk to village, and now is much more pleasant, neh?

"Oh, you don't know how pleasant. Because my whistles, it is warm, now they thaw out. They sing to me from every wild rose bush, from every blue spruce tree. Even ze snow, dripping from the branches, serenades me. I pretend the thawing whistles, zey are ze voice of my lover.

> *"I've loved you so long—*
> *I will never forget you."*

"That's horse puckey," said Jim, with a big grin.

"Says the world's biggest maker of horse puckey," said Sam.

"Whoo-oop! Lookee here!" Jim mock-roared. "I am a grizzly b'ar crossed with a mountain lion. I can outrun, outshoot, and outride, and outfight any man what takes breath within a thousand miles of the Missouri River. And I am the world's biggest maker of horse puckey," he concluded triumphantly.

"All right," he went on with buttery charm, "now, I got a story. . . ."

IN THE FAR, wee middle of that night Third Wing asked to hear the tale of how Sam got Coy.

"His medicine coyote," said Gideon.

"His familiar spirit," said Beckwourth.

"He's just my friend," said Sam.

"You aren't friends," said Beckwourth. "You're the master, he does what you say."

"We're friends," insisted Sam quietly. He thought a moment. He didn't believe Coy was his medicine animal. If he had a medicine animal, or should claim one, it was that buffalo cow back on the Platte, the one he entered into and joined with. Though he wasn't sure what a medicine animal was.

He did think he could tell the story of how he got Coy. It was related to the buffalo story, but not the same story.

"I was camped in a cottonwood grove on a little creek several miles north of the Platte. Alone—that was when I was doing my walk down the river to Atkinson."

"Baptism of fire, plains style," said Gideon, a veteran of the same walk.

"I shot a buffalo just before dark and got her gutted out. Woke up just before dawn, it looked like the sun was rising in the northwest, so bright and red it was. Until I smelled the smoke I didn't figure out what was happening. Prairie fire coming my way.

"I put it together fast as I could. Huge, huge prairie fire, wind whipping it straight toward me. Too wide to outrun to either side, too far to the river. I tried to get in the little creek, but there wasn't enough water—left half of me sticking out. Did get good and wet, though. Pawing around with no place to go, I heard a mewling sound. It was this pup here, only smaller, and he was poking at the slit in the buffalo, like he wanted to get in.

"Seemed crazy. I looked up at that fire. It was going to hit the grove right quick, and when it did the trees would turn into torches—you wouldn't have to touch flame to get burnt, 'All right,' I said to myself, 'It's crazy but it's the only chance.' I crept right into the buffalo belly, took the pup with me. Hell, all of me didn't even fit. Knees stuck out. When they got too hot, I turned over and my tail stuck out. Got burned pretty good.

"When the sound eased away—you can't imagine how loud a

prairie fire roars—I waited and waited some more and finally crawled out." He thought of telling them about the strange feeling he had, like being born, but decided against it. "Everything was turned black. *Every*thing. The stink was beyond belief, and it stung your nose. Most places you couldn't step, even in a moccasin—too hot.

"Later I butchered out the buffalo—meat was good, even if it was toasted around the edges. Kept the pup. Fed him. Figured the pup saved my life."

He picked Coy and hugged, dog back to human chest. "This pup is my friend."

No one spoke, maybe out of respect, Sam thought, or maybe because the story wasn't a stretcher like they wanted.

"Up at Slave Lake, hell of a way to ze northwest and gone," began Gideon, "I came across a sow grizzly, and sudden I wondered where her cubs were . . ."

Third Wing egged on Gideon and Beckwourth, and they never stopped telling stories until the sun rose over the hills to the southeast. Then the four men and coyote slept all New Year's day. Sam didn't figure this country often brought in the new year so sunny and mild and pleasantly lazy.

Chapter Seven

SAM SPAT HIS freezing hair out of his mouth—the hair was crinkled with ice. The weather was so nasty he had Coy up in the saddle with him, curled against his belly and around the horn.

It was three weeks and two days since they'd left the Ashley men at the forks of the Platte, according to his counting stick. He knew the tipis of the Crow village were in the cottonwoods along the river ahead. But on this bitter evening he couldn't see even their silhouettes, or any hint of a fire. His left ear ached from the wind and sleet slashing that side of his face. The hand leading the pack horse was too stiff either to grip or let go—the rope was wound several times around the hand. And his white hair, now finally grown back to decent length, was whipping ice into his mouth and eyes.

He had made it to Meadowlark's village, but at the moment he didn't give a damn.

"Riders," said Beckwourth.

Sam held up a hand, and all four stopped. Odd, though the youngest, Sam was a sort of leader here. He and Gideon had lived in this village last winter, but Sam alone spoke the Crow language. (Gideon had a few words of *amour*.)

Five horsemen came out of the lacing sleet and stopped facing Sam's party. Sam thought he recognized one figure.

"Ohchikaape." It meant, "Greetings after a long absence." "We come from General Ashley in friendship."

"Sam?" cried a voice in English. "Welcome back, Sam. I'm glad to see you."

"I'm glad to see you Blue Horse!" chimed in Sam. He felt a twinge of guilt at always thinking of Meadowlark and seldom of her brother, his noble-looking friend. He wanted to say lots of things to this comrade, but he forced himself to stick with business. "We want to speak with Rides Twice."

The young men with Blue Horse held the horses of both groups. Sam stopped to put Coy on a leash, which got him strange looks from whites and Indians alike.

The trappers limped into the village on numb feet that made them weave like drunken sailors. Their march had not a shred of dignity, but Gideon was still strong enough to lug the panniers, full of presents. "You can make a tent with the other young men," offered Blue Horse in English. He was still keeping one wary eye on the coyote.

"Pitch a tent," said Sam. He was acknowledging their former pact to help each other, one with Crow, the other with English. "We will do that tonight. Thank you."

A tent, though, was not what he wanted. He longed for the coziness of a real tipi and a center fire, preferably with Meadowlark in the buffalo robes at the rear.

As they approached the council lodge, Sam made himself remember the details of the Crow way of handling the sacred pipe, the proper Crow words to use in offering the smoke to the four directions. The presents would make the trappers welcome. These trade items were great luxuries to the Crows, who had no other access to them. He assumed the Crows would accept Third Wing. Both Crows and Pawnees were long-time enemies of the Sioux, and that should do it.

The problem was Coy. When they got to the lodge, Sam regretfully tied him to a lodge stake outside. Then they waited until Rides Twice and several Big Bellies went in. Sam ducked through the flap behind them. The lodge was cold, but a good center fire was already started. He wanted to crawl into a corner, wrap up in a buffalo robe, and sleep. *Right now I don't even want Meadowlark there with me.* He gave a crookedy smile. *Well, maybe I do.*

Rides Twice sat in his accustomed place behind the center fire. He motioned for Sam to sit to his left, and the others in the trapping party to Sam's left, and the Big Bellies to their left. He said in the Crow language, "Welcome, Sam, we are glad to see you again."

Sam lowered himself beside the chief. It was going to be a good winter.

EARLY THE NEXT morning Sam was sitting quietly by the river, on a cottonwood felled by a beaver, rubbing Coy's ears. The early morning fog half hid the two of them. His breath swirled up to join the fog. *My breath, the earth's breath,* he thought. He took off his other glove and changed hands. Coy's fur warmed his fingers better than the gloves. He watched the figures moving ghostly through the fog, to the river bank and back. He wasn't interested, though, in any figure except one, Meadowlark, and she didn't appear.

Beyond him the river was easy to get to, and the water formed a pool. Every morning the mothers and grandmothers sent the young women here to get water. But no Meadowlark yet.

When the weak winter sun had burned the fog off, Meadowlark's mother, Needle, came down the trail carrying a bucket. *Another trade item they need from us.*

Sam was miffed. The other young women must have told Meadowlark, or Needle, that the white man was waiting for her. *I'm sure she wants to see me.* Maybe it was her parents . . . *Maybe she still hasn't done the ceremony . . .*

Needle was usually merry. This time she walked with her eyes straight ahead, apparently seeing nothing but the path and the pool. Sam couldn't even tell whether she knew he was there. When she was gone, he and Coy traipsed back to the village. There would be meat for breakfast at the tent, and coffee. Sam had gotten to where he loved black coffee with sugar in it.

By midday the trappers had traded for a lodge cover and lodgepoles. Now they struggled to erect the tipi and get the cover on nice and tight, without wrinkles. Third Wing laughed a lot, Sam kept saying he didn't know what to do, Beckwourth gave instructions despite knowing nothing about tipis, and Gideon kept saying, "This is women's work." Except for Third Wing, they'd never have gotten the lodge up.

Sam remembered grumpily what happened last winter when he and Gideon put up their first lodge. Needle and her daughters came to help out, full of giggles at the white men's ineptitude. *Now we're just as clumsy, so where are you? Why don't you help?*

The four men stood back and looked at the small tipi, erect beside the brush huts of the young men. Altogether they'd done a half-assed job, but they would get by. Sam looked longingly toward the main circle. Like these men without families, the trappers weren't part of the circle that made these people a village, where everyone was arranged according to their relationship with everyone else.

Sam thought of what family he had. A brother who'd stolen Sam's girl and married her, and now hated Sam. A mother who loved both her sons in an ineffectual way, and wouldn't live long. Two sisters who loved Sam but were probably glad he was gone from the country and not causing trouble. Altogether, no one who wanted to see him coming.

Sam didn't see Meadowlark all day long.

"LET'S GET GOING," said Blue Horse, happy and proud to speak English again.

"We'll do it right here in front of the lodge," said Gideon.

Though the sun was about to drop behind the Wind River Mountains, they had a good while before dark—those mountains were high. It was a clear, windless afternoon, pleasantly cool before the plunge of the January night.

The four trappers and Blue Horse spread the blankets in front of the lodge and laid the trade goods out for display. Coy curled on a corner of the blanket. Soon Crows were bumping shoulders to see.

Sam had asked Blue Horse to help. Sam wasn't quite that sure of his Crow language.

The most popular item was a free cup of whiskey, as lubrication for the trade. Having neither Crow nor sign language, Beckwourth was assigned to play bartender and instructed to pour everyone a fair two fingers. "That don't make sense," Jim said with a laugh. "The cups are all different sizes." These cups were occasionally tin (luxury items) but mostly made of horn.

"Just do it," said Sam. He and Gideon had prepared the whiskey as instructed by Ashley—one part raw alcohol to four parts creek water, seasoned with tobacco and pepper. The Crows were so avid for it, men and women alike, that Sam was glad it would soon run out. Gideon had told him tales about Indians when they were really drunk—daughters seducing their fathers, husbands raping their daughters-in-law, men fighting with knives or tomahawks until someone was hurt bad or dead—every sort of behavior that forgot they were one people, all related.

Sam, Gideon, and Third Wing traded all manner of things for Crow beaver. Since the fur men had spent last winter with them, some

Crows had taken to hunting beaver, not with traps but spears and clubs. General Ashley liked Crow beaver. He said the plews (the men's common word for the hides) were thicker and heavier, so he got a better price for them. As the men put it, Crow beaver was *some*.

The favorite Crow purchase was a blanket. The trappers had the good thick ones manufactured by Witney in England. Each small black stripe woven into the rug indicated a cost of one plew. The smallest blanket was three plews, and a really big one six.

The prices of other items were not openly declared, and so depended on the bargaining skill of buyer and seller, and maybe the inebriation of the buyer. Gideon was fair and firm in his prices and didn't bargain much. Since he spoke only a few words of Crow, it was mostly point, gesture, and shake your head yes or no. Sam was cordial and less particular about price. Blue Horse checked with Sam before he made a trade—he seemed to take pride in helping the trappers by getting good prices. Sam reflected again that everything about this young man seemed noble. He was going to be a leader.

The Crows seemed uninterested in one item. At Atkinson Ashley had paid Indian women to sew the Witney blankets into coats with hoods—capotes, the men called them. Sam wore a beauty made of a blanket with narrow red stripes on a white background. But the Crows seemed to want the blankets as they were.

It was Third Wing, oddly, who turned the trading into entertainment. He'd take a piece of calico cloth, hold it up in front of himself like a shirt, and do an ain't-I-a-handsome-fellow strut. Then he showed them what the wool strouding, red with blue and yellow stripes down one edge, looked like when wrapped like leggings. He put vermilion on his cheeks as rosy makeup, modeled a string of sky-blue seed beads as a necklace, and did a sexy woman's walk. This drew hoots from the women. He conducted a mock fight, butcher knife against cottonwood trunk, and threw a tomahawk into the trunk with a force and accuracy that scared Sam.

Sam jumped up and added to the show. He got Coy to sit, roll over, and jump for a bite of meat held in Sam's hand. Since the Crows hadn't seen the coyote pup before, and had never seen even a dog obey commands, they were delighted.

The women (most of the customers were women) soon ran out of beaver pelts to trade and started offering buffalo robes. Ashley wanted some of these, and the four trappers would use them as warm bedding against the rest of the cold winter. The Indians also brought forward river otter skins, a bear hide, and thick wolf hides, all worth something, but not as much as beaver plews. After a while they were mostly offering to trade jerked meat and pemmican, the sausage-like blend of fine-ground dried meat and buffalo fat, with berries or rose hips mixed in. It was a nourishing food and would last forever—the men were glad to trade for it.

When dark came, the trading dropped off but continued slowly by the light of the nearby cook fires. Now Needle and Gray Hawk came. Needle was mostly interested in beads, which seemed more special as decoration than porcupine quills to the Crows, and in cloth, which was a complete novelty.

Sam stared at the two with one thought: *I haven't seen Meadowlark at all.* Even Blue Horse hadn't mentioned her. For that matter, Sam hadn't seen Meadowlark's sister either, or her younger brothers. He felt a chill: *She did the goose egg ceremony, married a River Crow, and is living with her husband far down the Missouri. And they don't want to tell me.*

Carefully, he insisted to himself that this was irrational. He didn't know anything about Meadowlark yet. Still, most of the tribe's women and many of the men had stopped by to trade, but not her. She loved beads, vermilion, wool strouding for knee leggings, and other white-man aids to looking good. He peered at the top of Needle's head as she bent over, lifting strings of different-colored beads. He looked into the impassive face of Gray Hawk. *You aren't about to tell me. So what's going on?*

He decided to tie Coy in the lodge, slip away without Blue Horse, and find her. He took a string of Russian blue beads, the finest beads they had, as a gift. Something else General Ashley would take out of his pay.

*   *   *

THE MAN WAS tall and well formed. Sam backed carefully between the tipis, outside the lodge circle and around it to another angle. When he came back into the circle, he saw the man's face by firelight—it was Red Roan, the son of Chief Rides Twice. *Damn.* It was an unusually handsome face belonging to a splendidly built fellow in his mid-twenties. Sam remembered now, he was a widower—his wife and son were taken by the Blackfeet. Meadowlark stood next to him, although she didn't let him wrap her in his blanket. Clearly, she had performed the goose egg ceremony and was accepting suitors. Red Roan was good-looking and much respected—a great catch. *Damn.*

He still couldn't see Meadowlark's face. Though he felt sure, he had to make certain. But Red Roan's big body blocked her features from behind, and from this direction the back of her head was to Sam. *Maybe they aren't courting.* But Sam knew this was a silly hope.

He hesitated, screwed up his courage, and walked up close. *Yes, it's Meadowlark.* He studied her face past the big man's shoulder. She was lovely, far lovelier even than he remembered. Sam shivered inside his red-and-white striped capote. He knew the custom. A girl would flirt with one suitor for a while, and others would patiently wait their turn. Sam was next. She was looking up into Red Roan's face in a way that looked adoring. *Oh, dammit, dammit.*

He stomped his cold feet, he fidgeted, and he fussed. In a few minutes—it was rude to monopolize a young woman's attention unless you were promised to each other—Red Roan meandered away. He had the swagger of a man who expects to get what he wants in life.

Meadowlark turned to go into her lodge, but Sam stepped forward and lightly took her elbow through the blanket. She turned to him, and he saw she was blushing a furious scarlet.

"I love you," Sam blurted. Since she couldn't understand the English, he unwisely added, *"apxisshe."* Though it meant "snubby nose," in Crow it was a term of endearment used by a lover. He had declared himself.

She lowered her head into her hands. When she looked back into his face, she reached out with one hand and touched the *gage d'amour* she'd given him, as though affirming something. Then she said in the Crow language, "I'm glad to see you."

That was enough for Sam. He was sure they'd be sharing a lodge within a couple of weeks.

He fished the string of Russian blues out of his capote pocket. "For you," he said.

She gasped. She looked up at him, her eyes lighted in the way every man wants to see.

"I'm sorry I didn't come to the village last summer." In summer these Crows rode down the Wind River, through a canyon where for some reason it changed its name to the Big Horn River, and north to a river called the Gray Bull. This site they regarded as a summer paradise.

She said nothing. Her face seemed to say, 'A maiden knows she will be disappointed sometimes.' He hated that. He couldn't tell whether her face shone in the moonlight, or shone because she was looking up at him, or shone in his mind only.

"I got lost," Sam said. "My companions sent me ahead to scout and then didn't come up. Some Arapahos stole my horse." Arapahos were enemies of the Crows. "I walked all the way down the Shell River," the one whites called the Platte, "to where we have a . . ."—he wondered what word to use for "fort"—"big house on the Muddy Water River." The Missouri, if he was speaking English.

He saw the question in her face. "I walked about seventy sleeps," he told her, "alone." He didn't mention having only eleven balls for his rifle, not being able to hunt much, and damn near starving to death.

"Seventy sleeps! You're a hero," she said.

Now Sam blushed. Wanting to cover up with some words or other, he broke out with, "Did you lead the dancers in the goose egg ceremony?"

Seemed everything either one of them said was embarrassing. "Yes, our relatives on the Muddy Waters River came to visit us and we danced."

The River Crows, Sam translated in his head, who lived on the upper Missouri in a village he'd never been to. *Thank God, you didn't marry one of your cousins.* He blundered forward, "Do you ever go to visit your relatives on the Muddy Waters?"

Now her eyes grew merry. "Rides Twice would never go down the Muddy Waters. One of our dogs, he likes to say, would not drink such water."

The eyes enchanted Sam. He wanted to kiss her—he was dizzy with wanting it. He reached out to draw her to him.

Just then her father stuck his head out the flap. "Meadowlark, it's time to come inside," Gray Hawk said abruptly, almost harshly.

With his hands on her upper arms, Sam felt Meadowlark stiffen. She turned away from him, then looked back over her shoulder. "Goodnight," she said. "I'm glad you're here."

Chapter Eight

SAM FUMBLED HIS way across their lodge, around the slumbering forms of Gideon, Beckwourth, and Third Wing, and pushed open the flap to the outside world. In front of him stood a spirit horse—it reared and tossed its head. The rising sun shot off the white coat in dazzling beams, and turned the mane and tail into long, flowing strings of black silk.

Suddenly, a dark figure darted from underneath. Sam flinched a little. Then he recognized the silhouette and, yes, the smile of Blue

Horse. "Wake up, sleeping head," Sam's friend called loudly.

"Sleepyhead," corrected Beckwourth as he peered out over Sam's shoulder.

"Sleepyhead," echoed Blue Horse dutifully. "Sam Morgan, rise up. I have brought you a gift."

Sam crawled out of the lodge, shivering in the dawn air.

Blue Horse led the mount in a circle. Sam saw now that it was the finest-looking Indian pony he'd seen, white with extraordinary markings—a black cap around the ears, black blaze on the chest, and black mane and tail.

"She's what we call a medicine hat pony, from the black on her head." The hat was almost a perfect, dark oval around the ears. "This blaze," he indicated the blaze on her chest, "we call the shield. She has hat and shield."

"She's gorgeous."

Blue Horse put the reins in Sam's hand. To the Crows reins meant a rope tied so it held the head and formed a loop around the lower jaw.

"A gift?" murmured Sam.

"I give Sam Morgan this horse," Blue Horse said ceremoniously, "in thanks for saving my life." He cocked an eye teasingly. "Or have you forgotten?"

Last winter, hunting in a brushy draw, Sam came on Blue Horse and a gray-hair lounging half-exhausted in front of a sweat lodge. About ten steps away a coyote was slinking toward them, shaking and frothing at the mouth. Sam shot the rabid coyote. Scared the devil out of Blue Horse and the gray-hair until they understood why he did it.

"Bell Rock also has a gift." Now another man stepped forward smiling—the gray-hair. Sam hadn't remembered his name. He had to be a medicine man, since he conducted sweat lodges. A medicine man built like a frog.

Bell Rock spoke in Crow in a deep, commanding voice. "I give you teaching this horse, and its rider, how to run the buffalo."

After a hesitation, Blue Horse added, "That's just as big a gift."

Sam took the reins of his horse and admired it. The mare was beautifully conformed, and from her teeth only two years old.

Beside Sam, Gideon said softly, "*Belle,* zis horse, she is *belle.*"

"You understand," said Blue Horse in English, "Bell Rock is good rider and very good horse teacher. Our men, they give him robes so he teach horses run buffalo. You let him teach."

Sam ran his hands up and down the neck of the animal. Coy crept stiffly out of the tipi and nearly got under its hooves. Sam snatched up his pup. He fondled the horse's muzzle. He checked all four hooves. The horse was sound. He thought of how he'd seen the Crow men ride their mounts right into the midst of the buffalo herd, both hands occupied with bow and arrow, guiding the horse with the knees only. The mounts made incredible adjustments, constantly saved the lives of horse and rider. "Good," he said. "This mare and I will learn from you."

"You eat," said Bell Rock in rough English, "we go."

"THIS HORSE," BELL Rock said, "is all raw. No human ever touch her back. Yesterday I teach her to lead." He mixed Crow and English, with Blue Horse sometimes helping out. Just then Coy nipped underneath the mare's hooves, and the pony skittered sideways. Sam nudged Coy off to one side and stayed between the pup and the horse. He was carrying his saddle and apishemore, a saddle pad made of buffalo calf skin—why, he didn't know. No one was going to be riding this animal anytime soon.

They walked toward the river, and the mare now followed on the lead rope docilely.

"How'd you get her to lead so quick?" Back in Pennsylvania they taught horses to lead when they were still too small to pull you around.

Bell Rock smiled enigmatically. "You have to be smarter than the horse, and sometimes quicker. When a horse fights, you can't try to overpower it. But when it rears or crow-hops, you can use that moment. It's off-balance. And more tricks, many more."

Sam looked at Blue Horse. "You coming along?"

"I also learn to train a horse for buffalo," said Blue Horse. His

English was always pronounced slowly but well. Sam could hear the concentration on imitating each part of each word just right.

They stopped at a deep pool in the river.

"Give me the saddle and apishemore," said Bell Rock. "Now lead her into the pool." Bell Rock gave a sidewise grin and handed Sam the lead rope. "It's cold for her too," Bell Rock said. "That's good."

The instant Sam pulled on the rope, the medicine hat reared. Blue Horse and Bell Rock shooed the upright, pawing animal, and the mare bounded into the pool.

Sam got jerked in head over heels.

The cold was a universe he'd never known. It felt not like liquid, but a weight, an immense, crushing weight. In one instant he knew he was going to die, and the next instant he burst out of the water for breath.

When the water reached only to his waist, it was merely agonizing.

"Lucky you hold on to the rope," said Bell Rock.

Coy looked for a long moment and then jumped into the pool. He skittered out just as fast.

The medicine hat stood in the pool up to her withers. Her eyes rolled and she trembled all over. Maybe it was from the cold, or maybe from being held on the lead by Sam—she was looking at Sam insanely.

She couldn't rear or crow-hop or buck, or act up any other way. The deep water put a stop to that. Now Sam began to get what Bell Rock was doing.

Bell Rock stuck the saddle pad out at Sam. "Put it on her."

Sam did.

The medicine hat shivered when the pad hit her back. But she stayed still.

Sam reached to touch her muzzle and the horse threw her head. "Won't let me touch her."

"Be glad she's not trampling you," said Bell Rock. "Lead her around in a circle."

Sam did. Unexplainably, his legs sort of worked.

"Put your hands on the apishemore."

Sam did. The medicine hat twitched, but no more than that.

"Take this rope, tie the apishemore on." He handed Sam about ten feet of line braided from rawhide.

Sam had to dip arms and shoulders down into the cold to bring the rope around. He wanted to screech. But he knew if the mare wasn't deep in water, she would have been kicking the hell out of him.

"Enough for now," said Bell Rock.

At the tipi they staked the mare with the saddle pad still tied on.

Sam got out of his wet clothes and into his capote. Then he straddled the low center fire for a long moment, feeling the warmth climb up his legs to the middle region. He sighed loudly. After a couple of minutes he rejoined his friends outside.

"Look," said Bell Rock.

The medicine hat had lost interest in what was on her back and was munching on some winter-brown grass.

"Let's give her bark of the sweet cottonwood." They did. Of the two kinds of cottonwood, horses liked the bark of this one. "You will always stake her by the lodge, always bring her food, never turn her out with the horse herds."

Sam nodded. He got it. Not that he had any horse herds to turn her out with.

When they went back to the pool later, they got the saddle on the medicine hat, and left it on. That evening Sam tried to uncinch the saddle, but the mare kicked at him and crow-hopped in every direction. Back to the pool, back into the cold, and off with the saddle.

The next day they left it on all the next day and scarcely worked with the horse, except to lead it around. When the sun was almost behind the mountain, Bell Rock said, "Soon comes the great moment."

THAT EVENING SAM stood fidgeting near Meadowlark's lodge. His feet were freezing, so he stomped them. "They'll never be warm again," he told Coy, and cursed the river.

Coy whimpered. Sam could never tell what that meant. He thought maybe it was, "I'm sorry I don't understand what you're saying, friend." Coy sat patiently, his butt on the chill earth. Snow seldom stuck in this high valley of the Wind River, but the ground was plenty cold. It didn't seem to bother Coy. "Lucky fellow, you grow your own coat." It was thick, too. First winter on Earth, but Coy knew what to do to stay warm, or accepted the cold as part of living.

Tonight Red Roan was taking his time, seemed like all the time he damn well wanted, with Meadowlark. Sam's practice now was to stand with his back to them and glance over a shoulder once in a while. He couldn't stand to see Meadowlark looking happily up into Red Roan's face, maybe even adoringly. Every night when Red Roan walked away, Coy yipped a little to let Sam know.

Sam looked around at the lodge circle. Every tipi had a fire inside, and they glowed like lanterns in the midwinter darkness. Children were playing games in those tipis. Stories were being told. Women were beading moccasins, or other clothing. People were sitting close to the fire, or cozying between buffalo and elk robes. Sam stomped his feet hard.

A tap on the shoulder.

He made himself turn slowly, unbelieving. Yes, Red Roan.

The chief's son said slowly in the Crow language, as though speaking to a child, "You are training the horse. Good. Soon I teach the young men to shoot bow and arrow well. You want learn?" A big smile accompanied the invitation.

Sam thought how desperate he had been when he had only eleven balls left for his rifle, how near he had come to starvation. Though making arrows was laborious, going to the settlements for ammunition was harder.

This invitation seemed generous. "Yes."

Fear bit at his breath. Was this some trick?

"At the half moon," the big man padded away, light on his feet.

Sam stepped close to Meadowlark, wrapped in her blanket. Now he could forget about his feet. "I love you," he said. This was the way he began the courting each evening.

"I am glad to see you," she answered with a smile. She looked at him adoringly. Every night he tried to figure out whether this was the same look she gave Red Roan, but he never could.

He reached out and took the hands that held her blankets clasped. She squeezed his fingers, reached down, and picked up Coy. At about eight months the pup was getting big to pick up, though it seemed he was going to be a small coyote. Still, Meadowlark picked him up every evening. Sam wondered if that was her way of preventing him from embracing her, kissing her. He watched her nuzzle Coy with her face. Yes, she liked him. Sam had seen the delight on her face when this little animal responded well to Sam's commands. Crows didn't train their dogs like this, or pet them. She buried her nose in Coy's fur and rocked him. *Maybe she is avoiding holding hands with me.*

He told her about his day, what his progress was with Bell Rock and Blue Horse to train the medicine hat as a buffalo runner. He laughed at himself about the awful cold of the river. After a look of surprise—did Crow men confess weaknesses like this?—she laughed too.

Then he took a risk. "Red Roan offered to teach me, along with the other young men, how to shoot the bow and arrow well. Is he trying to fool me?"

"He's a good man," she said.

But there was something she wasn't saying.

"And . . . ?"

"I trust him." She smiled like a pixie. "He and Blue Dog are rivals, maybe a little. Red Roan is a war leader. My brother wants to be." After a moment she added, "My brother is a natural leader. Everyone has high hopes for him."

She gave him the news of her day. She was sewing elk teeth onto a dress. Sam knew it took a long time to collect enough of these rear teeth to decorate an entire dress. When she was finished with that, she would trim the yoke, sleeves and neckline with red wool strouding her mother had traded for. She gave Sam a look like, You're special because you brought this cloth to our village. The dress, altogether, would be very beautiful. She would save it for an important occasion, he knew. He hoped she would save it for the day she came to him and they set up their own lodge, together.

Coy mewled. Gray Hawk was sticking his head out of the lodge. "Time to come in," he told Meadowlark.

She gave Sam's hand a squeeze, set Coy down, and darted into the tipi.

Sam stood and looked at the sides of the lodge, shaped into flat planes by the poles. The fire was lower than half an hour ago. The family would sleep soon, and sleep warm, the parents in the robes at the back, the two daughters on the north side near the door.

Sam wished he had a family.

He strode out of the lodge circle, toward the quarters of the young men and the lodge of the trappers. There a fire would be waiting, and meat, and stories. Gideon, Beckwourth, and Third Wing were such storytellers that Sam could only listen, amazed.

He turned and looked again at the circle of relatives, peoples who made their lives together. The fires were low, making the lodges ghostly pyramids against the black night.

Again Sam wished he had a family.

THE GREAT MOMENT Bell Rock promised . . .

All right. Sam took a deep breath, or as deep as he could get, standing waist deep in this river. The cold made him want to scream.

Blue Horse held the medicine hat's reins. The friends grinned at each other, comrades in being foolish enough to get into this river in midwinter.

Bell Rock handed Sam the saddle pad and the saddle. The use of this saddle was Bell Rock's concession to Sam's being white. He arranged and smoothed the pad, taking his time. He set the saddle loosely on the medicine hat's back. No sense in hurrying when your next job is to . . . He just did it, as quick as he could. Ducked down into the water, grabbed the cinch, slid it through the double ring, pulled down hard.

Stand up! Out of the crush of the cold! He looked at Bell Rock, glad his teacher didn't know how poor the cinching job was.

He thought, bit his lip, ducked down again, and pulled the cinch tighter. The worst thing he could do, the first time on this horse, was to step in the stirrup and pull the saddle underneath her belly.

He gripped the saddle horn, stirruped the foot, and swung onto her back.

The mare stood still.

Maybe she rolled her eyes at Blue Horse, standing in front of her muzzle holding the reins. But she didn't buck. Couldn't, actually. He felt her quiver. He grinned madly. She was overloaded. The cold pummeling her senses. A man invading her back. And the deep water keeping her from doing what every instinct screamed for—to buck this man off.

He sat there, triumphant. He looked at the Wind River Mountains on the southwest, their snowy summits remote against a crystalline sky. He looked at the crazy jumble of red hills on the northeast, footstools of the Absaroka Mountains, strange, barren mazes. He grinned at Blue Horse, then at Bell Rock.

He swung down. The cold made his bones holler at him. He stepped around to the mare's muzzle, looked her in the eye. He put a hand on the muzzle.

For the first time she didn't throw her head.

"Trade breath with her," Bell Rock said.

Sam looked up at him.

"Bend down, nose to nose. Let your breath go into her nostrils. Let her breath come into yours."

He did. Warm breath, warm muzzle—it was almost like kissing. He forced himself not to laugh. He looked into the mare's eyes. *Do we understand each other better, the breath and spirit of you in me, the breath and spirit of me in you?*

A memory seared him. The first night he dreamed of melding with the buffalo, the buffalo melding with him. One creature. "Samalo," he murmured then.

He stood back. Once more, now confident, he stirruped the foot and swung up. She quivered less this time. Once more he surveyed the world from horseback. Then he swung down and waded fast out of the water.

His lungs quit squeezing against the cold. He breathed normally for the first time in long minutes. "Enough," he said to Blue Horse, and his friend brought the mare up.

Coy ran up and jumped on him until Sam petted the pup.

Getting on was achievement enough for Sam this morning. He would give her sweet cottonwood bark now, a thank-you.

"Let's go get warm, Coy. Let's stand by the fire." He wanted to fill both their bellies with meat and the hot liquid it floated in.

"You conduct the sweat lodge ceremony?" Sam asked Bell Rock. They sat behind the center fire of Sam's lodge, dipping meat from the pot. It was their custom, the three of them, to lunch together after the morning's training session.

"Yes."

"What does it do?"

Bell Rock looked away and slowly put out some words. "The sweat lodge is the womb, our mother. We go inside and invite the powers to come, the four directions, Mother Earth, Father Sky. . . . Whoever is in the lodge with me, he maybe asks them for something. He asks for help for his family and his people, that they have good lives. If someone's sick, he asks for healing. He's uncertain, he asks what to do. He has a problem, he asks for guidance. If he's a young man, he asks for a vision, then he goes on the mountain and looks for it."

Bell Rock looked into the pot for a moment, like he saw something other than meat in its rich juices.

Sam blurted out, "I had a dream. Will you help me understand it?"

Bell Rock said gently, "You ask me? Why not ask other beaver men?"

Sam felt like his tongue was lashed to a post. He stammered three or four times before he got out any words. "Hannibal McKye. My friend. Six months ago on the banks of the Missouri River. I told Hannibal my dream of . . . this buffalo." He started to say something about the mystic buffalo, but some sense said *no—keep it for the sweat lodge.*

"Hannibal's the only person I ever told. Hannibal said, 'Do a sweat lodge, tell a medicine man.' "

Sam looked at Bell Rock and Blue Horse. He reached for Coy and slid the pup onto his lap.

"Tell me more."

Now Sam must descend into a morass, or was it ascending into realms of fantasy? The Missouri River was within Bell Rock's ken, but Dartmouth College, a school founded in New England to teach Indians? Latin and Greek?

He blundered forward. "Hannibal McKye is an important man in my life. He's the son—it's hard even for me to believe it—of a man who teaches languages at a school for Indians, that man and one of his students, a Delaware woman. Delawares are Indians who live a hundred sleeps away, near the water-everywhere to the east. Hannibal reads a lot of languages, but he hunts and tracks and wears hides like any Indian. He *is* an Indian. And a white man, all at once. I met him by accident, it was like he was an angel." On top of what must already mystify Bell Rock, "angel" wouldn't do. "A spirit messenger." Sam spread his hands in futility. "He said, 'Do a sweat lodge, tell a medicine man.' "

Bell Rock waited, looking into Sam's eyes, maybe hunting for something. "You ask me for a sweat lodge, I do it as a gift."

"Ordinarily," said Blue Horse, "you give a medicine man a horse in return for this ceremony." Blue Horse's way was always to be a little formal and do things entirely the right way.

"As a gift," Bell Rock repeated, "I help you with your dream."

BELL ROCK UNTIED the thong that held his breechcloth up, and it dropped. He stepped out of the last of his garments, his moccasins. He and Blue Horse looked expectantly at Sam.

"It's ready. Go in, crawl sunwise around the lodge, and sit by the door." Bell Rock made a clockwise circle with his hand to indicate the way Sam should go.

As Sam slipped out of his hide trousers, a flash of memory hit him.

When he had first been naked with a woman, Katherine, now his brother's wife, he had flushed with embarrassment. She laughed at how his pink skin looked against his white hair.

He knew he was flushing now. Off with the shirt, off with the moccasins, stand naked in the February cold. He shivered in one big jerk. It wasn't just the cold, but what was coming—or maybe the fact that he had no idea what was coming. He studied the lodge, which looked a bowl turned upside down. The inside would be low and dark, room only to sit or crouch. And it would be very, very dark.

That feeling lightninged. Once in a while it came up—*I'm living among an alien people. One day will they . . . ?* It always gave him a flicker of panic.

What was really going to happen behind that lodge door? Blackness, chanting, strangeness, maybe a kind of madness. From here he could see the lava rocks in the hole in the center. Some spots glowed faintly red, like a warning. He knew Bell Rock would pour water on them and make steam. He had heard it got really hot.

"Your dream is waiting for you," said Bell Rock.

Sam sucked in his breath, thought of the buffalo, dipped low, and went.

The lodge was pleasantly warm. He crawled to the spot instructed and sat. Close to the lava rocks, his shins felt half ready to blister.

Bell Rock slipped in and sat on the other side of the door.

Coy yipped, and Sam saw Blue Horse grab him and pull him back. "No dogs in the lodge," Blue Horse shouted in English. Bell Rock grinned and called out, "Might as well talk to him in Crow—he speaks both the same!" Sam laughed and felt better.

Blue Horse handed in a bucket and dipper.

Sam smiled wryly. The bucket—at least there was something white-man in this place.

"Wet your hair if you want," said Bell Rock. He dipped his hands in the bucket and slicked his own with the water. Sam followed suit.

"Close the door," called Bell Rock. Blue Horse did. Bell Rock told him where to tuck it at the bottom. In moments the sweat lodge was as dark a place as Sam could remember. He couldn't see his own knees. "Now I'm throwing cedar on the rocks," Bell Rock said.

A sharp smell hit Sam's nostrils, pungent but good.

"First I'm going to warm up the lodge." Sam heard a faint splash of water and then a big *h-i-s-s-s*. Steam ate at his nostrils.

"I'm going to pour four rounds," said Bell Rock. "Four pours the first round, seven the second, ten the third, and the fourth uncounted." Sam wasn't sure what he meant by "pours." Dipperfuls?

"This is your first time. You may get uncomfortable. If you do, put your head down on the ground. It will be cooler there. If you get really uncomfortable, put your nose in the corner, where the lodge cover meets the ground. Try it."

Sam did. Right there the air was almost cold.

"Now you know you can take care of yourself."

H-i-s-s-s! A roar came from the rocks. Steam erupted around Sam's face and chest, almost scalding. He forced himself to stay upright.

Bell Rock began to pray. Sam couldn't remember most of the prayer later. He knew Bell Rock called to each of the four directions and invited them into the lodge.

H-i-s-s-s! Sam thought, *I don't know if I can stand this.* He told himself he had to stand it. If he embarrassed himself, everyone would hear about it, Meadowlark included. The feeling of being closed in was oppressive, maybe worse than the heat.

Bell Rock asked blessings on various groups of people, the unborn, the young, the mothers, the old—Sam didn't remember all of the ones the medicine man made supplications for.

H-i-s-s-s! Sam flopped sideways and put his nose to the ground. *I'm not going to make it.*

Later he remembered nothing of what Bell Rock said after this third pour.

When the lodge felt a little less hot, Sam sat up again. He was glad Bell Rock couldn't see him in the darkness.

Finally Bell Rock called out to Blue Horse, "Take the covers off."

A blazing shaft of light shocked Sam's eyes. After a moment, as the buffalo robes slid off the willow framework and onto the ground, the steam rose to the sky. Cool, delicious air curled into the lodge.

Blue Horse brought water, and Bell Rock and Sam drank, murmuring thank-yous to the powers.

When they had drunk enough—actually, Sam could have sucked down gallons of water—Blue Rock put the robes back on. Little by little, Sam returned in body and mind to the darkness, and the fear.

H-i-s-s-s! This time Bell Rock spoke a long prayer. In the intense heat, and maybe his worry, Sam's mind failed him. The Crow language suddenly sounded alien to him, and he didn't understand what Bell Rock was saying. He tried to count the number of times the medicine man dipped into the bucket and poured. Somehow by his count there were not seven pours as promised but ten or eleven. By a fierce act of will he kept himself upright until Bell Rock cried out for Blue Horse to remove the covers.

When Sam and the medicine man had cooled off, Blue Horse ceremoniously brought Bell Rock his sacred pipe, filled with tobacco and a plug of sage on top. This pipe wasn't like the ones Sam had seen before. Instead of red, its bowl was of black stone, and carved into the shaggy shape of a buffalo. The stem did not have elaborate decorations, like feathers or brass studs, but was unadorned. Sam was glad it was a buffalo pipe.

Then Bell Rock stunned Sam. He reached into the fire, picked up a red-hot coal with his bare fingers, and without hurry dropped it onto the tobacco in the bowl. He sucked, let a cloud of thick smoke float out, and with one hand brushed it onto his head. Then he lifted the pipe skyward and began to pray:

"I offer this smoke to the east, where things begin." After each direction he drew on the pipe and blew the smoke out. By turn, going sunwise, he invoked the south, the west, the north.

Again he held the pipe high and touched it to the ground, to one of the lava rocks. "Sun, we make this sweat lodge for you. We seek your great power, to see many things. Great mountains, rivers great and small, I offer you this smoke. Beings above, beings in the ground, I offer you this smoke. Earth, I offer you this smoke, and I offer smoke to the willows. I ask you to let us see the next time when the leaves come out, when they are fully grown, when they turn yellow, and when they fall—may we see each of these seasons again and again for many snows. I ask that wherever we go we may find things to eat that are fat. Wherever we go, may we blacken our faces." Sam knew that the Crows rubbed charcoal onto their faces to declare victory in battle. "Wherever we go, may the winds blow toward us." Sam guessed this was so the game would not smell the hunter.

"Today a young man lays before you what he saw in a dream. He cries for your help in understanding it—he cries for your help."

Now Bell Rock turned the pipe in a full circle and handed it to Sam. "Hold the pipe up," he said, "then touch it to the earth. When you're ready, cry out for the help of Sun in understanding your dream."

Sam did exactly as he was told. He raised the pipe to the infinite sky. He touched it to Mother Earth. He didn't know whether he believed in what he was doing, and was even unsure what believing might mean. Then he pointed his arms and the pipe directly to the sky and declared loudly, "Sun, I cry out for your help!" Amazingly, his voice broke.

His mind leapt in and interfered. *At least you're praying to something real,* it said, *the sun is real.*

Be quiet, he told his mind, *and let me do my work.* He threw his head far back now, far enough that the low winter sun struck his face fully, and ran down his chest. He thrust the pipe back over his head. "Sun, I cry out for your help!" His voice broke, but that was no longer amazing.

"Offer the sun some smoke," Bell Rock said quietly.

Sam did, and watched in intent silence as the smoke rose through the branches of the lodge and evaporated into the blue, blue sky. Pictures from his dream rose into his mind, sharp and clear. He focused on them.

When Sam finished smoking, Bell Rock said, "Put the covers back on."

Blue Horse did, and Bell Rock began the third round, the round of ten pours. This time he sang a song, a song that sounded extravagantly emotional, plaintive. Sam held the pictures of his dream in his mind, his attention entirely on them. He did pick up one phrase of the prayer several times—"Take pity on us."

This time Sam felt no need to lie down and reduce the heat. He lived in his dream.

"Take the covers off!"

This time Blue ripped them off with a big whisk, and cool air rolled onto Sam like spring rain.

When they had drunk some water, Bell Rock said, "Now tell me what you saw of the spirit world."

At this Blue Horse considerately walked out of hearing.

For a moment Sam was taken aback by these words, and couldn't speak. Then he brought himself back to the task at hand. He told his dream, and what led up to it.

"Before the dream, I was caught in a prairie fire. No way out—I was going to die. The animals all around me were fleeing toward the river, deer, coyotes, rabbits, mice, buffalo, everything. But the fire was on us, and they were being eaten.

"A coyote pup, the one right outside this lodge, came scrabbling desperately for a place to hide. There was a buffalo cow I'd just shot and gutted out. The pup scratched at its slit belly, trying to get inside. Just as desperate, I took the lesson and crawled inside the cow, dragging the pup with me. That saved us. When I saw the scorched land afterwards, I knew that almost all the other four-leggeds died, and whatever two-leggeds were in the path.

"A few days later I dreamed. I saw a buffalo cow laying on her side, and somehow she looked like she was waiting for me. She wasn't the same cow, though. This cow was whole, healthy, waiting for me. What she wanted, I couldn't tell. There was something special about her but I didn't know what it was. I was simply drawn to her, powerfully drawn.

"So, without knowing why, I laid down next to her in the dream, my back to her belly. Then it happened. I passed through her flesh into the center of her. Not just her middle, the center of everything she was.

"I began to change, or we began to change. I became her or she became me, I didn't know which. My hair turned into her fur. My arms reached up, my legs stretched down. I moved into her forelegs and her hind legs—my bones knitted into hers."

Sam looked at Bell Rock to see if the medicine man was laughing at him. Bell Rock showed no expression but high and grave attentiveness.

"My muscles, they joined up with hers. My belly swallowed her food. Then the amazing part. My heart pumped in the same rhythm as hers, and then my heartbeat was her heartbeat, not two sounding as one, but one beat, just one. Her blood was my blood. When I breathed, I smelled buffalo breath in my own nostrils."

He gazed into Bell Rock's eyes, and he could not have said what passed between the two of them.

"Then I stood up from the buffalo cow, except I wasn't just me. I was us. I looked around the world and wanted to set forth into it, ramble around, and I was man and buffalo.

"I woke up. I hugged Coy close. And I said something. 'I am Samalo.'"

"Samalo?" It was the first question Bell Rock had asked.

"My name, Sam, combined with the word for buffalo in English. Samalo."

Bell Rock nodded. He sat, saying nothing, his eyes far off. After what seemed a long while, he said, "Blue Horse, bring us some more hot rocks and put the covers back on."

The fourth round, the round of uncounted pours, went on forever. Bell Rock lifted an impassioned plea to Sun, more chanted than spoken. Sam's mind drifted into a netherworld. It felt lost, like it was floating on the steam he couldn't see, swirling this way and that without knowable reason. Part of his mind was moved, maybe, by the Crow words and phrases—*"Take pity on this young man, grant him . . . Heed our cries. . . . Send us . . . Reveal to us. . . ."*

The heat came at him in waves, and he refused to lie down. A big part of mind was occupied with enduring. He told himself repeatedly that he was making this sacrifice of pain in exchange for a blessing to the spirit. And part of his mind was pleading, *Let it end, let it be over.*

"Take off the covers," yelled Bell Rock.

Blue Horse was quick about it, maybe knowing how it felt. The air felt as good as ice in the mouth on a hot day. Sam got a picture of himself cannonballing into the deep spot in the freezing river, and loved it.

They drank. Now Sam had lost his embarrassment, and poured four or five dipperfuls into his belly.

Once more Bell Rock called for the sacred pipe, and they smoked.

When they were finished, the medicine man asked, "What do you understand from this dream?"

"Nothing," Sam blurted out. Then he corrected himself. "I guess it means the buffalo are important to me. Maybe my connection to the buffalo, or animals in general, is important to me."

Bell Rock waited.

Sam had nothing more to say.

Finally Bell Rock spoke. "There's a lot for you to learn here. Maybe I can guide you a little. But mainly I can help you arrive at it yourself.

"You're right, the buffalo are important to you. The powers have sent you a messenger that took the form of the buffalo. Only you can really understand what the messenger is telling you. I can point out some directions, but really it's up to you.

"From now on you should watch the buffalo for what they might be able to teach you. Watch for spirit messengers in the form of buffalo cows, yes, but also observe all ordinary buffalo. Study them, see what they do. Observe the wisdom of their everyday ways.

"Since you're a man, watch the bulls and what they do. For example, when they fight, the bulls are not quick, they're big and heavy, but they never flee. A bull will fight until he wins, or he will fight until he is defeated. But one thing he won't do—run away. You should think, maybe, whether that's the way you ought to conduct yourself when you go into battle.

"Remember, always look for buffalo cows that might really be messengers. If they are, listen with your heart open.

"Also watch the eagles. Eagles often bring messages from Sun."

Though all this seemed overwhelming to Sam, he repeated the words in his mind and held on to them carefully.

"Understand, the buffalo cow was sent to guide you. Animals are often people's guides. Most Crow men, almost all of us, have seen an animal in a vision, and those are our guides, our medicine. Probably every man wears something in tribute to his guide, a claw, or tooth, or feather, maybe. Or he paints something on his body. Perhaps you should think of doing something like that. Some men who dream of buffalo make hats out of buffalo hide and horns.

"Sometimes picture in your mind the buffalo cow of your dream. Ask her questions—maybe she will answer. Ask her for help. Listen to her without asking questions. Invite her to come to you, and just watch the way she comes, how she walks—sometimes there's a message there. Pay attention to whatever feelings you get, and whatever words surround them. Lots of times these messages are little feathery things, made of almost nothing, like the seeds that float down from the cottonwood trees. But like these seeds, the wispy messages sometimes bear great fruit.

"Return to this dream again and again in your mind. Don't grill it, like an attack. Hold it gently. Feel it. Listen to it. See if, over the years, it has messages you haven't understood yet."

Bell Rock waited and thought. "Anything else you want to ask about right now?"

"I dream about snakes, too."

"What about them?"

"I'm bad afraid of them."

Bell Rock smiled. "We'll leave that for another sweat, another time."

Bell Rock waited a while and then went on. "I think your connection to all animals is important. You should pay attention to that. I study you white men, and I see beliefs that are strange to me. For example, you seem to see yourselves as apart from the animals, made separate in some way. You even think you are supposed to dominate the animals. You treat them as things to use, like a hatchet or a knife.

"We Crows see it differently. We think the buffalo and all the four-leggeds have their ways, which we must honor. The two-leggeds, we have our ways, but we are not the owners of everything. Maybe you think about that some."

Bell Rock waited. "We also think each animal has something to teach us. Maybe you think about that. The buffalo has something to teach you. So does the snake."

"I don't know if I can remember all this," said Sam.

"You'll remember what you need to know now," said Bell Rock. "One thing you haven't mentioned. You are male, the buffalo female. Maybe in some way you joined with the female in that dream, or maybe you should look for ways to include the female in your life path. I don't know how this might work."

Sam nodded. The female part, it seemed like too much.

"I come back, though, to the two most important things. Whatever message this buffalo brought you, only you can know it. Maybe you won't know it in words, maybe just something you feel in your heart. That's good.

"Also, use the buffalo cow as your helper. Ask for her guidance. Listen to what she says.

"Anything else you want to ask me?"

Sam didn't dare.

"Now comes a good part. You need a new name. You are not the same fellow as before your dream.

"A Crow man gets a new name when he does something worth-while. Maybe when he gets a war honor, or does something else big."

Sam was excited.

"Let's go to my tipi."

When they crawled out of the sweat lodge, Coy bounded all over Sam. "How did Blue Horse make you behave so well?" Sam cooed, rubbing the pup's head vigorously. "How did he get you to act good?"

At the tipi Bell Rock painted Sam's face red on the right side, blue on the left, the colors split right down the nose. "This will give you power," he said. "You must wear this paint tonight as a sign to all that you intend to do something. That will be to kill a buffalo cow from horseback and give the meat and the robe to old people who are poor and need it. When you have done this, I will give you a new name."

"All right," said Sam. He wanted to get to the river and look at his new, painted visage in the water.

Then he had an impulse. He said eagerly, "I'll kill a buffalo from the back of the medicine hat." Almost the moment the words were out, he was sorry. *Ahead of myself as always,* he thought. *I can't even ride the medicine hat.*

Chapter Nine

SAM KEPT WORKING with the medicine hat in the mornings and standing with Meadowlark by her lodge at night.

The mare progressed. After letting Sam sit on her in deep water, one morning she stepped gingerly out of the freezing river with him on her back—he just whacked her lightly with one hand on the rump and out she went. There she stood on the riverbank sand, looking around nervously, uncertain what to do when a human being sat astride her. Sam wanted to let out a war whoop, but didn't dare.

Coy darted up and nipped at the mare's heels.

Sam landed *ker-plop!* in the river. O-o-w! He wished he'd come down in deep water. He stood up rubbing his bottom.

Now Blue Horse had Coy tucked under one arm. Bell Rock held the mare by the lead rope. "Lucky she didn't get away," he said. "Get back on."

Sam made a wry face and led the mare back into the deep water.

"Calm, easy," said Bell Rock.

Holding the lead rope again the horn, Sam swung back into the saddle. He let the mare just stand for a long moment. Then he tapped her rump with a hand, and she walked gingerly out of the river.

Man and horse shivered in the down-canyon wind.

"Slip down off her," said Bell Rock, "and get right back up."

Sam did. The mare stood still, bewildered.

"Slip down."

They stopped worked for the morning. Sam was excited.

He made a little progress with Meadowlark, too. Every evening Sam waited for Red Roan to finish romancing her. Even when Sam went early, cutting his own supper short, Meadowlark stayed in the tipi until Red Roan arrived and stepped quickly to him, barely flicking her eyes in Sam's direction. Sometimes Coy barked, like he was trying to get her attention. More likely, Sam thought, he was protesting standing out in the cold while two men flirted with Meadowlark. Coyotes didn't fool around with flirting, he was sure of that.

This evening the wait was even longer than usual. At last Sam took his turn. They stood wrapped in a single blanket, and Meadowlark let him hold her hand. They gave each other the news of the day. They smiled moonily. They looked at the snowy peaks to the west and watched the evening star rise above them. Meadowlark pointed out what she called the Seven Stars, which Sam knew by the name Seven Sisters. She told him how the Seven Stars gave her grandfather an arrow bundle, and now her father was the keeper of that sacred bundle.

Though Sam was puzzled at what a sacred arrow bundle might be, he gave her his mother's story about the same stars. They were seven sisters, all but one in love with gods. The one who loved a mortal was embarrassed, and because of her mortification was the dimmest of the seven. Meadowlark liked this story. Sam liked realizing that his culture had fanciful tales to explain things, just like hers.

"Coy," he said to the coyote pup near his feet, "talk." This was a trick he'd been working on for a week.

Coy sat up on his haunches and raised his head to the night sky. *"Ow-o-o-o-o-o!"* he howled. *"Ow-o-o-o-o-o!"*

Dogs all over camp set up a howl. Angry exclamations came out of tipis.

Sam and Meadowlark looked into each other's eyes, giggling.

"When the Seven Sisters rise at dawn," Sam added, "that's in the spring, they're telling us it's time to plant the crops."

Then he had to explain what crops were, more than a little tobacco planted along the river, and how white people grew their food instead of hunting it.

Meadowlark said, "White people are full of wonders."

Awkward pause. Sam knew she meant her words and was also trying to be nice.

"I couldn't live white ways myself. They're *too* strange."

The two lovers broke into giggles. Gray Hawk coughed loudly in the lodge, Meadowlark's signal to go inside for the night.

She squeezed his hands and disappeared.

He and Meadowlark were not lovers, of course. As Sam neared his lodge, he felt grumpy. Here came another night of listening to the amorous adventures of his buddies. Gideon, Beckwourth, and even the Pawnee Third Wing apparently had no trouble getting mates regularly for little trips to the willows, and they enjoyed torturing Sam with endless recountings while the center fire died down, night after night.

It was clear that the Crows saw no particular virtue in chastity. Men chased whatever woman they had a yearning for, and that was regarded as natural, what a male of any species does. Women were less obvious about their adventures, but the beaver men soon learned that various married women had boyfriends. Their husbands disdained to notice, as jealousy was supposed to be beneath their dignity.

And even more women would take a lover for an hour, especially if enticed with a string of beads.

Sam ducked through the lodge door and discovered, to his relief, that his lodgemates were all asleep. He stripped and crawled beneath his own blankets and on top of two buffalo robes. Coy was already curled where Sam put his bare feet.

The next morning, though, Gideon, Beckwourth, and Third Wing made their stories ricochet around the lodge again. While Sam built the morning fire to take the chill off, they lay in their blankets and traded stories of adventures among the willows. The way Third Wing told it, he pleasured a young woman named Muskrat every evening. Sam pretended not to hear.

"Hand me the *charqui*," Gideon said. He made it sound like a mock order.

Ignoring his tone, Sam picked up the parfleche box of dried meat and handed it to Gideon.

"Me too," said Third Wing.

"Me too," said Beckwourth.

Sam gave all of them a look, but handed the box from bedroll to bedroll. When Coy mewled, Sam gave him some meat too.

Third Wing took out a dried stick and held it stuck out from his groin. "Oh, Muskrat, Muskrat," he cooed.

Beckwourth did the same, crying "Oh, Sweetheart, oh, Sweetheart."

Suddenly Gideon stopped the laughter with a loud, "Sam needs a woman."

"That's right," said Third Wing.

"Damn right," said Beckwourth.

"Enough!" Sam growled.

"No, I mean it," Gideon went on. "You need to take a woman to the willows. If you don't, the Crows are going to think you're a weakling."

Sam ducked out of the lodge and came back with an armload of aspen for the fire.

"You need to think on this," said Beckwourth.

"Think on getting jollied in the willows," said Gideon.

"You're afraid it would make Meadowlark mad," Third Wing said.

"Actually, it would make her respect you," Gideon said.

"When in Rome," said Beckwourth.

"Half of the men are married to two women," Third Wing said.

"Makes you more of a man."

"Shut up," said Sam. The truth was, he'd made a resolution not to touch any woman until he got Meadowlark. Why, he couldn't have said. But he wanted it that way.

Scratch-scra-a-a-tch!

The beaver men looked at each other. They couldn't remember when anyone had scratched at their lodge flap, which was the Crow way of knocking on the door.

Sam called, "Come in."

A shadow darkened the entrance. Then the big form of Red Roan loomed, and Sam saw he was smiling.

"You want to learn the bow and arrow?" These words in Crow were aimed at Sam.

"Sure."

"Come at midday, over by the big yellow boulders." He motioned to the southwest. Sam knew the place.

"Good."

SAM AND COY walked toward the big yellow boulders in good spirits. A week or two ago, when Red Roan first mentioned working on bow and arrow, Sam gave Blue Horse a butchering knife to make him a good bow. Though Blue Horse was only twenty-two winters, everyone agreed he had a knack for making bows. At the same time Sam made a dozen arrows in the slow, meticulous way Blue Horse taught him last winter. He had to throw away several, but the dozen left were good. When he showed Blue Horse the arrows, Sam asked why Red Roan would help him with his archery. "He's a good man," Blue Horse said, "and he must teach his sisters' sons to shoot the bow and arrow."

Sam was sorry Blue Horse, who'd gone hunting, wouldn't get to see this new bow shoot.

On a flat area in front of the big yellow boulders, Red Roan, Blue Horse's younger brother, Flat Dog, and five twelve- or fourteen-year-old boys were shooting arrows at a target of grasses tied together with rawhide. They stopped immediately. "Time for our game," said Red Roan.

"Who wants the white man?" teased the biggest kid. "He won't be able to hit anything."

Sam gave the kid a look and got nothing but impudence back.

"This one is called Stripe," said Red Roan. "He has no manners." Red Roan gave Sam the names of the others. Sam knew Little Bull, the youngest brother of Meadowlark and Blue Horse, but he felt frozen in his brain and couldn't remember the others' names.

"We're going to play a game, rolling the buffalo chip," said Red Roan. He picked up a chip off the ground, an ancient one, very dry. A hole about the size of a boy's fist had been punched in it and in a stack of others nearby. "It's a simple game. I roll the chip across in front, and you boys shoot at the hole."

"The hole," Sam muttered in English. He also found it odd, at twenty, to be included as one of the boys.

Red Roan rolled a chip as a demonstration. Stripe pantomimed taking a shot at it.

Coy pranced forward and grabbed the chip in his mouth.

"Coy, no," called Sam in English. The pup looked back, chip poking out of his mouth.

"Coy, come."

The pup did.

Sam took the chip and handed it to Red Roan.

"Sit," he said.

The pup did.

"Stay put," Sam said.

"What did you say to him?" asked Flat Dog in Crow.

"I said no, uh, come, sit, and stay there."

"In your language?"

"Sure."

"Would dogs do that?"

Flat Dog had a face that looked put together out of mismatched pieces and a half smile that said everything in life is funny.

"Yeah."

"If you told them in Crow?"

"Yeah."

"What if you told the coyote in Crow?"

"No, he learned in English."

"The game," Red Roan interrupted. "If you miss, you let your arrow lie. If you hit the chip, you get your arrow back, but you don't get anyone else's arrows. If you put an arrow through the hole, you get to pick up all the arrows on the ground."

Sam nodded that he understood. "I probably can't hit a moving chip," he said.

The boys all looked at each other and nodded, like "We know."

"First we divide into teams."

Uh-oh, Sam thought, *bad news.*

"The game's over when one team gets all the arrows."

"And they keep them?" asked Sam.

"Sure," said Stripe, like "What do you think?"

"So Stripe and Little Bull, you choose sides," said Red Roan.

"I don't play," said Flat Dog softly to Sam. "Too old."

"Stripe, go first," said Red Roan.

"Beaver," said Stripe. A youngster as wide as he was short went to stand by Stripe.

"Straight Arm," said Little Bull immediately. He was a skinny kid with an angry face.

Stripe looked lingeringly over the faces of the two players remaining. He had a superior smile. *I'm going to be the last one chosen,* Sam told himself, and it made his gut ache. "I choose Spotted Rabbit." This was the youngest-looking kid, with a big smile and baby fat still in his face.

"You belong to the other team," Stripe told Sam. He flashed a giant smile that made Sam sick. "White man."

"My name is Sam," he said.

Coy whimpered.

"Sam," Stripe repeated softly, almost laughing. He gestured for Sam to stand by Little Bull.

Sam looked at Flat Dog, hideously embarrassed. He was willing to bet any of these boys could outshoot him. And he was older even than Flat Dog.

The two teams faced each other.

"Sorry you were last," said Flat Dog quietly.

Sam tried to shrug nonchalantly.

"The truth is," Flat Dog said, "no one wants to lose his arrows."

Sam was beginning to catch on, and he didn't like the setup one bit.

Red Roan put a stop to their talking with, "Who wants to go first?"

Stripe said, "Go ahead, show us what you can do, white man."

Sam ignored the gibe and took a shooting stance. About twenty steps away, very carefully, Red Roan rolled the chip across his front, giving it a good thrust so it wouldn't curl off one way of the other.

Sam let the arrow go, and his heart jumped up.

No, a miss. The arrow slipped by just behind. He felt good at coming so close.

Beaver shot first for the other team and put the arrow right through the hole. The chip spun a little on the arrow and stood up, pinned. Beaver collected Sam's arrow, and his own, without even a glance at Sam.

"That's all right, white man," said Stripe, "you have plenty of arrows to lose."

Then Sam noticed that the other players had only six or eight arrows each. "My name's Sam," he said.

Stripe flipped him an indolent smile and walked off without a word.

"Nephew," said Red Roan, "treat our guest respectfully." But the two grinned at each other.

"Should we have everyone start with the same number of arrows?" Little Bull asked.

"No," said Stripe, "the white man will need all he's got."

Straight Arm shot and ticked the edge of the chip, knocking it over. Red Roan tossed his arrow back.

Spotted Rabbit shot, a clean miss.

Little Bull hit the chip and knocked it into fragments. He collected his arrow.

"Are you ready, Stripe?"

Stripe nodded his head yes. Red Roan hurled a chip fast across the flat ground. Stripe nailed it with a perfect shot. He strode forward in a silky way to get his arrow and Spotted Rabbit's, no swagger but lots of feline arrogance.

Stripe hurled the arrow of Sam's captured by Beaver into the ground point first. "First round finished, your side loses one arrow," he said. "Come on, fellows, we have to get their arrows quicker than that."

Red Roan said, "Get us started again, white man."

"My name is Sam."

But he got into position to shoot. This time his arrow sailed a little sideways, but it knocked the chip down. When Red Roan flipped him the arrow, Sam breathed a sigh of relief.

Altogether in the second round, no one lost any arrows, and no one gained any.

The third round, though, was a disaster. The first five players missed, and Stripe hit, winning all five arrows. "Lucky for you we're on the same side," he said to his teammates. "Go to it, white man."

"My name's Sam," said Sam.

"What is a 'sam' in your language?" said Flat Dog.

Red Roan looked at Sam curiously.

Sam saw his chance. "He was a hero. His name means 'chosen of. . . .' Sam had to hesitate. His mother had said "chosen of God." In the Crow way of seeing things, the Creator was Old Man Coyote; but the supreme deity seemed to be Sun. Sam let it go. "Chosen of Sun."

"What did Sam do?" Spotted Rabbit was really interested.

"Sun revealed to him who should be chief of the Israelites, a man named Saul, so Sam anointed Saul as chief. Later, even though Sam was dead, he came back and charged Saul with failing to follow holy law."

"After he was dead?"

Sam nodded yes.

Spotted Rabbit's eyes grew very round. Little Bull looked impressed, too.

Sam said, "My culture has traditional and fanciful hero stories, just like yours does."

"Very good," said Stripe, and then he deliberately added, "May we win some more of your arrows now? White man?"

Later, when the last arrow was painfully extracted, Stripe said casually, "Thanks for the game, No Arrows."

Sam understood how complete his humiliation was when, in front of Meadowlark's tipi that night, Red Roan left with the words, "Good night, No Arrows."

Sam took his place next to Meadowlark and started to tell her about the game.

"Everyone has heard your new name," she said stiffly.

That night she cut their conversation very short.

THE NEXT TWO weeks Sam simmered. A number of Crows—far too many—called him by the name No Arrows. All he could do was ignore them. He spent all his physical energy on training the medicine hat, and all his emotional energy yearning for the moment Bell Rock would give him a new name. Nothing less would end the humiliation.

Every night he stood outside Meadowlark's lodge while she and Red Roan courted. When the chief's son walked away, Sam turned his back and refused to notice him. It was a piddling gesture, but all he could do. Once he heard Red Roan chuckle as he walked away.

Meadowlark seemed to cut their evening talks shorter and shorter.

Sam waited as a burning, spewing fuse waits.

Every day, all day, he trained the mare. He taught her to accept the improvised rope bridle easily, hand-feeding her sweet cottonwood bark each time she cooperated. And slowly he taught her to neck rein.

This was the crucial step. Feel the left rein on your neck, turn right. Feel the right rein on your neck, turn left. Part of it was also leg pressure. He moved his right leg forward and let her feel the pressure when she turned left, the opposite when she turned right. Eventually, she would respond to the pressure of the knees alone, leaving both of his hands free. Then she would be a buffalo horse.

He got to know her. He learned the feel of her back. He got to know when she was about to shy, or crow-hop, or do anything unexpected. He learned when she was tense and when relaxed. He got to where he knew her moods through her flesh.

One afternoon when Sam was cooling the mare down, Blue Horse asked, "Why are you in such a hurry with this horse?"

"I'm going to hunt my buffalo from her."

"You could use your other mare," said Bell Rock.

Sam said stiffly, "I'm going to hunt buffalo on this mare. I'm going to get a cow and give the meat and the hide to old people who need them." He looked hard at Bell Rock. This was the task the medicine man had assigned him.

"Then you'll earn a new name," Bell Rock said.

After she was neck-reining reasonably well, Sam tried her at different gaits. A cluck and a heel boosted her up to a trot, another cluck and heel to a lope, and yet another to a gallop. Sam found the rocking balance for her lope, and the forward balance for the gallop.

She learned to respond quickly to the feel of the bridle bringing her head back, slowing down, stopping.

After two weeks Sam showed Gideon. The mare responded quickly to all instructions from Sam's hands and legs. "She's a nice saddle horse," said Gideon.

"Not finished out," said Sam.

"A long way from a buffalo horse," said Bell Rock.

Sam knew that.

"Let's see what speed she has," said Blue Horse.

Sam, Blue Horse, and Flat Dog rode upstream to a nice, big flat. There they raced the three mounts all out. Flat Dog edged out Blue Horse, and Sam was a horse length behind.

"Let me ride her," said Flat Dog. He showed the funny, half-smile his face always wore.

Sam hesitated. No rider but him had ever been on her back. Then he swung down and held the reins while Flat Dog mounted.

The three raced back the other way along the flat. The medicine hat won by a horse's length.

"You need a little better balance when she's running all out," said Flat Dog.

"It will come," said Blue Horse.

Sam reminded himself that they had ridden even as children, and he'd essentially started a year and a half ago.

That evening the scouts brought in a report. A small herd of buffalo was ten miles down the valley.

Chapter Ten

THE NEXT MORNING the Wind River valley was a swamp of fog, the cottonwoods along the river hazy, dark lines, the peaks on both sides lost in the gray swirl.

Sam woke up irritable. First he'd sat up listening to four medicine men sing for the success of the hunt. Then he had to watch while they chose Red Roan as the leader of the hunt. One man of medicine had seen the herd in a dream and told the scouts where to look. That medicine man picked Red Roan as the leader—he'd been successful in the past.

After the singing, Sam lay sleepless in the lodge, or had wild, chaotic dreams when he did drift off. But he forced himself—got the medicine hat saddled, pulled her picket pin, and led her to where the hunters and their women were assembling. After the men killed, the women would butcher.

When he appeared, some hunters suppressed mocking smiles. Others threw worried glances at the medicine hat.

Sam knew a bad horse, one who stumbled in the middle of a rampaging herd, or got gored, could kill his rider, and maybe get riders behind him killed.

Sam reached up and rubbed the mare's black hat and ears—she always liked that. He looked down at Coy and said, "Good pup, good pup." The little coyote now had sense enough to stay out from under the horses' hooves.

Bell Rock and his wife rode up beside Sam. The medicine man just nodded at him. No words were necessary. Both knew what Sam was taking on was dangerous. And both knew there was no way Sam wouldn't ride her on this hunt.

Blue Medicine Horse and Flat Dog slipped their mounts in next to him. Sam understood that their smiles were meant to be encouraging, and he appreciated that.

Stripe edged up and gave Sam an ironic smile.

Sam had a strong sense of foreboding. A message thumped in his chest like his heartbeat: *This is not a day for good things to happen.*

Gideon, Beckwourth, and Third Wing eased their horses in behind Sam. "Good day to hunt," Gideon said.

Sam resisted shaking his head no. Maybe a bad day for a lot of things, but he didn't care. No telling when another chance to run buffalo would come. Maybe next week, or maybe not until summer, when he got back from the spring trapping season. He couldn't take a chance on being No Arrows that long. He was about to lose Meadowlark even now. So today he was going to run buffalo, shoot a buffalo, and do what was required to get a new name. If a medicine man told the people he had earned a new name, the Crows would honor it.

He did not let himself know how much he yearned for honor.

*   *   *

A COUPLE OF miles away from the herd, the scouts rode up and gave their report. Where the herd was grazing, the river wound along the northeast side of the valley. The buffalo were on the southwest side of the stream, above a high, steep bank. It was a small herd, maybe fifty head.

"Is the bank high enough to run them off of?" said Red Roan.

Three of the four scouts thought so. The fourth agreed, but didn't think the fall was enough to kill all the buffalo. "Some will be killed, some hurt, all of them confused," he said.

"That's what we'll do," said Red Roan.

Sam felt a pang. If they herded the buffalo off the cliff, he wouldn't get to run the mare among them today. Or maybe he was relieved.

Red Roan and the scouts drew with sticks in the dirt and came up with a plan. The wind was directly up the canyon, from southeast to northwest. So when anyone flanked the buffalo on the downstream side, they would break the other way.

The hunters had divided themselves into three warrior clubs. Red Roan called out the plan. The four scouts and the Muddy Hands would ride along the river on the southeast side, out of sight in the cottonwoods. They would go a couple of miles beyond the buffalo, spread out on a long flank, and ride hard to the herd. Red Roan made sure Jackrabbit, the Muddy Hand leader, understood what to do.

The Kit Foxes, Red Roan said, would go into the aspens on the southwest side and stay well hidden. Today, since Blue Medicine Horse and Flat Dog were Kit Foxes, the white men were invited to ride with these hunters. The chief's son himself would lead the Foxes, and he almost glared at Sam when he repeated, "Well hidden." When the buffalo smelled or heard the hard-riding hunters from the south, the Foxes would cut off any who broke toward the west and turn them toward the river. Otherwise they would move all the buffalo lickety-split toward the river. "We'll run them hard, straight at the drop-off," he said.

The Knobby Sticks, about a dozen hunters led by Bull-All-the-Time, would remain on the upstream side and push the animals toward the river from that direction.

The Foxes and Knobby Sticks would wait for the Muddy Hands to make the buffalo break. Then all hell would break loose.

SAM HAD TO hold the medicine hat firm. She felt the tension mounting—everybody did—she was ready to run. That was good, he hoped.

The fog had gone up to Sun. The day was crystalline, under a sky that was deeper and higher than any Sam had ever seen in Pennsylvania. *Today*, he told himself, *I'm going to earn a new name.*

Or get bad hurt. The memory of the leg broken by a ball at the Arikara villages was still painful. Being flat on his back, then on crutches, then hobbling, weeks of being a cripple . . .

Pictures flitted through his mind—him and the mare flying off the cliff, black shadows leaping into blackness. He tried to ignore the clutter. The mare turning in the air and landing on her back, Sam being speared by the saddle horn underneath her. He could already feel his chest being crushed.

The buffalo were still grazing placidly. The Muddy Hands needed a lot of time, evidently. Jackrabbit would take no chances. . . .

An old bull, one of the biggest, raised his head. He held his muzzle into the wind. As suddenly as a leaf drops off a branch, he galloped upstream.

"*Hi-yi-yi-yay! Hi-yi-yi-yay!*" The Knobby Sticks charged the herd from Sam's left.

Suddenly the horses around Sam ran like hell. He jumped the mare to a gallop to catch up. Excited, he slapped her rump with hand. Now the cry was all around him— "*Hi-yi-yi-yay! Hi-yi-yi-yay!*"

He was dodging aspen trees at incredible speed. The mare was doing the job herself, without guidance, gliding left, veering right, occasionally jumping a downed tree. All that was a damn good sign for running buffalo.

When they burst out of the grove, the closest buffalo were no more than twenty yards away. "*Hi-yi-yi-yay!*" everyone yelled, or something like that. Red Roan galloped in front, hollering the loudest.

When the big bull broke, all the buffalo did. They ran in all directions at once, like balls scattering on a billiards table. One bull ran straight at Red Roan. Then the monster turned and headed downstream, but had to veer off to avoid the Muddy Hands. *"Hi-yi-yi-yay!"* It was a war cry and a declaration of triumph to come.

Sam yelled *"Hi-yi-yi-yay!"* right in the mare's ears, and suddenly she put on an extra burst of speed and took him to the front. Sam hadn't imagined a horse could run this fast. *"Hi-yi-yi-yay!"* he cried.

Faster, harder, faster, harder!

Riders closed in from the right and the left. The buffalo dashed first in one direction, then another. They milled. They bleated. At last they set their muzzles on the only direction open to them, straight toward the river. *Faster*, thought Sam, *faster. Run them so hard they go right off that cliff! Faster!*

A great noise, like a thousand people stomping their feet on a wooden floor. Rumps and shaggy heads rose and fell in rhythm. Horses screamed, buffalo bellowed. Mud clods the size of huge fists flew. A giant one hit the medicine hat in the muzzle—she trumpeted a complaint. Sam kicked her flanks and she ran faster.

Dung squirted out of buffalo bottoms and flicked backward from hooves. A green gob hit Sam in the corner of his right eye. The sting made him shout in pain. He wiped at it with a sleeve and urged the mare to go faster.

He was giddy with the chase.

Screams—incredible guttural screams!

Buffalo were pitching off the cliffs!

Others, he could see, tumbled into a ravine on the right that opened onto the river. Muddy Hands from downstream reined in at the rim and shot arrows into the gully.

All the damn buffalo don't need to go off the cliff, Sam told himself. *I can shoot one on the run.*

He dropped the reins—the mare did better without them—and knee-nudged her toward a cow to his left. They couldn't catch the cow. Sam kicked the mare, and she went faster, but not close enough for a shot.

Sam reminded himself, *It needs to be in the brisket just behind the right shoulder.* He bellowed at the top of his lungs.

Somehow the mare drew almost even with the cow.

Sam sighted as sharp as you can sight bouncing up and down on a galloping horse. He saw the brisket in The Celt's sights.

The cow went over the cliff.

The medicine hat wheeled right, screamed out a whinny, and fell over the cliff sideways.

In midair Sam got his left leg out from under the mare and kicked away.

Whummpf!

Slanted ground cracked his back. He rolled head over heels into a melee. The mare clipped his right ear with a hoof, and his mind spun like a dust devil. Another kick smashed his left hand. Screams—horse screams, human screams, buffalo screams, his own screams—tore his brain.

He got up on one knee. A buffalo bull charged straight at him, horns lowered.

The mare ran at the bull and collided with it hard, shoulder to shoulder.

She went down hard. The bull veered off, shook itself, and slowly turned to face Sam again.

The mare clambered to her feet.

The bull charged.

The mare reared and flashed her hooves in his eyes.

The bull stopped. It glared. Just as it was making up its mind to gore the medicine hat, the air glimmered, and an arrow quivered in its brisket. A second arrow passed straight through the chest and vibrated in the cold ground beyond.

Sam touched his right ear, and his hand came away thick with blood.

The bull stood, fierce, aroused. Its rump lowered for a charge.

Two more arrows whumped into the brisket.

The bull huffed air out, like blowing pain away.

Sam looked up and saw Bell Rock, Blue Horse, and Flat Dog drawing back the bowstrings hard.

He felt the blood split into two streams on the divide of his shoulder and curl down his chest and his back.

Blasts of gunpowder hammered his ears. Gideon and Beckwourth were doing their part on the bull, too.

The mare ran at the bull and bit him on the snout.

The buffalo stood still, like nothing had happened, or he had turned into a tree stump.

Sam scrambled up the steep dirt cliff as high as he could get. He started reloading The Celt, but his left hand would barely hold the rifle. He managed to shake powder into the muzzle—too much powder, he knew, but he had to do something.

A young bull ran at the medicine hat, horns lowered. She skittered away easily, but tripped on a fallen cow. The mare flipped over the cow and sprawled headlong. Sam's heart leapt out of his chest. The young bull stood over the cow like he'd lost interest. The mare scrambled back to her feet.

Sam rammed a ball down the muzzle, eyes fixed on the bull, which was still glaring at him.

The old bull buckled to one knee.

Sam lifted The Celt and held the bull's head in his sights. Then he remembered what Gideon said. 'You can't kill one straight on in the head. The skull bone is too thick.'

The bull struggled back to four feet and planted them wide. His eyes rolled in horror. Blood gouted out of his mouth and nose.

Sam gushed his breath out. He knew that story—bull on the ground, from all the shots.

He shook his head—he was a little light-headed. He looked around. Everywhere buffalo were dying or struggling to live. They staggered around on three legs. They bleated, each cry as loud as ten stuck pigs. Yearlings ran around lost. One cow waded deeper and deeper into the river, as though looking for a place to drown. Arrows whistled down from the clifftop.

Sam knew he had to stay clear of those arrows. He looked up. Bell Rock Flat Dog, and Blue Medicine Horse, almost shoulder to shoulder, were still whanging arrows into buffalo flesh.

Twenty yards from Sam a cow stood still in the midst of the tumult, solid on three legs, the near foreleg raised neatly, like a little finger stuck out from a cup of coffee. Sam figured the leg was broken.

He leveled The Celt right at the spot behind the shoulder. Ignoring the bolt of pain in his left hand, and pretending not to notice the rivulets of blood on his chest and back, he let fly.

The blast knocked Sam down.

The cow toppled like she'd been clobbered by a steamboat.

I got my cow.

Bell Rock grinnned down at Sam.

His head swimming a little, Sam looked around for the medicine hat. To his surprise she was on the cliff slope, half a dozen steps away. He edged over and took the reins. Evidently, once her personal enemy was down, she withdrew from the fight.

Carefully, Sam picked his way along the loose dirt of the slope toward the ravine.

The sides of the ravine were too steep to walk on, but the hunters were finished here. Half a dozen buffalo lay dead. Sam weaved his way up the middle of the gully, a drunk leading a horse. Soon the ravine sauntered up to level ground.

He half-stumbled out onto the plain, dizzy with whatever had happened. He collapsed onto the earth. *Oh, things happened.*

Chapter Eleven

HE WOKE TO a tongue slobbering on his face.

Coy. I forgot Coy. The whole time. Where was Coy?

He tried to jerk his head away, but something held it in a vice.

This realization was knocked to smithereens by a stabbing pain in his ear.

"O-o-o-w!"

"You t'ink to bleed to death, *ami?*" said a calm voice.

Another stab. "O-o-o-w!"

"Easy. Half done."

Sam opened his eyes. Coy licked his mouth, but when he tried to move, the grip tightened.

Gideon bent close over his face. Against the sky, Beckwourth, Blue Horse, and Flat Dog. On their knees next to him, Bell Rock and Third Wing. If he believed the looks on their faces, he was in trouble. The beaver men didn't speak Crow and the Crows didn't speak English, but they didn't need to.

The medicine hat stomped her feet and flabbered her lips, like asking for attention.

"That mare done saved your ass," said Beckwourth.

"She was your *paladin*," said Gideon, with the French pronunciation.

"O-o-o-w!"

Third Wing was holding Sam's head hard.

"Remember Diah, when ze bear got him? Ze ear?"

Diah meant Jedediah Smith, the Bible-reading brigade leader, and that was one of the big days of Sam's life. The griz rushed out of the bushes, knocked Diah down, and got his head in its mouth. After everyone shot at the bear, they checked Diah's head. His scalp was cut to quilt pieces, and his ear was about to fall off. James Clyman sewed it back onto his head, more or less. That ear was nothing Diah would want anyone to see, ever again.

That was all before Sam got Coy, who now sat a step away and whimpered.

"Your ear is not so bad. I am your Clyman. I, how you say . . ."

"Stitch," said Beckwourth.

Sam saw now that Bell Rock was carefully studying what Gideon's hands did. Next the medicine man would want to trade for needle and thread.

"O-o-o-w!"

"Be still," snapped Gideon.

Sam wondered if he cared whether he messed up Gideon's sewing job or not.

"You about lost too much blood," said Third Wing.

"We won't say 'Hold on to your hair' to Sam," drawled Beck-wourth, "we'll say, 'Hold on to your ear.' "

"Very funny. O-o-o-w!"

Gideon gave a big, exasperated sigh. Beckwourth knelt beside Third Wing and helped him clamp Sam's head. "Do it."

Sam hollered "O-o-o-w!" about half a dozen more times, and it was over.

"Let us see you stand up," said Gideon.

Sam rolled over, raised onto all fours, tented his bottom up, and slowly stood . . . until he buckled to one knee.

The knee got Coy's paw. The pup yelped and skittered away.

"I don't know if he is good in ze head."

"Nothing important there," said Beckwourth.

Sam gave a lopsided smile and stood up. He rocked like a sailor on a pitching deck, and then steadied. Coy rubbed against his leg.

"We get the buffalo?"

"We're finished butchering them out," said Beckwourth.

Blue Horse spoke in Crow. "We're going to pack some meat back to camp now. We'll walk and lead the horses. Some of us will stay here tonight, until we come for the rest."

"But you will ride back," said Bell Rock, just like a doctor.

"Tied on," said Third Wing, like a mother.

"I got a cow," said Sam. He looked woozily from one face to another. "I got a cow."

"Are you giving the cow to an old couple?" asked Bell Rock.

Sam nodded. "Whoever you choose."

"Pack the meat on a travois. Lead the pack horse to their lodge. Drop the travois on the ground."

"We'll pack the cow back for you," said Third Wing.

Sam nodded that he understood all. Coy looked at everyone brightly, like he understood too.

"You earned a new name," said Bell Rock.

"What name?" blurted Sam. He would have shown better manners, except that his head wasn't right.

Bell Rock smiled and shrugged. "You'll find out."

"Next time," said Beckwourth, "don't near get killed for a name."

Sam squatted—going down felt risky—and petted Coy. "What about the mare?" said Sam. "Can she get a name too?"

Bell Rock gave Sam a look, like "Medicine men don't name horses." Blue Horse had a similar look. *All right, I know, Crows don't name horses.*

"So I'll name her. Hey, white people do." He ruffled Coy's head fur and thought. "What's a good name?"

"Bull-killer," said Beckwourth.

Sam shook his head and found out it hurt to shake it.

"Paladin," said Gideon. "How you say in English? Paladin? Is ugly that way."

"What's it mean?" asked Sam.

"Knight, a champion for his leader."

Sam nodded his head slowly, so the ear wouldn't hurt. Paladin sounded pretty good.

"Protector," said Third Wing.

"Guardian," said Beckwourth.

"Savior," said Third Wing.

"Save your what?" asked Beckwourth. Third Wing had gotten a little Christianity during his trading post years, and Beckwourth always mocked it.

"Our Lord and Savior," replied Third Wing with dignity.

"More like 'Save Your Ass,' " said Beckwourth.

Sam gave them all a wide, nutty grin. "Save Your is not bad."

Bell Rock butted in. "I name her."

The others looked at each other. "All right," said Sam.

"She is special horse, champion for Sam. Her name is Paladin."

The others checked each other with their eyes. "That's good," said Sam.

"But Save Your Ass would have been more fun," said Beckwourth.

So in a March twilight, while the people were at their cook fires, Bell Rock sent Sam and the village crier around the circle of lodges. "This young man has a new name," called the crier. "His name is Joins with Buffalo, which in his language is 'Samalo.' The crier boomed out the words "Joins with Buffalo" like a flourish of trumpets.

Sam walked behind the crier slowly, ceremoniously. Coy traipsed behind. He looked hangdog, but he went everywhere Sam went.

"This young man has a new name," boomed the crier over and over. "He killed a buffalo cow and gave it to the elderly, who have great need. He is given the name Samalo, which in his language means, Joins with Buffalo."

Meadowlark and Blue Medicine Horse came out of their family's tipi and stood at something like attention while Sam and the crier passed. Their parents, Little Bull, and Flat Dog all came out and stood next to Blue Horse and Meadowlark.

Sam kept his eyes front. He felt like a fool, and at the same time giddy with pride.

IT CAME TO him some time that very night, some time in the wee hours. It was not a cracked dream, nor was it a broth of lost blood and a thunked head. *I can ask Meadowlark to marry me now.* He was sure of it—a man who had won a name could.

He pulled Coy close to his chest and belly. They liked to sleep cuddled up.

And when Sam woke the next morning, in an empty tipi and under a gray sky, he was still sure he could.

His neighbors said the other beaver men had let him sleep while they went to bring the meat back. They were worried about his injuries.

I will do it today.

He ate. He rested. He shook his head to see if anything felt loose. He fed the mare some cottonwood bark by hand, rubbed her muzzle, and called her repeatedly by her new name. "Paladin, want some bark? Paladin, you're a good woman. You saved my ass." He also laid his plans.

That night he caught a break. Since Red Roan and the meat party weren't back, Sam was the only man courting Meadowlark.

After a gray day the sunset wiped the sky clear. The night was so crystalline it felt brittle. When Meadowlark came out, Sam opened his blanket and wrapped her into it with him snugly. She smiled at him like he was special. Coy rubbed against both their legs and lay down. Sam looked up into the dark sky and pretended to count a thousand of the million-million stars. On moonless nights in the high mountains many, many more stars glittered against the darkness, four or five times as many as you ever saw in Pennsylvania.

He had to do it right away. He sucked a great, cold breath in. "Meadowlark, will . . . ?"

It wasn't right. He took both her hands in his. Still wasn't right. He turned Meadowlark away from Coy and got down on one knee. She giggled at this, but he said it was the way of his people, and she put on a straight face. It struck him that she knew what he was about to do.

"Will you marry me, Meadowlark?" The actual Crow words were "share a lodge with me," but Sam knew what he wanted to say.

She pulled him up by the hands, raised him until she could look upwards into his eyes. "I want to share a lodge with you," she said. More stars shone in her eyes than in the spangled sky.

He heard a dreaded "but . . ." in her voice. He waited.

"You will have to ask my brothers for me."

Blue Medicine Horse and Flat Dog, maybe Little Bull too. *This will be a cinch.*

He stood up. He lifted her chin and kissed her. The kiss was so long, Sam was surprised the sky was still moonless when it ended. Then he told himself, well, maybe one whole moon passed during the kiss.

"Every day now, will you teach me English?"

They kissed a lot more, rehearsing the good times to come.

Much later, when she saw Red Roan coming, Meadowlark slipped out of Sam's blanket and back into her tipi. Then she stuck her head back out the door and gave him the shiniest smile he'd ever seen.

Sam's blood fizzed with happiness.

*   *   *

"Eight horses," said Blue Medicine Horse.

"Eight horses," echoed Flat Dog. Whatever Flat Dog said always sounded like a joke, somehow.

"Eight horses?" Sam said slowly. As a gift for the bride's family, it was out of line. A chief's daughter wouldn't bring such a price.

Sam ran his eyes from brother to brother. As though to answer his skepticism, Flat Dog repeated, "Eight horses." Blue Horse sounded uncertain, maybe embarrassed, but Flat Dog was definite. Sam eyed him and got nothing back.

The Crow custom was that a young man seeking a girl's hand made a gift to her brothers, or sometimes to her father. Sam was expecting such a request, but . . .

I want to take Meadowlark with me on the spring hunt.

"There's no way I can get eight horses until summer."

The brothers nodded, as much as to say, "We know."

So maybe your parents are putting me off, he thought. *But why?*

Maybe Gray Hawk and Needle are pushing her into Red Roan's arms.

Maybe she got carried away in the moment and has changed. . . . He put a stop to that line of thought.

"I leave in a quarter moon."

They nodded.

Everyone could see and feel the weather changing. Ice was off the river now. South-facing hillsides were clear of snow. Nights were less bitter. For the Crows this meant the coming of the sign that marked the change: thunder would soon be heard in the mountains. That would put an end to the season of storytelling, winter, and bring on the season of hunting and fighting. The village would join with other Crow villages for the spring buffalo hunt. Young men would gather into warrior clubs and plan what raids they would make against their enemies, Shoshone in the west, Blackfeet on the north, and in the east their most bitter foes, the Sioux, the ones they called Head Cutters.

For the beaver men, it meant the spring trapping season was at hand. Sam, Gideon, Beckwourth, and Third Wing would leave in a quarter moon for the Siskadee, to join their brethren.

Sam looked at the brothers, stupefied.

"Tell him." This was Flat Dog.

"We want to go with you," said Blue Horse.

"What?"

"We want to go with you," repeated Flat Dog.

"Trapping," said Blue Horse.

"With the white men," said Flat Dog.

Sam felt more stupefied, or maybe stupid.

"On the way back to the village," said Blue Horse, "we will get your eight horses and a lot more."

"If you take us," said Flat Dog, "you get your eight horses. If not . . ."

Cornered.

Sam grinned.

THAT NIGHT HIS friends' attitude around the center fire of the lodge was clear enough.

"Why not?" said Gideon, in a Gallic, it-makes-no-difference to me tone.

"Six men are safer than four," said Third Wing, ever the protective one.

"Think they'll still call us the white men?" asked Beckwourth.

They looked at each other. Beckwourth, a mulatto. Gideon, a French-Canadian Jew. Third Wing, a Pawnee. Sam, the only white.

And they were thinking of adding two Crows to the party.

"I'm losing track of white," said Sam.

In his buffalo robes through the night, Sam pondered on all of it. He didn't know. But he had to get the eight horses for Meadowlark.

"FRIEND."

This was Blue Horse, with Bell Rock and Flat Dog right behind him, squatting at the open door of the tipi.

Sam drained his coffee. Gideon, Beckwourth, and Third Wing were already out and about. Sam was lingering over the last of the coffee—he'd grown fond of the sweetness.

"Welcome."

"We have an invitation for you."

They came in and sat.

Sam waited.

"Would you like to be a Kit Fox?"

Sam really didn't know what the Kit Fox club was all about, or the other two main men's clubs, Knobby Sticks and Muddy Hands. They acted as police for the village, and in warm weather made war parties. He did know that almost every Crow man was a member of one club or the other. *If you want Meadowlark* . . .

"Yes, thank you. I am honored."

"Then you must spend today in the lodge," said Bell Rock. Sam knew the club lodge well, an oversized one. "First we must teach you a song."

The words were simple, but the feeling behind them was big:

iaxuxkekatū'e, bacbi'awak, cē'wak

Bell Rock's voice was passion, with strains of melancholy.

"You dear Foxes, I want to die, so I say."

"It is the way of the Fox," said Blue Medicine Horse. "We are made to die."

"Old age is an evil, bedeviled by many ills," said Bell Rock, in the tone of a ritualistic statement. "A man is lucky to die in his youth."

Sam suppressed a smile. He suspected that this ideal was like chastity, honored more in word than deed.

"Sing with us," said Bell Rock.

All four men lifted the song to the smoke hole and up to the sky.

You dear Foxes, I want to die, so I say.

The three Crows sang the words as though they were sacred. Sam did his best to bring conviction to them. He was willing to risk his life for his family, but he damn well didn't intend to die. The words "I want to live" rolled over and over in his head, tumbling with "I want to die."

They sang the song, and sang it again, and again.

At last Bell Rock was satisfied. "When you're finished with Paladin come to the Kit Foxes lodge."

Sam led Paladin to water first thing every morning.

"It's a big day," said Flat Dog. For once the joker seemed excited.

Lots of men milled around outside the lodge. Blue Horse, Flat Dog, and Bell Rock came to Sam immediately. "You may come in," said Bell Rock.

And just like that, without ceremony, it was done. Sam's mind teetered a little. Am I becoming a Crow?

He corrected himself. *When I marry Meadowlark, our children will be Crow. And white. Both. So I must be Crow and white.*

The inside of the lodge looked ordinary, but the men did not. Red Roan and others wore the gray or yellow-brown hides of kit foxes as capes. Younger men carried long staffs, either straight or hooked, wrapped full length in otter skins, and otter skins also hanging from the shafts as decorations. Some of them had painted their faces, one side red and the other yellow.

"We'll explain everything," said Blue Horse. "For now just go with Flat Dog."

Instead of the usual seating pattern, a main circle around the fire pit with others seated behind, there were three clusters of men in the big lodge. Bell Rock went to one, Blue Horse to another, Flat Dog and Sam to the third.

They sat with the youngest group of men. Several looked at Sam oddly. He was the one man in the lodge, he supposed, who hadn't been born Crow.

"Blue Horse sits with the Little Foxes. They're second oldest. Bell Rock is a regular Kit Fox." He wiggled his eyebrows. "That either means they're too old, too lazy, or too smart to do the fighting. They pick us young guys for that.

"We are the Naughty Ones," Flat Dog went on. "We're younger, and we're not supposed to be able to think for ourselves." He smiled slyly. "They actually assign older men to us to do the thinking. To humor them, sometimes we act like kids and play games. It's fun. Until it turns serious."

Sam watched for a few minutes. Some of the older men were consulting. Aside from that, everyone just seemed to be gossiping. "No meetings all winter?"

"The clubs get going in the spring."

"What's the purpose of today's meeting?"

"To choose leaders. For the summer action."

As though Flat Dog's words were a cue, two of the oldest men got up, carrying tobacco-filled pipes in their left hands. Some younger men joined them. These groups went to two young men of the Little Foxes, particularly good-looking fellows, each of them. An older man presented each of them a pipe. Each chosen man took the pipe and smoked it ritually, first offering smoke to the four directions.

"Those two will be the leaders until cold weather comes again," Flat Dog, "or as long as they live. In war they go first." He sighed. "Luckily, neither of them refused the pipe."

Sam soon saw what this meant. Next two old men approached other young men with pipes. "They are asking these men to be the straight staff bearers." Flat Dog nodded at a man carrying a straight staff, also wrapped in otter skins and about three feet long.

Since one of the two was a Naughty One, Sam could hear what was said. The older man spun the pipe in a full circle and offered it to the young man.

Instead of taking the pipe, the young man looked the older full in the face and said, "Please do not bring me this responsibility. I'm afraid I'm weak. I might flee."

"The bearer of a straight staff," whispered Flat Dog, "is expected to plant it in the ground at the first sight of an enemy. Then, no matter what happens, he must make a stand there and not run away. If a fleeing friend pulls the staff up for him, then he may run. Otherwise he has to stay and fight."

The older bearer of the pipe then offered it to another young man.

This man also declined the honor. But the pipe bearer did not take no for answer easily. He presented the pipe again and was again refused.

Now a younger man began to harangue the honoree. "Smoke the pipe," he urged. "You're a brave man—smoke it."

"That's his brother," Flat Dog said softly.

A third time the pipe was presented, and a third time refused.

"You're the right age to die," the brother went on. "You're handsome. All your friends will cry. Your family will mourn, they will fast, they'll cut their hair. Everyone will remember your courage."

The pipe bearer offered the pipe the fourth time, holding the stem directly in front of the honoree's mouth.

"This is the last time they'll ask," Flat Dog said.

The honoree looked at the pipe but didn't take it.

"He's afraid to die," said Flat Dog.

Abruptly the brother reached out, pulled the young man's head down and forward by his hair, and forced his lips to the stem.

"Now he must smoke," Flat Dog said.

The young man smoked.

"He thinks that if we encounter enemies," Flat Dog said, "he is sure to die."

Another young man, one of the Little Foxes, had accepted the pipe and was smoking.

"Ten altogether. Two who go in front," said Flat Dog, "two straight staff bearers, two crooked staff bearers, two who come at the rear, and two who must be the bravest of all."

During the smoking, which took a lot of time, Flat Dog explained the duties of each of these club officers. The front and rear men weren't marked by any special insignia, and their jobs were simply to lead and bring up the rear. The straight staff men had to sink their staffs into the ground the moment they spotted the enemy and make a stand there, not retreating. The crooked staff bearers had the same duty, except that they were allowed to run back a little before making their stands. "Those who are the bravest of all," Flat Dog, "must throw their lives on the ground. Because of that, they get to pick their food first at any feast, and eat before others begin."

Sam knew that among the Crow, warriors got killed far less often than their stories suggested. Even one death was a cause for the whole village to mourn extravagantly. He itched to know the odds of survival of a season as a club leader, but dared not ask.

Suddenly the pipe was put in front of Flat Dog. He looked up into the face of the pipe bearer, then quickly across at his brother. Blue Horse nodded.

"I am a Kit Fox," Flat Dog said in a tone of sincere recitation. "I want to die. But I must say no to this pipe for this season. Blue Horse and I plan to go with the white men on the beaver hunt."

A murmur swept through the Naughty Ones.

The pipe was proffered a second time, a third, and a fourth. It seemed the bearer held no expectation of a positive answer. Each time Flat Dog said a quiet no.

The Naughty Ones buzzed with the news, and many of them looked at Flat Dog and Blue Horse with surprise or amusement, admiration or disapproval.

Flat Dog didn't look at Sam.

Sam didn't know what to think.

During the next couple of hours two or three young men did refuse the pipe successfully. As far as Sam could tell, this was no great shame.

At last all ten leaders were chosen. Each of the staff bearers now carried a bare stick as a symbol of his leadership to come. The straight staffs were peeled poles of pine tapered to a point. The hooked staffs had the same body, with willow limbs tied to the top and curved.

Finished choosing their leaders, all the Kit Foxes marched out of the lodge. First came the two who go in front, then the straight staff bearers, then the drummers. The rank and file, including Sam and Flat Dog, came next, then the most brave of all, the crooked staff bearers, and the rear ones.

They paraded through the camp, singing several Kit Fox songs. People came out of their tipis to watch. The families of those chosen darted back into their tipis to fetch otter skins, or offered their neighbors something in trade for the skins.

Flat Dog told Sam, "We can't quit dancing until they come up with one whole skin to cover each staff."

After many songs had been sung, they sang the one Kit Fox song Sam knew—

"You dear Foxes, I want to die, so I say."

He joined in enthusiastically, sending the words up to the sky over and over. He wasn't sure what they meant, but he swooned into them, and in a certain way meant them.

Then everyone went to their lodges. Blue Horse fell in with Sam and Flat Dog. "The men honored with staffs, at their parents' lodges a man will come who has carried that staff in the past. He will sew the otter skin on. Then they will all come back out dressed in their best clothes. Kit Foxes who have done well with the staffs in the past, they'll come up to these young bearers. Maybe they'll take the staff and smoke with it. Then they'll say something like, 'When I carried this staff, I killed an enemy,' or 'When I carried this staff, I went straight through the line of the Head Cutters and they weren't able to touch me,' and wish the new bearer the same good fortune." "Head Cutters"—that was the Crow name for the Lakotas, the ones the white men called the Sioux.

At his lodge Sam invited Blue Horse and Flat Dog in to eat.

They helped themselves from the pot outside and sat by the fire inside.

"Let me understand this," Sam said. "You've fixed things so I have to take you with me on the beaver hunt. Right?"

The two brothers smiled at him. "Exactly right," said Flat Dog.

SAM WAS PONDERING things the next evening when he heard some scratching at the bottom of the lodge cover. The Crow young men played a game Sam thought was rude. They'd sneak up on the lodge of a girl they fancied at night, when she was sleeping. Then they'd worm a hand underneath the lodge cover and grope the girl, if possible in a private place. A touch meant victory. *No girls in this lodge,* thought Sam. And right now he regretted that.

A hand edged under the lodge cover. He started to whack it hard. Then he saw a feminine hand. A hand he knew.

He reached out and touched Meadowlark's fingers. She turned her hand over—yes, he knew this palm—and offered him a pouch. He picked it up. It was a medicine pouch, and beautifully beaded with the tiniest beads made. It was gorgeous.

He grasped the hand, but it slipped quickly back under the cover. He heard a giggle and quick footfalls.

He clutched the pouch to his chest. *She loves me.*

Also, he now had a pouch for medicine that would always remind him of his real name, Samalo, or Joins with Buffalo. He would tie up a swatch of matted hair from a buffalo head and keep it in the pouch.

Suddenly he was filled with good thoughts. Maybe this whole thing was going to work out. Meadowlark loved him—she would wait for him. Next summer, with Blue Horse and Flat Dog's help, he would come back to the village like a hero, eight horses in hand, or more.

Meadowlark's parents had thrown a glove on the ground.

Sam took up their challenge.

Part Two

STALKING BEAVER

Chapter Twelve

BLANK. EMPTY. MOUNTAINS well off to the west, mountains well off to the east. Big river in the middle, with desert scrub all around it.

No sign of the brigade.

Sam was sure his count was right, or close. It was April 14, or maybe a day or two later. The phases of the moon, full, half, and new, had made it easy to keep track of the weeks on his counting stick. Sixteen weeks and a day since they left Ashley on the Platte.

Sam looked around. Desolation in every direction, including his heart.

Memory: Last June he went ahead alone, with a promise to meet Diah and Fitz and the boys where the river got deep enough to float. He waited eleven days. They never showed up.

Then his imagination ran wild. They were all killed by Indians. They got lost and would never find their way home. In this vast, apparently endless landscape, desert horizoned by mountain followed by desert and again horizoned by mountain, a man could never find his way home. There was no such place as home, not anymore, not for the men who came out here to hunt beaver.

On the twelfth day he'd set out downstream for the settlements. He had only eleven lead balls left, and so would seldom be able to hunt. He wasn't sure whether this river was the Platte or the Arkansas, whether he would hit the Missouri four hundred miles above St. Louis or the Mississippi three hundred miles below it. In other words, he was good and lost.

He damn near starved to death. He got captured by Indians who would have tortured and killed him, except for Third Wing. He got caught in a prairie fire and survived by hiding in a buffalo carcass with Coy. After more than two months of wandering, he stumbled into Fort Atkinson.

Maybe in the end, the reality had been wilder than his imaginings.

Here he was again, waiting for a brigade that didn't come. He looked around at his five friends, Gideon, Beckwourth, Third Wing, Blue Medicine Horse, and Flat Dog. Coy, too, panting there in front of Paladin. Sam felt a throb of gladness next to his pang of fear.

This time coming over the South Pass had been easy. Mid-April, mid-March, an entirely different story, new grass instead of deep snow and howling winds. They crested the continental divide, came onto the headwaters of the Sandy, a pathetic stand-in for a river, and followed it here to the Siskadee. All the way they looked for sign of Ashley's horses, nearly fifty of them. Not a hoofprint. At the junction of rivers they looked for the cairn Fitz said he would leave. Nothing. No sign of human beings, not even Indians.

This was Snake country. Crows and Snakes were longtime enemies. Snakes had run Sam's outfit's horses off this time last spring, not far from here. Not a place to be wandering around carelessly in a small party.

They settled in to wait.

COY SENSED THEM first. On the fourth day Sam was taking evening watch on top of a sandstone outcropping, stroking Coy's back. Suddenly the coyote pup jumped up and pointed ears, nose, and eyes up the Sandy. The wind was blowing down the little river.

Sam stood for long minutes before he saw anything. *But,* he thought, *twenty-two men and maybe forty horses make a lot of sound and smell.*

Finally, one rider skylined on a ridge. By the silhouette Sam recognized Fitzpatrick.

In seconds, it seemed, all six of them were hightailing it up the river.

Whoa. Here came the outfit. But it was in poor shape, most of the men walking and leading heavily laden horses.

Still, the welcome was warm.

"Look who's still above ground."

"This nigger thought them Crow women diddled you to death."

"Glad to see you, hoss."

"Look who's still got his hair!"

" 'Bout missin' an ear, though."

These greetings from Ashley, Fitzpatrick, Clyman, Zacharias Ham, and all the others, every man looking hale and hearty.

Blue Horse and Flat Dog hung back, uncertain. Sam waved to them to come up and meet the general.

After the introductions Ashley said, "Looks like you came through well."

"You, too," answered Sam.

Ashley shook his head. "Lost seventeen of my best horses to the Crows. Recently." The general couldn't help throwing an odd glance at Blue Horse and Flat Dog.

"Wasn't our Crows," said Gideon. "All of us been layin' 'round camp lazy all winter."

Now Flat Dog showed off his English. "Some of our young men think, run horses off is most fun anything."

Zacharias Ham threw a woolly look at the two Crows. "We'll learn 'em what's fun."

"You men are welcome in camp," said Ashley.

"They want to trap with us," put in Sam.

"Welcome to that, too," said the general.

So it was settled. Sam had never known he was nervous.

Quickly the camp settled into fires against the evening chill, roasting meat, and stories.

First the Ashley men caught Sam and the fellows up on what had happened since they left. January the brigade spent toiling up the South Platte until, at last, they got within sight of the Rocky Mountains— that brought a cheer. February was given mostly to waiting in a cottonwood grove and looking at the spectacle of snow and ice ahead. At the end of the month they forced a crossing of the main range, a bitter three days struggling through snow. Then they emerged onto the Laramie Plains, a fine country along the North Platte, full of game. The next range, the Medicine Bow Mountains, turned them back. But it was March now. They slowed down and moved northward, trapping the creeks of the east side of the range. The next pass led to a paradise of game, the valley of the North Platte River.

April now, time to head for the Siskadee. The Wind River Mountains lined the western horizon. Fitzpatrick, though, told how the horses got run off, and how he led a party to get them back. They came on two animals so weak the Indians had abandoned them, but never caught up with the rest.

That's how the brigade came to the Siskadee half worn-out. Plenty of smiles, though. The horses were loaded with plews aplenty.

Sam, Gideon, Beckwourth, and Third Wing gave back their own stories. The favorite was about Paladin. Blue Horse told in good English how Sam trained her in the freezing river. He still chuckled about how cold Sam looked standing rib deep in that river.

"But his mind," said Gideon, "it always point to the day he ride her against ze buffalo. When he shoot a buffalo riding her, he get new name. Medicine man, he promise, new name."

Sam was embarrassed, so he took over the telling, and got as far as when the buffalo stampeded for the river. "I rode hard at those buffalo. I could hear bellowing as they went off that cliff ahead. And then . . ."

Abruptly, Beckwourth jumped in, "And then, he got the brightest of his bright ideas. I can shoot a cow right now. Riding hard, he takes aim, he gets her in his sights just perfect and . . ."

"Off the cliff goes!" hollered Gideon. "Cow, horse, and rider."

The beaver men applauded.

Sam retreated to petting Coy.

"Sam, mare, cow, all topsy turvy over ze cliff." Dramatic pause. "He lands in middle of the buffalo driven off ze cliff."

"They ain't all hurt," Beckwourth put in. "This one old bull, he lowered his horns and looked at Sam between 'em just like sights. He charged."

"And ze mare," interrupted Gideon, "she save his miserable life. She run at buffalo—boom—knock him off balance."

"The bull," Beckwourth burst in, "he gets his feet back under him and lowers that head."

"Then Blue Horse, Flat Dog, and ze medicine man, they shoot him a little bit wit' arrows. We shoot him a little bit with lead. Ze mare, now she run up to ze bull and . . ."—Gideon opened his arms wide to his audience—"she bite him on the snout!"

The men cheered.

"So the one that earns the new name," said Beckwourth, "is the mare. Paladin. But we oughta called her Save Your, short for Save Your Ass."

The men roared.

After a while, in the following silence, Sam said, "I got a new name, too."

"You did," Gideon allowed. "Ze medicine man gave him a name."

"What are you called now, Sam?"

"Joins with Buffalo," said Sam.

Men made faces. One farted loudly, causing a bubble of laughter.

Fitzpatrick went up to Sam and clapped him on the shoulder. Sam kept his hands on Coy.

"To your fellow mountain men, lad, to us you will always be known as *mi coyote*."

TIME TO GET serious about the spring hunt. Ashley divided them into four outfits. Fitzpatrick would take his south, to trap the mountains visible on the horizon. Zacharias Ham would lead men west to those mountains easy to see. James Clyman would lead his north along the Siskadee and trap its headwaters, right where they'd gone before.

Himself, Ashley would do a journey of exploration. He wanted to know whether this river was the Colorado, which flowed into the Gulf of Mexico, or the Multnomah, which emptied into the Columbia, or the Buenaventura, which emptied into the Pacific near Monterey, California. The men said nothing. Everyone knew that if this was the Buenaventura, the road was open to the Golden Clime—fur men would be the first to reach Alta California by land!

Sam quietly asked Clyman to choose him and his friends to make an outfit together. He knew Clyman wouldn't mind a multicolored brigade.

James just nodded.

THE TRAPPING FELT good to Sam. Up in the morning at first light, coffee, get mounted, move out. Ride with your partner up a creek coming down from the Wind River Mountains to the east. Watch for slides, dams, chewed cottonwoods, any beaver sign. Pick a likely spot to set a trap, especially one out from a slide. Move downstream, splash into the creek, which right now was snow run-off from some of the highest, coldest mountains in the nation. Wade up to the spot and set your trap. Put a big stick through the ring at the end of the chain, so the beaver can't swim off with it. Dip a small stick into your horn of castoreum and bait the trap with it. Attach a floating stick, in case the beaver, despite all, swims off with the trap. Move upstream to the next likely spot, keeping an eye out for Indians all the way.

Sam's partner was Blue Horse, which made "keeping an eye out for Indians" funny. Sam took Blue Horse, Gideon took Flat Dog, and Beckwourth took Third Wing, in each case an experienced hand showing the ways to a new man, what they called a pork-eater. Clyman kept the camp.

Later you would raise your traps and ride up the creek, or on to the next stream, depending. After you trapped the wily rodent and he drowned, you still had plenty of work to do. You skinned out your beaver, taking only the pelt and the tail. Back in camp you scraped the hide free of fat and stretched it on a hoop you made from willow branches. The tail you threw in the coals for eating, a delicacy. Your pack horse would bear your plews, or you'd cache them for retrieval later.

In this way the little Clyman outfit worked its way up the river they called the Siskadee. Sam knew that just across the mountains he was working, on the east side, was the winter camping place of the village led by Rides Twice, the village where lived his love, Meadowlark. By now, surely, the village had moved down the Wind River, made its big turn to the northeast, worked their way through the big canyon, and come to where it changed its name to the Big Horn. There they would do the spring buffalo hunt. There, sometime this summer, Sam would ride into the village leading eight horses and claim her hand.

For now, though, the creeks were running full, the pelts were prime, he had good comrades, and it was time to make a living.

SAM THOUGHT IT was the weirdest thing he ever saw.

They had worked their way north along the Siskadee to where she came out of the mountains, no longer a big, fat, slow snake of a river but a sprightly colt. He and Blue Horse trapped their way up a creek half the day and down it the second half. They were riding into camp an hour beyond sunset, in the very last of the light. And he distinctly saw three fires instead of the one there should have been. And the men around those fires, where Clyman and their friends should have been, were . . .

Indians!

He looked at Blue Horse guiltily.

"Snakes!" his friend hissed.

Sam dismounted. They tied the horses to a cedar and put Coy on a lead rope. Sam jerked his head to the left, and they eased up a sandstone outcropping.

When they got there, Sam chuckled. Beyond the Indian camp, clear enough to the eye, was the camp of the fur men. Sam counted five figures—everyone accounted for.

"We've got company," he said to Blue Horse.

Just in case, they rode a wide circuit around the Indian camp.

"Snakes," said Clyman.

"How many?"

"Fourteen."

"How many guns?" said Sam.

"Two that I saw."

"They're friendly," said Beckwourth.

"Say they are," corrected Clyman. "Want to trade."

"What can we trade them?" said Sam.

Everyone knew what was in their panniers—a few beads, a little jerked meat, some good twists of tobacco.

"We need horses," said Clyman. "We gotta try."

The entire brigade had been short of horses from the start.

"I will trade my pistol for a horse," said Gideon.

Clyman shrugged. "We'll try."

All the men looked at each other warily. From their expressions, Sam judged, the Crows trusted these Snakes even less than the mountain men did.

"We'll hobble the horses and make a rope corral too," Clyman said. "We'll also set a double guard."

"And tomorrow," said Beckwourth, "we'll do some old-fashioned horse-trading."

SAM CLAMPED HIS teeth together to keep them from chattering. He wiggled his toes, left foot, right foot, left foot, right foot—the toes were likely to freeze. Damn Rocky Mountains in the springtime.

The sky wasn't any lighter than a few minutes ago. In an hour the world would be warmer, and his time on watch would be over.

One by one, he poked each gloved finger up and down, the left fingers on the barrel of The Celt, right fingers on the stock. He pulled the hood of his blanket capote tighter around his face. He wanted to stomp his feet, but didn't dare. Guards were supposed to be absolutely silent.

He reached down and patted Coy. While the others slept, Coy went with Sam on watch every time.

His eyes probed the darkness. The half moon let patches of light through, but the cottonwoods threw big blotches of blackness. Chances were better for hearing an enemy than seeing one.

Probably nothing will happen. Nothing had ever happened while Sam was on watch. Yet he took standing guard with complete seriousness. He would always take it seriously, and would always be scared.

Tonight he was also worried about Third Wing, the other guard. His friend . . . Sam didn't know. Maybe he thought Third Wing hadn't spent enough time at this duty. Maybe he thought Third Wing had too motherly a way about him to fight hard. Maybe . . .

Sam was worried.

Third Wing's job was to stay by the horses penned in the rope corral. Sam's was to stand in different spots around the camp, each one with a good vantage point. To keep his eyes and ears wide open, and if he saw or heard anything, to yell like hell.

The silence made Sam's ears ache.

Now the sky was a shade lighter. The half moon made only gray shadows. The world was no longer black but dark gray.

"Hunnh!"

Instantly, Sam yelled, "Indians! Indians! Indians!"

He shouldered his rifle—this light gray spot, that dark gray spot—seemed like he was pointing it in every direction at once. He saw no one.

"Indians!" he bellowed louder.

Damn! That "hunnh" sound, it was a human being getting hit hard by something, and it came from the horse pen.

I better get over there.

"Blam!"

Sam heard it and felt it at the same time. He grabbed the left side of his chest.

Godawmighty, I'm shot!

But it didn't hurt.

Why?

He looked around. Dark human shapes were darting around the horse pen.

Shouts came from his camp. "Indians! Indians!" Help was coming.

Get going!

He wiped his right hand on his face. Dry, not wet. No blood.

He ran lickety-split toward the horse pen.

The mounts were jostling around, but they weren't running. For sure the rope that made the corral was cut. *We fooled you! When you cut the corral, you thought you could run the horses off. But they're hobbled.*

He saw human arms, legs, heads here and there. He tried to sight on one, but knew he was more likely to hit a horse than a thief.

He almost stumbled over a moccasined foot sticking out of a gray shadow.

He bent over it—Third Wing, unconscious. He groped for the head. Both hands came away gooey with blood.

"Horse thieves! Horse thieves!" That was Gideon roaring. Sam recognized the blam! of Gideon's .58, largest of all the men's rifles.

Lots of footsteps coming toward the horses.

Sn–n–i–i–i–ck!

Flame seared his chest!

He felt his right ribs. Blood. An arrow, probably . . . *My blood!*

He went berserk. He ran crazy-legged into the shadows in the direction of the arrow.

"You bastards!"

I will die with your blood on my hands!

Movement. Maybe movement, going away from the horses. He slapped The Celt to his shoulder and fired in the direction of the flicker in the half light.

Damn! Stupid! Now his rifle was empty.

He dashed to the horse pen. The corral rope was on the ground. Paladin was still there, cross-hobbled. Gideon's horses too. Every man had his own way of not ending up afoot.

The beaver men ran around the horses, looking for horse thieves to shoot.

Sam reloaded. *I'm going to kill someone before I die.*

"The Indian camp! The Indian camp!" Clyman shouted.

Sam and Beckwourth sprinted out of the cottonwoods upstream toward the Snake camp.

Arrows flew around them like flocks of birds.

Sam dashed back into the trees. He gasped for breath. "All right!" He shouted to Beckwourth. "I'm all right."

He knew he wasn't, he had a mortal wound, but he hadn't been gored by the burst of arrows. "I dance past death!" he roared. It was unbelievable, like running through raindrops and not getting wet.

He realized Beckwourth was standing beside him.

They looked around the trees.

A red ridge blocked their view of the Indian camp upstream.

"Let's charge the bastards!" said Beckwourth.

"Yeah!" said Sam.

"No!" said Blue Medicine Horse in English, coming up.

"Let's get high and shoot down on them," said Flat Dog.

"We'll get up that ridge," Clyman said.

Every man stopped and looked at the leader, then nodded.

"Sam, you're hurt. Let me see."

Sam raised his right arm. A finger poked at his ribs painfully. Something bit the back of his arm.

"You're lucky. Arrow gouged your ribs, bounced off into your arm. You'll be all right."

Sam was hugely relieved, and maybe half-disappointed.

"Beckwourth, Blue Horse, Flat Dog, go with Sam," said Clyman. "I'll help Gideon watch the horses. And take care of Third Wing."

"Third Wing's near dead," said Beckwourth.

"Bad hurt," corrected Clyman. He fixed Sam with ice-gray eyes. "You can help him later. Remember, Sam, you're in charge."

Me?!

"Let's go kill Snakes," said Medicine Horse.

THE FUR MEN ran fast to the top of the little ridge. They crept up and looked over without showing themselves too much. "Down!" Sam ordered Coy. The pup circled and curled up.

From there the Snakes' dilemma was obvious. Their camp was on the south side of the creek. Across from it, in a finger between two low ridges, some boys held the Indian party's mounts ready. No doubt, as soon as the trappers' animals were loose, the Snakes had intended to stampede them off. Which had turned sour on them.

Now the Snakes were mostly pinned down in the cottonwoods where they'd camped or in the brush along the creek. If they tried to ride off, they'd have to bring the horses out from that finger of land between the two ridges. Then the trappers would have clear shots, and this ridge made a nice shooting angle.

The mountain men looked at each other, faces set hard. Third Wing's blood cried out for vengeance.

"How many do you see?" asked Sam.

Everyone saw two or three boys, probably, holding the Shoshone horses far to the back. Out of range.

Blue Medicine Horse said he saw two men hidden behind the trunks of cottonwoods. Within a couple of minutes the other trappers saw a hand or a bow or a flap of clothing stick out. Two men in the trees.

The brush stirred here and there. Nothing visible to shoot at.

Sam got a chill. He looked around. No, this was the highest point for about a quarter mile. No one could shoot down at him.

"We could work around and take the boys and steal the horses," said Beckwourth.

Everyone said "Yeah" before they thought. Getting even, that sounded good.

"We don't know where all the men are," said Sam. "Half of them could be laying a trap to get us if we go for the horses."

And what if they come up behind us, or from the side? Maybe every man had the same thought at the same time. All four of them looked around warily.

Sam said, "Blue Horse, back down off this edge a little. Keep a lookout," said Sam. "All the time. Make sure no one comes up on our backs."

Blue Horse nodded and went.

"We'll take turns at that."

Coy mewled, like he was agreeing.

Sam turned back to the Indian camp. He, Flat Dog, and Beckwourth laid flat on their bellies, peered over the lip of the hill, and looked sharp. "A bunch of them is down in that brush somewhere," said Beckwourth.

Flat Dog said in a heavy accent, "Or somewhere else."

Rocks exploded in front of Sam's face.

"Boom!" spoke a rifle.

A big puff of black smoke fizzed up from the brush.

Sam rolled several feet down the hill, brushing at his face.

Beckwourth fired beneath the smoke. Just then they saw a figure with a rifle scurry into another bunch of willows.

"Waste of DuPont and Galena," said Beckwourth. Trapper talk for powder and lead.

Looking across at Sam, Flat Dog said, "You got some little flecks of red war paint."

Sam brushed at the bleeding scratches. Coy licked at them.

"We better stay here and not go looking for trouble," said Sam. "And we have to make damn sure of our targets," said Sam. His blood was singing revenge in his ears.

No one had DuPont and Galena to waste. Blue Horse and Flat Dog carried maybe a dozen arrows each. Sam had the bow and arrows he wasn't so good with.

Sam grabbed pieces of sandstone in each hand and shoved them up in front of Beckwourth and Flat Dog. "Build something for us to hide behind."

In ten minutes it was done, a low wall with gaps between the rocks to look through, and to stick the muzzle of a rifle through. Sam, Beckwourth, and Flat Dog stretched out behind and watched. Coy curled up at Sam's feet.

They settled in.

"What I think," said Jim, "is that it's going to be one hell of a long day."

NOT ONLY LONG, it turned out, but hot and thirsty. They were exposed on an outcropping, in full sun without a hint of shade, a swig of water, or a breath of wind. The Rocky Mountains proved once again they would freeze you all night and broil you all day. Coy whimpered. The pup didn't like it when they stayed far from water.

Sometimes the trappers saw movement in the brush. Occasionally Beckwourth shot at the movement, and once he thought, from an outcry, that he killed a Snake.

About midday Flat Dog, standing watch, said "Here comes Gideon."

The big French-Canadian ran a zigzag pattern from cover to cover, carrying a small, flat keg. Then he looked around, shrugged, and walked up the open hillside. "Sorry," he said when he reached them, "Clyman and me, we not think until now, you no got water."

Every man drank his fill, and Sam cupped hands for Coy to drink.

"You go down now," Gideon said to Sam. "I take over here. You go see Third Wing."

IS HE DEAD? He wasn't moving. His skull was broken open, probably by a stone axe or a tomahawk. Streams of blood made cracks down his face, like a stone broken by a sledge hammer. Blood tangled his black hair, and red stained the big hanks of Sam's white hair tied into it.

Brought low.

Coy uttered a whine and laid down between Third Wing's feet.

Sam sat next to his friend, wet a forefinger, and held it in front of Third Wing's nostrils. Air cooled the finger.

"He won't last," said Clyman.

"Hugh Glass lasted," said Sam.

Sam stepped over to the creek. Coy followed and lapped. Sam drew air in big and let it out big. He felt as though, in all that vast Western sky, his lungs couldn't catch breath. When he was calm, he fished in his shot pouch and brought out a rag, a piece of cloth he used for tearing patches for his rifle. He wet the rag in the cold running water, walked back, and sat down by his friend. He squeezed drops of water from the rag into Third Wing's open mouth.

The parched lips made no movement. The dry tongue gave no sign. Sam saw the eyelids flutter, though, and that gave him hope. He put his hand to the medicine pouch around his neck.

Clyman moved around, rifle in the crook of his left arm. He was padding from tree to tree in the cottonwood grove. From every station he studied the plain for sign of enemies. Luckily, the campsite offered no good cover for sneaking up.

Sam put his mind deliberately on Hugh Glass. Everyone knew Glass was dying. Major Henry left two men to bury him while the brigade rode on. They abandoned Glass. The old fellow came to and started crawling back to the fort where they started, a couple of hundred miles away. He made it.

Third Wing was going to make it.

*   *   *

COY HEARD CLYMAN'S footsteps before Sam did. Sam refused to look up. "Don't kid yourself," said Jim, "Third Wing's luck has run out."

Sam said nothing. He reached down and took Third Wing's hand. Maybe his friend would take comfort from that. Coy licked the joined hands.

"Why don't you take a snooze?" said Clyman. "You look tired. It's going to be a long night, and I'll need you for two watches." He padded away on his rounds.

Sam certainly wasn't going to nap while his friend struggled for life. He took his patch cloth, wet it from a keg, and dribbled water into Third Wing's open mouth. No response except for ragged breathing.

He leaned back against a cottonwood and took Third Wing's hand again. It was a fine afternoon. The sun felt good on his face, the little breeze felt good, and he liked the small rustling of the cottonwood leaves. A good day. Death danced "Skip to My Lou" around the edges.

HE WOKE WITH a start. How long had he slept? *Why is my hand cold?*

Oh. He shook his hand free.

It was Third Wing's hand that was cold.

Coy crooned out a moan.

Sam just sat. Death had wiped his mind clean.

When he heard footsteps, Sam said softly, "James."

Clyman came up, looked from Sam to Third Wing and back. "You want to do the burying?"

"That would be hard."

"Me and Beckwourth will do it. Go relieve him."

NOTHING WAS A whit different on the ridge. Not a shot had been fired since Sam left. "Them Snakes moved around a little," said Jim, "but too quick. They're waiting for dark."

"And then what?"

Beckwourth shrugged.

Gideon was asleep on his back, wheezing like a bellows.

Blue Horse and Flat Dog lay behind the low rock wall, eyes on the Snake camp.

"Go down to Clyman," Sam told Jim. "Tell him I'll take care of Third Wing."

Beckwourth rose, whacked the red dust off his leggings, and headed down the hill.

"Down, Coy," said Sam. Last thing he wanted was the pup to sky-line himself and get shot. He looked at the sun. Midafternoon, maybe five hours until dark. Too damn long.

Sam took Beckwourth's place as lookout.

A couple of hours later he thought time was moving the way dust particles blew off this hill. Tiny bits moved, and they didn't go far. The sun would go down about the time the hill changed shape one half of a smidgeon.

He saw a willow wiggle. *Clumsy bastard you are,* he thought, *to bump a tree that hard. You deserve to die.*

He stuck The Celt's muzzle through a slot in the rock wall and drew sight on the willow. Then he thought how dumb this was. His chance of hitting anyone was small, his chance of killing almost nothing. He might end up wishing he had this lead ball later, and the powder to shoot it. He might end up out of ammunition, just like he did last summer.

To hell with it, he'd lost a friend and he was angry. He held his sights low down on the bush and pulled the trigger. Boom!

The branches and leaves wiggled. *My Indian name should be Slayer of Green Leaves,* he mocked himself.

Beckwourth came back up the hill and sent the two Crows down. "You need a break," he said, "sit in the shade."

"We don't need a break," said Blue Horse. He and Flat Dog were still watching the Snake camp with infinite patience.

"Get gone," said Beckwourth.

They did.

Sam took their place behind the rock wall. "What's going to happen tonight?"

Jim shrugged. "They'll attack us or they'll clear out."

Both men thought on this.

"I'm sorry about Third Wing."

"He saved my life," said Sam. "I liked him. I'll miss him."

A raven swooped close overhead. *"Cra-a-w-wk."* Maybe the raven thought this was too many people in his backyard.

"Know what else?" said Beckwourth.

Sam looked at him curiously.

"You ever think, ninety of you went up the Missouri last spring, fifteen got killed by the Arickarees? Seven of us come up here trapping, one got killed so far." Jim paused. "You ever think . . . ?"

Silence.

At length Sam said, "The next one is gonna be me?"

"No, me," said Beckwourth.

They looked at each other, wordless.

ALL NIGHT FOUR trappers slept and two stood guard. Clyman gave Sam the first and last watches. The night was perfectly quiet, eerily quiet.

At first light Blue Horse and Flat Dog were already on the ridge overlooking the Snake camp. They'd gone up in the darkness to avoid being spotted.

After a look they stood up in plain sight and walked down.

"They're gone," said Blue Horse. Which everyone had figured.

A search of the camp, the brush, and the horse pen showed they'd left nothing, certainly not a dead man to even up for Third Wing. Sam did get to learn the print of a Snake moccasin and set it down firmly in his mind.

They sipped coffee and ate jerked meat.

"What you boys thinking?" asked Clyman.

"Time to move," said Beckwourth. "Six is not enough in Indian country." Jim didn't look guiltily at the Crows when he said this, but Sam did.

"Right," said Clyman. "Let's go find Fitzpatrick and trap with him."

Sam said only, "Third Wing."

"I want to say some words for him," said Clyman.

Sam felt the pang again. When he learned to read, he would have words for important occasions.

Blue Horse and Flat Dog didn't want Third Wing planted in the ground. The others agreed. No one had to add—"He's not a white man." There were no trees in sight, except here along the stream.

"I think," said Sam, "Blue Horse and Flat Dog should have his horses."

"One horse, each of the three of you," Clyman said. "The rest of us, we'll divide his weapons."

Silence was assent.

So Third Wing's grave turned out to be a cottonwood tree indistinguishable from any other, in a cottonwood grove barely distinguishable from any other.

They hoisted him up, the two Crows below and Sam on the lowest branch. It was an embarrassingly awkward and intimate piece of work. Sam could hardly believe how, well . . . It didn't seem decent that something so *bodily* could be the remains of his friend. Didn't seem decent that what animated Third Wing could be so completely gone, gone, gone.

He got Third Wing propped across two branches. Poor, but the best he could do. He looked long at the face. Then he reached out, grasped the hanks of his own white hair one by one in Third Wing's, untied them, and put them into Third Wing's hands.

Blue Horse handed up the robes, and Sam tied them around Third Wing, head to toe. They would keep the birds off, for a while.

"Words," he said to Clyman.

"In the midst of life we are in death. Earth to earth, ashes to ashes, dust to dust; in sure and certain hope of the Resurrection unto eternal life."

"I have some words," Gideon put in. The bear man hesitated. "This is a prayer of my father's people, the Hebrews. We call it the Kaddish, and it is a prayer for those who mourn the dead. It exalts the name of God and asks that His kingdom be established on earth in our lifetimes."

Gideon began to recite. The words themselves meant nothing to Sam, but he found himself swept up in their rhythms. Meaning surrendered to incantation, thought to feeling. For those long moments Sam swam in sounds of memory, longing, grief, love. For those moments death seemed less hideous.

When Gideon finished, no man broke the silence, and they rode on.

Part Three

RENDEZVOUS

Chapter Thirteen

SAM COULD HARDLY believe this business of finding someone in a wilderness a thousand miles high and two thousand across, but it worked. They picked up the trail of the Fitzpatrick outfit easily, a dozen or so horses following the Siskadee. They even found Fitz's camping spots. Soon the two groups joined up and trapped the Uinta Mountains (the men had named them after the Indians who seemed to be called Uintas, or Utahs, or Utes).

Ashley was still gone down Green River with an exploring party, Fitz said.

"What the devil's Green River?" asked Sam.

"What the general calls the Siskadee, *mi coyote*. That's its official name now, the map name."

"What's wrong with Siskadee?" said Sam.

"It's not the white man name," Fitz said. It was the Crow word for the river, and meant sage hen.

It was time to make a living. Sam liked roaming the country and getting to know Indians better than he liked trapping. When you came back the the trap you'd set in the cold creek, if you were lucky, a beaver had inspected the stick to see if a rival was coming into its territory. CLAMP! No matter how it struggled, if you'd done your work right, the beaver would drown. Now the work began. You skinned it out. Back in camp you scraped the fat off the hide and stretched it on a hoop made of willows. The results of your labor were two: you stunk of blood and fat, and you had something to trade to General Ashley for supplies you needed to survive another year in the mountains.

In mid-June they set out for the place General Ashley had appointed for a midsummer rendezvous of all his mountain men.

Ashley told his three captains, Fitz, Clyman, and Zacharias Ham, that on his way down the Green River, he would mark a meeting place in a certain way. Fitz had written it down. After going at least forty or fifty miles downstream, he would cache all his trade goods and unneeded baggage at some conspicuous point. If a river entered on the west, that would be the place. If there was no river, it would be some place above the mountains the river seemed to pass through. Here Fitz had down Ashley's instructions exactly, including spelling. "Trees will be pealed standing the most conspicuous near the Junction of the rivers or above the mountains as the case may be——. Should such point be without timber I will raise a mound of Earth five feet high or set up rocks the top of which will be made red with vermilion thirty feet distant from the same——and one foot below the surface of the earth a northwest direction will be deposited a letter communicating to the party any thing that I may deem necessary."

Fitzpatrick commented that the general would never be celebrated for his literary style. Sam wasn't sure what that meant.

What Sam couldn't believe was, it worked. Here they were, all the American trapping outfits from all over the west side of the mountains—Pacific drainage, all of this, maybe the wildest country left on the continent. By a mark simple as a mound of rocks they came together on a broad flat on this stream they were calling Henry's Fork, above the general's Green River.

They came in one outfit at a time, and greeted friends. Ashley's men had been in the mountains only three years, but the friendships felt strong and deep.

"This child is glad you're still wearing your hair."

"Glad to see you, old coon, I heered you'd gone under on the Salt River."

"Good to see you above ground, hoss."

Sam observed quietly that a lot of them, sun-darkened white men for sure, called themselves "this nigger" and others "you nigger," without any implication of race at all. *Strange,* he thought. But then races here were a jumble: American whites, French-Canadians, Mexicans from Taos and Santa Fe, blacks, and Indians.

The man Sam most looked forward to seeing was Jedediah Smith—Cap'n Smith to some of the men, Diah to those, like Sam and Gideon, who'd known him before he became a captain. Diah acted glad to see Sam, too, almost effusive for this restrained Yankee. He said he'd spent the winter going clear to some place called Flathead Post on some river named Clark's Fork of the Columbia, far to the northwest.

Bill Sublette was also in, after wintering on Bear River with Captain Weber, and young Jim Bridger with them. Sam wasn't clear how well he wanted to get to know Bridger.

A party of men under Johnson Gardner had fallen in with Weber— free trappers they called themselves, not employed by Ashley or anyone else. Sam wondered what that was like, operating without the protection of a big outfit like the Ashley men, having no one to issue you horses or supplies, trapping wherever you wanted to, and owning a hundred percent of your fur at the end. He wondered if those free trappers would make more money than he did.

And the Weber-Johnson outfit brought a surprise—twenty-nine French-Canadians who used to work for the Hudson's Bay Company in the far Northwest. Gardner had offered them $3.50 a pound for their beaver, and prices for supplies far lower than the John Bulls offered. Immediately they'd come over to the American side. They were old hands from their look, men like Gabriel, in the beaver country a long time. Most of them had Indian wives, Indian children, and Indian ways. Sam watched them carefully, and enviously.

Eight horses for Meadowlark.

THE TRAPPERS SPREAD their camp under the cottonwoods on a flat alongside Henry's Fork of the Green River. There wasn't much need for shelter, for here the country was more desert than mountain. Bedrolls and some tents, brush shelters, and tipis were scatted near mess fires. The talk over morning coffee was about where the Ashley party might be—every other brigade was into rendezvous. The general had set out to find out where Green River went.

"Maybe it went to hell," someone offered.

"Maybe the general got lost," Gideon said.

"Maybe he got seduced by the maidens of California," said Beckwourth.

Blue Horse gave Sam a look like, "Explain this to me later." Sam knew Blue Horse spent time explaining things to Flat Dog, too; but the younger brother's English was improving.

Sam said nothing in answer to the maidens of California remark, but wondered whether so small a party, eight men, might have been stalked and killed by Indians. "Killed by Indians" was a phrase that sang wickedly through his mind more and more, and through his dreams.

"I hear you got to be a hero," boomed a voice behind him.

Sam wheeled. Micajah.

Sam jumped to his feet and shook Micajah's paw, careful to keep the clasp light and quick.

Micajah and his brother Elijah were the biggest men Sam had ever seen. They weren't big like trees, tall and limb-shaped, but like kegs. Their thighs were keg-sized, their upper arms similar, and their enormous chests and bellies were full-sized barrels. Maybe they were signs that the Bible stories about giants were true.

Way back on the Ohio, Micajah and Elijah had been working crew on the keelboat that brought Sam to the West. Captain Sly Stuart took on one passenger, a sassy madam named Abby. In Evansville, Indiana, Micajah and Elijah attacked Abby, Sam, and his friend Grumble, intending to steal the gold coins sewn into the stays of Abby's corset. In the big men's view, their proposed victims were a boy, a whore, and a gambler. The boy, whore, and gambler turned out to be more dangerous than expected, especially the whore. Micajah ended up fleeing, and Elijah ended up dead.

"I don't know what you mean," Sam mustered. He didn't like being called a hero.

When Sam ran into Micajah months later by surprise, Micajah was blaming him for Elijah's death. But when Micajah got sober—there wasn't enough liquor in the wilderness to keep him drunk—they made up.

"They tell a big story about you," Micajah went on, "walking the whole Platte River by yourself, starving, coming out to Atkinson all right." There was sneer in the tone.

"The hero's Hugh Glass," said Sam. "I just did what I had to to survive."

Coy sat next to Sam's legs and stared fixedly at Micajah. Sam marked it down as strange behavior, but kept his attention on the big man.

"Wal, hoss, you're my hero," Micajah said, and exposed his big, yellow teeth in what was supposed to be a smile. "What's this?" He pointed at Coy.

"My pup," said Sam. He didn't want to say "coyote."

"Looks like a damn prairie wolf to me, Hero." It meant the same as "coyote," but Sam disliked both terms equally. Coy was Coy. "You want a prairie wolf for a pet?"

"Saved my life on that long walk," Sam said. "Maybe we ought to call him Hero."

Micajah gave out a roar of a laugh. "Maybe we oughta. A prairie wolf hero, ain't that the cat that caught the cradle?" He clapped Sam hard on the shoulder. Sam stumbled sideways, tripped over Coy, and went ass over teacups into the dirt. Coy skittered off making little yelps.

"Come on, Hero, get up, we're gonna have some fun over by the river. Men competing." Micajah grabbed Sam's hand and yanked him to his feet.

"See you over there," Sam said, and turned his back.

Blue Horse gave him a look like, "You have funny friends."

THE NEXT MORNING Micajah interrupted their morning coffee. "Sam," he said, paused dramatically, and squatted. "You and me, we oughta do something. Show each other we're friends. I know you'll play the comrade to me—that's the kinda man you are. And I am your friend, but you don't seem sure of that."

Micajah waited, one eyebrow cocked.

"What do you have in mind?"

"A little shooting show," he said, tapping the butt of the pistol stuck in his belt.

"Not pistol," Sam said. Sam didn't have one. And a pistol might be a sensitive matter. At the Crow village, winter of '24, Micajah and Gideon fought best two of three falls, and Gideon won Micajah's pistol.

"Naw, not pistol. For this you'll want it accurate as it can get." His face looked full of good humor.

"What?"

"We shoot the tin cup off each others' heads." It was an old and favorite trick of the alligator horses of the big rivers, the keelboat men. It was used to show how strong a friendship was, or that one had been patched up.

"Hell, no," said Sam. That was something he'd never do, not with anyone. Even if he had perfect confidence in the other fellow, it was too risky. Hell, what about the wind? It was a game for drunks and wild men.

"It's safe. You've caught me sober."

Sam shook his head.

"I challenge you, as a matter of honor." That was supposed to be the invitation that couldn't be refused.

Sam didn't want to play. "Not a chance," he repeated.

"You don't, I'll take it unkindly," said Micajah.

Gideon threw words in fast. "I'll do it. Sam's not that sure of himself. I'll stand in for him."

In the strange world of river honor, this was allowed, and Micajah couldn't refuse it.

"Let's get at it," said Micajah, and stood up.

They picked an open spot within view of most of the mess fires. Fifty paces apart they stood, and they weren't long paces.

Micajah was genial and kept it light. "You take the first shot," he told Gideon. "Since we have no whiskey to make our pledges," he mock-complained, "we'll do it with the best drink in the world, Rocky Mountain creek water."

He downed a cup, and so did Gideon. Then Micajah took Gideon's hand and said, "In this way, I pledge everlasting friendship between you, me, and Sam."

Gideon said the same words in a light-hearted tone.

Sam felt damn weird, but he had no intention, ever, of playing this game, especially with Micajah.

They took their positions. Micajah looked sassy as he waited, hips cocked. Just as Gideon's flintlocker came level, no hesitation, BLAM!

The tin cup flew. Micajah danced a jig.

Micajah's shot was just as quick and accurate.

Dozens of men grinned at each other.

Gideon and Micajah joined arms at the elbows and danced around.

WAITING FOR ASHLEY, the trappers held competitions—foot races, horse races, wrestling, and whatever else they could dream up. They played euchre endlessly with the few decks of playing cards in their possible sacks. They made bets on contests of knife-throwing and tomahawk-throwing—take seven steps back and throw at a piece of cloth pinned on a tree. Sam watched and decided he had something else to practice during the long winters, learning to throw a knife or tomahawk accurately enough, and hard enough, to stop an attacker. He was damn impressed with the realization that this was a dangerous country.

Some men also hunted. Some fished. But mostly they did what all their successors would do during the long evenings while the twilight glowed and the sun rimmed a western range on the horizon with gold. In a country without newspapers, and almost no books, they talked.

Every kind of talk. Shop talk—where such and such a creek heads up and what river it flows into. Where you can cross a certain mountain, and where it peters out into plains. What spring might save your critters and your own hide on a long, dry crossing, if you know where it is. What berries are good to eat, and when; which ones tastes all right in a stew, if not by themselves. What roots are nourishing, and which ones might make a poultice, or a remedy for headache or looseness of the bowels.

Endless talk of animals, too. What the habits of Old Ephraim, the most dangerous animal of the country, seem to be; how prairie wolves act different from wolves. How you catch up with an ermine or a river otter and what their hides are worth in trade to Indians, or worth in dollars back in the markets of the States. Where elk can be found in spring, summer, autumn, winter. How, if you hang your shirt or hat from your ramrod, you might get an antelope to walk right up to you.

How antelope hide makes a fine shirt for dress up in front of squaws, but deer hide is better for leggings, moose hide for winter moccasins, buffalo to wear like a blanket in winter.

Talk of weather, too, a rain so hard it opens a gully right in front of you. Lightning that dances on the horns of the buffalo. A dust storm that will choke you if you stay out in it. A night's blizzard deep to a mule's muzzle. A flash flood that swept away our horses, beaver packs, possibles—everything.

Indians: What tribes were usually friendly, meaning the Crows and to Sam's surprise, the Snakes, which some of the men called the Shoshones. Those "friendly" Indians still might kill your friend and steal your horses. Which tribes were never friendly, meaning the Blackfeet. Which made the most durable moccasins, which tanned hides the finest, which did the best beadwork, and which had squaws most eager to go to the willows, and were most fun when they got there.

The news got handed around. Sam thought the most dramatic was Jedediah Smith's story. Trapping to the north and west of the Green, he and his half-dozen men had come on a bedraggled party of Hudson's Bay fur men led by a fellow who called himself Old Pierre. These men were from Flathead Post, on Clark's Fork of the Columbia, far to the north and west. They hailed originally from the region of the St. Lawrence River, all the way beyond Montreal, they said, but some of them had been on western waters for more than a decade. Bearing names like Godin, Godair, and Geaudreau, they were French-Canadians—half-breeds—and the American fur men called them by the tribe they said they came from, Iroquois.

These trappers, separated from their main outfit, had been harassed by Snakes, and the Indians were aroused because a chief had been killed. Would Captain Smith, they asked, in exchange for the hundred and five furs they had, escort them to the camp of their leader, Alexander Ross?

Jedediah Smith knew an opportunity when he saw one. The combined party would be safer than either outfit alone, and he would be guided through country he didn't know and get paid for it. And then he could follow the main outfit in safety all the way to their home post, mapping out beaver country all the way.

Now he was back, with knowledge of lands with plews aplenty. But his tale, along with Johnson Gardner's, meant bad news as well as good: The British were trapping the prime Snake River country to the northwest. Here on the west of the mountains, the territory was disputed. Both the U.S. and Britain claimed it. Whoever got the beaver first would carry the day, and neither side would do the other any favors.

Now a realization began to dawn on Sam and everyone else. This rendezvous wasn't a one-time thing. It was *the* way for all the men who roamed the mountains to get together. Summer, like winter, was a time you couldn't be out making a living—the beaver pelts were too thin to be worth taking. So why not rendezvous? See your friends, and note which ones you wouldn't see anymore. Get the stories of what happened to everyone, and be warned, or know where you would likely have a welcome. Rendezvous would be like a giant bulletin board, keeping all men up to date on doings in the fur country.

Now they were impatient for Ashley to show up, so they could trade their year's catch for all the things they needed, powder and lead, maybe a pistol or another trap, coffee, sugar, tobacco, and blankets, cloth, beads, bells, vermilion, all the foorfuraw that gave you entrée in a village because the squaws wanted it.

Some of the men saw that they were accomplishing something else, too. At this first rendezvous in the summer of 1825, they started to build their community's body of knowledge. Hard-won detailed facts about a land of daunting vastness and astonishing topographical complexity, creek and plain, mountain and badlands, and all the creatures who inhabited it, four-legged, winged, rooted, crawlers, and most important, two-legged. As carpenters knew about different woods and about tools, the mountain men needed to know about a country that was equal parts inviting and hazardous to your health.

Also, during these long evenings, they told stories. Some of them were simple. How Antoine got drowned in the Milk River. How Manuel and Ezekiel rode up the Mariah and never came back. How

Joe and John got surprised by Injuns but outran them and warned the camp.

Some of these stories Sam knew. How he and Clyman and Sublette survived a bitter night on South Pass. How old Glass found the grit to survive after being left for dead. (No one told this one in front of Bridger, and mostly they didn't name young Jim as one of the men who abandoned Glass—Sam wondered why.) How Sam, and then Fitzpatrick and Gideon with others, got put afoot and walked down the whole length of the Platte, seven hundred miles, near-starving all the way. Several men clapped Sam on the back after this one was told.

And here, finally, Sam heard the story of John Colter and his escape from the Blackfeet told properly. Some of the American hands here had been in the mountains for fifteen years before the Ashley men came. Some of the French-Canadians had been here for several generations. Auguste, a graybeard with two Mandan wives, told the tale:

"Colter," Auguste began, "he was *some*. He come out wit' Lewis and Clark and stay, he *stay*—ze only man who don' go back to ze settlements but by God *live* in ze mountains. When old Manuel Lisa, ze Spanyard, he come upriver, here is Colter to show him ze ways and ze creeks and passes. With Colter's help, Lisa get on wit' ze Crows good. When ze Crows get into a big tussle wit' ze Blackfeet, though, Colter, he fight on Crow side and ze Blackfeet spot him—enemy.

"Soon not long Colter and a trapper name Potts go trapping in Blackfoot country, keeping zeir eyeballs skinned.

"One morning zey work a creek near Jefferson Fork in canoe when, all of ze sudden, zey see Blackfeet on both banks. Not just men, women and children too, which is a good, means is no war party. An Injun, he motion for zem to come ashore. Right quick Colter head in—no other place to go. He hope maybe zey just get rob and let go.

"Colter, he step out canoe and sign he come in peace. When Potts start get out, an Injun jerk his rifle out of his hands. Colter snatch ze rifle back an' hand to Potts, who push ze canoe to midstream. 'Put in,' Colter says to Potts, 'right now. Ain't no place to run. Let 'em see you ain't afeered of 'em.'

" 'You crazy?' says Potts. 'You can see zey going kill us. Torture us first.' Blackfeet, they be bad Injuns for torture.

"An arrow hits into Potts' thigh. He ups rifle and shoots Injun as grab his rifle. Right quick Potts is pin cushion for arrows.

"The women, now they send up grieving cries the way zey do, the men start whoop and yell for revenge. Colter, he know what comes. Hands grab him and he no resist. They take everything he own and rip off his clothes, but he don' fight it. Warriors come at him shaking zeir tomahawks, and he act like he don' notice. He means to stay calm, no matter what.

"The Blackfeet, zey sit in a council. Not so long a chief comes to Colter and ask if he is fast runner. Colter, he consider his answer—you don' hurry talk wit' Injuns. Looks like maybe a chance here, poor as a gopher agin a griz, but a chance. 'No,' says he, 'I'm a poor runner. The ozzer Long Knives, zey think I'm fast, but I am no.'

"The Injuns chew on this. Soon ze chief takes Colter out onto a little flat. 'Walk out past that big boulder,' he signs—'zen run and try to save yourself.'

"Colter sees ze young men is stripping down for race. So he walk. He keeps walking past ze boulder, knowing zey start when he set to running. Finally zey whoop and he take off.

"He head for Jefferson Fork, about five, six miles off. Don' make much sense, but nothing make sense. He no outlast 'em on land, Blackfeet be good trackers. Maybe he can get in river and wipe out his track and. . . .

"At least he give zem a run for it.

"He just run. Eyes see, legs run, that's all—run. Way that child figure, while you run, you live.

"He no look back, not for long time. When he take ze chance, he sees Injuns spread out all over ze peraira, 'cept one. That one is mebbe one hundred yards behind, and carry spear.

"Right here, this is when Colter begin to t'ink mebbe he have chance. He gives thought to Jefferson Fork, probably two, three miles ahead more. He pick up pace a leetle. The mountain air come in and out of his lungs big and good.

"He feels dizzy sometimes, and sick to his meat bag sometimes, but that Colter, he keeps runnin'. After a while his back, it starts prickle, like it is expecting ze point of that spear. He no help himself, he must look back.

"The Injun is only twenty yards behind and ze spear, it is cocked.

"That does it. Colter turn to Injun, spread his arms, and holler out in ze Crow language, 'Spare my life!'

"That Injun, maybe he is took by surprise. Anyhow, when he tries stop and throw ze spear all at once, he stumble and fall on his face. The spear sticks in ground and breaks off in his hand.

"Old Colter, he pounce. The Injun holler for mercy. Colter grab that busted spear and drive it right into his gut.

"Then Colter, he take a big look around. No sign of Injun anywhere. Shinin' times. Off he runs wit' a spring in his step, head for ze river.

"Not so long he hear whoops, which mean ze Blackfeet find zeir dead comrade. He just run harder.

"When he finally see Jefferson Fork, he spot an island down a little wit' a pile of driftwood at ze top. He has idea. Right quick he dive in— damn, that river so cold!—and goes wit' ze current down to ze driftwood.

"Now he dive down like beaver and come up in ze pile. Thick logs sticking every which way, blue sky up above, O *sacre bleu*! If Injuns get too close, he can duck down in ze water.

"Those Blackfeet splash all around and whoop and holler to *le bon dieu* in heaven, but not one sees Colter. They disappear downstream and come back, so zey probably know his trail no come out of ze river. After a while zey quit.

"Old Colter, he wait until far after dark. Then he ease out and swim wizout no splash down ze river, float down a long way, in case zey check for his track agin.

"What is ahead, that is a job for a mountain man. Walk two hundred miles naked. No rifle, pistol, nor knife. Nothing but roots and bark to eat. Sun and wind burning and drying ze skin.

"Finally he come to Fort Lisa, and ze gate guard not know

him—he is so gaunted and sunburned, all scratched and bloody. After they hear his story, all men say, 'Colter, zat hoss have hair of a bear in him.' "

A SHLEY CAME IN late on the last day of June, and brought some surprises with him. Leading the Ashley men to rendezvous was a brigade out of Taos. Reports of trappers working from Mexico echoed through the mountains, but this was the first outfit Sam had seen. Etienne Provost was the leader.

Sam watched them unload and set up camp. They spoke three languages, Spanish, French, and English. They were Frenchmen from Canada (not French-Canadians but white Frenchmen) and dark Spanyards; that's what the men called them, though Mexico had gotten her independence four years ago. These trappers were different, and their outfits were different, these men from Taos. Some of them carried ponchos instead of capotes, and they lifted odd-looking saddles from the backs of the horses, the saddle horns as flat and big as saucers. Sam reflected that a fellow could sit around the fire tonight and trade stories in a handful of languages—there were Americans, an Irishman for a different accent, Frenchmen, about thirty Iroquois, French-Canadians who spoke Cree, two Crows, a couple of dozen Mexicans. Coy sat close by Sam and glared at the strangers and growled.

Then Sam heard a voice in English that seemed familiar. Coy jumped up and trotted forward, dodging horses, and jumped up on . . .

Sam sprinted forward and gave the man a bear hug so hard it was almost a tackle.

"Hannibal McKye," he stuttered out.

"Sam. I knew you were close when I saw Coy."

"Glad to see you above ground."

"Hail, friend," said Hannibal. His speech was always a little strange. What could you expect of the son of a Dartmouth Classics professor and one of his students, a Delaware girl?

Coy squirmed around Hannibal's legs until the Delaware petted him. "Have you turned into a mountain man?"

"No," said Hannibal. "After I saw you at Atkinson"—Hannibal had found Sam on the trail near the fort, passed out from starvation—"I went back to St. Louis to get outfitted again." Hannibal's profession, or one of them, was trading with the Indians. Oddly, he did it alone, apparently not afraid of having his scalp taken or his horses or trade goods stolen. "Had a good winter, partly because of some friends of yours, Abby and Grumble."

Abby the madam and Grumble the con man, two of the finest people in the world. Sam couldn't stay in the mountains all the time, if only because he had to see Abby and Grumble once in a while.

"What is this?" Sam had never seen a horse the color of the one Hannibal's saddle came off of. It was a stallion, slate blue, with dark stockings and tail, and a dark stripe on the back.

"The Mexicans call it a *grulla*," said Hannibal. "His name is Ellie."

"Ellie?" A girl's name for a stallion? Also, it was Sam's mother's name.

"Short for elephant. Hannibal was a general from Carthage. He marched against the Romans on elephants."

"Oh, well, Ellie is some good-looking," said Sam.

"And an athlete," said Hannibal.

Again, Hannibal seemed to have the finest in horse flesh.

Sam grinned into the eyes of his friend. "My fire's over by that cottonwood, just this side. When you're ready, come and sit and tell your story."

A while later (time in the mountains was never measured in minutes) Hannibal staked the *grulla* nearby, keeping the horse in sight. He helped himself from the coffee pot on the fire and sat.

Sam began with, "I never thanked you properly for what you did."

Hannibal cocked an eyebrow at him.

"That Christmas Day," Sam said.

Hannibal nodded and smiled.

Christmas Day, 1822, Sam often thought, was the most important day of his life. It seemed to be the worst and turned out the best. The day before, Christmas Eve, was just the opposite.

On Christmas Eve, his birthday, he'd gone to his special place in the forest near his home, which he called Eden, to remember his father. Lew Morgan died in Eden that day in 1821.

In the middle of his reminiscing, Katherine turned up. She was his neighbor and the girl he secretly fancied. As a birthday present, she'd brought him a picnic and, as it turned out, the first act of love of his life.

The next day, Christmas, was emotional acrobatics. At Christmas dinner Katherine and Sam's big brother, Owen, announced their betrothal. Sam wanted an explanation from Katherine, but got none. He fled—and ran into Hannibal.

Across a fire, with the aid of some food, Hannibal helped him come to terms, partly, with what had happened. And helped him, gently, see into his own heart. What Sam wanted most in life was to go to the West, adventuring.

Incredibly, nudged imperceptibly by Hannibal, he went that very night, straight from the campfire. He followed his heart's compass to the Ohio River, down it to the Mississippi, up to St. Louis, and signed on to go to the Rocky Mountains as a mountain man.

Madness. Divine madness.

"You said something that night," Sam said across the flames. "I didn't really get it. Something about a wild hair. What was that?"

Hannibal grinned. "I've said it several times, mostly to myself. 'Everything worthwhile is crazy, and everyone on the planet who's not following his wild-hair, middle-of-the-night notions should lay down his burden right now, in the middle of the row he's hoeing, and follow the direction his wild hair points.'"

Coy squealed and looked at Sam pathetically. The two men sat with the embarrassment of too many words about things that are hard to talk about.

"I'm crazy, you know," said Hannibal.

Coy barked.

"The pup agrees," Hannibal said.

Sam raised his eyes over rim of his coffee cup and said, "You were going to tell me about Taos, and how you ended up here."

Hannibal shrugged. "There was an outfit heading for Santa Fe to trade. I went, I traded, I made a few dollars. Up in Taos, where I went for the devil of it, I met Etienne Provost's partner LeClerc. He was bringing supplies up to Provost in the Ute country, and I thought I'd like to see it. When I met Provost, I liked him and wanted to get to know the Utes, so I stayed . . ."

They both laughed. The narrative of bouncing around in one direction after the other . . .

"Hell," Hannibal, "I never know what I'm going to do next."

"I guess you live without planning."

"I guess."

They were both laughing too much. Coy made simpering noises.

When they looked up, Blue Medicine Horse and Flat Dog were standing next to them, waiting.

Sam introduced the two Crows to Hannibal, who offered them coffee.

After the Indians sat carefully—Sam noticed how mannerly they always were—Blue Horse said, "Everyone wants to know about that horse."

That brought on a discussion about Hannibal's *grulla* that only horsemen could appreciate. Though he was interested, Sam felt half left out. He did, however, learn how good Flat Dog's English was getting.

"Your horse looks excellent, too," said Hannibal. The three had stepped over to inspect Paladin. This brought Sam's mind back to the discussion.

"She's a good horse," said Sam.

"And she saved your ass," said Blue Horse. He and Flat Dog had learned that "ass" was a slightly vulgar word, and got a kick out of using it in English, which they would not have done in Crow.

Sam told Hannibal the story of how Paladin saved him from the buffalo bull. He finished with, "She is a good horse, but how can you tell?"

"Horses are athletes, or not, just like people. This animal doesn't look strong, but she has fine grace and balance."

Sam twisted his mouth in a pretense that he understood.

"In a race, for instance," Hannibal went on, "a clumsy horse will lose distance. A well-balanced horse covers the ground more efficiently, and therefore faster."

Sam could see that "efficiently" and "therefore" were too much for Blue Horse and Flat Dog, so he explained.

"So how about a race?" asked Blue Horse.

Coy barked in apparent approval, and they laughed.

"Several men want to run against you," said Flat Dog, a good English sentence for him.

"Including us," said Blue Horse.

Flat Dog began, "And some want to . . ."

"Bet." Blue Horse supplied the word.

"You got a race," said Hannibal.

BEFORE THE RACES the next day, most men got their business done with General Ashley. The general, typically, wanted to get his trading done in one day and start back to civilization.

This very first rendezvous made Ashley a believer. Summer was the best time to get a trade caravan to the mountains and back. The men had to have supplies. For survival, they needed fire steels, powder, lead, and flints; for their sanity, tobacco, coffee and sugar, plus an occasional trap, rifle, pistol, knife, tomahawk, or coat, and all the items they traded to the Indians. If Ashley brought these goods to the mountains, the men wouldn't have to spend months going all the way to St. Louis, or at least to Taos, to outfit themselves.

Ashley saw that and more. He realized that bringing trade goods to an annual rendezvous would be less risky and more profitable than running fur brigades. So he sat down with Jedediah Smith, the young captain who had impressed everybody in the mountains, and offered Smith a partnership—Ashley to supply from the city, Smith to lead in the mountains.

Diah said yes. He didn't tell his partner that his ambition ran far beyond profit. He said nothing of his desire to see what was over the next hill, every hill in the West. Nothing of his yearning to be the first man to cross the continent to California. Nothing of his desire to use his compass and his eye to make pencilled maps, rendering the entire West for cartographers. He just agreed to a business proposition.

For Ashley this day's agenda was trading. He kept a careful record of what he traded to everyone. He gave the free trappers three dollars a pound for their beaver pelts, these plews weighing on average two pounds. He sold them tobacco at $1.25 per pound, coffee and sugar at $1.50, cloth at six to eight dollars a yard, two yards of ribbon (something to make an Indian woman smile) for a dollar; he exchanged a dozen fish hooks for two dollars, a dozen flints for a dollar; he sold butcher knives at $2.50 each, wool strouding at five dollars a yard, earrings, bells. The old types of muskets, *fusils,* went for $20 each— these were for trading to the Indians, since mountain men demanded the newer, more accurate guns, with rifling in the barrels.

One outfit, Gardner Johnson's, actually bought razors, scissors, and combs. The other mountain men chuckled at the idea that Johnson intended to have his men groom themselves.

The general settled up with his hired trappers at reduced rates for their beaver, because they were being paid wages as well.

Sam waited his turn. This was the moment, the occasion for which he'd stood in cold creeks until his knees and scraped hides until he smelled worse than a dead rodent. But like every other man, he needed DuPont and Galena. He needed trade items for the Indians. And much of what else was in Ashley's packs. He bought more than his pelts would pay for, and ended up in debt to the company.

Some of the men grumbled at the prices, which were five and ten times what Ashley had paid for the goods at St. Louis. The brigade leaders, though, defended Ashley. The cost of transporting goods to the mountains was huge in time, effort, and dollars, and was sometimes paid in blood as well.

Ashley kept one fact to himself. In the first three years his fur trade operation had lost money. Now he was heading to St. Louis with plews worth nearly fifty thousand dollars. He was becoming a rich man, and back in Missouri and important man.

The fur men of the Rocky Mountains were miffed about one big gap in all this trading. Ashley had no alcohol. Nothing to drink now, when they were in the mood for a party, to celebrate surviving the year; and nothing all year long, when they were working hard; and most important from a practical viewpoint, no liquor to trade the Indians. Booze made the trading much better.

Dozens of men groused at Ashley as they walked away, "Next year bring whiskey."

THE FUN DIDN'T stop, though, for Ashley's trading. The men set up a race course that circled the tents and tipis. It wasn't the smooth sort of course set up in towns and cities. In fact, a dry wash running toward Henry's Fork cut through it twice, the second time only fifty yards from the finish line.

There were a couple of hundred saddle horses in camp, and a score that the men wanted to watch run, or that their owners believed fast enough to race.

Not that others weren't valuable. Buffalo horses, for instance, needed a lot of bottom. A buffalo would outsprint a horse for a quarter mile, and might hold the lead for a mile, but eventually a horse with endurance would bring the hunter alongside for a shot. The strength of these animals wasn't a burst of speed around the camp.

Trail horses had their own value. They needed to be calm and sure-footed for some of the steep, narrow mountain tracks.

These were excellent horses, but not race horses.

The men worked it out. Every competitor put up a pound of tobacco as an entry fee. The horses would run in pairs. If you lost a race to any other horse, you were out. Everyone could bet, and you could make side bets on your horse. But the big prize was winner-take-all. You had to win every race to win all the tobacco.

"Enter," Hannibal said to Sam. "Paladin is fast."

"I've never done this."

"So learn."

"Do I have a chance?"

"Against every rider but me."

Down at the mouth, sure he'd lose, Sam put his tobacco on the pile. James Clyman, running things, acknowledged his entry with a nod.

Tom Fitzpatrick walked up with tobacco, too. He was leading his fine sorrel Morgan.

Blue Horse entered his paint mare.

Flat Dog said tobacco was too valuable to throw away.

Coy slunk behind Sam, as though he was ashamed of Flat Dog.

Godin, one of the Iroquois, came forward on a small horse the men called a "cayuse," a term Sam hadn't heard. "Pony bred by them Cayuse Indians up to the Columbia River," someone said. "Sure-footed little things."

Two other Iroquois brought up Indian ponies. Everyone distinguished between Indian ponies and what they called American horses, which were brought out from the States, and larger.

Several men led forward horses that looked nondescript to Sam.

"They don't look like any racers," said Sam.

"They aren't," agreed Hannibal.

The eighteenth and last entry was Micajah, with a grin that said he was sure of winning. He rode up on a big, powerful-looking bay. The horse looked every bit of eighteen hands high, a horse truly big enough for Micajah's immense bulk. He handed down his tobacco from high in the saddle. "Meet Monster," he said, "the hoss of the mountains."

"Is Monster the one to beat?" Sam asked Hannibal.

The Delaware shook his head. "Micajah's a clumsy rider who tries to jerk his horse around."

Sam didn't really understand that.

"That man mean as he looks?" said Hannibal.

"He is when he's drinking," said Gideon. He and Beckwourth had just walked up.

Hannibal appraised Micajah and said, "Good thing we don't have any liquor."

Coy made a loud yawning sound.

"Maybe pup's a booze hound," said Hannibal.

The riders loped around the course, checking footing and obstacles here and there. When they came to the dry wash each time, they picked places to cross. Most of them ran their mounts back and forth to get them used to diving into the wash and clambering out without losing much speed. The two crossings would be tricky moments of the race.

After most of the men headed back to the starting line, Hannibal was still repeating the jump into the wash. Sam took his cue and did the same until James Clyman hollered for them.

Beckwourth provided Clyman with a deck of playing cards. James shuffled just the hearts and spades, deuces through tens, and tossed them in a hat for the men to draw. Sam drew the deuce of spades, which meant he raced the fellow who drew the deuce of hearts, Art Smith, on one of the nondescript horses.

"I'm lucky," said Sam.

"Your whole time in the mountains," said Hannibal, "you've been walking in luck."

"Except with women," Gideon joked.

The first race was intriguing. Blue Horse was to run his paint against Micajah and Monster. The riders minced their horses up to the starting line. Blue Horse's mare was fidgety, but Monster kept so still he might have been bored.

"David and Goliath," Hannibal said.

Clyman stood off and threw his hat in the air. When it hit the ground, the racers were off.

Blue Horse whacked the paint's hindquarters with his quirt. The bay got off half a step behind, and Micajah seemed in no great hurry.

Flat Dog cut loose a Crow war cry. *"Hi-yi-yi-yi, Hi-yi-yi-yay."*

Blue Horse whipped the paint again. "Looks like he means to get in front and stay there," said Hannibal.

The horses approached the dry wash, Blue Horse about two horse lengths ahead. The mare shifted her gait to go into the wash just right. At that moment Micajah whipped the bay and roared like a boulder crashing down the mountain. The bay charged hard and bumped the mare as she got her footing for the leap down, right in the hindquarters.

Blue Horse and the mare went a-tumble.

Micajah roared again, and Monster powered across the wash and up the other side. The big man was putting the whip to the bay now, and Monster showed his speed.

"Good horse," said Hannibal.

Coy yipped a protest.

Amazingly, Blue Horse was on his feet, back on the mare, and sprinting after Micajah.

"Never will he make it," said Gideon.

"We'll see," said Hannibal.

On the far side they only caught glimpses of the racers in between tents and tipis. Sam could make out that Blue Horse was riding like a fury and catching up.

As Monster came to the edge of the wash, Micajah's balance seemed uncertain, and the bay hesitated.

Blue Horse closed fast. Sam thought maybe Blue Horse intended to bump the bay. No, Sam saw, that was just his jump-off into the wash.

As the paint neared the edge, Micajah slid to the right and blocked the way.

The paint pulled up and pranced off. The edge crumbled. Horse and rider rolled into the wash.

Coy sent up a mournful howl.

Blue Horse was on his feet instantly. Sam was relieved—he thought the mare had rolled on Blue Horse.

The rider grabbed for the reins, but the mare threw her head, and the reins whipped out of reach.

Blue Horse lunged and caught them. Up the opposite side of the wash they bolted.

Micajah had a big lead now, though, at least half a dozen horse lengths with about a hundred yards to run.

Blue Horse came on hard, positioned high toward the horse's neck and whipping her hard.

"Look at that," said Hannibal. "Blue Horse is perfectly balanced and Micajah chugs along like a keg tied to the saddle."

Micajah won by two lengths.

Sam turned to Clyman. "He cheated. Micajah cheated. He bumped Blue Horse and made the paint fall."

Clyman looked at him with long-nosed amusement. "We didn't set any rules, as far as I can recollect."

"That's an educational remark," murmured Hannibal.

Gideon and Beckwourth grinned at each other.

Blue Horse caught Sam's eye and shook his head no. "I didn't know how whites do it," he said. "Next time I will."

Sam couldn't believe he wasn't mad, but Blue Horse seemed calm and easy.

They watched two races between indifferent horses. Sam knew he could get Paladin to run better than that.

"What did you mean about Blue Horse being high and Micajah chugging?" Sam asked Hannibal.

Hannibal and Blue Horse smiled at each other.

"Blue Horse had a good position in the saddle," Hannibal said. "High, balanced, sending the horse messages only with the reins and the whip."

"And speaking in her ear," said Blue Horse.

"Micajah had his big weight bouncing up and down hard on the horse, which works against the 'run fast' message and, worse, throws the horse off balance."

"What should I do?" asked Sam.

"You're a good rider. Shorten those stirrups, 'cause you're going to gallop or sprint all the way. Rise out of the saddle and really move with the horse."

Some of the races were interesting, some weren't. Sam noticed that the Iroquois on those cayuses won their races against the American horses.

Fitzpatrick ran against Godin. It was a terrific race until Fitz swung wide as they headed for the finish line. Suddenly Sam heard a loud crack! Horse and rider went ass over teacups.

The horse didn't try to get up. Fitz looked at it, checked out the ground where it down, came back and got his pistol.

"Prairie dog hole," said Hannibal.

Bang! Black smoke roiled up from the pistol. The horse made one convulsive movement and went rigid.

"Bad luck," said Sam.

"Bad luck and poor observation," said Hannibal.

And, for an average trapper, half a year's earnings lost.

But it was time for Hannibal, who'd drawn the seven of hearts, to race. His opponent was the leader of the Iroquois, a fellow known to all, apparently, as Old Pierre, and he was riding a cayuse.

Sam felt nervous at the start. He had no doubt Pierre was wily, and was dying to know how Hannibal would run the race.

At the starting line Hannibal rose up close to the *grulla's* left ear and spoke softly. Clyman's hat sailed into the air. When it hit, Hannibal angled Ellie to the outside, well away from Old Pierre. He didn't use the whip, but the stallion ran beautifully.

At the crossing Ellie bounded into the wash in one leap, and out in another—no clawing up and down for this horse.

Pierre started yelling in French. Gideon said, *"Mon dieu,* he is angry."

On the far side Hannibal and Ellie had several lengths on Old Pierre, and their lead was growing. Ellie Elephant leaped into and out of the wash the second time in the same way. "That horse won't be beat," Blue Horse said.

"Unless he's out-tricked," said Sam.

Hannibal let the *grulla* run home, fast but comfortable. He never raised the whip in his right hand.

"My God, what a horse," said Beckwourth.

"And rider," said Gideon.

Sam's race was the last of the first round. "Take your position on the outside. I'd try to get right ahead and stay ahead," said Hannibal. "When you get to the wash, veer away from the other horse, so he can't play any tricks."

"Sam Morgan," said Sam to the other rider. He looked like a Kentuck man. He didn't take Sam's offered hand, but muttered, "Asa."

The race was pure fun. Paladin showed plenty of speed at the start and got a lead. Sam took Hannibal's advice and kept well away from the other horse when crossing the wash. By the time he came to the second wash, Sam had enough lead on Asa not to worry about where he was.

Paladin made the sprint to the finish in fine form.

Asa led his mount away grumbling, without a word to Sam.

"That man's just not having any fun," said Hannibal.

"I want to quit," Asa told Clyman loudly, "and I want my tobacco back. My horse is acting lame."

Coy stood up and bristled at the man. Everyone else stared at him. They were all gathered near Clyman, holding their mounts by the reins. No one had seen any sign of lameness during the race.

"Seems the fellow doesn't like losing," said Hannibal softly.

"Dammit, I said I want to quit. And I want my tobacco back."

"Well, hell, Asa, you already bet."

"Shut up, Cam," said Asa. "I'll whip you all unless I get my tobacco back."

Hannibal whispered to Sam, "Looks like some of the men have liquor."

"Quit your damned whispering. I say I want my tobacco back. What do you say?"

"More power to you, my friend," said Hannibal.

Clyman intervened. "We do have nine riders left, which is unhandy. If we had eight, an even number, it would work out better."

"Quit mouthin' and give me my tobacco back."

"My friend, I'll make you an offer," said Hannibal. "If I win, I'll return your pound of tobacco."

"Not good enough. Do you all say the same?"

"I do," said Sam.

Godin did too. One by one, each winner agreed, until they got to Micajah.

Micajah grinned fiercely and said, "To hell with you."

"Then I'll whip you and take it."

Micajah laughed nastily and said, "That's a deal."

"Is it settled, then?" said Clyman. "The winner will give Asa his tobacco back, unless Micajah wins."

"Which I will," said Micajah.

"I'll enjoy kicking your ass," said Johnny.

"All right," Clyman went on, "four races this round, two next round, and then the final."

Everyone nodded. Coy barked like a town crier making an announcement.

Sam's next opponent was Godin. His cayuse was a wiry thing, hard-muscled, looking like it had been through a lot of battles, and the losers of those battles were dead. Godin himself looked at Sam with a glint of amusement.

"He has a thousand tricks," said Gideon.

"You can't be ready for all of them," Hannibal said. "He saw you steer clear of Asa, so he'll be expecting that. If I were him, I'd jump out hard and all the way inside, get a lead. Then, if you catch up, he'll probably whip Paladin's face. That means you'll have to go far outside to pass him, and run a longer distance."

Sam's heart sank. "So what would you do if you were me?"

Hannibal told him. Sam didn't like it.

"He's right," Gideon said. Beckwourth nodded.

"Let's get going, Sam," said Clyman.

Sam swung up into the saddle. He looked hard at Hannibal, who was smiling big.

"Just do it," said Hannibal.

Sam decided he would.

Sam gave Godin the inside position. The riders smiled at each other like predators. Both horses pranced, ready to run, about to fight the reins.

Up went the hat.

When it knocked up a puff of dust, Sam turned Paladin right into Godin's cayuse and whipped her hard. Her front shoulder banged into the cayuse's hind quarters.

After a moment, the horse and rider caught their balance. The cayuse wheeled and snapped at Paladin.

Sam and the horse, though, were already a step in the clear, taking the far outside.

The cayuse came after Paladin like a rocket, neck stretched out, head lowered, teeth bared. One length, three, five, the cayuse attacked ferociously. Paladin fled like mad.

The cayuse was getting close. Sam shifted his weight to the inside and reined Paladin sharply that way. As they turned, the cayuse nipped Paladin's left hip with his teeth. Paladin bounded forward with a speed Sam didn't know she had.

Instantly, they were hard on the wash. Sam nudged Paladin to a crossing spot that was difficult but possible. This time she leaped, took two jumps in the wash, and hurled herself up the other side.

Sam didn't need to give her whip again. She could probably hear the cayuse on her outside and coming up. She ran like hell.

The cayuse shrieked. That horse was never going to quit.

For a little while Sam thought Paladin might just outrun the cayuse. In the far turn, though, opposite the starting line, the critter managed to get close.

Sam put the whip to Paladin, but was careful to give no sign until he executed his plan. When the cayuse's head came alongside Paladin's rump, he slashed the animal in the face, hard.

The cayuse veered sideways, screamed, and pulled up. Then he collected himself, urged by Godin's shouts, and set out in pursuit that was hotter yet.

Too late. Paladin had more speed anyway, and now she was running beautifully. The cayuse had shown the moxie to put on a burst and catch up once, but not twice.

Sam took a safe, quick route across the wash and kicked her home.

The biggest grin on the field belonged to Hannibal.

Sam jumped off the mare before she was fully stopped, threw his arms in the air, and yelled *"Yi-ay-ay-ay, Yi-ay-oh!"*

Coy made the best imitation of that cry he could manage.

Godin was full of dark looks. He had to rein the cayuse away hard. That horse still wanted to fight.

"Don't mind him," said Hannibal. "You give him a chance, he does the same to you."

Suddenly Paladin began to limp on her front right foot. Hannibal went to her quickly and lifted the foot. He poked at it and flipped something out. "A pebble in the frog," he said. "She should be all right."

Sam checked Paladin's left hindquarter. The hair was rubbed all wrong, the skin scraped but not broken.

"I'm sorry," Sam told her.

The mare took a step on the front right foot, a little gingerly, as though to say, "This is where the hurt is."

Blue Horse and Flat Dog walked up. They'd borrowed buckets and brought water from the river. "Let's rub her down," said Blue Horse.

All three of them did. Sam also gave her a drink from the crown of his hat, just a little. Coy insisted on getting a drink from the hat too. When Sam slapped the wet hat back on his head, it felt great.

Paladin still put that foot down as though it was tender. "Walk her around," said Hannibal. "Let her work it out."

Sam hardly saw the next two races. He was too busy with Paladin, and too concerned about her. Hannibal won easily. Micajah won.

While two Iroquois on cayuses got ready, Hannibal said, "Come out here."

Sam led Paladin alongside Hannibal to the second wash crossing. "Micajah's the spade four, so you're gonna get him. He'll pull every dirty trick there is. You've got to stay away from him."

Hannibal led the way up the wash a little. "Not bad," he said. This place to cross was not too steep and had fair footing. Coy dashed back and forth as though to demonstrate. Hannibal stomped the edge, knocking dirt down and making it smoother. Then he surveyed the area, the distance back to the inside along the tents, and how far it was to the finish line.

"All right, stay to the outside, let him lead, and stay on his tail.

Halfway through the race, on the back side, start moving up. When she begins to really run, take her well outside. Angle straight for this spot." He surveyed the distances again. "You'll be running four or five lengths further than Micajah. But Paladin has the speed, and the way Micajah rides slows Monster down. I think you can do it."

"Long way," said Sam, eyeballing the same distances.

"If you get close to him, he'll pull something on you."

Clyman hollered for the winners to gather round.

"Just a minute," called Sam.

"Now!" ordered Clyman.

Coy headed for the starting line. Sam and Hannibal followed.

Hannibal and Jacques rode first. It was no contest. Hannibal led by a wide margin all the way. Horse and rider finished looking casual. The Iroquois whipped his horse to the finish cussing, man and mount drenched in sweat and crusted with dust.

While they ran, Sam stewed.

When his time came, Sam asked Blue Horse to hold Coy away, on an improvised leash. Sam lined up well to the outside. Micajah came right with him. Sam reined Paladin around to the inside. Micajah crowded in on him. As Sam tried to get back outside, Clyman got tired of waiting and sailed the hat into the air.

When it hit, Sam threw caution to the wind and slapped Paladin for a quick burst of speed. He got a lead and decided he would go hell for leather and keep it.

At the first crossing of the wash Paladin altered her pace a little to get ready for the plunge downward.

Wham!

A huge collision—the world lurched upside down. Paladin was above him. Where was Earth? . . .

Whumpf! They hit on the slant of the cutback. Paladin tilted over him, and Sam felt the saddle horn gore deep into his stomach. Darkness, darkness. Sam accepted death.

Death was strange, dizzy, slowly spinning around. What death was, was . . . No air, a place without air. You waited a little, and then you died—no air at all, no air . . .

His chest heaved, and air gushed in. He lay there, accepting its sweetness. When he had drunk his fill, he opened his eyes.

Coy licked his face. Paladin stood looking down. Her reins tickled his ears. "Hello, friend," he said.

Then he thought, *My champion was almost a killer. My killer.* This struck him as funny beyond anything that had ever been funny. Laughter shook him, he was like a leaf shaken on the frothing water of laughter.

Someone . . . His shoulders.

Suddenly he was sitting upright, held by Hannibal and Blue Horse. "I'm all right." It came out as a squeak, so he said it again in a shadow of a voice. "I'm all right. I think. Maybe."

"She rolled right over you," said Hannibal.

Blue Horse lifted Sam's shirt up to his heart. A round spot just below his ribs dotted his flesh crimson and white. "The saddle horn got him right there," Blue Horse.

"It's going to get purple," said Hannibal.

"Let's get you on your feet," said Blue Horse.

They did. Sam felt shaky as a one-year-old taking his first steps.

They boosted him out of the wash. His first sight back toward the starting line was Micajah finishing the race on Monster and waving his hat triumphantly.

Some of the trappers actually booed. Others cackled.

Sam toddled back, supported on both sides. Coy whined. Paladin followed calmly.

When they got back to the starting line and walked in front of the mounted Micajah, almost touching Monster's muzzle, Sam told Hannibal, "Get even for me."

Micajah snickered.

WHEN HANNIBAL CAME to the starting line, Ellie's saddle was gone. Hannibal would ride bareback, with just a rope of braided buffalo hide around Ellie, in front of where the saddle should sit.

He didn't look at anyone, not Sam, not Clyman, not Micajah. It was as though he were waiting alone.

Right off, Micajah started crowding Hannibal the same way he'd done to Sam. Looked like he was getting away with it too, staying with Hannibal wherever he went. When James Clyman cocked back the hand with the hat, they were far to the inside, Micajah bumping against Hannibal.

When the hat reached its zenith, Hannibal abruptly pivoted Ellie straight around and kicked. They passed so close the riders bumped stirrups as Ellie dashed to the outside.

The hat saucered to the ground. Hannibal reined Ellie to the left and charged for the first crossing.

Micajah chugged along behind, not taking the inside but straight at Hannibal.

Coy whined, and Sam caught his breath in fear of what would happen at the wash. At the edge Ellie suddenly wheeled to face Micajah, reared, and flailed his legs at Monster's face.

Monster reared and kicked.

Ellie, his feet back under him, made a quick move to the left, a quick one to the right, and crashed into Monster.

Horse and rider went tumbling. The lip of the wash gave away and they rolled down, six legs kicking the air.

Hannibal turned Ellie and bounded across the wash. Then Ellie began to run as only a splendid horse can run, smoothly, powerfully, freely.

At first Monster skittered away from Micajah. Finally the big man got hold of Monster's reins and heaved himself into the saddle. He stared at Hannibal and Ellie, already halfway around the course. He turned and walked Monster back to the starting line. Jeers greeted him. Coy howled triumphantly, and everyone laughed.

Hannibal approached the finish line. Some trappers began to cheer. Gradually Ellie slowed to a lope, and Hannibal stood on his back. It was beautiful, a man erect on horse's back, both moving together.

Now everyone cheered.

When Hannibal crossed the finish line, he jumped to the earth on Ellie's left side, holding the hide rope with his right hand. From the ground, he bounded cleanly over the horse, landed on the other side, and bounded back across.

After three or four jumps he sat on his back again and took the reins. He brought Ellie back to the starting and finishing place and grinned hugely at his admirers.

Chapter Fourteen

"WHERE IN THE hell," said Sam, "did you learn that?"

Blue Horse, Flat Dog, Gideon, and Beckwourth were crowding as close as Sam, and as avid.

"I didn't tell you what I did when I ran off from Dartmouth," said Hannibal. He led Ellie away with a grin. "I was very tired of studying Greek and learning about this war or that under Caesar. I wanted some fun. So I got a job at the circus."

After a pause Blue Horse said, "What's a circus?"

"I'm not sure," said Sam.

Hannibal set his victory tobacco on the bank and led Ellie into the river. He drank. "I worked for the John Bill Ricketts circus, the big one in Philadelphia."

Everyone waited impatiently.

"In a circus a horse runs circles in a ring and the rider does tricks on his back."

"Like we just saw," said Sam.

"Yeah, and lots more. Jumping through a paper hoop, for instance. Someone holds up a big hoop, you ride toward it, dive through, and do a flip back onto the horse."

The three innocents stared at each other.

"Make a hoop with your fingers," Hannibal told Sam. He did. Hannibal made a horse and rider with his fingers, and showed how the rider did a somersault through the hoop.

Six eyes got as big as eyes get.

"How do you control the horses without reins?" said Blue Horse.

"They're trained to respond to your voice. We call them 'liberty horses,' horses that run free without reins or saddles and do what you tell them."

"You did this riding yourself?"

"I started taking care of the horses, though I didn't know a thing about horses. If you're an Indian, they think you're a horse man. Then I became a trainer, and finally got to do the riding. It was fun."

"And you quit doing this?" said Sam.

"Everything wears out its welcome."

Sam took several deep breaths. "Will you show me how?"

Hannibal smiled at him.

"Me too," said Flat Dog.

"We've got time now," said Blue Horse.

Hannibal regarded them all. "Sure, why not?"

GIDEON JOINED IN and they made a ring from ropes and stakes. "A ring," Hannibal repeated. "Round pen training. Forty-two feet across, exactly forty-two." No one knew why, but they built it.

Then Hannibal demonstrated a lot of tricks that could be done—not only standup bareback riding and jumping from one side of the horse to the other and back to a mounted position, but also doing somersaults to and from the back of the horse, and doing a handstand on its back. He also showed them how to make a horse do maneuvers by itself, guided by verbal commands or hand signals.

The three young horsemen watched mouths agape. Gideon gave them a smile and sat down to watch from the sidelines.

"What do you want to learn?" said Hannibal.

They hesitated.

"Come to think," Hannibal went on, "let's figure that out after lunch."

While they ate the buffalo stew that always simmered over the fire, and threw bits to Coy, the three students talked it over. None of them saw much advantage in knowing how to jump from one side of a horse to the other. Not much advantage in riding a horse standing up either, but they all wanted to learn it. "I'd love to parade through the village, the three of us," said Blue Horse, "standing up on our horses."

The main thing, they all agreed, was learning to command a horse when you weren't on its back. They didn't know exactly what they could use that for, but it looked very handy. They would also teach Paladin to come to Sam's whistle, which they knew was handy. "We'll be horse kings," Sam cried.

They started that afternoon and spent the next week training their horses, then another week. And, as Hannibal said, training the riders. Coy, unfortunately, had to be tied off to one side.

First they taught the horses to respond to commands of voice and command. This was done in the round pen. The owner of the horse acted as trainer, giving the commands from the center. Gideon on the outside used a whip lightly to get the horse to go in the right direction. When the horse did the right thing, the trainer rewarded it with a handful of sugar.

Sam, Blue Horse, and Flat Dog took turns as trainer.

"We're not gonna have sugar for our coffee for a whole year," said Sam in mock complaint.

They couldn't get any more because the general had packed up his caravan and headed for St. Louis. Jedediah Smith, his new partner, had gone with him, saying he'd be back in the mountains by winter. Jim Beckwourth had gone along.

Third Wing dead, Beckwourth gone. Sam missed them. He wouldn't see most of the other trappers until next year's rendezvous, set for the same time on Bear River, north and east of the Salt Lake.

Outfit by outfit, most of the trappers drifted toward wherever they planned to trap that autumn. They didn't hurry. There was plenty of time.

Sam, Hannibal, Gideon, and the two Crows stayed. Their training days ran long into the summer evenings. One night over a late supper Gideon asked, "What we gonna do this autumn?"

Sam looked around at his current outfit, three friends, himself, and Coy. Not a brigade you could take on a big trapping expedition.

He raised a questioning eyebrow at Hannibal. "I'll be going back to Taos."

"Still maybe fifty men here," said Gideon "We could hook up with someone."

Sam shook his head. "I'm getting married. Soon."

Gideon chewed on that. He knew it meant a raid on some tribe for that eight-horse bride price, and a return to Rides Twice's village.

"This child will go along. I guess we are free trappers, then."

Sam smiled. His outfit for the raid and going back to the village would be Gideon, the two Crows, and himself. A small party, maybe not a safe one. But Sam felt daring.

"What's a free trapper?" asked Flat Dog. He was more forward than his brother.

"We aren't working for anybody," said Sam.

"What's working for anybody?"

"Doing a job someone else wants us to do, and getting money in return."

Flat Dog and Blue Horse gave each other odd smiles. "No Crow would do that," Flat Dog said. His expression said it would be demeaning.

"What it means is, we're on our own," said Gideon.

"For better or for worse," put in Hannibal.

"Like us," said Flat Dog, grinning.

"If we work our tails off," said Sam, "we could go back to rendezvous with a lot of plews and be rich."

Everyone mulled on that. Finally Blue Horse spoke up. "You want to be rich?"

"I want to get married. And stay in the village all fall and winter with my new wife."

"We gonna trap in the spring?" said Gideon.

"I thought we'd trap the Wind Rivers, you and me, and Blue Horse and Flat Dog if they want. Fall and spring. We ought to do all right."

Gideon nodded. It was his judgment, unspoken, that there was no point in speaking up against young love. "Free trapper," he said. "An equal shot at being rich, broke, or dead."

Everybody chuckled, but not much and not long.

THAT EVENING HANNIBAL suggested that he and Sam take a walk along the river. They stopped on the edge of the Henry's Fork, Coy at Sam's heels. Sam found a flat stone and skipped it across the slow-moving water, one, two, three skips.

"This has been a good time," said Hannibal.

Sam nodded yes. The sun was nearly down now, near the rim of the western hills. The evening cool would be a relief. He hoped Hannibal wasn't going to wax philosophical.

"I want to show you a trick," Hannibal said. They stood near some willows. It was a plant Sam had learned to love, the red branch with green, finger-shaped leaves. It grew along water courses in the West, and so was always a good sign for a man with a dry throat.

"Stand by that willow." Sam did. "Now take out your knife and hold it at me. Pretend you've disarmed me and are holding me."

Sam slipped his butcher knife out of his belt and it held it on the Delaware.

"Watch carefully." Hannibal held out his hands to show that they were empty. Then he raised them and put them behind his head. "Remember, Indians will mostly accept this gesture. They've learned that it's the way white men surrender." He grinned. "They like that."

Hannibal's right hand slashed out near Sam's face.

A thin willow branch tilted. The top turned end over end as it tumbled to the ground."

"What . . . ?"

"That could have been your face."

Hannibal did something with his hands and opened a palm to Sam.

There lay a piece of polished walnut, about four inches long and thick as a finger. On each end four rings were carved, and painted red, yellow, black, and white, the colors of the four directions. A hair ornament, Indian style.

"Take it."

It was light, smooth, well-oiled.

"Open it."

Now he saw the thinnest of lines in one of the rings. He pulled on the two ends, and the ornament came apart. One end was a wood sheath, the other a gleaming, wood-handled, double-edged blade an inch or two long.

"Feel it," said Hannibal.

Very, very sharp.

"A knife I had a gunsmith make for me. I have two of them." He rummaged in the pouch until he found a second one. "I'll give you that one."

Sam was mesmerized by the little weapon.

"Keep it really sharp. That's what makes it work."

Sam slid it apart and put it back together. It pleased him, and reminded him of Abby's hidden knife. Hers was the size of an emery board and looked like part of the hem of her dress.

"Here's what I do with it." Hannibal turned his back to Sam. He slid his piece of wood into his thick, black braid, and adjusted it just so. It looked good as a hair ornament.

Now he slipped it out. Only the knife part came, the blade catching the light in the last of the sun. Hannibal made a pretend slash, and another willow stick flew off. "It makes a hell of a cut, lots of blood. But it's the shock of getting sliced right across the face, maybe the eyes, that makes it nasty."

"I love it," said Sam.

So they sat on some rocks and Hannibal let Sam learn to braid hair. He undid and then rebraided Hannibal's black thatch several times.

Coy got impatient and jumped into the river to play.

As Sam worked, Hannibal said, "Do us both a favor. Don't show any of your friends this knife trick. Or else these knives will be all over the mountains, and the Indians will learn the trick. And the whites and French-Canadians and Spaniards."

"Not a word."

After three learning sessions on Hannibal, Sam braided his own white hair. He inserted the walnut hair ornament and practiced sliding the blade out easily.

Finally he nodded several times. "It works," Sam said.

"Keep it sharp," said Hannibal.

"I guess I'll be braiding my hair every morning."

Hannibal smiled, knowing what Sam was thinking. "Or find a woman to do it for you."

THE NEXT MORNING Sam spent teaching Coy to ride Paladin.

It was frustrating. Oh, the little coyote caught on quick enough. It was something else. When they stopped for lunch, Sam munched until he'd figured out what. He went and found Gideon, Blue Medicine Horse, and Flat Dog and told them all the same thing. "Let's go."

By midafternoon, they set out for Powder River country. They had a pledge to steal those eight horses.

Part Four

GAINING THE PRIZE

Chapter Fifteen

"IT'S THE RIGHT setup," said Gideon.

Nobody used a word like "perfect." Too many things could go wrong.

From a timbered ridge they looked down on the small village tucked into a curve of Crazy Bear Creek, soon after the stream dropped from the mountains to the plains. It was a dozen lodges.

Scouting, they had found a much bigger village of Sioux—Head Cutters, in the Crow language—further down Powder River. But they wanted a small one. The best way, Blue Horse said, was to find the horses held in one place, so you could drive them all off. That way they couldn't come after you, or at least you could get a big advantage. "Many lodges, many horses, more pursuit," he said.

Here there were maybe forty horses, about a quarter mile upstream from the village on some good grass.

"They'll still have their buffalo horses," Sam said. These were staked by the lodges.

"No pursuit, no fun," said Flat Dog.

They put camp by a little rivulet well off the ridge. A small fire would be safe here because the aspen would burn smokeless. They couldn't relax for a moment, not in Head Cutter country.

"Let's stake the mules up the trail," Gideon said. "Five miles maybe."

While the two brothers watched the village, Sam went with Gideon. They found some water and good grass and hobbled and rope-corralled the mules and Blue Horse's and Flat Dog's mounts. "Be embarrassing," Gideon said, "to go to steal someone's horses and have them steal yours."

Not just the horses, either. Saddles, traps, extra powder and lead, blankets, coffee, goods to trade to the Indians—all their possibles, everything that made life in the mountains more than a desperate scrape-by.

"Is this far enough?" said Sam. He was picturing stopping for the animals while pursuing Head Cutters filled the air with arrows.

"We don't leave 'em behind in five miles," said Gideon, "we got bigger troubles than losing our horses."

When they got back to the little camp, Blue Horse was staring into the fire. Sam knew he was worried. He'd been hinting.

Sam helped himself to coffee and jerked meat.

Blue Horse said, "To go to war, a man must see something."

The four eyed each other across the little fire.

Flat Dog nodded his agreement with his brother.

Sam and Gideon knew what Blue Horse meant. Crows went to war because of medicine. One man had a dream of success, or in a vision saw enemies falling, or many horses. If he had a history of strong medicine, if his war parties had succeeded before, other men would agree to join in. Or some would consult their medicine and see that this was not the time for them to go to war.

No one in this outfit had proper medicine for war.

Lying in front of his knees, Coy looked up at Sam pathetically.

Sam pondered. Then he said, "I think maybe I have seen something." He waited. "I've dreamed about this constantly. Not running the horses off. Driving them into the village, everybody looking at us, Meadowlark being proud."

He sipped his sugarless coffee. Actually, he hadn't dreamed it. More like daydreamed it. "Is that medicine?"

After a little bit Blue Horse shrugged. "White men are different," he said. "Maybe that's how your medicine comes."

Nobody spoke for a moment. "You with me?" Sam said.

Blue Horse smiled and nodded. "You are my friend."

Sam looked quizzically at Flat Dog.

"I'm always good for a fight."

"Wagh!" exclaimed Gideon.

Now they were looking down on what seemed like a good situation. "This timber's good cover," said Sam. "Let's make a plan and move in the morning."

"Not too much plan," said Flat Dog. "Action."

Coy yipped. Sam let him yip. Anywhere in the West there was nothing suspicious about a coyote yipping.

SAM WATCHED BLUE Horse and Flat Dog get up, gather their weapons, and wrap their blankets around their shoulders. The Big Dipper said halfway between midnight and dawn, and the night was chill.

He shook himself. He wouldn't be able to sleep while they were getting started. The rest of the night was going to feel long. He sat up. Coy looked up with accusation in his eyes, 'What are you doing?'

The brothers looked across the remains of the fire at Sam. Their smiles were plain in the light of the three-quarters moon. "It is a good day to die," said Blue Horse in Crow.

"Die or fly." That was Flat Dog, always the wise-ass.

With that they were off.

Sam held a hand close to the ashes. Warmth, therefore coals. He could get fire easily. He added small twigs, blew, and soon had flame.

He rummaged in his goods and found the sack of roasted coffee beans. He put them on a flat rock and ground them carefully with another rock, taking his time, mashing them all the way to powder. As he did it, he was full of big thoughts.

"Coffee would feel about right," said Gideon from his blankets.

The usual rejoinder was, "I'll bring you breakfast in bed, too." But Sam said, " 'A good day to die,' what does that mean?"

"Don't know," said Gideon.

Sam added the fresh ground coffee to the grounds of several previous days in the pot. Then he poured water in and set the pot on the fire.

"What do you figure?"

"Something like, 'Let's go live so grand, so extra grand, it would be good to die like this.' "

"Mmmm."

The smell of coffee wafted on the night air.

He wished he had some sugar left.

Coy whined like he did too.

SAM COULD HARDLY stand it. The sky was getting light, but he couldn't see.

Early morning fog smeared itself over the creek. Somewhere below, Blue Horse and Flat Dog were slipping toward the horse herd, and toward the sentry. The one sentry, they thought. But they would check carefully for a second.

"We Crows," Flat Dog had said, "like to count coup on Head Cutters."

Sam looked across at Gideon. He was behind a boulder too. It would be good cover when the time came. Between them was a well-used pony drag trail running up the creek. Soon it would turn south, parallel to the mountains. In half a day they'd turn west up a creek and cross the mountains to the basin where the Big Horn River ran, and where Rides Twice's village would be. It wasn't a subtle escape route, but it would be wide open and fast. If Sam and Gideon did their work well, being quick was what they needed. Four men, more than forty horses, and one coyote racing across the mountains.

Rumble!

At first he wasn't sure he heard it. Yes, *rumble!*

Sam grinned at Gideon. The horses were on the move. No outcry from the sentry. Blue Horse and Flat Dog had done it perfectly.

"Yi-ay, Yi-ay!" they would be yelling to make those ponies run. They would snap their blankets at the horses too, but Sam wasn't close enough to hear.

The Sioux, who preferred to be called Lakotas, would hear the racket. Asleep or not, they'd jump up and come hard after the herd.

He grinned. The few with horses to ride would come hard.

He thought he saw movement at the edge of the fog. Yes, ponies going headlong for the timber, right up the trail.

He checked The Celt's priming. Everything ready. He had to make the first shot count.

Soon the ponies roared past, manes and tails flying, hooves throwing clods of dirt and clumps of pine needles into the air. Right behind them came Blue Horse and Flat Dog on stolen mounts, riding bareback, running the herd hard.

We did it!

Sam watched the edge of open ground between the fog and the timber. One Lakota rider. After a long moment, two more.

Another long moment, two more. Now every horse staked in the camp was in the action.

The first rider galloped furiously up the trail, whipping his mount.

Sam took a deep breath and sighted on the horse. *No horse, no pursuit.* He relaxed, and as he let the breath out pulled the trigger.

Blam!

For a moment he couldn't see through his own black smoke. Then he saw—horse gimping around, rider running into the trees. *All right!*

He started reloading fast.

The next two riders came around the bend.

Sam was just beginning to ram the ball home. He wouldn't be ready for a while.

Gideon let them get close. Sam knew he intended to create the impression of two shooters on that side of the trail.

Blam!

One rider pitched off the horse backward. The horse skittered off into the woods.

"Way to go!" yelled Sam, still ramming.

Blam! This was Gideon's pistol.

The horse reared, and when it came down fell onto one side.

Off jumped the rider, down behind the animal.

The horse struggled back to its feet, unable to use one front leg. Sam thought, *Shot in the shoulder.*

Coy sprinted toward the horse and rider, barking furiously. "Coy!" shouted Sam, half in a panic. "Come! Come, Coy!"

The coyote turned, looked at Sam, hesitated, and started trotting back. Sam breathed again.

Two more riders came around the bend.

Sam rammed furiously. He wasn't ready, and both of Gideon's guns were empty.

The riders stopped. Seeing the lame horse and the rider behind it, plus the downed rider, they figured out what was going on. Off into the woods they sprinted.

"Let's go!" shouted Sam.

He sprinted toward Paladin, Gideon right behind him.

In a flash Sam was in the saddle and whipping Paladin up the trail. He could hear Gideon coming too.

He dropped the reins—he could depend on Paladin now—and rammed that ball home. They were going to need it.

Sam felt Paladin's speed under his butt. Nothing could feel better right now.

He turned to look at Gideon. Dammit, Gideon's horse was falling back a little. They had some time—the woods would slow the Lakotas down—but not much.

Coy was dropping back too. But no one would bother a coyote, and he would come along.

Sam kicked Paladin and hollered to her for speed. He was thinking hard.

He kept looking back. Gideon wasn't too damn far behind, but . . .

On the third or fourth look he saw the Lakotas well behind Gideon, smack in the middle of the trail, coming as fast as they could.

About a quarter mile on he whirled Paladin off the trail and dropped her reins. He gave thanks now that she would respond to his hand signals or whistle. He dashed behind a tree.

When Gideon passed, Sam hollered, "Go like hell!" Coy ducked behind Paladin.

Within seconds the Lakotas were in sight.

Sam leveled The Celt. He didn't want to let them get too close. Finally he took a long shot.

The Lakotas bolted in opposite directions, into the trees.

He'd missed, but Sam was satisfied.

They wouldn't charge forward now. They'd circle and come up on the place where his smoke hung in the air. And Sam would be long gone.

SAM AND GIDEON picked up the brothers' mounts and the pack mules, no problem. Before long they caught up with Blue Horse, Flat Dog, and the stolen ponies. The four grinned at each other—*we did it.*

Still, just in case, they ran the horses hard for three or four hours. It was fun, the herd like one huge galumphing animal, bodies, necks, legs, manes, tails, everything flying along, cavorting through the air, and the rumble of more than 150 hooves, noisy as a waterfall. The

August day would be hot by noon, so this was the time to move along. They figured safety lay in getting the hell out of there.

Sam and Coy dropped back every so often to wait and put fear into the pursuers. The trail was crossing plains here, and the visibility was good. The first three times, he just scared the two Lakotas at long range. Finally he let them get close, almost too close, and shot one of the mounts square in the chest. "One horse left," Sam said to himself, and ran like the devil with his empty rifle.

He jumped into the saddle. An arrow ripped open his shirt sleeve and his forearm. He put the whip to Paladin but good. Two more arrows flew just out in front of him. Finally, Paladin's speed took them out of range.

He caught up at a creek where they were letting the horses drink a little. There Gideon poulticed Sam's arm with a concoction he swore by.

Now Gideon waited and laid the ambush. He didn't catch up for a long time. "Nobody comes anymore," he said.

"We can't take that for granted," said Sam.

"Let's give the horses a breather," said Blue Horse. There was some good grass, so they did.

Sam took thought. This break would be short. Blue Horse and Flat Dog had been up and moving since maybe 3:00 A.M. There was good visibility from the rise behind them. "I'll watch for a few minutes," he said.

But Sam saw no rider. *One man won't try to take us. If there is one left.* He stretched and worked the muscles in his bloodied arm.

After half an hour they hit the road.

TWO MEN TO drive the herd, a lookout well to the front, another to the rear. That's how they ran it, the two Crows front and back, the white man and French-Canadian with the herd.

The trail wound down toward another drainage, a nice little creek edged by leafy cottonwoods. Here they would leave the main pony trail and head up the creek into the mountains.

When they rode into the shade of the cottonwoods, Sam took a deep breath of the air, cooler here along the creek. Coy dashed into the water, lapped some up, and pranced around in it.

Then Sam saw Blue Horse come riding slowly back toward them. He tensed. *What the hell is wrong?*

Warriors stepped from behind almost every cottonwood. Lakotas. Their bows were drawn, their few rifles cocked.

Blue Horse kicked his pony a little and came back closer to Sam. A terrible smile scrawled itself across his face.

A voice sounded in a strange language. Blue Horse turned to the right toward it, looked into the trees.

An arrow rammed through Blue Horse's chest. Sam saw the point come out below his shoulder blade.

Slowly, Blue Horse teetered out of the saddle backward. He hit the earth head first. His neck bent at a terrible angle, and his body crumpled.

Several warriors kicked their ponies up to Blue Horse to touch his body first, or second, third, or fourth, so they could claim the honor, the coup. First was an arrogant-looking man with a two-horned buffalo headdress, second a pock-marked man. At ceremonies they would brag about this deed.

From the creek Coy whined plaintively.

Gideon whipped his horse straight into the trees and bellowed like a madman. Arrows whipped through the air. One must have hit the horse, for the beast screamed. Another sank into Gideon's hip, and he bellowed louder.

Sam wheeled Paladin and dashed straight back along the trail.

No one shot an arrow, fired a ball. *Maybe they really want Paladin.* Fire rose up Sam's gullet. *Maybe they'll try to catch me, we can outrun . . .*

Two sentries walked their mounts into the trail ahead of him.

Sam wheeled Paladin to the left, just beyond the cottonwood grove.

A half dozen riders trotted out in front of him.

A half dozen more flocked behind him.

Live for an hour and you may live until tomorrow.

He dropped the reins. He set his rifle butt on the ground and held the muzzle lightly. He made his mind blank and very clear. *They don't know Paladin will respond to my voice.*

Riders from behind came up close.

Two arms ripped Sam backward out of the saddle and slammed him to the ground. The arrogant-looking, two-horned Lakota smiled down at him. *Strong man,* Sam realized through his dizziness. The pock-marked warrior threw a loop around Paladin's neck. Two Horns seized Sam's rifle.

Other Lakotas seized Sam and hauled him to his feet. A loop settled around his neck and pulled half-taut. The pock-marked warrior held the rope and grinned sardonically at Sam.

Blue Horse dead.

Gideon hurt bad, likely dead.

Sam hoped Flat Dog wouldn't ride blindly into this disaster.

Paladin stolen. Coy stolen. The Celt stolen. All our possibles stolen.

I messed up.

I'm dead.

WARRIORS WALKED UP to Sam, their faces lit with satisfaction. One took his shot pouch. Others grabbed his butchering knife, his hat. Someone stripped off his cloth shirt and belt. His breechcloth fell into the dust. His moccasins went—since they were Crow made, they would be saved and worn, or traded for value. Someone snatched his *gage d'amour,* his emblem of Meadowlark's affection, and ripped it off. Last, someone took his medicine pouch, with the buffalo hair. Joins with Buffalo had lost his buffalo medicine.

He stood totally naked. He showed no emotion. It would not do to show anything.

They waited. No one said or signed a word to Sam. He felt like trail dust.

Coy trotted over to him. Sam petted the little coyote, then decided to put him through some tricks. By turns, Coy laid down, rolled over, and jumped up to touch Sam's held-out hand with his muzzle.

Some of the Lakotas watched curiously. But the bastard who took Sam's rifle, Two Horns, growled something and they looked away.

In a few minutes an entire village of Lakota came up, all their belongings trailing behind pack horses on pony drags. Big Bellies, women, old people, children, and a phalanx of warriors.

Now Sam understood what had happened. They had ridden headlong into an entire village of Lakotas on the move. He feared something worse. The way these people were headed, they might even be joining the village whose horse herd Sam had stolen. *Good Godawmighty.*

Bad luck. "No, mountain luck," said Hannibal's voice in his head, "which runs just as bad as good."

The Head Cutters . . . Sam reminded himself that they wanted to be called Lakotas. They had young men from the warrior societies out in front as scouts. Instead of Blue Medicine Horse spotting them, they had somehow spotted him. No one would ever know how that happened. Warriors sign their mistakes in blood.

It is a good day to die.

The entire village moved up the trail. Sam walked behind the pockmarked warrior, tethered like a mule. Paladin and the pack mules walked nearby, tethered to pony drags. Coy minced along behind Sam, whimpering.

Where is Gideon? Sam hadn't seen him since he charged off into the cottonwoods, an arrow jacking up and down in his hip. Probably his friend ended up fifty yards down the grove, a hundred at most, arrows sticking out of his back like needles from the branch of a pine tree.

Again, Sam hoped like hell Flat Dog wouldn't come riding into this mess. If Sam knew a god to pray to, he would ask now that Flat Dog see the advance scouts, or the village itself, and get the hell gone. But Sam wasn't sure the God of his childhood held sway out here.

He walked. He paid attention. He cleared his mind, so he could see any opportunity for escape. All day, no opportunity. Before the sun dropped behind the Big Horn Mountains on the west, the parade rode right into the village Sam feared.

His heart went rigid. *Damn well no mercy from these people.*

He stood, rope around his neck, while the women put up the tipis and unpacked their belongings. The pock-marked warrior who held the other end of the rope watched Sam idly. Carefully, Sam showed no particular interest in anything he saw.

Two Horns, now holding The Celt, faced Sam. 'The people will talk about you in council,' the fellow signed, with an indolent smile. Sam knew how that would come out. Tomorrow he'd be turned over to the Lakota women, well bound. They would begin the delicious torture, making his death come as slowly and painfully as possible, giving him every chance to be immensely brave as he died in stoic silence.

"Tonight we will hold you in a small tipi," said Two Horns. "Don't try to get away. Two men will stand guard. Outside, where you can't get at them. If you come out, they will kill you."

IT WAS A small tipi, maybe a travel lodge. Sam was bound, and had to lie on his back the whole time.

The first problem was getting untied. He'd give a lot now to be able to get his hands on the hair ornament knife in his braid. *A weapon.* The thought stirred his heart foolishly. *A weapon.*

There was nothing at all inside, so nothing Sam could use. No stones encircled a fire pit. No fire pit. No wood to build a fire with. No flint and steel for making a fire. Nothing but the poles, the lodge skin, and the rope that held the tipi down against strong winds.

Sam snorted. They didn't want the little lodge to blow over and let him escape. Hannibal's voice said in his head, "Even the wind can be your friend."

He laughed.

Sam snorted. They didn't want the little lodge to blow over and let him escape. Hannibal's voice said in his head, "Even the wind can be your friend."

He laughed.

He rolled over. Rolled over a couple of times the other way. Found out that was the limit on his freedom, rolling over.

He thought. He didn't feel afraid to die, not especially. He looked around the tipi in the dwindling light, and on the panels of stretched hide between the poles he saw parts of his life, like pictures hung on the walls of a home. Himself and his father, wandering the woods, Sam learning. The feeling the night he untied the painter on the boat there at the family landing, and let go into the current and into the wide world, one of the best feelings he'd ever had. The piercing loneliness of the week and a half he'd waited for Diah and Fitz and the fellows and they didn't come. His dream of melting into the buffalo, so he and the beast were one. The village crier circling through the lodges, declaring that a young man had earned a name, Joins with Buffalo, or in his language, Samalo.

These experiences were his life. If it was time to quit living . . .

He felt it like a gut burn. No. Because they didn't include sharing love with Meadowlark. No.

He snorted, and felt a spasm of stubbornness. When he breathed back in, his breath smelled like buffalo breath. He gave a crazy chuckle.

"Buffalo is your medicine." That's what Bell Rock told him. "Watch the buffalo and see what they do. Notice that when the bulls fight, they are not quick, they're big and heavy, but they never flee. A bull will fight until he wins, or he will fight until he is defeated. But one thing he won't do—run away."

Sam thought of his medicine pouch, with his swatch of buffalo hair. Gone. But he didn't think he needed it. He thought of the bulls and what Bell Rock said about them. They fight until they win or die, but they never run away. He wondered how . . .

And finally he had a thought. The center rope was anchored to a gnarled piece of limb driven into the ground as a big stake. *I could, maybe I could . . . scrape the ropes of braided rawhide on the head of the stake, and scrape them and scrape them, and maybe they'll slip down.*

He inch-wormed to the stake. He lifted his legs and after a couple of tries caught the bottom strand of rope on its head. Then came the job. He jerked. And pulled. And jerked. And wriggled. And jerked and pulled and jerked and wriggled again. *I don't know or care how long it will take.*

At last the bottom strand slipped over his heels.

He heard a peg being pulled out of the door opening.

What if they see?

He rolled quietly away from the center stake and lay still, facing the door. He pointed his feet inconspicuously the other way.

The last peg slipped away, and Pock-Marked ducked in. They looked at each other in the last of the twilight that seeped down from the center hole at the top of the poles.

"Are you afraid?" signed Pock-Marked. "I suggest you spend the night wrapped in the blanket of your fear. In the morning, when you ask, I will save you all that pain with a quick cut of your throat."

He laughed. "We permit men to be cowards." He disappeared.

From the inside the door appeared to reassemble itself.

Now that the bottom strand had slipped over his heels, Sam got the rest off easily.

He stood up. It felt good.

In the new darkness he knelt, backed up to the center stake and started working his hands against it hard.

He didn't know how long it took him. It was the most frustrating task of his life. Catch—pull—nothing. Catch—pull—nothing. Catch—pull—nothing.

When he finally found a way, it took a lot of skin off his thumbs. He stuck the sore digits in his mouth and tasted warm, salty blood.

He stood now, moved around silently, swung his arms, and stretched his cramped wrists and fingers. He tied the rope around his waist. Might come in handy. He took out the hair ornament knife and ran his fingers along the sharp edge. Plenty sharp to cut a throat.

Then he stood on his tiptoes and looked up at the center hole. No sign of the moon, Big Dipper out of sight, no idea how much night was left.

Half the night, he guessed.

How do I get out of here?

Pull the stake and use it as a club.

He no more had the thought than he rejected it. If he began to pull out the pegs that held the door together, that would take a lot of seconds, and both guards would be standing there laughing when he stuck his head out.

He wanted to pace but didn't dare. Sometimes he looked up in the hope of a glimpse of the moon. Finally he sat down cross-legged. He remembered not to think. That's what Hannibal taught him. If you keep your mind still, you get ideas.

Where is Flat Dog?

It didn't matter. Since Blue Horse died—since Sam got Blue Horse killed with his horse-stealing scheme—Flat Dog probably wouldn't try a rescue. Sam couldn't blame him for that. Regardless, Sam could not wait to be rescued. Tomorrow morning death would open the tipi door.

When the idea came, at last, it came as a picture.

Without any special thought, he acted. He grabbed hold of the center rope and began to shinny up. Half way to the top his arms started screaming at him. He had to rest—he almost let himself drop to the ground. Then he realized. One chance. Arms never fresher than now. One chance. Reality: Do it or die.

At the top he stuck a foot way out. He squirmed and pushed and nearly fell before he got a toe in behind the lodge pole. A little more squirming and it was wedged between the pole and the lodge skin.

He seized the pole with his exhausted left hand. He took a deep breath, then another. At last he let go of the rope with his right hand and swung free.

Reprieve!

Now, though, his muscles were getting used up fast in a different way. *Time running out.*

The lodge skin split under the blade of the hair ornament knife. He gushed out relief.

Quick!

He made the split longer and stuck a leg through. Silently, he slipped his head and shoulders through.

He was in the world again. In the light of the moon he could even see. His own moon shadow angled down the lodge cover.

This position was damned awkward. He . . .

Sam slid to the ground and went tumbling.

On your feet! Now!

Running footsteps.

He rolled behind a sagebrush.

Pock-Marked ran up, knife ready. In the moonlight he looked up and saw the gaping hole in the top of the lodge.

And saw nothing more, ever.

Blood gushed all over Sam's knife arm. He held the limp body for a moment. Then he let it fall and looked briefly at the bloody neck. *You offered to cut my throat.*

A raised tomahawk caught the moonlight as it swung down.

Sam dodged and rolled.

He looked up and saw the dark figure raise the tomahawk again. Sam ducked inside its arc and rammed his head into the man's chest. As they went down, he tried to slash the man's back with his hair ornament knife, but couldn't tell if he got deer hide or human flesh.

Tangled arm and leg, the dark figure and Sam slashed at each other.

SLAM!

Someone else whammed into them. All three men rolled in the dust and darkness. Sam spilled away onto his back. His mind hollered, *Run!* The new man lifted a tomahawk.

Sam's arm was caught. He looked up into the tomahawk and swallowed his own scream before he died.

The blade swung down and crashed into the Lakota's skull.

"Let's go!"

It was a loud whisper—in the Crow language!

Sam followed the figure into the sagebrush. It paused and turned, and in the moonlight Sam saw Flat Dog's face. He motioned into the darkness, and Sam followed him at a run.

SHOUTS SOUNDED BEHIND them. Quickly the Lakotas would discover their dead comrades, and the escape.

They ran.

Suddenly there was Paladin, staked. Coy danced toward Sam.

Flat Dog jumped onto his mount. "Let's get out of here."

Sam jumped onto Paladin. No saddle, and Paladin would be fine without a bridle.

"Let's slip off quietly," Flat Dog said. "They can't track us in the dark."

After a hundred yards Sam said, "I gotta get my rifle."

"Forget it!"

Sam realized he didn't know where it was anyway. *The Celt is gone.* His one legacy from his father.

"I got Paladin for you, and Coy with him," Flat Dog said, as though to say, "And that's enough."

They came out onto the trail downstream of the village. "This trail, they won't be able to see any tracks. With luck they'll look for us the other direction," Flat Dog said.

They walked the horses all night. Sam half froze. Even August nights are cold when you're stark naked.

When the sun came up, they concealed themselves in a willow thicket and slept.

Late in the afternoon they gathered juneberries and ate them. "I'll hunt tomorrow," Flat Dog said. The only hunting weapon they had left was his bow.

"Where are we going?"

"We'll follow the mountains north. There's another pass up that way, and we'll cross to the Big Horn."

They rode all night, and Sam froze again. Being naked had its disadvantages. He thought glumly that when they started riding during the day, he'd sunburned all over. Then he grinned at himself. All over except for the small strip where the ropes belted his belly, a funny sight.

Flat Dog killed a doe. They ate all they could that night and the next morning carried the hind quarters and left the rest. "Gotta get out of Head Cutter country," said Flat Dog.

Sam pondered his situation. He'd lost everything he owned except his horse, dog, and hair-ornament knife. Rifle gone, knife gone, clothes gone. No more powder and lead, no more pemmican, no more coffee. No traps to get beaver with. No bow and arrows. Nothing to trade to the Indians.

He'd lost his friends.

Ghastly.

A clear, rotten thought clanged into his mind. *Instead of getting eight horses to win Meadowlark, I killed her brother.*

He spent the rest of the day getting sunblistered and swimming in remorse.

That night and morning they gorged themselves on the hindquarters and ended up picking the last flesh off the bones. Amazing how much you could eat when you knew no more food was available. Coy looked back at the bones as they rode off. "Better to go hungry than get scalped," Sam told him.

Up came a mental picture of Coy scalped. Sam started laughing and couldn't stop. Paladin turned her head and gave Sam a queer look. Flat Dog looked at Sam. He laughed the way a spring bubbles out of the ground, and he didn't know whether the water of his laughter was sweet or alkaline.

FROM THIS CAMP they could see where the Big Horn River flowed, and where it cut through some mountains to the north. According to Flat Dog, the village now would be where the Stinking Water River flowed into the Big Horn. Later the big buffalo hunt, with several villages gathered together, would be held near the Pryors.

Sam was learning where the mountains lifted up and how the rivers ran, all a big picture in his mind. He wished he could write it all down, like Jedediah did, and make a map. Which was a damn funny thought for a man who didn't read or write, and didn't own even a scrap of paper.

But on this warm evening in August, in a pleasant camp on a nameless creek, that wasn't on his mind.

"I'm sorry I got Blue Medicine Horse killed."

"Don't use his name," said Flat Dog.

"I'm sorry."

"You didn't do it. The one who isn't here, he made a mistake."

Silence. As if that was enough.

"I feel terrible about it."

This drew a flicker of sharpness in Flat Dog's eyes. "Warriors pay for their mistakes."

Silence.

"I found all the signs," Flat Dog went on. "I could tell a lot of what happened. The one who isn't here, it was his job to see anyone we were riding into. He didn't."

"He was my friend." Then Sam thought that Blue Horse was Flat Dog's brother, and felt ashamed of himself.

"I took care of him. Wrapped him in his blanket and put him in the fork of a tree. After one or two winters I'll go back and put his bones in a rocky crevice."

Sam started to ask if Blue Horse was scalped, but he already knew the answer to that.

He tried to find something good about their situation. Well, on the trip home he would learn to ride bareback, since his saddle was gone. And he would train himself and Paladin always to turn with pressure of the knees instead of the reins.

He wished they had coffee. He wished they had food. He wished he didn't have to ride into the village tomorrow dead poor and stark naked.

Now that he thought of it, literally naked was too much of a problem. "Big favor," said Sam.

Flat Dog looked up at him.

"I need a breechcloth. Don't see anything to use but your shirt."

Flat Dog looked down at his chest. It was a perfectly good deerskin shirt but nothing special. He stripped it off. "You owe me a shirt."

Sam started cutting a breechcloth from the tail of the shirt. The very sharp hair ornament knife worked well. "This is going to be one very short breechcloth," he said.

"Cut two. We'll find someone to sew them together."

Sam looked at the material. "I'll have enough for a couple of pairs of moccasins, too." Barefoot could get painful.

He took off a sleeve and sliced part of it into a belt for the breechcloth, the rest into strips to braid into another rope.

"You owe me a shirt," Flat Dog repeated, laughing a little.

"I owe you everything."

Part Five

PASSAGE THROUGH DARKNESS

Chapter Sixteen

MILES FROM THE village, Sam felt his flesh redden. In his imagination he saw that, sunburned as he was, his skin would glow redder yet when they entered the village. Red Roan would watch him and smile. Gray Hawk and Needle, seeing they had lost a son, would turn their backs on Sam and refuse to look at him. Meadowlark would run into her lodge and weep.

He lived in this moment of humiliation all afternoon, running it over and over through his mind. He told himself that the real moment only had to be lived once, but he couldn't help rolling it through his mind again and again.

They spotted the village across an open plain, on the south bank of the Stinking Water. The moment was coming. Sam steeled himself.

Then, for some reason, no more than two hundred yards away, Flat Dog had said, "We have to go up on that hill."

When they got there, Flat Dog's words surprised him again. "You have to sit here." Sam dismounted and plopped his breechclothed bottom down. Coy joined him and looked up at Sam anxiously.

The hillock overlooked the camp. Flat Dog dismounted, walked the few steps to the crest, and waved his blanket in a big circle. "I have to get the people's attention," he said.

This seemed odd—the sentries surely had told the camp that a small party was coming in.

"Now they know someone has been killed," he said.

He waved his blanket toward the Big Horn Mountains. "That tells them what direction we're coming from," he said.

He flung one end of the blanket to the ground at his side, once. "Now they know we've lost one."

One? Six men rode out of this camp, and two were returning. Beckwourth was just gone somewhere else. Third Wing, Gideon, and Blue Medicine Horse were dead. Dead.

Flat Dog walked over and sat down by Sam. "Since they've seen me," he said sadly, "they know which one."

Sam pondered what that meant.

In a few minutes Red Roan and two other young Kit Foxes showed up. Coy stood up, bristled, and growled. Sam calmed him down.

The three sat and asked questions of Flat Dog, disregarding Sam. Flat Dog answered very factually and very fully. It seemed to Sam that he recounted every little thing they did after they left rendezvous to steal horses from the Head Cutters. The session seemed to last for hours.

Sam noticed nothing in particular that reflected on him except one story. Flat Dog told how Blue Medicine Horse had worried that no one in the party had medicine to go to war. At that point Sam told about his daydreams. Blue Horse and Flat Dog thought maybe that was how white men got their medicine and decided to go against the Head Cutters the next morning.

Not one of the interviewers looked directly at Sam, but he had never felt more thoroughly condemned.

At last Red Roan and others rose and walked down the hill to camp.

"We stay here," Flat Dog.

That evening the wives of Kit Foxes brought them food and water. For some reason they weren't allowed to touch the cups that held the water. The women put water to their mouths like they were small children. No longer having a hat, Sam had to ask them to bring a small bowl for Coy to drink out of.

One woman brought a buffalo robe. Without looking at Sam, she dropped it on the ground and said, "For Joins with Buffalo," and walked away.

When they were alone, Sam went to Paladin, then turned and looked at Flat Dog expectantly. Flat Dog shook his head no. "We stay here," he said, "until the village finishes mourning."

He sat on a silvered cedar log and took an arrow from his quiver. He gazed off toward the Big Horns for a minute or two. Then, suddenly, Flat Dog stabbed himself in the left shoulder with the arrow point. Then he stabbed himself about a dozen times on the left arm, each cut making a trickle of blood.

He began to weep. At first he cried softly, moaning a little. The moans grew in volume. They grew in intensity. They swooped up and down. They squeezed soft and bellowed loud.

As he moaned, he changed hands and stabbed himself on the right arm. Over and over, seemingly without counting, he inflicted small wounds on himself.

His moaning grew extravagant. It was as though he was trying to gauge the depth and breadth of his grief for his lost brother. He pitched on an ocean of sorrow, rode a swell of fierce pain upward and dropped down into a trough of anguish. Then the next pain lifted him high into the bleak vista of his heartache.

With the arrow he wounded himself about half a dozen times on each cheek.

At last he sat rigid, frozen by the prospect of a loss as wide and deep as any ocean.

Sam heard the drums beating in the village, and the voices joined together in a great song of woe. Now what he had seen in two winters of living with the Crow people came home to him. He had seen men and women with wounds like those Flat Dog just scarified himself with. Men and women with joints missing from a finger, where they had expressed violently their sorrow, and their anger at their loss. Women who lost a close relative chopped their hair almost to the roots, and mourned until it grew to its original length. Families gave away most of their belongings, and grieved formally for two moons, or sometimes an entire year.

When a relative was killed by an enemy, Sam remembered, the family mourned until a member of the offending tribe was killed in vengeance. It hit him hard—until a member of the offending tribe was killed in vengeance.

Flat Dog emerged from his seeming trance and once more began to give voice to his sorrow. Long into the night rose the beat of the drums and the village songs of mourning. Long into the night rose Flat Dog's wail.

The next day Sam realized that they were in a kind of exile. All day they sat on top of that little hill, and then another day and another. Sam lost track after three. Every day they sat on the hilltop, all day. Flat Dog sat looking mournful, or far away. Sam waited. Or thought about his dead friends. Mostly waited.

Coy looked at them peculiarly, and jumped onto his food and water gratefully when it came.

It was the second night that Sam began to grieve. He started with a kind of madness. He began to moan along with Flat Dog—he didn't know why, just had the impulse to make a kind of duet. Flat Dog sang high and loud, Sam soft and low.

Tears came.

True, hot tears.

Thoughts of Blue Medicine Horse swam through his head. How hard he worked, so exactly, to learn English. How he opened his heart to Sam because of that rabid coyote. How he helped Sam train Paladin, and helped save Sam's life during the buffalo hunt. How he counseled Sam wisely on how to behave in a way acceptable to the Crows. This man's duty was to protect his family, but he brought the stranger into their circle of acquaintance, tragically.

Most of all, Sam couldn't help thinking of Blue Medicine Horse as the man who risked his life to help Sam get eight horses to win Meadowlark's hand. And lost his life.

Sam's mourning lifted him high into anguish, low into despair.

He thought of the brother who could not help to assure the safety of his younger brothers and sisters. Who could no longer help feed his family. Who would be unavailable to defend the tribe against enemies. Who would never delight a young woman with his love. Who would never add to the life of the tribe through his issue.

A human being lost.

A new wave lifted Sam, and he knew how far his sorrows reached beyond the death of Blue Horse. He had lost Gideon, his first real friend in the mountains. He'd failed to protect Third Wing, the Pawnee who saved his life out of pure generosity.

He lifted his lament to the night sky.

The memory of his father, Lew Morgan, washed over him, tumbled him head over heels in a flash flood of sadness. It had no words, only pictures of his father's kind face, or his compact body doing work, lifting a deer onto his shoulder, carrying a ham in each hand, walking behind the mule and forcing the plow blade into the soft, spring earth.

He wailed and wailed.

Worse, Sam himself had become a killer. He had killed the Pawnee sentry Two Stones. He had slain Pock-Marked, his Lakota captor. Altogether he had walked the halls of the drama of life and death as one who sheds blood. He recognized, with the heaviest of hearts, that he walked the earth with bloody hands.

In this fullness of recognition, he knew that the earth was, forever, the cradle of birth. It was equally, and also forever, the cold arms of death. He knew himself as the bearer of both life and death, and knew that he bore in his blood his own death.

He wailed long into the night.

Chapter Seventeen

LOW ESTATE.

That was Hannibal's phrase. Hannibal was always using words no one else knew. When Sam asked him what it meant, Hannibal said, "Down and out."

When he and Flat Dog finally went into the village, Sam found out what it meant, really, to be in low estate.

He had sewn the two pieces of breechcloth together, so his nether end was more or less covered. He had no shirt or hat, and, worse, no shoes. No shelter. The buffalo robe was his on loan. He had no food and no weapons to hunt with.

It stung, also, that he had lost his *gage d'amour* and his medicine pouch. They were the only gifts he'd ever gotten from Meadowlark. And the medicine pouch held the matted hair that was his buffalo medicine.

The Celt was gone. The Celt. . . . His bow was gone.

What did he have in place of all his possibles, everything he owned?

Guilt.

Flat Dog got them shelter. They moved into a brush hut with two other Kit Foxes, Naughty Ones like themselves, he said. These turned out to be Stripe and Straight Arm, who inflicted the name No Arrows on Sam.

Bell Rock invited them to supper at his lodge that evening. He didn't have to say it was to fend off starvation.

Around the brush hut Stripe and Straight Arm hardly spoke to him at all. Sam was glad.

The next day Flat Dog left to join his family in mourning. They would live out somewhere alone for some weeks, Sam knew. At least he didn't have to face Gray Hawk and Needle, not yet. He also wouldn't get to see Flat Dog. Or Meadowlark.

He felt defeated.

The first job, he made himself decide, was to get food. He used his single weapon, the hair ornament knife, to cut finger-thick willow shafts along the river. He peeled them and laid them out to dry. They would make arrows. He'd learned from Blue Medicine Horse—the memory twisted his heart—to use thick ones. The small ones would get too thin when they were scraped straight.

Owning almost nothing, he dried extras to trade for arrowheads and sinew to lash the points on.

While they dried, he rode out with Paladin and Coy to gather serviceberries. Since he had nothing to carry them in, he picked double handfuls, devoured them, and rode to the Stinking Water to drink. He liked the taste of the red and purple fruit, and the cool river water. Though the river got its name from hot springs upstream, the sulfurous taste was long gone here. Coy and Paladin liked it, too. Sam would have napped in the sun by the river, but he was afraid of what he might dream.

Gathering berries was women's work, but Sam refused to care. Tonight he would put serviceberries into the stew Stripe and Straight Arm would have. Though he was sure they wouldn't let him starve, he wanted to make a contribution. Tomorrow he would find a good root-digging stick and dig up some Jerusalem artichokes.

He was mostly worried about getting through the night.

The next day, doing that, he made a discovery. Life was simple. Necessity: Find enough food for today. There were no other necessities.

He made another discovery. He liked life this simple. It had clarity. Find food or starve. The finding wasn't so hard. He liked life this way.

He started to wonder why anyone ever made it harder.

The answer came quickly. Winter.

He knew he deserved to be poor.

Winter would come.

When Sam brought his contributions to the supper pot, Stripe and Straight Arm nodded their approval but still didn't say much to him.

Sam understood. The way the village saw things, he had taken a party on a raid, come away empty-handed, and gotten a man killed. In fact, that was exactly what did happen. He would have shunned himself.

Stripe and Straight Arm, though, frowned at Sam when he fed Coy meat from the pot. Almost as if he understood, the little coyote started hunting chipmunks and squirrels. Sam's sense of justice was offended.

In the dark of the night, whether he slept or waked, his sense of justice also condemned him.

After several days Sam borrowed a deer shoulder blade with a hole drilled in the middle. Slowly and carefully, he used the bone to scrape the willow shafts to a single diameter. When he returned the shoulder blade, he gave the owner several straightened shafts and borrowed a piece of basalt with a groove worn in it. With this tool he took the knots off and rubbed the remaining shafts smooth.

The next part tested his patience. He heated the shafts over the fire and rubbed oil on them until they were supple. Then, borrowing a bone with a hole in it from Straight Arm, he used that as a lever to straighten the shafts slowly.

Last came the most trying part. He held each shaft a long time while it cooled.

He had no skill at lashing the points on. So he begged for help from Bell Rock. It was one of Bell Rock's sons, Weasel, who showed Sam how to get tight lashing. Sam gave the young man two finished arrows for his help.

Bell Rock chuckled at that and said, "Do you think you could accept a dinner for nothing?"

Sam didn't think he deserved it, but he accepted.

He had three finished arrows. At the end of dinner he had to ask for the loan of one of Bell Rock's bows.

Bell Rock reached behind him and unwrapped an object Sam had paid no attention to. It was a bow fashioned from the thick, heavy horns of big horn sheep. He handed it to Sam.

"It's yours. A gift."

Sam turned it over and over. It was a stiff, powerful bow, and would take a strong draw.

"Let it make you strong," Bell Rock said.

Sam pulled on the bowstring. He needed all his arm power to get the string back to shooting position.

"I want you to have that," Bell Rock said. "I believe in you. You're a good young man."

Sam felt a gush of relief. Then he reminded himself, *I got Blue Medicine Horse killed.*

He practiced all the next day, shooting his arrows at a circle drawn into the soft earth of a hillside. When he went to bed, his right arm ached. When he slept, his dream tormented him.

The next morning the arm was screaming at him. At dawn and dusk he watched for deer, observing the paths they took to the water. Midday he spent gathering gooseberries and wild onions.

The following day he got up before first light, excited. He left Coy tied to a tree near Paladin. A coyote might scare the deer off.

In half an hour, big bow in one hand and three arrows in the other, he stood utterly still beside a boulder alongside the Stinking Water. He'd picked this spot out when he watched two does and their fawns drinking last evening. The abundance of heart-shaped tracks said they came here a lot, and others too.

He hoped he looked like part of the boulder.

He wished he could hunt bucks instead of does. It was his father who taught him to take the bucks. "The does will bear the young," Lew Morgan said. But Sam would take whatever came.

Now his days of hunting in Eden came back to him strongly. It hadn't been a real Eden, just a spot he and his father liked. They named it that because Lew Morgan had once told his younger son, when Sam wasn't old enough to hold a Pennsylvania rifle steady, that he could play Adam and give names to all the animals and plants. The names were original. Deer were mooshmen. Trees were starks. Wild roses were garbies. A bear was a woze.

That was a good day. Sam remembered lots of good days with his father. He didn't think about the lousy days after Lew Morgan died, and Sam's brother Owen took over as head of the family.

It was Lew Morgan who taught Sam how to become absolutely still in the woods, how to make yourself part of things, so that after a while even the birds would forget about your presence and return to their songs. Then all the animals would relax—and the deer would come.

I had a rifle then.

He hadn't let himself think about the rifle his father willed him since it got stolen. What did it mean to him? He'd had the gunsmith Hawken engrave C∈Lⱦ on a brass plate on the stock and circle the name with Celtic love knots. That said it all.

What would Sam do? Some Lakota—Sam was tempted by the hand-slap name the Crows used, Head Cutter—was walking around with his father's rifle. That couldn't be, simply couldn't be, allowed.

There's nothing I can do about it now.

He felt a tingle.

Doe. One fawn. Picking their way through the cottonwood grove, noses up and alert.

They would get no scent of Sam. The wind was upcanyon, and he'd picked his spot upwind of the tracks.

Slowly they came. When they stepped out of the trees and onto the bank of the river, he might get a shot.

The doe changed directions, heading a little left.

Damn. That would make the shot longer.

Frustrating. If he had The Celt, a hundred yards or so would not be an issue. But this big-horn bow was another story. He couldn't brace it against a tree trunk, and he couldn't hold it steady for long. He wouldn't be able to take his time on his aim.

He considered trying to slip closer, and rejected that. Even when she had her head down to drink, the doe would be too alert for a significant move. He would wait and hope.

The two deer came half out of the trees. The doe sniffed the air carefully. She looked upstream and down.

They emerged and walked steadily to the river. Into the stream. Drinking.

Sam couldn't stand it. The bow had plenty of power for this distance. It was up to him to make a good hold.

Check of wind, arrow nocked, now drawn. His forearms and biceps screeched. Steady. . . .

The arrow flew a couple of feet over the doe's back.

She bolted, and the fawn behind her. They ran in their upright, prancing way until Sam could barely catch an occasional glimpse of a white tail flicking through the cottonwoods.

The arrow could be found later. He might get another shot. Carefully, he lined up the boulder he stood by and a tall cottonwood across the river. The arrow would be on that line, maybe in the water.

When he did get another shot, it was even longer. This time a doe and two fawns. The arrow sailed behind the doe, and a little above. A gust of wind, maybe.

She just stood.

Quickly, Sam nocked his last arrow and drew. *Steady!* he shouted at himself inside his mind.

A clean miss.

The doe ignored anything she might have heard or felt, drank a little more, and then trotted daintily back into the cover of the trees.

Sam wanted to stomp the bow.

He didn't.

He spent an hour hunting the arrows. One was in the soft sand of the opposite bank. One was in front of a head-sized rock in a riffle, the shaft broken. The third he never found. Maybe it landed in a deep spot and floated away. But he didn't find it washed up downstream either.

One morning's hunting, no meat, one arrow left.

Dejected, he went and got Coy. They walked along the river to cut more willow shafts to dry.

SAM WATCHED THE evening shadows lengthen. They were closing in on him, the gentlest of traps. He felt as though he could almost hear them whisper. He wished he could make out the words. But he knew the message was mockery.

No meat for you.

He sniffed. He'd waited since sundown, no deer. Still no deer. Not a one had come to water, or not this water.

He stroked his single arrow, felt the smoothness of the shaft. He ran his finger along the serrated edge of the flint. Sharp enough.

Come, deer, come.

A shadow stirred.

No, he'd imagined it.

The shadow edged forward.

Deer.

Yes, a doe and a spotted fawn.

They ghosted forward one step at a time, as though they knew better.

Now the wind came downcanyon, and Sam was downstream of the deer. They stopped twenty feet from the edge of the trees, suspicious, feeling the predator they couldn't smell.

The doe turned straight toward Sam. The fawn echoed her stance.

He stilled himself, maybe even his heartbeat. *This is a chance.*

The doe faced straight toward him. She lifted her muzzle and sniffed.

Wrong sense.

She turned back the way she'd come, and stopped. The fawn imitated her.

Sam held his breath. He didn't have a decent shot. A sapling blocked the doe's middle. The fawn stood in front of her. Small target.

They're going to run.

Sam hefted the bow and instantly let the arrow fly.

A hit! A sort of hit. Sam thought the arrow had actually ricocheted off the back of the fawn and into the doe behind the shoulder blade.

For an instant the doe stood quivering.

Deciding whether to die?

Then she bolted.

Sam dropped the bow and ran like a maniac.

She hadn't been hit hard. The arrow worked up and down in her ribs like a pump handle. But maybe she wouldn't go far, couldn't go far.

When he cleared the trees, the doe and fawn were standing on the prairie, looking around. They saw Sam and ran upstream, their bottoms bouncing in the last of the light.

Am I going to lose her?

Sam ran like hell and shrieked like a banshee.

Out of pain, or shock at the sound, the doe stopped.

Sam ran and roared.

When he was a dozen steps away, she ran directly away from the river.

He veered that way. He would have hollered but was out of breath.

The doe stopped and pivoted.

She's crazy with pain or fear.

The doe dashed straight at him.

They collided. Shoulder bounced off shoulder. For a split-second Sam thought the arrow would actually stick in him.

The doe went down.

Sam pitched to the ground, rolled, and found his feet.

The fawn skittered a few steps, stopped, and looked back, quivering.

The doe clambered up and started to run.

Before she got three steps, Sam jumped on her back.

She bolted upward, like trying to jump onto the moon.

Sam held on.

He jerked the ornament knife out of his braid, reached around the doe, and slit her throat.

She crashed down. Sam went tumbling through the grass. He sat up. She wasn't moving. His right forearm was covered with blood.

Sam looked at the fawn. It danced lightly away.

Sam did as his father taught him, and said, "Godspeed."

Then he bellowed, "Hallelujah."

Chapter Eighteen

IT WAS A comedy. He'd broken his last arrow, probably when he banged the deer's shoulder. He gutted her out with his ornament blade, which was the length of a finger joint. Butchering required a butcher knife. Still, he got it done.

He staggered into camp, exhausted by her weight. Sam dunked himself in the river to get the dust caked with blood off. Straight Arm and Stripe gladly helped finish the butchering. Sam took the heart and liver, his by right, and broiled them on a stick over the flames. He thought that was the best meat he'd ever tasted.

As the others finished the butchering, he wondered if his dreams would be haunted again. Or did action, maybe, chase away the phantoms?

He thought of tomorrow. He would spend the day on women's work—cutting the meat into strips and slowly drying it over low flames.

Now they fed on the back straps, share and share alike. He gorged himself.

He broke ribs off and gave them to Coy, as many as the little coyote wanted.

Tomorrow he would also set about making new arrows. He'd trade the deer hide for a pair of moccasins. Which would still leave him poor. He had no rifle. He had no traps to take beaver to earn money for a rifle. Or powder and lead, or a butcher knife, or coffee and sugar, or anything else that would make him a white man.

He was so belly-heavy he could barely move. He crawled to his buffalo robe.

I have meat against the winter.

And guilt enough to last a lifetime.

IN THE MIDDLE of the night Coy mewled and woke Sam up. He wondered if the little coyote was hungry again. He reached down and petted Coy's head. Suddenly, he had one clear thought: *That meat, actually, won't last the week.*

He also thought that being poor wasn't all right. It didn't shine, as Beckwourth would say.

Sam was in a big hole.

He needed to trade for things. Material goods. White man stuff.

He took stock. He owned Paladin, as much as any man could own her. But he would never trade her. The tricks she could do, they dazzled his mind and lifted his spirits. And no one else could get her to do them.

He didn't own Coy, who was no good in trade anyway. He gave the coyote's ears a good rub and lay back down.

He had his legs, arms, and brain. And heart. What would that get him?

He could shoot some beaver, probably, with arrows. That was the hard way, compared to setting a trap and coming back later. If the beaver swam for its lodge, what would he do? Swim into the lodge? With maybe several beaver there, that idea didn't shine.

A few of the Crows had traps the fur men had traded them for almost nothing, in the hope that the Indians would learn to be fur hunters. They weren't, not to amount to anything. Sam could take deer and trade hides and meat for traps. Yes, that's what he'd do.

Then he'd spend part of the fall and winter getting enough plews to trade for . . .

Just a minute. Was he going to *trade* for a rifle?

He couldn't do that. Had to get The Celt back, some way. Had to get The Celt back.

He shoved that out of his mind. He heard the inside of his mind whisper, "Too damn dangerous."

He had to work hard, work like hell. He had to get stuff, had to prove himself.

Because Meadowlark would never marry a poor man, a disgraced man.

He turned over in the buffalo robe. He looked at the blackness of the sky through the leaves and branches of the hut. He wished it was light, so he could get going.

MEADOWLARK AVOIDED HIM. Everyone in the Gray Hawk family avoided Sam, even Flat Dog.

At midday they'd returned and set up their tipi in the lodge circle. They said little to anyone, and few approached them. Maybe that was a way of honoring their grief.

The family shunned Sam. They refused even to look in his direction. He rode Paladin upriver, Coy following, to a willow patch to cut more shafts for arrows. By God, he was going to become an arrow manufacturer. The only way he could rise in the world, now, was to make arrows. Trade them or take deer with them. No other way.

In the evening Sam waited in the cottonwoods and watched the other young women come to the river to get water. Meadowlark didn't come. Needle made the trip, surely to keep Meadowlark away from Sam.

When Sam got back to his brush hut, though, Flat Dog sat there talking to Stripe and Straight Arm. He shared a deer hindquarter with the three of them. Sam had hung it up, thinking the cold September night and cool day wouldn't spoil it, not in one day. Sam showed Flat Dog the gift bow from Bell Rock, and described his deer hunt for comical effect. Flat Dog said very little in return.

When they were finished, he said to Sam, "Let's build a brush hut."

Sam smiled big. "First thing in the morning." At least two Crows were treating him decently.

"First thing," said Flat Dog, "we hunt. I'll lend you some arrows. Then we build the brush hut."

Two weeks later the village moved. Everyone marched down the Big Horn to the Pryor Mountains. Along with the other Kit Foxes, Sam rode as a policeman. He felt good to be doing the job along with Flat Dog, Bell Rock, and Red Roan. They kept order in the long line of pony drags, and watched out for the enemy. The trip was uneventful. Sam was glad the Kit Foxes still treated him as one of them.

Other villages met them near the foot of the Pryors. Together they made one great camp, a series of lodge circles up and down the river. Sam was, sort of, one of over a thousand of Crow people.

He was still a poor man, but not desperately poor. He owned a dozen arrows and an otter skin quiver, two pairs of moccasins, a shirt, and two buffalo robes. The robes were rubbed half hairless by wear, and wouldn't get him through the winter.

In another way he was desperate. Meadowlark avoided him

completely. She didn't stand outside her lodge in the evenings to meet any suitors at all, not even Red Roan. She didn't sit outside in the afternoon sun, sewing with her friends. She didn't mingle with the people of the other villages to trade news of what had happened since the spring hunt. She seemed never to come out of the tipi. The entire Gray Hawk family, except Flat Dog, was keeping to themselves. And they were keeping Meadowlark away from Sam.

Flat Dog confirmed it. "My mother and father haven't forgiven you for leading that raid. May never."

The raid where "the one who isn't here" died. Flat Dog never used Blue Medicine Horse's name. No one did.

Sam didn't use it. But he dreamed about Blue Medicine Horse.

He tried to keep his voice casual. "Not Meadowlark either?"

Flat Dog seemed to ponder while he chewed a slice of blackstrap. "I don't know."

They were broiling the backstrap on sticks over open flames. They ate fresh deer meat most evenings now, and Sam was killing his share. His arms and shoulders were getting noticeably bigger, the muscles more defined.

Sam looked at Flat Dog straight in the eyes. "I dream about him."

Flat Dog looked at Sam questioningly.

"The one who isn't here."

Flat Dog lowered his head.

"Maybe it's me that can't forgive."

Flat Dog snapped his head up.

"Forgive myself."

"It wasn't your fault. It . . ." Flat Dog sounded frustrated.

Sam said slowly and clearly, "Forgive myself."

Flat Dog thought for a long moment. "Tomorrow we better go see Bell Rock."

SAM, FLAT DOG, and Bell Rock were sitting naked outside the sweat lodge, sweat pouring down their bodies. The evening was cool, soon to be cold, and Sam was glad for it.

Sam looked at his friends. He had told Bell Rock, simply and truthfully, that the death of the one who was not here was disturbing him, even disturbing his dreams.

Bell Rock said they would sweat.

Between rounds they smoked the pipe. After offering the smoke to the four directions, the sky, and the earth, Bell Rock asked for wisdom for each of them, to know how Sam might be healed.

At the end of the sweat, Bell Rock said in his usual way, acting offhand about what was important, "You should think about holding a sun dance."

Sun dance. Sam knew vaguely about it. A ceremony where men put skewers through their chests and hung by ropes from lodge poles. When he thought there wasn't so much difference between him and Indians—began to think maybe he could be Indian—he thought of the sun dance, shuddered, and knew he was white, white, white.

"Maybe you should ask for all the buffalo tongues to be saved."

To another Crow, Bell Rock would have said those words without mention of a sun dance. Characteristic Crow indirection, Sam knew that much, but he didn't know what tongues had to do with it. He decided to keep his mouth shut and his stupidity hidden.

He did know the autumn buffalo hunt, the big one where they joined with other villages and got meat for the entire winter, was coming in the next few days. Men were making medicine to bring buffalo to the people. Scouts were out looking for the great, shaggy creatures.

"Save the tongues from the hunt that's coming up?" he asked.

They were all embarrassed that Sam didn't know. But they all understood it was because he was new to being a Crow. His friends were good about taking the time and trouble to explain. And then, after one explanation, expected him always to know.

"We hold a sun dance sometimes," Bell Rock began, "when one of us has been killed by an enemy, and someone has a great thirst for revenge."

"That would usually be a relative," said Flat Dog. After hesitating, he added, "It might be a close friend."

"The man who asks for the dance, he's called the whistler."

"He doesn't ask for the dance directly," said Flat Dog. "He tells someone we should save all the buffalo tongues, and that someone tells the chief, and the chief tells the herald to spread the word."

"Why buffalo tongues?"

"During the ceremony, which takes a number of days," said Bell Rock, "the whistler must give buffalo tongues to the principal families, and to all those who help him."

Sam nodded.

Bell Rock and Flat Dog looked at each other a long moment.

"All right," said Bell Rock, "for now we will answer your questions about the ceremony. Then you will ask your heart, and ask the grandfathers and grandmothers, and the four directions, and all the powers, whether you should do this."

"Why does the whistler do the ceremony?"

"He seeks a vision," said Bell Rock.

"He is hoping for a vision of revenge," said Flat Dog. "He blows the eagle-bone whistle and asks to see an enemy killed. Then he rides against the enemy and fulfills the vision."

"Whose help is needed for the ceremony?"

"The effigy owner, mainly," said Bell Rock.

"Some men own effigies that have the sun dance medicine."

"The owner, we call him the father. The whistler is the son."

"The sun dance is not just for one man," said Flat Dog.

"Other young men will sacrifice their blood for a vision."

Yes, the ones who skewer themselves, Sam thought. It gave him the willies.

"The sun dance is for all the people. They join in with all their hearts, and share in the blessings."

Sam took a long moment to think. "I don't know how to decide such big stuff."

Bell Rock said, "First, ask your heart, not your head."

"And," said Flat Dog, "I have something that may help you." He reached for a bundle wrapped in a deer hide and handed it to Sam. "A gift."

First Sam found a hide bag made from sheepskin. It was a very simple bag, rectangular, with a thong fringe but no bead or quill decoration.

Inside was a pipe stem and a bowl of red stone. The stone was carved into the shape of a T, with four rings around the part that held the tobacco. These, Sam knew, represented the four directions.

He also knew that a big moment had arrived. Flat Dog and Bell Rock were inviting him to become a carrier of the sacred pipe, as every Crow man was.

Sam looked at Flat Dog. He knew the hours required to shape the stem and the bowl, and the expense of getting a woman to sew the bag. He also knew that a quiet statement was being made. This was not an elaborate pipe; it was barely decorated at all, and it was short. Not the pipe of a man of consequence, but of a beginner.

"Thank you," he said to Flat Dog. Breath in, breath out. "I accept."

"Then," said Bell Rock, "we will dedicate your pipe by smoking it."

"From now on when you can't decide something, or you need special strength," said Flat Dog, "you'll ask your pipe."

ON THE NEXT evening Sam came back to Bell Rock. The medicine man asked if he wanted to smoke.

"Not tonight," said Sam. "I just want information."

Bell Rock waited.

"Will the people save the buffalo tongues if a white man asks?"

"They will if I support it."

Sam nodded. "Will an effigy owner consent to be my father?"

"I will."

Now a long pause. "Will the people join in with all their hearts, if a white man is the whistler?"

"Most will, some won't."

Sam grimaced and thought. "This will make it all right, what happened?"

"He will never be here, and you will always miss him. But it will be all right."

"Anything else you want me to think on?"

Bell Rock smiled. "Maybe you should think of yourself more as a man, not just a white man."

THE NEXT EVENING scouts came into the camp with news. On the other side of Pryor Gap, on Lodge Creek, they had found buffalo, many thousands of buffalo.

That night the heralds walked around the camps crying out the news: "There will be a big buffalo hunt."

The next morning experienced men rode out to see the herd and the country around it. Maybe they would set up a jump, where the buffalo could be driven off a cliff. Or maybe no jump would be handy, and they'd decide on tactics for a surround. For a thousand mouths and a long winter, they needed a lot of buffalo.

That evening Sam Morgan, a pipe carrier and no longer just a white man, spoke a few words to Bell Rock.

Bell Rock sent Flat Dog to the chief, Rides Twice.

Though Rides Twice may have been surprised, he merely nodded. Even a chief did not ask questions when Spirit spoke.

Within an hour the camp herald made their rounds of the lodge circles, crying, "Save all the tongues. Do not let the children have any. Save all the tongues."

To say it more directly—"A man is going to hold a sun dance. His name is Samalo, and he comes from Rides Twice's village"—that would have been entirely improper.

Since a sun dance was a rare event, the people asked each other who had pledged to make this ceremony, who the whistler would be.

At first it seemed that no one knew. Then the news was traced to the village led by Rides Twice, and the name Samalo came forth.

Samalo? It was a name no one recognized.

Some said that it meant Joins with Buffalo in the white-man language.

"White man?" people whispered to each other.

"Samalo?"

Many people were skeptical. Why would a white man seek to become a whistler? Why would he seek a vision of revenge? What relative of his died at the hands of the enemy?

The answers were vague and contradictory. Sometimes the words "son of Gray Hawk" were spoken, but no one was sure.

Many asked, "Should we join in a ceremony where a white man is the whistler?"

Some answered, "If the Effigy Owner brings the medicine, we must."

Young men said to themselves, "Should I shed my blood in a lodge where a white man is the whistler? Seek a vision?"

Some answered, "The medicine of the effigy is not often with us. I must seek a vision."

More answered, "This is very strange."

Fortunately, there were buffalo to hunt. Thousands of buffalo.

Chapter Nineteen

THE HERD SPREAD itself out over thousands of acres, over plain, through ravine, in the creek, up the hill, hard against the canyon walls. Vast as a forest, it covered the earth to the end of sight in three directions. Unlike a forest, it could get up and haul tail. When it did, it would be the biggest, wildest, stompingest beast . . . Sam couldn't even imagine it.

He grinned sideways at Flat Dog, and his head did a little dipsy-doo.

Meat for the winter. Also, a chance to prove Paladin was a fine buffalo runner.

They were lying on a low cedar ridge on the southeast edge of the herd, overlooking it all. Lodge Creek, meandering through the middle, was visible only because its cottonwoods stood tall and yellow-leaved above the dark brown mass. Most of the Kit Foxes of Rides Twice's village were near Sam and Flat Dog, some on the ridge, some a hundred strides back holding the horses. Those were the orders.

Red Roan's sister held Coy well back from the action. Red Roan gave a strict order, unwilling for the coyote to come anywhere near the herd.

That was the other part Sam could hardly believe. Of all human beings he'd been around, the Crows were the least likely to give anyone orders, or take them. Even in a battle, each man fought individually, according to his own lights. They didn't seek victory as a group, but honors as individuals. In anything you did, if you said your medicine was that you should act in such-and-such a way, no one would bother you about it.

Apparently, the buffalo hunt was run just the other way.

The hunters divided themselves into their soldier clubs, Kit Foxes, Knobby Sticks, and Muddy Hands. Each club in each village was assigned a position and a strategy.

Those buffalo in that draw? Cut them off from the others and shoot them from above.

That bunch of cows? Disguise yourself in wolf skins, or as bushes, creep as close as you can, and shoot silently.

Slip around into those trees, ease up close, and get as many as you can without stirring them up.

Most important: No one was to show himself on a ridge top on horseback. No one was to shout or wave a blanket. If anyone had a gun, he was not to fire it too soon. No one was to make a ruckus.

Inevitably, at some time, the herd would get agitated. They would chuff and stomp. They would mill about. They would run.

A herd of several thousand head at a full run, hooves flying, tails waving, heads bobbing, horns waving menacingly. Sam wanted to see that, and he was scared as hell of being in the middle of it.

His Naughty Ones were assigned to wait and watch. The quiet killing would be done by the most experienced hunters among the Little Foxes. When the stampede began, so would the chase.

Sam could see Little Foxes from his village sneaking toward an edge of the herd. They held big pieces of sagebrush in front of them as they crawled over a low ridge. In the coulee, out of the sight of the buffalo, they ran swiftly. On the next ridge they became sagebrush again, and wormed forward slowly.

Others were wolves, padding forward on all fours, their faces hidden behind wolf muzzles.

After a long while Sam began to see arrows whizzing through the air. Cows faltered. Some fell. If the opportunity was right, every hunter would shoot at cows—bull meat was tough and stringy.

In eerie silence the hunters tried to strike mortal blows, but not to finish the buffalo now. Plenty of time for that later.

When a cow would fall, the animals near her would mill around her body, poke her with their horns, and kick at her. They clustered around any fallen one, sniffed, bawled out plaints of loss.

Twice some bulls acted wild, like the smell of blood from their kind drove them mad. They ran forward and licked the wounds. Once two of them lifted a dead cow off the ground with their horns. Tongues thick with blood, eyes aglow, the bulls were an awful spectacle.

But they didn't run off. Everything but that. Sam remembered that the trappers sometimes called slow-minded people "buffler-witted." Now he knew why.

Finally, one bull pawed the ground and let out a terrible roar, deep and wild. He ran out toward the hunters, threw his rump in the air as he pivoted on his big front legs, and dashed back to the herd.

A few more arrows . . .

The herd fidgeted. Cows ran around directionless. Two bulls charged each other and banged heads fiercely. Sam felt like he should hear collision, but it was too far away.

Suddenly Red Roan jumped onto his horse. He yelled, *"Yi-ay-ii-ay,"* and galloped toward the herd.

The Kit Foxes flung themselves on their mounts and charged. Everyone yelled and waved blankets.

The herd hesitated, quivered, and ran.

In headlong panic beasts sprinted in every direction. They crashed into each other. They attacked the horses bearing down on them. With wonderful agility the mounts evaded the slashing horns, and the riders maneuvered into position alongside for a bow shot, or the thrust of a spear or lance.

Far to the left, far to the right, all around this end of the herd, Sam heard the hunters shouting as they attacked. Clots of buffalo here and there began to run, like arms and legs of a single great beast.

Suddenly, as though a gong sounded in the brain of every buffalo, they all ran north along the creek.

Sam heard something he'd never heard before. He felt it in his skin—it vibrated in his bones. Ten thousand buffalo hooves pounded the earth in a fury. It seemed as though the earth itself, under the great tramp, trembled.

Suddenly, a bull pivoted at full speed and charged a rider in front of Sam. The horse hesitated, or perhaps stumbled. A horn caught a hindquarter. A terrible whinny squealed out against death. The rider was down and out of sight, perhaps trampled, perhaps running for his life.

Paladin sprinted headlong at a speed Sam didn't know she had. He used no reins, but she responded perfectly to his knees. As though by instinct, without guidance, she drew alongside a good cow.

Sam drew the big horn bow far back and whizzed an arrow into the cow.

Hit! And well hit! She staggered.

Now he could see only about a hundred buffalo, a dozen riders. The air grew rank with the smell of dust and dung, blood and urine. Sam drew, aimed, shot, drew, aimed, shot. His veins sang an exultant and terrible song of slaughter.

Abruptly, the trap was sprung. A score of buffalo closed in on him.

Pretending only to stampede, they crowded Paladin, penned her in, bumped her. Was she going down?

Sam got a flash of his brain being trampled by hooves.

Paladin eased her stride and slid out to the right.

Clear! Safe!

The trap again! Buffalo thick about him, so close a hand couldn't pass between them, jostling, screaming, and always pounding forward in headlong panic.

Crash!

Sam pitched off.

Insanely, he sprawled over the back of a buffalo and bounced. He kicked wildly, slammed onto the back of another one. He roared with crazy laughter. *Maybe I'll walk on buffalo to the edge of the herd.*

Whumpf!

He hit the ground ferociously. His breath was knocked away. Before he could pass out, his mind screamed at him to get on his feet.

A cow nearly ran right over him. His dodge was slow, and her shoulder knocked him headlong.

On your feet!

He charged against the stream of buffalo, waving his bow. Dashing about, he stuck two fingers in his mouth and pierced the air with his shrill whistle.

Could it be heard? In this tumult nothing else . . .

Suddenly Paladin was alongside him.

He made the highest, cleanest leap of his life onto her back.

They got the hell out of there.

Two cows sprinted away from the herd at a tangent.

Sam galloped after and whanged an arrow into one.

But a fever seized him. He had to be part of the great, running, weaving beast of madness again.

He steered Paladin into the herd. He rode, he shot, he rode, he shot, addicted to the pell-mell of blood and death.

Until he ran out of arrows.

Then he arced out of the herd. Slowly, drained, he looked around. Black carcasses dotted the earth behind him. Women and children flocked around them like birds drawn to carrion. He rode slowly among them. The women slit the great animals from throat to genitals. The guts spilled out into the dust. Huge flaps of skin, pulled onto the prairies like tables, held heart and liver, glistening.

He looked for his arrows. Some laid on the ground, but most stuck out of buffalo flesh, usually several in one animal. He found three of the great masses of meat he had felled. He didn't have to think about the meat. He'd asked Flat Dog to give all but one to his family.

Flat Dog brought back this reply: The family wanted no meat from Joins with Buffalo, but their women would butcher it and give it to the elderly.

He watched the women butcher out tens of thousands of pounds of meat. They would load it on pack horses to haul back to camp, and everyone would feast.

He retrieved his arrows. Most would be fine to use again.

A woman he recognized from Rides Twice's village walked up to him and held out something bloody. A huge, raw piece of liver. He took it with both hands. It wanted to slither away and plop into the dust, but he sank his fingers in. Blood and juices ran over his hands and down his arms. He lifted the liver to his mouth, sank his teeth in, and swallowed a big piece raw. Something primal thrummed in him.

Chapter Twenty

THE PEOPLE STAYED in one big camp to dry the meat on head-high racks over low flames. Also, with mixed feelings, they stayed to prepare for the great ceremony, and be part of it.

True, they did save the tongues, but some talked against it. "This isn't right," they whispered. "One man, Bell Rock, has no authority to decide for the whole tribe. Joins with Buffalo isn't a Crow." That was all, but it was plenty.

They also told and retold the story of what happened on that ill-fated raid, how Sam led a good young man to his death. "A man who would go to war against the Head Cutters without medicine. What is he, crazy?" People snorted and spat in disgust.

The meat on the racks drove Coy wild. Sam found him scraps. When Coy did a good job of riding on Paladin's back, he got rewarded.

Bell Rock brought it up to Sam directly. "This talk is no accident," he said. They were broiling hump ribs over the supper fire. It seemed to Sam that all he did now was work on arrows between huge bouts of meat consumption. He threw Coy a half-eaten rib and looked questioningly at Bell Rock.

"Two people, Yellow Horn and his wife Owl Woman, they started all this talk, and they're spreading it."

Yellow Horn and Owl Woman. Sam knew vaguely who they were. They lived in Rides Twice's village. Sounded like he should find out why they were causing trouble. He said, "Maybe I should talk to them."

Bell Rock shook his head. "After the dance." He gnawed. "Or after the raid."

After the raid. Bell Rock spoke like his confidence was perfect. But Sam's wasn't. Maybe in the ceremony he'd get a vision of revenge, maybe he wouldn't. If he didn't, he damn well wasn't leading any raid of revenge. He'd learned that lesson. He rubbed Coy's head.

Bell Rock said, "I have a lot to do to get ready for the dance."

So Sam spent time learning how to make pemmican from Bell Rock's wife, Coming-from-the-Water. Her daughters smiled at Sam learning women's work, but he figured he'd better learn how to do everything he could. He was living on a thin edge.

What the Crow people made from the buffalo was astounding. It was nearly their entire diet, roasted, boiled, jerked, or stored as pemmican. The organ meat was treasured, the liver often eaten raw, the gall drunk as spice. The bones were cracked for marrow. The intestines were kept to make boudins, a sausage some white men thought the finest of all Indian delicacies. They saved the tallow as butter, and sun-dried strips of back fat for a gourmet treat.

The list of what they made other than edibles seemed endless. Men used the thick skin of the head for shields, or turned the horns and head into a hat. A horn might become a container for powder. A good hide, beautifully tanned by a woman, became a calendar. Men recorded each year's happenings as pictures on these robes.

Beyond that, it was women's work. Winter hides, finely tanned with the hair on, became blankets to sleep under, or wraps to wear, thick moccasins against the cold, or surfaces for the geometrical paintings made by women. Summer hides, with the hair removed, turned into lodge covers. After they'd served their purpose as lodge covers, they became parfleches, handsomely decorated boxes where family belongings were kept. Or summer moccasins. Or leggings. Or they could be put to all the uses of rawhide, even making dolls for children.

The hide was just the beginning. The sinew became thread, and splitting it for thickness was a valued skill. The hooves became rattles, or were boiled to make glue.

It was all more than Sam could remember.

The business at hand, though, was making sure of enough pemmican. First he dried the meat thoroughly, which took several days. Coy and the camp dogs went around with their muzzles up during the drying—the smell of the meat drove them wild. But it was spread in strips on racks as high as a tall man's head.

Then Sam pounded the dried meat into small shreds. For some reason, Coy thought this was funny, and made playful runs at the meat while Sam whacked it on a flat stone. Meanwhile, he had fat melting in a pot. While the fat was getting runny, he and Coy gathered chokecherries and serviceberries. Then, still under instruction, Sam dumped in handfuls of the berries into the fat and mixed that concoction with the meat, equal parts by weight. Last, he stuffed the whole tightly into a skin sack and sewed it shut.

The result was kind of like a sausage made by the Pennsylvania Dutch, Sam thought. "It will last for months, even years," said Coming-from-the-Water. "Especially if you don't feed it to the coyote."

When Sam showed Bell Rock a sack of pemmican he'd made, Bell Rock said a little gruffly, "It's past time for everything but your journey to the lodge of the sun. Sit down and we'll smoke a little."

Sam patted the ground behind him and instructed Coy to sit. The little coyote had gotten good at keeping still for long periods.

They smoked Bell Rock's pipe this time, observing all the small rituals that were proper. Then Bell Rock went into his lodge and came back bearing something wrapped in deer hide. With an air of respect he set it between them.

"The sun dance effigies," he began, "they came to the people in the following way. Dances Four Times was fasting on a mountain when he saw, to the west, seven men standing on another mountain."

Sam knew that "fasting on a mountain" was an oblique way of saying, seeking a vision. Lots of what the Crow people talked about, if it was important, they spoke of at a slant.

"Before them a woman stood, holding an effigy in front of her face. The men beat drums with skunks painted on them and sang songs. Dances Four Times memorized the songs.

"He looked away for a moment, and when he looked back, they were standing on a closer hill. When he looked away and then looked back again, they were walking across a nearby bluff. When he looked away the fourth time, he heard a noise where he was, and there they were sitting beside him.

"The Moon—for the woman was the Moon—stood with the effigy wrapped in buckskin in her hands. Again the men began to sing. At the close of the first song, without any movement from Moon, the effigy's head popped out of the wrapping. At the end of the second song, Moon shook the bundle and stepped back. The effigy revealed its arms. When the third song was finished, it exposed itself to the waist. At the conclusion of the fourth song, the effigy appeared wholly, in the form of a screech owl."

Sam stared at the bundle in front of him, curious about what the effigy looked like.

"The owl perched on Moon's head, and then on the chest of the one who lay fasting.

"One of the visiting men suddenly drew a bow and nocked an arrow. 'Screech owl,' said the woman, 'this man will shoot you. You better make your medicine.' It rose up and flapped its wings.

"The man shot at the bird. Instantly the bird flew into his chest and started hooting from inside."

Coy mewled. Sam patted his head, and the coyote quieted.

"Then Dances Four Times saw a sun dance lodge. Moon and the seven men walked toward the lodge. Four times they stopped and sang a song, and then went into the lodge. In the lodge, on the north, was a cedar tree with an effigy tied to it. At the foot of the tree lay a whistler.

"Once again the seven men sang four songs. With each song Moon lifted up the whistler a little and then laid him back down. At the end of the fourth song she pulled him all the way up. She gave the whistler the effigy. He put it back on the cedar tree. Then they sang and danced to the effigy.

"The effigy represents the Moon, and the lodge is the Sun.

"Now, when anyone wants a sun dance, he asks an effigy owner to direct it." Bell Rock gestured to the bundle in front of him. "You have asked me.

"You and I and our helpers have many tasks. First we must, with guidance, choose the place for the dance. Then, in four movements, the people go to this site. We must perform ceremonies in the whistler's lodge. We must choose the proper trees for the Sun's lodge, fell them, and then with many ceremonies build it.

"Finally, we will enter the lodge.

"Joins with Buffalo, you seek a vision of revenge. For that vision you will go without eating from the day we begin with ceremonies in the whistler's lodge. Then, when we enter the sun lodge, you will neither eat nor drink until the vision comes."

Sam's stomach flip-flopped. "How long?"

"No food for several days before we go into the sun lodge. After that, no food or water for however many days are needed until your vision comes. Maybe it will come the first night, maybe the fourth or fifth."

Sam thought maybe he couldn't go four days without water. Or a week without food.

"We will call on the spirits, and they will give you strength."

Coy crept over against Sam's thigh.

"Why are you doing this for me?"

"You have a good heart."

ON A BRIGHT mountain morning Sam walked toward a small tipi with Bell Rock and Coming-from-the-Water. He wore nothing but a breechcloth, so the cold air dimpled his skin.

This was his tipi during the ceremony. Nearby women were putting up a lodge for the buffalo tongues.

They walked without speaking, for this was an occasion of high seriousness.

Coy was tied up for the ceremony, taken care of by Flat Dog and other Foxes. "I don't want him there to remind you of who you are, or think you are."

Inside Coming-from-the-Water, in her formal role as the wife of the effigy owner, dressed Sam in a deerskin kilt and moccasins. The kilt had been sewn by a virtuous woman, a wife completely faithful to her husband. When asked to make this kilt, a woman might decline by saying, "No, I have a hole in my moccasin." If she didn't speak up, yet had been unfaithful, her lover would shame her publicly.

Coming-from-the-Water slipped moccasins blackened with charcoal onto Sam's feet. They had been sewn by the wife of a man who killed and scalped an enemy. Black, which would be everywhere during the ceremony, represented revenge.

These two women, and almost everyone who helped with the ceremony, would receive a buffalo tongue. So would many warriors of distinction.

Bell Rock spoke solemnly. "On purpose I have told you very little about the actual dance. It may be difficult for you. Listen to me very carefully.

"This ceremony . . ." He seemed to take thought. "This ceremony has many, many songs, many, many deeds, many, many parts. They won't make sense to you."

He looked Sam hard in the eyes. "So I'm asking you, for a while, to give up sense, or what you think is sense. I ask you join in without question."

He let that sit. "More, I ask you to do everything I say with the greatest attention and caring. When it seems trivial, do it anyway, and exactly as asked. Exactly as asked.

"Nothing is going to be terrible. You will not be cut, wounded, anything like that. I believe strongly that a great blessing waits for you in this ceremony. A great blessing. If you give yourself up to it.

"Do you agree?"

Sam felt committed. "Yes."

"From now on you will eat nothing."

Coming-from-the-Water took a skunk skin, slit it, and draped it around Sam's shoulders and chest.

"Come," called Bell Rock.

A half-dozen men came in, some carrying drums. Immediately, they started a song.

"Attention," said Bell Rock.

Sam sank his mind into the music.

From within the music, he only half-noticed what was done. Bell Rock painted all of him, head to toe, with white clay. He drew something on Sam's chest and back, and something below his eyes, and performed other rituals. Sam would remember the plaintive music perfectly.

After all this, the fourth song ended. Coming-from-the-Water handed Sam a small mirror. He looked at his own face and saw a stranger. His entire body was as white as his hair. On his chest were crosses, which he knew represented the morning star. Beneath his eyes flashed lightning bolts.

Sam felt like a stranger had stepped from within him, and was him.

The whistler's tipi was taken down, and the tipi holding the tongues. All the people rode and walked a couple of miles to a clearing Sam hadn't seen before. The dance site.

Bell Rock instructed two skilled hunters to go out and bring back one buffalo bull each. The bulls must be killed with only one arrow, he cautioned. If the arrow went clear through the buffalo, making two holes in the skin, the hunter was to leave the carcass and hunt another animal.

Bell Rock sent scouts out to look for enemies. Women busied themselves putting up the two ceremonial lodges. When the scouts came back, the people mock-treated them as enemies. Young men took their weapons and counted coup on them.

Then Bell Rock tied the effigy to a willow hoop, gave it to Sam, and said, "Walk alongside me."

Carrying the effigy, Sam led all the people to a cottonwood that had been chosen, for reasons he didn't know.

Again a woman who had no hole in her moccasin came forward. "This is a big gesture for her," Bell Rock said softly. "After she acts as our tree-notcher, if her husband dies, she cannot marry again."

The woman touched the cottonwood four times with the tip of an elk antler. A man painted a black ring around the three. Another one cut it down.

Suddenly, everyone rushed forward gleefully. They hit the tree with their hands, with sticks, with lances, and proudly counted coup. The tree represented the enemy.

The young men found twenty lodgepoles and dragged them to the dance site. Then, if they were among the first, they ran away, or pretended to run. But the Kit Foxes, acting as policemen for the dance, rode after them and brought them back.

Carefully instructed, Sam now painted the faces of the first four and brushed them all over with the effigy. By consenting to this ritual, these men accepted a great honor and responsibility—never to retreat from an enemy. The herald announced their commitments of courage to all the people, and the women trilled their acclaim.

Bell Rock chose a spot to erect the sun dance lodge. There he planted a small cedar tree and tied the effigy to it.

Before Sam lay down in the whistler's lodge for the night, he asked Coming-from-the-Water for a drink. She gave it, adding, "Drink as little as you can. The more you sacrifice, the more quickly your vision will come."

The next morning they built the sun dance lodge, which was huge. Bell Rock blackened his face. He and Sam wore cedar headdresses. Sam kept feeling more and more odd, like he wasn't himself.

The women cut willows. This lodge would be enclosed not with hides but limbs, and a head-high space would be left open so the people could watch.

First, though, a half-dozen groups of men came one at a time. "War parties," said Bell Rock quietly. They marched into the lodge and pantomimed fighting. "They hope the effigy's medicine will give them a vision of a dead enemy," said Bell Rock.

Sam watched. He tried to give his undivided attention to the mock war, and to everything. He wanted to see, listen, smell, take in everything that happened, know completely what his sun dance ceremony was.

But his mind kept wandering. Sometimes he felt sleepy. As one group left and another entered, Sam smacked himself in the head with his own hand. He blinked his eyes several times and shook his head.

"Hard, isn't it?" Bell Rock gave him a half smile.

The worst was that his mind kept nagging at him. *Why are you doing this? This is absurd. You aren't an Indian. This is all superstition. Worse, it's savagery. What the devil are you thinking?*

"What you want," said Bell Rock, "is not to think. Just lose yourself in observing." He paused. "Some of the difficulty, though, is that you're weak from not eating. Tomorrow or the next day, that will get better."

Sam wondered why, as he got further and further from his last bite of food, his weakness would ease off.

THE NEXT DAY, it turned out, was the first of the great days. That's what Sam called them to himself. True, he didn't know why they were great, or even have a clear sense that they would be. He simply made up his mind to call them that, purely as an act of faith.

Dressed ceremonially in his kilt, skunk hide, and black moccasins, Sam left the whistler's tipi and, stopping four times, carried the effigy to the sun dance lodge. There Bell Rock met him and tied the effigy to the cedar tree at the height of Sam's eyes.

"From now on you will drink nothing until your vision comes," he said.

Coming-from-the-Water (no other woman was permitted to be near Sam) built a center fire, hung pots, and put buffalo tongues in them to cook.

Warriors entered the lodge one at a time and reenacted their fights against enemies.

At last Flat Dog appeared, carrying two hide ropes. Sam hadn't seen him since the ceremony began. Dressed only in a kilt, he came to be first to make the sacrifice of his blood.

Altogether seven young men came bearing hide ropes. They tied their rigging high on lodge poles, painted themselves white all over, and lay down on buffalo robes. Bell Rock went to Flat Dog, and afterward each man in turn. He handed Flat Dog an eagle-wing fan. Flat Dog put the hide handle in his mouth and bit down on it, Sam supposed to keep from crying out.

Between the nipple and the collar bone on each side, Bell Rock made two shallow, parallel cuts. Then he slipped a wooden skewer beneath the skin, so that it stuck out from behind the flesh of the chest on both sides. Finally he tied the ends of the ropes, which were fashioned into a Y, onto each skewer.

One young man, a tall fellow with a piratical scar on his face, sat calmly while Bell Rock made cuts on his back, above his shoulder blades. Bell Rock fixed the ropes from these skewers to buffalo skulls, and the young man danced out of the lodge, dragging the skulls behind him. He would dance until the skulls broke the skin and pulled free.

The drum began, and the day's first song swirled through Sam's mind. The young blood sacrificers danced. Sometimes they leaned back on the ropes and stretched their skin away from their chests. But always they danced. They would dance, Sam understood, as long as the musicians played, to the end of the day. Blood rivuleted down their chests and into their kilts.

Warriors came into the lodge, and went with the skull-dragger, to help. They recited their own brave deeds in the face of the enemy and added beseechingly, "May this man do likewise."

Now Sam came to it. He didn't understand, and he had to act. He faced the sun dance effigy tied to the cedar. He stared at it. And slowly, to the beat of the drum, he began to dance. He did a simple toe-heel step, repetitive, monotonous, soon automatic and forgotten. He blew the eagle-bone whistle, sending an eerie piping above the music of the singers.

At the beginning he repeated in his mind Bell Rock's words: "The people have been wounded. With or without fault, you brought that wound. Now you can gain the strength to heal it."

Soon, though, he lost track of all words, and of language itself. His mind drifted into a state . . . He could not have described it. The drum pounded, the songs rose, the men's blood ran down their chests, and Sam's mind ran headlong into the effigy.

The lower body of the effigy was wrapped in buffalo hide, hair turned in. The face had eyes and mouth roughly drawn in black. The hair was parted in the woman's way, and sprouted feathers in every direction. And the whole was littered with morning star crosses. Sam stared into the crude, blank eyes of the effigy. "Give me whatever power you have for me," he said silently. He danced. He stared. He danced. He danced until he forgot he was dancing, and why. Dancing was all.

Songs were repeated over and over. Men came to recite their deeds and went. The seven making the sacrifice of their blood danced. Sam stared into the blankness, or mystery, of the sun dance effigy, and he danced.

Sometimes he failed, or thought he was failing. He got distracted. He remembered the day his brother Owen's fiancée made love to him, or the day he slugged Owen. He remembered cowering inside the buffalo carcass during the prairie fire. He remembered the massive Gideon's gentle wit, and missed him.

Suddenly, he would snap back to it. *Attention. What I must do is pay complete attention to dancing and to the effigy.* And his mind would flow again into the song and the motion.

At some point he imagined, or dreamed, or envisioned himself as a sac being filled with the voices of the singers and the beat of the drums. Like an ambrosial liquid it flowed into him, sweet and satisfying. The sac of himself swelled with the liquid of . . . he didn't know what and he didn't care. He swam on the sea of music, he floated into the air like one of Benjamin's Franklin's balloons he'd heard about, he drifted, joyous, fulfilled.

Suddenly—or it seemed sudden—the singers and drummers stopped. In his fantasy the sac that was Sam Morgan began to lose . . . whatever was him. The singers left. Fluid kept trickling out of Sam's sac. The tears leaked from his eyes. All his bodily fluids seeped away. Even his blood ran onto the ground, and he was a dry husk.

Those making the blood sacrifice leaned back against their ropes hard and broke free. Bell Rock removed their skewers. One by one, they departed.

Sam felt utterly deflated, drained of all energy, even of self.

Bell Rock helped him onto a bed of cedar leaves. He felt barely able to stagger, even with support. In his private world he had become a nothing.

Coming-from-the-Water put cedar on the burning charcoal at the foot of his bed, so the purifying smoke would drift through the lodge. And they left him, they thought to sleep, but in truth, as Sam felt things, to lie there empty.

It was the strangest feeling of his life, utter emptiness, everything gone that made up Sam Morgan, his memories, his feelings for people and places and things, his convictions, his skills, everything he had fashioned into a self. Yet in a way, it was pleasant.

He put his left hand out idly and felt something that shouldn't have been there. He picked it up. A pouch, a . . . A *gage d'amour*! Despite all, Meadowlark had managed to send him a message, one of love. Flat Dog must have left it here.

Now he decided to enumerate the things he was, things he could be glad of and grateful for. He was alive. He hadn't begged for water. Young men, though not as many as Bell Rock hoped, had used this sun dance to seek visions. The gods hadn't sent lightning bolts or an earthquake to punish him for presuming to dance like a Crow.

Then he switched moods. He railed at himself. He had no vision yet. He didn't even have a glimpse of what corner a vision might be hiding behind. Was he going to humiliate himself by failing to see anything? Was he going to thirst and starve and dance until he died, blind?

Now he had shaken the feeling of emptiness, but he was full of a mental business that was uncomfortable. He told his mind to gentle down, treating it like a skittish horse. After a while, it got out of the way, and after another while he slept.

EVERYTHING MAY HAVE been the same on the second day, but Sam felt changed, so everything was different.

He made up his mind not to think about whether he was empty or full or in any other state, simply to do the ceremony. Quietly, he let Coming-from-the-Water dress him as before, and Bell Rock painted him the same way.

As they walked ritually to the sun dance lodge, Bell Rock said softly, "Remember, whenever there is singing, you must dance. Later in the day that will get hard, very hard, but you must dance."

The first song rose up, Sam fixed his eyes on the effigy, and his feet moved.

Time passed, measured only in drum beats. The sun's shadow moved from northwest to north in the lodge, but Sam didn't notice. Seven pairs of feet, plus Sam's, were drawn to the earth as the stick was drawn to the drum.

Men came into the lodge and spoke words retelling their brave deeds. The people watched, and they hoped.

The music stopped. All the songs had been sung and repeated several times. The dancers rested. In a few minutes the endless motion began again.

During one break in the music Bell Rock cut a root Sam didn't recognize and held it to his nose. It felt like an elixir, and his spirits rose.

Music. Dance. Music. Dance.

The sun's shadow slid from the north side of the lodge to the northeast. Sam didn't notice. He danced and saw nothing but the effigy and heard nothing but the words, the melodies, and the thump of the drum. He swayed with the words, he undulated with them, he circled with them. He was the words and melody.

Sometimes pictures floated into his mind, every odd kind of picture, things not seen before on earth or in heaven, things he was seeing or dreaming or imagining now. Often he reminded himself to put his mind on the effigy and in the music. What worked best was to dance more vigorously. He lifted his knees high, bent his body double, threw his arms high, tried to dance himself to exhaustion.

Except that he was already exhausted. In his emptiness he didn't know where his strength came from. He asked the effigy for more strength, and felt it flow into his arms and legs. He felt it animate him. But the energy was the effigy's, or the music's, and he only borrowed it, as a wing borrows lift from the wind.

One more time the drum stopped. Four times they will stop, Bell Rock had said, and after the fourth you will sleep. Unless you have seen something.

Shadows rose on the brushy walls of the lodge—the wintering sun was falling.

The musicians rolled into a cadence that promised the last repetition of the last song. The day's dancing slid toward an end.

But the women would not let it end. They trilled their tongues, they cried out, they themselves danced—they forced the singers and drummer to go on.

And on they went, louder, stronger, firmer of beat, more passionate of voice. Sam swam into the lyrics. He heard no sentences but some words were Sun, Eagle, courage, blood, Grandfather.

When the singers rolled into the fourth repetition, normally the last one, the women again would not let them stop. In Sam's mind their trills turned into commands. "Dance, dance, fly, fly."

Harder and harder he danced, wilder and wilder, he knew not why.

Again and again the women insisted. Again and again the musicians roused themselves for one more time. Again and again Sam somehow, barely, found energy where there was none, and he danced, and danced . . .

He collapsed.

"Do not touch him!" the women cried.

Bell Rock sat quietly beside the fallen dancer.

SAM FELL FREELY. He saw nothing, heard nothing, couldn't know that he was falling, except for the sense within that he was . . .

Sam was within the earth. He grasped the tail of a snake.

My oldest enemy.

The snake looked back at Sam and smiled, a smile impossible to interpret, maybe inviting, maybe mocking.

It writhed forward, dragging Sam behind. *Unconquerable enemy.*

Sam scraped against nothing, felt no resistance—being dragged felt almost like floating.

They slid through a kind of tunnel.

Sam accepted whatever was happening to him, and accepted the snake as his guide. Within him all was acceptance.

They came to a widening, a kind of chamber. The snake turned. Gradually, it coiled itself—not round and round, as snakes do, but stacking itself upward, lining itself against the wall.

Instantly, the snake's face was hideous, eyes flashing evil. The tongue lashed out into Sam's face. Scornful laughter flash-flooded through the labyrinth of his mind.

Sam shuddered. He wanted to duck backward, but there was nowhere to go.

He thrust his face toward the snake. Abruptly, within the storm, he felt calm. Yes, calm. Confidently, he reached around the slavering tongue and grasped the body of the snake with both hands.

So quickly and deftly even he didn't know what he was doing, he tied the snake into knots.

He drew back and looked at his handiwork. He had tied his mortal enemy into Celtic love knots.

Sam laughed immensely, laughed at himself, laughed at his fear, laughed at life . . .

And woke gently into ordinary reality.

BELL ROCK WAS looking down at him in a kindly way.

"I have seen something," murmured Sam.

Bell Rock cupped a hand at his ear.

Sam realized he hadn't spoken out loud.

"I have seen something."

He was aware that Bell Rock was hoping for the traditional words, "I think things will be all right." But Sam wasn't sure what he'd seen.

Bell Rock gave Sam a drink of water. He felt some Jordan had been crossed, and drank of it.

"Now let's smoke and you tell me about it," said Bell Rock.

A FEW MINUTES, or millennia, later Bell Rock repeated slowly, "And Snake is your oldest enemy."

"Yes, the oldest enemy of all my people." Sam felt utterly weak. At the same time, if Bell Rock had challenged him to climb a mountain, he would have set out confidently.

Bell Rock nodded several times. "You have asked to see a small victory over an enemy," he said, "and have seen a great one."

He stood up and walked outside the lodge. Through the branches, across the twilight, Sam heard him call to the people, "He thinks things will be all right."

A tumult of trills and cheers lifted Sam. He swooped up on the wave of sound, and slid down the far side, and slept.

Part Six

COMING BACK

Chapter Twenty-One

"LET'S GET CLOSE," said Sam.

"Big risk." Flat Dog eyeballed him. But Flat Dog wouldn't fight it. Since the sun dance, Sam's medicine had been too good for that.

The Head Cutter village spread out along the Buffalo Tongue River where it came out of the Big Horn Mountains. The evening fires defined the circle of lodges. They'd found the right village straight off because Sam trusted his instinct. It was the very first village they came to. They knew because Blue Medicine Horse's pony grazed with

the horse herd. Flat Dog was impressed. Sam told himself to keep
trusting his instincts.

Since the sun dance, Sam's prestige had been high. When he said
there would be no large war party against the Head Cutters, just
two men, the Crows hid their disappointment and accepted that.
Flat Dog accepted it. People would have done whatever he said.
Sam got everything he hoped for except a chance to talk to Meadowlark.

Now he fingered his *gage d'amour.* "Let's go."

Coy slunk along with them. The coyote knew the silence of the
hunter.

The early darkness on this November night was halved by a gibbous moon. Sam wanted to stick to the shadows.

He had big problems. What Flat Dog wanted was only to take a
Head Cutter scalp. What Sam wanted was to get his father's rifle back.
The Celt belonged to Sam. So he had to find it. He hoped the man
with the two-horned buffalo headdress still had it. He had no idea
how he would set about getting it, none. Maybe he'd set fire to the tipi
and take advantage of whatever happened. No, that might do harm to
The Celt.

Since the dance, actually, Sam had the sense that if he kept things
simple, whatever he tried would work. He just needed to go straight
toward whatever goal he had, and act without question, and things
would go slick. That's what he was doing now.

They knew where the sentries were. They'd watched last night and
the night before. The village wasn't on high alert, not during a winter
camp. Winter was a poor time for raiding, unless your medicine was
particular in telling you otherwise.

Very, very slowly, they worked their way close. In the trees behind
the circle, not twenty steps from the lodges, they stopped. In his
usual way, Coy moved with them and stopped with them. Sam could
hear his own breathing, and made it slow and quiet. For a long time
he and Flat Dog stood perfectly still, their blankets helping them en-
dure the cold. They watched. Sam felt the danger in his nostrils, and
he liked it.

The evening was mild. People walked back and forth across the circle, ducking in and out of tipis.

After an incredibly long time Sam began to wonder if he'd lost his mind.

Just then Flat Dog nodded slightly to the south of the circle.

The figure moving—Two Horns. Was it really him? Sam recognized the body shape, but the moonlight didn't catch the face. Had he come out of the tipi with the two sleeping dogs in front?

He crossed to one of the two tipis at the circle's entrance. Someone important. He scratched the flap and slipped in. Almost immediately, he came out and crossed the circle back to the tipi next to the one he came out of. This time he just stuck his head in. Then he went back past the sleeping dogs and into his lodge.

Sam and Flat Dog nodded at each other. His lodge, probably.

A girl came out.

Sam was intrigued. The girl, a teenager by her looks, just stood in front of the tipi. Soon he saw girls standing singly in front of two other lodges, and young men beginning to move around. One young fellow came up to the pair in front of Two Horns' lodge and folded the girl into his blanket. Courting.

Sam sat through an hour or so of courtship, warming himself with thoughts of Meadowlark.

Suddenly he whispered to Flat Dog, "Hold Coy. I'm going to get closer."

Flat Dog shot him a *you're crazy* look.

Sam smiled and repeated, "Closer."

He had an idea. Now he needed to make sure he could recognize the face of Two Horns' daughter.

He stole carefully through the shadows of the cottonwoods. He planned to get the lodge between him and the two young lovers and then slip out onto the moon-shadowed side for a look.

On full alert, he stepped out of the trees. Nothing. He padded to the back of the lodge. He could hear the chatter of women's or girls' voices inside. Suddenly, a man's voice rose over the others, and the female voices went silent.

Sam inched around the lodge and ducked under the right smoke pole. He decided he'd better get low. He crawled out far enough to see.

Damn. The girl's back was to him. Her boyfriend's face was clear in the moonlight, but . . .

Two Horns' voice again, louder but further away.

Two Horns stepped out of the lodge and said something firm to his daughter. She turned, and her face caught the light perfectly, a round face with an impish smile.

She looked directly at him.

Sam wanted to turn into dry grass, or a slinking dog, or a buffalo dropping. He was caught. He brought his legs up under him, ready to run.

But the girl chirped something merrily, threw a final glance at her boyfriend, and ducked into the lodge. The boyfriend called something to her. Sam wished he spoke Lakota. Now he would probably know her name.

Two Horns looked straight at Sam. For a long moment he studied the shadow.

Attack! Sam's mind screamed at him. *This is your chance! Attack!*

His legs tightened but didn't propel him forward. *Where was The Celt?*

Two Horns ducked back into the lodge.

SAM HID NEAR the path that the women used to get water the next morning, waiting for Imp. He couldn't keep calling her Two Horns' daughter in his mind. To him, her name was Imp.

She walked by with an empty pail, back with a full one.

Sam waited and watched carefully, his hand on Coy. Then they slipped away.

He talked about it with his friend. Flat Dog looked full of unspoken words, and Sam knew what they were. "Dammit, you're taking too many chances."

But Sam also had his instincts, and he felt sure of when to take chances and when not. "The water path is not a good place," he said.

Sam saw his friend's face struggle. Flat Dog always wanted to pitch in, not hold things back. Since he couldn't go against medicine, though, he said nothing.

"Let's just watch today," Sam said.

Just watching almost cost them their chance.

The Head Cutter men stayed in camp, talking or working on weapons. A dozen women went out into a field a mile away and dug at the earth with root sticks. A creek separated the field from a wooded hill. Sam and Flat Dog watched from the timber.

"Prairie turnips," said Flat Dog.

At midday Imp and an older woman came. "Two Horns' wife?"

Flat Dog shrugged. Lying down, Coy panted and looked curiously from face to face.

They could only watch—too many women around.

About midafternoon the women all left at once. As they were walking away, though, Imp suddenly turned and trotted toward the creek. Her mother waited, then walked after the daughter. Imp started plucking something off the wild rose bushes, probably rose hips.

Suddenly Sam knew. This was their chance.

The mother was still walking toward Imp. The other women were a hundred yards ahead. The way to the village led through some trees. *Keep picking.* Sam looked at Flat Dog, jerked his head sideways, and the three of them slipped down the hill.

Edge of the timber. Women still picking. Wait.

Now take a chance. Cross the creek. If they look, rush them.

He motioned to Flat Dog.

As Coy skittered across and Sam and Flat Dog waded unsteadily ankle deep, the two women dropped to their knees and started pulling something out of the creek. Watercress, Sam saw. They wanted watercress.

Sam reached the bank and walked steadily toward the women's backs.

They kept their faces to the creek.

Closer, closer. Sam scarcely dared to breathe. He wanted to laugh out loud at his luck.

Two steps away he slipped the blanket off his shoulders. Flat Dog did the same. Sam pounced and wrapped Imp in his blanket. She shrieked, but he held her tight.

Flat Dog had the mother, kicking and screaming furiously.

"Let's get out of here."

Coy howled, maybe in triumph.

"GO GET THE horses!" Sam half-whispered.

Flat Dog left at a trot. Coy stood guard over the two women.

The mounts were staked in high willows on the back side of the hill. Sam hoped Flat Dog got back before Two Horns came looking. He told himself Two Horns probably wouldn't show up until twilight. That was probably.

Sam looked at the women. He'd kept them in the blankets and bound one with his breechcloth, the other with the belt that held it up. He felt odd standing around buck naked below the waist, and chill from standing around without his blanket.

The women were quiet. They'd given up on crying out.

All three of them, and Coy, were hidden behind huge boulders on the field side of the creek. Sam peered around the end of one boulder toward the village trail.

When Flat Dog got back, Sam used his bridle rope to tie the women and put his breechcloth back on. Then he had a quick talk with Flat Dog, speaking Crow. The women probably didn't speak English, surely not Crow.

"We won't hurt the women," Sam said.

Flat Dog's eyes lit up. One of the great coups, an honor you could boast about for a lifetime, was to kill an enemy's woman right in front of him. Wife and daughter both—this was an incredible opportunity.

Sam could see that Flat Dog was thinking wildly. "Is this your medicine? Or just your peculiar white-man ways?" The first Flat Dog would respect. The second he'd jump right over.

Finally, Sam said, "You will kill Two Horns."

Flat Dog nodded. Coy gave a little yip.

TWO HORNS CAME out of the trees. Yes, he was carrying The Celt. Sam let out a big breath. It was working.

Two Horns was riding a pinto, probably on the off chance that there was trouble.

The Celt. Sam could feel the heft of the half stock in his left hand, the smooth pull of the trigger under his right index finger.

Two Horns walked the pinto forward slowly. Though he was armed and mounted, his guard wasn't really up.

Wife and daughter. For a moment Sam lost track of his hatred. Then he thought of how the man counted coup on Blue Medicine Horse's body so thirstily, and got it back.

Two Horns was still a couple of hundred steps off. Sam thought he'd better act before he got within hearing distance.

He held Coy, because the coyote liked to play with Paladin. "Forward," he said in a tone the mare would recognize.

She walked out into the meadow and took a few steps.

"Circle left," Sam said, not too loud.

Paladin loped in a clockwise circle fourteen steps across.

Sam and Flat Dog looked hard at Two Horns, trying to guess what the man was thinking. Though he may have recognized Paladin, the horse was loose. Sam would bet Two Horns' mind was shouting, "Get that good-looking horse."

"Circle right," said Sam.

Paladin reversed course and loped out toward Two Horns and then arced back toward Sam.

Now Two Horns turned and rode away. Sam's heart lurched.

At the trees he stopped, dismounted, and tied his mount. He came walking forward carrying a short lead rope, in no hurry. He knew better than to rush toward the strange horse and scare her off.

When Paladin got nearest to them in her circle, Sam said, "Stand." Paladin did. Sam would say no more, afraid of being heard.

Two Horns now approached gently.

Flat Dog drew his bow string far back.

Two Horns uncoiled the lead rope and held it out in both hands.

The arrow struck deep into his belly.

WHILE FLAT DOG took the scalp, Sam reclaimed The Celt. He put his rifle to his shoulder and felt its balance. A very good feeling.

"Touch him," said Flat Dog. Sam hesitated, then realized. Flat Dog had already made the first formal touch, coup, and the second belonged to Sam. He performed it seriously.

Then he had to get his shooting pouch off the dying man's shoulder. Two Horns was glaring fiercely at Sam, or trying to glare fiercely. The force was slipping away. Sam worked the pouch off. He looked into Two Horns' eyes. It took a long time to die from a gut wound.

Coy sniffed at Two Horns' blood on his belly, and Sam told him no.

Sam took Two Horns' knife too. Then, calmly, he cut the man's throat.

When he stood up, he asked himself if he did it out of compassion. The answer was, Yes, mostly.

He walked across the meadow, untied Two Horns' pinto mare, and led her back. A horse was good booty.

Then he untied the women, took the blankets off, and retied them, avoiding their eyes. This time he made the bonds only half tight.

One look into the field and they knew what had happened. Though they said nothing, he felt the daggers from their eyes.

Five minutes to get loose, thought Sam, *and ten minutes to run to the village. It will be dark by then. Time enough.*

Flat Dog came up with the bloody scalp dangling from one hand and dripping blood onto the tawny winter grass. He and the women looked at each other darkly. Sam didn't like seeing their faces.

"Come," Sam called to Paladin. "Let's go," he told Flat Dog.

"Fast," said Flat Dog.

Sam mounted Paladin, the new horse on lead.

Two Horns' widow said clearly in the Crow language, "I will remember you with hatred."

Chapter Twenty-Two

THEY CAUGHT UP with the village at the big bend in the Wind River, just above where it changed its name to the Big Horn. The people were moving to their usual winter camping place in a long line of pony drags, policed by the Foxes.

It had been surprisingly easy. Sam and Flat Dog loped their horses all that first night on the wide Indian trail in front of the Big Horns, switching mounts to let one always run unburdened. They went so long and hard, Sam had to let Coy ride behind him on Paladin. The coyote had learned to balance very well.

At dawn they rested for a couple of hours. Then they loped the horses for hours more, walked them, and loped them a last time. With the head start they got, Sam figured no Head Cutter would catch them.

They turned west along the Owl Creek Mountains and made tracks for the river. In summer water might have been scarce, but not in late autumn. On the way Sam discovered that the pinto was a good riding horse, with plenty of bottom. He'd call her Pinto and make her his traveling mount. Now he had one for traveling and Paladin for running buffalo. For a man who'd been practically naked in August, he was getting outfitted.

Sam could hardly believe the way they were welcomed into camp. First Flat Dog went near the camp, leaving Sam behind, and found the sentries. "Tell the women to get charcoal ready." That was all he had to say.

Soon Bell Rock came to Sam and Flat Dog with charcoal. They blackened their faces with it. This was what everyone longed to see, the sign that they had killed an enemy.

At the end of the day they rode into camp. Sam felt like The Celt gleamed, Paladin gleamed, and he gleamed with what he had done.

All the people formed a circle. In the center Bell Rock told Sam what was to happen. First he and Flat Dog were to perform the long dance.

They did. The people were perfectly attentive, poised to hear great things.

Then, at Bell Rock's instruction, first Flat Dog and then Sam told the story of the war party. When Flat Dog told how he shot the arrow and it sank far into the enemy's belly, the women trilled. When he described making the first touch, the trilling rose to the clamor of a thousand ecstatic birds.

Sam thought it was the most exciting sound he had ever heard, and felt a pang of envy.

Flat Dog pointed out over and over, though, how Sam's medicine and wisdom had led them. By Sam, they were led directly to the right village. By his plan, they captured the Head Cutter's women and drew him out to search for them. By his plan and the medicine of his wonderful horse, they brought the Head Cutter within range of Flat Dog's bow. He spoke of Sam making the second touch, and again the women trilled.

Then Sam told his story. His account of the same event was different, as all tellings must be, and Sam thought the women sounded just as enthusiastic. When he finished with his version of making the second touch on the fallen enemy, his voice betrayed a sense of anticlimax. The women sang out with their tongues, but there was a sense of waiting, waiting for . . .

Bell Rock, as the "father" of the expedition, cried out. "Flat Dog has made the first touch of an enemy with his hand."

Enthusiastic clamoring.

"Joins with Buffalo has made the second touch, and has led a successful war party."

Exultant clamoring. Sam felt like it lifted him off the ground.

"Two young men have achieved some of the highest of the four great coups."

Now Sam realized. Four coups to become a war leader—to touch an enemy with your hand, to wrest a weapon away from him, to steal a horse picketed in the camp, and to lead a successful party.

Not quite twenty-one years old, Sam had performed two of them.

He felt giddy.

Now a clansman of Bell Rock came forward and sang praises of Sam and Flat Dog. The songs were beautiful and extravagant.

Bell Rock said quietly to Sam, "Normally, your clansmen would make him gifts for his singing. Since you have no clan, my clansmen will do that."

Though the songs ended the festivities for the night, they jumped to a new start the next morning. The herald circled the camp, crying out news of the start of the dance. All that day and the next were filled with drumming, singing, and dancing. Only killing an enemy was enough to make the women dance, Bell Rock told Sam—stealing horses was not enough.

At the end of two days even Sam felt glutted with glory.

THE NEXT MORNING, when Sam and Flat Dog were still sitting in their blankets and breaking their fast with some jerked meat, Bell Rock appeared. He said, "Come smoke with me and Gray Hawk tonight."

After months, that's how it ended, the shunning by the Gray Hawk family. Meadowlark's face, and memories of touching her, exploded in Sam's mind.

When Flat Dog walked off with Bell Rock, Sam asked Coy, "Now Gray Hawk will talk to me?" Coy offered, as comment, only warm eyes. Sam had seen Meadowlark dancing exuberantly during the last three days. His repute among the Crows, he hardly dared form the words in his mind . . . "I guess I'm too big to ignore," he told Coy. He allowed himself hope. His heart danced.

Sam had work to do. Two Horns had used up most of The Celt's powder and lead, maybe on the fall buffalo hunt, or maybe just trying the rifle out. Aside from horses and coyote, Sam was a pauper. He lacked flint and steel for making fire, and nothing could be more basic. A pot to cook in. Plenty of moccasins. A capote. A couple more buffalo hides to sleep on and under. A tipi. A saddle, and a calf hide for a saddle pad. Ropes to hold packs on the horses, and to picket them. A tomahawk to make firewood with. A pistol, the best complement to The Celt. Coffee and sugar. Tobacco. Most of all, maybe, goods to trade to the Indians. He was tired of living in poverty.

So he needed to spend his winter days setting his two traps and getting a few beaver. Very few, for beaver were inactive in the winter. Then he needed to have a spring hunt, even if he did it alone. Since he'd missed the fall hunt, he didn't know where his outfit was. When he thought of it, he supposed that Diah, Fitz, and the boys had given him up, thinking he'd gone under.

He spent this day making arrows, a necessity that seemed never to end. He listened for gossip about Gray Hawk and his family. He learned absolutely nothing before he, Flat Dog, and Coy arrived at Bell Rock's lodge that evening. At the door flap Sam told Coy to sit and stay.

Bell Rock sat in the center behind the fire, Gray Hawk on his left, as was proper. Sam and Flat Dog sat to the left of Gray Hawk.

In silence Bell Rock used a coal to light his pipe. He offered the smoke to the four directions, Father Sky, Mother Earth. Turning the pipe once in a full circle, he handed it to Gray Hawk, bowl in the left hand, stem in the right. Gray Hawk took it just that way and smoked. Sam and Flat Dog followed suit.

When the pipe was empty, Gray Hawk spoke without preamble. "My daughter's brothers told you to bring eight horses and ask for her. I ask you not to do that."

Slammed down. Defeated. Crushed.

Sam made his mind focus on what counted: Meadowlark was lost.

He got out one word. "Why?"

"You may think it is because of Blue Medicine Horse."

It was permitted, for reasons Sam didn't understand, to speak the name of a dead person when you were smoking the pipe. He felt the name like a stab. He knew that Gray Hawk felt it more deeply, and always would.

"That's not it," Gray Hawk went on. "You have made it possible for us to end our mourning for our son. Thank you."

Now the older man waited for a long time.

"A wise person," he finally said, "tells us Crows to have nothing to do with white men. White men will bring death to the people, it is said."

Sam gawked. Of all the tribes in the mountains and on the plains, the Crows were the friendliest to whites. This was a bad turn.

"Who?"

"A wise person," Gray Hawk repeated.

Bell Rock lit the pipe, and they smoked in silence. After a while Meadowlark's father started to stand up. On one knee, he glanced sideways at Sam, put his gaze back in the fire, and said quietly, "You are a good young man."

Then he left.

The moment Gray Hawk replaced the door flap, Bell Rock said, "Owl Woman."

Sam searched his mind. He associated the name vaguely with a heavy-set, middle-aged woman full of dark looks . . . Now he remembered that two people had started the talk against his sun dance. Owl Woman and her husband, Yellow Horn.

"A woman who sees things," Bell Rock said.

Sam translated this in his mind, making allowance for the Crow customs of indirection and understatement. A woman who had strong dreams, or visions, ones people paid attention to.

"I will invite her and her husband to smoke with you and me soon."

Flat Dog wanted to talk more, but Sam wanted to be alone.

Outside he clucked at Coy, and they walked across the lodge circle. At the brush hut he pulled the head end of his blankets outside. He rolled in and looked up at the stars. Coy settled himself on the blankets at Sam's feet. So many stars, so far apart, such emptiness in between.

"Boy," he said, "the stars are working against us."

Chapter Twenty-Three

WHEN THE LONG train of pony drags wound into the winter camping place, all eyes—those of the Fox policemen, the old men, the
women and children—were on one spot. There where the outfit led
by Diah had camped two winters ago, a solitary line of smoke rose to
the sky.

Sam and Flat Dog looked at each other. The scouts knew who was
there, or they would have warned the people. But who? White men?

Sam touched his heels to Paladin, and the mare flashed that way

with her wonderful speed. He could hear Flat Dog coming hard behind him.

Three horses picketed—Sam recognized none of them.

A lean-to backed against a boulder. White men, for sure.

Sam reined up in front of it. Buffalo robes and blankets within, a
fire in front.

Click! The dry click of a rifle hammer?

Sam looked up. Twenty feet above him a figure rose, silhouetted
against the sun and hard to make out.

"Sam Morgan, you done lost your top knot."

He knew the soft, kindly voice of the Virginian—it was James
Clyman.

Sam laughed out loud.

Next to him another figure, familiar but against the sun . . .

"This child is glad to see Joins with Buffalo hasn't joined with the
buffalo grass."

Gideon!

WINTER CAMP. A good fire, old friends, plenty of meat, the first
sugar and coffee Sam had tasted in months, and a good story. Mountain man heaven.

Sam and Flat Dog would hear of nothing except for Gideon to tell
the story of his escape and survival at full length. "Last time I saw
you," Sam said with a rush of feeling, "you were hightailing it south
with arrows in you and your horse and Head Cutters flying thick as
mosquitoes around your head."

"One arrow in me," corrected Gideon. "Here." He tapped his
right hip. From the look of the way he walked, that wound was still
bothering him. Maybe it always would.

"I can't believe you didn't get hit but once," said Sam.

Gideon made a snaky motion with his right hand. "We Frenchmen,
we fly between dangers, whether they be arrows or bullets or angry
husbands."

"You think you could tell this story"—Flat Dog searched for words—"in a true way?"

Sam was proud of his friend for learning to josh American-style.

Gideon sucked on his lower lip. "I get hit by two other arrows. One rakes across my back, leaves long scar, you will see. The other, it digs at my scalp, knocks my hat off, makes more blood than trouble."

He gave them all a wily look.

"What really happened?" Sam reminded him.

"Most ze Indians, they go toward you, Blue Horse, ze pack horses. Four devils, they comed after me . . ."

GIDEON POOR BOY whipped his horse like hell. He knew damn well he had no chance, so he meant to go under in high style.

When he cleared the cottonwood grove stuck bad in only one place, he roared. He wheeled his horse and raised his pistol. Four Head Cutters were on his ass. He aimed and dropped the front one clean. That would slow the buggers down. They knew he still had a loaded rifle. He kicked his drag-ass horse and worked at reloading the pistol.

A gravelly hill came up on his right. He rounded a curve and spurred the horse up it. He was possessed by an idea.

He turned hard to the right again—this horse wasn't going to be able to go for long. He galloped twenty yards back and hurled his mount and himself off the lip of the hill.

They careened straight into the three men after them. Gideon spurred the horse into the flank of the lead horse, and it knocked it ass over teacups. He ducked under the war club of the second rider, sped at the third man, knocked his lance aside, and buried his knife in the man's chest.

Without looking back, he spurred sideways and the second rider clipped his mount's hindquarters. Horse and rider went down. Gideon rolled and came up with his rifle raised. He fired almost point blank into the rider's gut, and the Indian flew toward heaven backwards.

Gideon lunged for the man's bridle. His hip stabbed him, and he screamed, but he got the rope. Unable to mount normally, he threw himself belly down across the pony's back, turned its head up the creek, and whacked its hind end hard.

When Gideon got into a sitting position, he looked back. Five or six more Indians coming, including the one he unhorsed, but well back.

His mind whirred. He laughed. A chance! This was even bigger fun!

GIDEON ONLY LISTENED. He dared not watch.

Knowing he couldn't outrun a half dozen Head Cutters, not hurt as he was, he veered off into the first coulee he came to. After a quarter mile it turned, and sandstone crags pushed in from both sides. That gave him an idea.

He pulled the horse up, slid off, and smacked its hindquarters as hard as he could. The pony started and then fled up the coulee.

Now the bad part. Gideon had to get into the rocks. The damned hip would fight him all the way.

Later he told himself, bragging, that it was like climbing out from the ninth circle of hell. But pain, what does pain matter to a man?

Half-dragging that leg, he hoisted himself up the sandstone, step by agonizing step, and around it into a little cleft.

He listened to the beat of the hooves. Probably they would gallop by, looking for the pony and rider. When they found the pony, they would hunt for the rider. Hunt up at the top of the coulee, if he was lucky. Eventually, very eventually, they would look hard at all the tracks in the coulee and trace him to these rocks. Then, well, a game of cat and mouse until dark, and another game of cat and mouse the next day . . .

Or one of them might have a superb eye. He would see the grass broken in a clump, and tracks more than a straight-running pony would leave. Then Gideon would be a mouse in a sandstone trap.

The hooves thundered by.

When they were halfway out of hearing, he grabbed the arrow with both hands, bellowed, and wrenched it out of his hip. His outcry would never be heard above the hooves.

He gazed morosely at the hip. "Heal, damn you." His uncle had dragged around a bad leg, and that always gave Gideon the willies. Nothing, to him, could be worse than being a cripple.

Up, up, he had get out onto the ridge. Damn, why had he chosen the one thing he couldn't do, walk? He forced himself to chuckle through the pain. *Because they think I can't do it.*

Across the ridge into the next crinkle in the landscape, which turned out to have a tiny tributary to the creek. He slid down the hill on his bottom, his left bottom, the one that wasn't killing him. When he got to the creek, he lay flat in the shallow water and drank. Drink, drink. Maybe no other drink for hours, for a day . . .

He walked up the creek, his feet carefully in the water.

He hoped it was the opposite of what they would expect. He was going up into a sweep of grassy, treeless hills, where a man might be seen for miles around. He was going away from water, for this rivulet would soon be . . .

A marsh. In a quarter mile it was a little marsh where a spring rose. He looked at the muddy ground. He studied the sparse growth of cattails. No cover, not a bit. No cover on the hillsides either. What had he gotten himself into?

Hellfire. He started up the hill, practically clomping on his bad leg. *Hurt, you bastard, hurt as bad as you can.* Up he chuffed, and up and . . .

Time to crawl over the ridge top. He needed to be exquisitely tiny. Across the top, he inched and looked down the other side.

Hope.

Not much, but hope. An outcropping of sandstone, with a split. Maybe not big enough for a man of his girth. No, maybe not. But the only hope.

He scooted down the hill on his left butt. He crawled out onto the sandstone, dropped his legs into the crack, and lowered himself.

It wouldn't work. Damn every pound of buffalo meat he'd eaten in the last year. Damn his father for having the build of a bear. Damn all his ancestors.

He heaved himself up.

Out of luck. He was stuck. And, due to gravity, getting more stuck every minute he stayed there.

He heaved mightily with both his immense arms.

Stuck.

He got an idea.

He rotated himself. He walked his feet up the crack, tilting his upper body down toward it. He braced himself with his elbows. He pushed with his left foot. That hip slipped upward a little. He repeated the motion, and slipped back a little, sideways into the crack.

Have to lift both sides out at once, the way I'm widest.

He used the right foot, gaining one excruciating inch. He braced the foot and knee on opposite sides, twisted his body level, and pushed up with both elbows.

Out he popped.

He crawled off the sandstone and down the hill. Below the sandstone he looked back to curse his personal Golgotha. And saw it. The cave of his resurrection. He crawled up.

It was just a bigger split, no cave. He could actually crawl into it maybe three steps before it narrowed.

When it did narrow, it squeezed together only at the middle and top. On the bottom was still a decent hole. He got down on his belly and slithered forward.

Behind the squeeze, a cozy little room crook-necked to the right. He sat down, back against the far wall, legs on the sand. Straight up the split slithered down to a hand span, and it curved. He could stand, but he couldn't see sky above. And no one above could see him.

It was cool. The sun wouldn't broil him. He had nothing to eat. Nothing to drink. He couldn't move around.

He touched his ear and his hand came away sticky.

Syrupy blood.

He felt of his head. Bloody, matted hair. He remembered the slash of pain from the arrow that furrowed him. Well, the bleeding was stopped.

He studied the hip. Couldn't tell a thing about it. *Mon dieu,* he said to himself, *don't let me be a cripple.*

He slept.

The morning sun woke him and brought riders. He listened, but the language of the hooves was babble to his ears. He stood up and pulled his throwing knife. He was pretty good with it. If someone crawled into his hideaway, the fellow probably wouldn't crawl back out.

The next day, more riders from time to time, close and distant. Waiting.

He'd wondered how Indians went for days without water on their vision quests. Mostly a trick of the mind . . .

So. He hadn't bled to death from his scalp or his hip. He'd stood the thirst for two full days. He would leave tonight. He would be afoot, wounded, half-crippled, and alone.

He grinned. Not bad fixings for a mountain man.

"AFTER ZEM TWO days," Gideon went on, "I take thought. You and Blue Medicine Horse are dead. Flat Dog, I don' know—hightailing over the mountains, if he have good sense. I think where the Crow village might be. On the Big Horn somewhere, upper end maybe. Ze Crows, will zey help me? Don' know.

"One more chance. Ze general and Diah, they take the furs down the Big Horn to the mouth, float them down the Yellowstone. Then many trappers, they come back up the Big Horn, go toward pass to cross to Siskadee. Maybe can find zese trappers.

"So I crawl. No can walk, hip is worse, all stiff. Crawl. In two days reach timber, get big stick, stand up and walk leaning on stick. Walk up creek, through pass, down mountain, across plains toward river. Walk maybe a hundred miles, maybe fifteen sleeps.

"Eat? It is August. Lucky. I eat berries. Sometimes wild onions. Rose hips. You ever have serviceberries and wild onions in mouth at one time? Pretty funny.

"I hungry, maybe starving, but not starving to death.

"Get near river, sleep, one morning zis *fou,* zis madman, he stand over me." He nodded at Clyman.

"The Frenchy was sleeping on the sand within ten feet of the Big Horn. I wanted to throw him back, but Fitz said he was big enough to keep."

Gideon went on. "After fall hunt, I t'ink, Sam Morgan, if he is still alive . . . Maybe I shouldn't hope. If still alive, he goes with village of Rides Twice this winter. I go there. I give him cussing he never forget. Lead me into ambush, get arrow in hip, lose horses and all possibles, ever' damn t'ing make me a man, not a beast." He put on his worst mock-angry face. "I cuss you," he roared. "Now, what you do since August?"

"On account of he led us into an ambush," said Flat Dog, "he has given a sun dance."

That changed the expressions on the faces of Gideon and Clyman. They knew what it meant.

The story took the rest of the night.

Chapter Twenty-Four

OWL WOMAN LOOKED straight into Sam's eyes. He saw then and there that she intended to tell him the truth, her truth.

Bell Rock, the host, waited with a neutral face. Yellow Horn, Owl Woman's husband, kept his gaze in the center fire, like he wanted nothing to do with this.

"Because Bell Rock asks me to," she began in the Crow language, "I will tell you what I saw, exactly what I saw.

"It does not have to do with you personally. I believe you are a man with a good heart."

She took a deep breath and let it out. Then she seemed to go into a trance and report from there. "I had a dream. I was lost. I looked around in every direction, my head turning this way, turning that way, and I didn't know where the people were. Yellow Horn, our children, our grandchildren, the village, all the people of Absaroka, I couldn't find anyone.

"I was by a small, pretty lake in the region of the stinking, bubbling springs. I knew it was said to be a special place. From there waters flow from one end of the lake into the great water-everywhere to the west, on the other end into the great water-everywhere to the east. It seemed a good place of green grass and thick stands of lodgepole pines, except that I was alone.

"I didn't know which way to go, what direction to start looking for the people. Soon, though, I heard something. It was hard to make out. Moans, maybe, deep, low sounds uttered by human voices, or voices that had once been human. I walked in the direction of those sounds.

"But before long, even the moans were lost. Instead I saw white people, lots of faceless white people, marching through the country on horses. They rode, they rode, they rode. They didn't see me. They didn't look at me or anything, they just rode with their blank faces pointed toward some horizon, somewhere far off.

"When I went in a different direction, I heard the human utterances again. I ran toward them. I lost them. I panicked. I heard them again and ran in another direction. I saw more faceless white people, riding, riding.

"Suddenly I was on a path alongside a pond, among the white people, marching, marching. They didn't see me, and I was alone. I could hear the moaning voices, soft, but close.

"On the pond were lily pads. Except that the lily pads were faces, the faces of the Absaroka people under a film of water. The faces were dead, the people were dead. In rows many, many of them, they lay dead. Their countenances were ghastly white, their eyes frozen open, their lips vermilion.

"I stood by the side of the pond and looked at the faces of all my people, dead. The white people marched by on their horses, not noticing. Forever they went on, forever and forever. And the people's death went on forever."

She emerged from the trance and looked at Sam. "I understood this to mean that the white people will come into our country and go past and keep coming and going past and keep coming endlessly, and because of them the people will die.

"I want our people to live. So it is very simple for me. I tell anyone who is willing to listen to have nothing to do with white men, nothing at all."

She sighed. "They do not listen, most of them. They want *things,* the many things you bring to trade. Needles, cooking pots, tomahawks, guns, cloth, blankets—all of these they want. Our women want them even more than our men. It will not stop. I cannot change everyone.

"But anyone who will listen, I tell them, 'Do not set your feet on this path. It is the path of death. And some listen. Gray Hawk and Needle, they listen. And they choose. Life, not death."

She heaved breath in and out once, as though she had run a mile. "Life."

Again she raised her eyes straight into Sam's. "Meadowlark's family respects you. I respect you. We know you mean no harm. But they see you, and I see you, the way we regard the first flake of snow in a pleasant autumn. The first sign of a long and terrible winter."

AFTER A FEW days Sam asked to speak with Owl Woman again. Yellow Horn sat with them, and once more Sam had the sense that the door of Owl Woman's heart and mind was in some way open, Yellow Horn's closed.

He felt like he had to deal with that first. To Owl Woman he said, "My heart is good toward you, and I sense that yours is good toward me. But Yellow Horn, I sense that your attitude is different. I ask why."

Yellow Horn scowled and worked his mouth but stopped himself from saying anything.

Owl Woman volunteered, "He has seen you work your power over the coyote and over the horse, so that they do your will. He believes that this power shows you possess a bad medicine. He thinks he, and all of us, should oppose this medicine."

She let Sam take that in. "I do not agree with him," she added, "and that is not what you have come to talk about."

Sam looked from Owl Woman to Yellow Horn and back to the woman. He accepted. He would pass by Yellow Horn's attitude.

He had thought and thought about what to say about Owl Woman's dream, and all his thoughts came to nothing. He ventured forth in ignorance.

"What you fear, I understand it," he began in the Crow language. "But it is a fear only, not a prophecy. Many dreams come to make us afraid, or give voice to our fears. They are not gifts of the spirits. They do not foretell the future. They are a child's fantasy only. On one breath of the wind of what is real, they blow away.

"Most white people will never come to this country. Never. It is not the kind of country they like. They want to plow the earth, plant, grow their crops, and harvest. They want to feed their cows, have calves, and eat the meat that grows inside their fences. They have no desire to follow the buffalo. That seems idle to them, worse than idle. And they would not like the earth here. It is dry. There is little rain. Never would they be able to till the soil and grow their food, as they like to do.

"This desire to grow things, to live in one place, to eat meat from animals they own—these wants live deep within them."

Owl Woman raised an eyebrow, and Sam knew she was reacting to the extraordinary idea that people could own animals. He pressed on.

"We white men who come here are rare exceptions. We like the life they hate. They hate the life we love.

"They have land in their own country, as much as they will ever want. Abundant land, waiting only for the axe to clear away the trees and the plow to cut the earth. They will never turn these arid plains into farms, or the high mountains into pastures."

Sam thought a moment. He was only saying what every mountain man knew. "As evidence I give you one fact. A few young white men come here. The women stay home. Home, a man's center, the place he belongs. Where his woman is, there is a man's home. No white women come here, or will.

"Some few of us beaver hunters will join with your women. Then the place where we live, where our hearts sing, it will become home to us as well. You will not become white. We will become red."

She nodded. It was an acceptance that Sam, at least, had become a Crow.

"Other beaver men, you will see, they will go home to their women and not come back. Already many have done that. Young men will have their sport, their great days of wandering and hunting. Then they will go home. You will see."

Owl Woman waited, gave Sam time to think whether he had anything more to say. He decided he didn't.

Finally she answered, "You speak with the voice of mind, I with the voice of dream. You tell what the two eyes of the head see. What I tell, that is seen only with the single eye that lives in the heart."

Chapter Twenty-Five

WHAT OWL WOMAN said about the eye of the heart disturbed Sam. He didn't know what to make of it. He spent that night telling himself that he and Meadowlark were finished. He spent the second night promising himself that he accepted this fate. *She isn't mine. She isn't mine. She isn't mine.* Maybe a little bit of him believed it, and grieved.

The next morning he ordered himself to stop maundering and get on with his life.

Regardless of what the future might bring, Sam had a present to get straight. He and Flat Dog, having nothing to trade for a lodge, cut poles and built a lean-to that shared one wall with James and Gideon's. That was shelter for the winter. Pemmican from the fall hunt, and the elk they would hunt in the snow, that made enough food.

Then the future. Sam didn't know what Flat Dog wanted, but he and Gideon needed plews to trade at rendezvous. He felt half-desperate to get a decent outfit again.

By comparison Gideon was lucky. When he escaped from the Lakotas, he wasn't stark naked. Aside from clothes, he had the gear he wore on his person, his rifle, pistol, shot pouch with powder, a few lead balls, and a vial of beaver medicine, throwing knife, butcher knife, patch knife, flint and steel, even the pipe and tobacco in his *gage d'amour*. Right pert fixin's, some of the beaver men would have said.

Sam needed all that and much more.

Luckily, Clyman was willing to let the two of them use his traps. Unless a man was desperate, the few winter beaver weren't worth the effort.

Sam and Gideon laid plans to work the nearby creeks in pairs. Up one creek, down another, back to the village.

So imagine when, in the twilight of their second day of work, they came into camp to find Needle and Meadowlark sitting at the mountain men's fire, talking to Flat Dog and Clyman.

Sam sat down and, keeping his eyes down, helped himself to the meat in the pot.

It was proper, in a way. Proper for a mother and sister to come talk to Flat Dog. Proper for a young maiden to talk to friends of her brother's, if she treated them like other brothers, and there was no prospect of courtship.

There is no courtship, is there?

Half an hour later, when the women got up to leave, Sam got up with them. He walked them back to their lodge. Needle had promised him three pairs of moccasins for an elk hide. Now she was going to draw around his foot with charcoal on deer skin to get his size.

When Needle came back out with the charcoal, Meadowlark came with her. While Needle was bent over Sam's foot sketching, Meadowlark mouthed three words to Sam. They were in English, a language she had never spoken a word of. But she had heard Sam say these English words many times to her: "I love you."

He looked into her face, and she opened it to him. He saw nothing there but sadness, and in her eyes infinite sadness. Having let him see, she tucked her head away, turned, and slipped back into the tipi.

SAM USED FLAT Dog. That made him feel guilty, but he could see no other way to do it. The message was simply, "Meet me under the overhang at midday."

He stood half crouched, though there was no reason to crouch. His blood thrummed with anxiety. Would she come?

This was a place the river had undercut the bank in the spring, when it was high. A fir tree stood on the point, and some of its roots were exposed below, where Sam stood. In another spring or two the river would cut too much dirt away, and the fir would pitch into the melt-swollen waters.

Now the river had backed away, winter-thin. The overhang was cold. The sun, low in the late-winter sky, never reached this cave. Sam shivered. He looked along the sandy strip upstream, back toward the village.

The corner of his eye caught the fall of a shadow, and he jerked his head the other way. Meadowlark, with Flat Dog. She reached for Sam's hand, as she knew he liked, but she wasn't smiling.

"Better to be alone?" he said in the Crow language.

Flat Dog's face stayed impassive.

"It's better if my brother's here."

"I love you," Sam said in English.

"I love you," she answered, and maybe her lips did start to smile.

In Crow he went on, "Let's go away together. I have traded Muskrat Woman for her travel tipi." It was a ragged affair, and they both knew it. "Spring is coming, and warm weather." He paused, unable to think of what to say.

"I love you," she began, then proceeded in Crow. "Joins with Buffalo, I cannot go outside the will of my family, my people. I will live my life in the circle of a Crow village. In that circle are safety, caring, warmth, companionship, everything that matters. I will raise my children here.

"Many people believe Owl Woman's dream. Especially my mother and father believe it."

Sam wanted to rage that this was impossible. The beaver hunters were a couple of hundred men, the Indians ten of thousands. But he knew better than to argue.

"Unless you can change their minds . . ."

She turned away slowly. For a moment he thought she would turn back and say something more, something different. But she set her shoulders back the way she came, and in an instant was out of sight.

Sam looked into Flat Dog's eyes. There he saw compassion. In that moment he was sure that he and Flat Dog would always be friends.

"I'm sorry," said Flat Dog. "For both of you."

WEEKS PASSED, FOR Sam, in a fever. He and Gideon trapped. Sam and Flat Dog hunted elk. Sam made arrows to trade for small items. Around their nighttime fires, the beaver men told stories, sometimes stories of the frontier back in the States, a land of fable kinged by alligator horses who could whup ten panthers at once and eat their whelp for breakfast. More often now they told stories of their own kind, the men variously called mountain men, mountaineers, and beaver hunters, men of the white, black, brown, and red tribes, men who had done things that would be remembered, that people would look back and tell stories about, tales with heroes worthy of big stories. John Colter's run from the Blackfeet. Hugh Glass's crawl across the plains. Diah Smith and the griz that bit his head. And they knew, wordlessly, that they themselves were doing deeds worth remembering and telling stories about. Sam wondered if he was a hero.

He barely heard these stories, though. His mind was in a roil about what to do about Meadowlark. He saw her often, but never alone. He looked at her when he thought no one would notice. Sometimes she looked at him, and he saw in her eyes that she grew sadder and more hopeless by the day.

He had no idea what to do, until he asked himself what would happen in one of these big stories.

HE HAD NEVER been so frustrated in his life. Three straight days. Normally Meadowlark came to the river for water in the time between sunset and darkness. One woman from each lodge did. The first evening, though, she came with another girl, both talking gaily, so Sam did nothing. The next evening Needle came instead. The next evening, the same. Sam knew very well that Meadowlark usually made this trip, not Needle. He asked himself over and over if they had figured what he was up to. But they couldn't possibly. He had been very careful.

It wasn't happening. He was ready, and beyond ready.

This evening no one had come. Full darkness was gathering, and no one had collected water for the Gray Hawk household tonight. An impossibility, yet it was true.

Squatting out of sight, he fidgeted.

A shadow. It glided along the path, flickering between trees. He couldn't see who it was. In the near darkness, it grew close and passed. The figure seemed to be running. He never did see who it was. Unbelievable. It was the right size and shape for Meadowlark, but most young women in the village were about that size and shape.

What to do?

He hurried to the path and from there walked openly toward the river. If it was Meadowlark, well and good. If not, he would give a casual greeting and keep going like nothing was . . .

Meadowlark, almost in his face. In the last of the light he saw several emotions on her face, pleasure in meeting him, sadness, pain, and more.

He smiled at her and stepped aside to let her pass.

She squelched a smile and walked forward.

He acted swiftly. From behind he flung the deer hide around her mouth and between her teeth, threw a quick knot, and pulled her back tight against him.

Her body felt so good along his. It had been so long . . .

She flailed.

Go!

He seized her behind the knees and shoulders, lifted her, and trotted through the cottonwood trees. Paladin and Pinto were tied about a hundred yards away, and he could carry her that far on the run.

He lifted her and seated her on Pinto. The pony was tied on a lead to Paladin, in case she might try to bolt.

He took both her hands, looked directly into her eyes, and said, "I'm kidnapping you. I want you for my wife."

Coy mewled in a way that sounded like, "Ple-e-e-ease," and Sam couldn't help smiling.

He tied Meadowlark's hands behind her. "Are you going to scream?"

Hesitation. Wild eyes. Thought. At last she shook her head no.

Good. Safer this way. He took the deer hide off her mouth. A sentry would pay no attention to two Crows riding on a trail in the darkness. No one would miss Meadowlark for a while, and then it would be too late.

He mounted Paladin and started off at a walk. A quarter mile on, he kicked the horses up to a lope. The trail was easy going, and Coy kept up comfortably.

Before too long, they left trail and turned up Black Creek. Riding at night was slow, but they were headed for a good place. The best place, he thought—a wide, well-watered valley on Black Creek within sight of the great Absaroka peaks to the north. The mountains would be snowy, but the valley floor, mostly free of snow, would be full of elk. In a week or two the grass would come green. When he and Flat Dog had first come here, they watched a hawk hunting in the open meadows. As they watched, the sun set, and the hawk's broad wings caught its evening colors gloriously. They named it Ruby Hawk Valley.

The travel lodge was already set up there, and it would do for a while. He had chopped, split, and broken up plenty of firewood. He had brought pemmican enough for a couple of weeks. He had traded for a blanket to sleep under, in addition to the buffalo and elk robes. He had made a household, one of poverty, but his. Theirs.

AT THEIR CAMP he gritted his teeth until his molars ached.

She didn't say a word. She hadn't spoken since he abducted her, and she didn't speak while she got water from the creek and watched him build the fire. He spread their bed robes near the flames so they could sit a while. Coy snuggled up next to her leg, but she ignored him.

Sam didn't know what she might need to say, or hear. What he needed to say, he'd said by bringing her here.

She looked at him funny. It was odd, in the Crow way of things, for a man to be arranging the inside of the lodge. He assumed they would get used to each other, if. . . . A big if.

He sat behind the fire, took his white clay pipe from the *gage d'amour* she had given him, packed it, and lit it. This gesture, at least, she would be familiar with. Now she petted Coy's head, and he accepted that.

She looked at Sam, just looked. He couldn't tell what was in her face. Nothing, it seemed. Or maybe it was everything, held very still.

He looked back at her. And smoked. And looked.

His bowl of tobacco was gone, burned. He tapped the ashes onto the edge of the fire. He looked around the lodge. The glow of the fire made the lodge skins rise. In the light Meadowlark's face glowed.

He reached for his woman, put his arms around her, and kissed her. He kissed her passionately, and in a moment both of them were kissing passionately. Their embrace lifted him up, and time spun away.

After a while he stroked and caressed her in various places. Later still he slipped her moccasins off, and then her dress, gently. He looked at her, all of her, and noticed that she enjoyed his look.

He took off his own clothes, lay down beside her, and folded her into his arms.

They began as in a slow waltz. First they explored one possibility, then another. Hour revolved upon hour, embrace upon embrace, body upon body. Through the night they did everything they wanted to do. Coy slept like nothing was happening. An hour or so after sunrise, they dozed off and slept until midday.

Then Meadowlark pounced on Sam.

THEIR FIRST FULL day was different, what was left of it. When they woke, Meadowlark went to the creek for water, and Sam built a low fire in the lodge. They nibbled on pemmican, and fed Coy more than they ate. They made love. This time they played melodies like yesterday's, and the harmony was the same, but the tempo was slow, relaxed, indolent. The feel shifted from fiery to languid, from stormy to sweet. Again, toward dawn, they slept.

When they woke, they stood, somehow, on a shore where they had never been.

They took care of tasks without speaking or looking at each other—water, fire, food.

When they finished, now stretched out naked on their robes and close to the flames, they looked long, each at the other, and saw the same friend, lover, spouse. The eye-holding looks grew longer. Though they couldn't have said what these looks meant exactly, they held something new, something more than lust, more than play, more than laughter, more even than love.

Light drained out of the tipi. In the smoke hole, the sky turned the color of a dove's breast. The air they breathed was melancholy.

Sam breached it. "The one who is not here?"

Meadowlark nodded. "My brother, Blue Medicine Horse." In the use of his name, somehow, coiled defiance.

"I miss him."

"And I miss him."

"Feels like he's here." Sam felt the risk in his words, sharp as razors.

"He is as real to me as the warmth of the fire."

"I'll never stop missing him."

She just nodded.

Sam felt the guilt seep into his heart like chill water into a cellar. "I'll never stop feeling . . ."

She saw it and put a finger to his lips. "You were not to blame. Flat Dog said . . ."

"Flat Dog forgave me. I don't know if your parents did." Then he said the hard part. "I don't know about you."

She cocked her head like a doe, half-startled.

He made himself speak directly into her eyes. "I brought agony into your life." Nothing abject in the words, only honesty and pain.

She shifted into a sitting position and looked down into his face. After a few moments, she asked him to put his head in her lap. He did.

"Did you ever have a big grief before?"

He looked like she'd slapped him. "I did. When I was a kid, my brother died. His name was Coy."

She smiled in recognition of the name. She stroked his hair. "Tell me about Coy."

As though misunderstanding, Coy the coyote slid up onto his haunches and began to howl softly. His cry took the shape of the word "ho-o-o-wl."

Sam spoke as though content with the coyote's accompaniment. He remembered ramblings in the Pennsylvania forest. Turtles found and brought home. Rides on the family mule. Swims in the river. Fights. Watching the stars and giving them names, special names, names to be held only between two brothers. His words sounded childish as he spoke them, commonplaces, things all siblings shared, pennies without polish. But it felt good to say them.

Sam stopped. The coyote renewed his call, louder, more echoing. Sam pictured the sounds wandering in all the lonely places of the planet. Then, for whatever reason, the song ended.

"When he died, what did you . . . do with him?"

"We put him in the ground." He thought that probably sounded barbarous to her. It felt barbarous to him.

"Did you sing?"

"Yes, hymns." He took thought and added, "Songs to wish him well, songs to say good-bye. Dad got a preacher man—medicine man—out from Pittsburgh, first preacher I ever met, to say some words. Big words about the big things, living and dying."

She stroked his face. "Do you remember any of the words?"

"Bible words, words from our . . . sacred stories. I wish I could bring them back clear. Maybe some day I'll learn to read and find them."

She bent down and kissed his face lightly. Her long hair caressed him.

He flinched at the sudden memory. " 'Beauty for ashes'—that's what the preacher said. He said he'd come to comfort those of us that grieved, to give us beauty for ashes, and the oil of joy for our mourning."

He looked up between her small breasts into her face. There he witnessed, in the soft light of the fire, a radiance that was beyond all eloquence. He saw love. He saw the gift that passes understanding, peace.

Her fingers stroked his forehead and cheeks. "Sam," she said, "the man known as Joins with Buffalo, my husband. For this death I forgive you. Accept my forgiveness. Beyond that, I offer you my heart. Find in my love beauty for the ashes of your grief, and the oil of joy for the pain in your heart."

During that long night, their loving explored a universe far from the previous night's. Where there was play, now came tenderness. Where eagerness, deliberation. Where excitement, unity and completeness. Near dawn they slept as on a boat upon the great and mothering sea. They were lifted, eased, lifted, eased, and infinitely at rest.

SAM LAY BACK on his robes, beneath his blanket, Meadowlark sleeping next to him. Usually, when he was single, he woke up at first light, well before the sun rose. Maybe she liked to sleep in. Coy nestled by her head, choosing her way, not Sam's, which tickled him.

He knew damned well he'd never felt this good.

Three days, living in a new world. A life of discoveries ahead.

And a life of lovemaking ahead. He didn't want even to think any of those other words, not about what he and Meadowlark did. He'd had some experience of sex before, and for him it always had a flicker of aggression in it, sometimes of anger.

With Meadowlark it was . . . Even if he could read books, and quote Shakespeare like James Clyman, even then he wouldn't have the words for it.

For once he'd done the right thing. Finding the woman for his life and attaching her to him, that was the most momentous thing a man could accomplish. Doing the right thing, when you've done a lot of wrong ones, felt incredible.

Meadowlark was open about not being so sure they were doing the right thing. Maybe Rides Twice's village still wouldn't accept them. Maybe they'd have to live in another Crow village. Her mother's original village wintered well to the east, on the edge of the Wolf Mountains. Needle only saw her parents and brothers and sisters once a year, at the big fall hunt.

Or maybe, Sam said, we'll spend some of our time with a fur brigade, hunting.

"Maybe," Meadowlark said.

What each of them knew was simple and clear. They would always be together, as close as back and belly when they slept, as close as mingled breath when they made love.

He cricked his neck and rolled his shoulders. He always felt energetic first thing in the morning. Two of the three days he'd made the morning trip to the creek to get water. Meadowlark protested sweetly—he mustn't do women's work, that was unseemly. He thought she'd get used to it.

He slipped from under the robes, looked at his sleeping wife, and at the pup asleep by her head. They loved each other, which was damn good. Sam looked at the fire, long since out. He would start it when he got back from the creek. Right now he was thirsty.

He slipped the pegs out of the lodge door, bent, and duck-walked outside. This time of year, near the equinox, the sun rose straight to the east, and lodge doors always faced that way. Just as he looked, the red-orange sun gathered itself from a sheet of light along the ridge top into a bright ball. It blinded Sam a little, and he laughed with pleasure at the light and warmth.

Yi-ii-ay!

Sam got slammed hard to the ground on his side, a body on top of him and pinning his arms to his ribs.

He screwed his head back and saw . . .

Flat Dog's face.

"What the hell are you doing?" Sam yelled nose to nose with his friend.

"Saving your life," said Flat Dog mildly.

Half a dozen men stepped up, led by Red Roan. Several had arrows pulled back and pointed at Sam. Two had war clubs raised. Yellow Horn was holding a lance and growling.

"If you raped Meadowlark," Red Roan told Sam, "I'll kill you." Anger coiled in his voice like a rattler.

Meadowlark rose out of the doorway, protecting her modesty with their blanket. She bristled at Red Roan, and her eyes turned to fire. "Everything that was done, we did together. I wanted what he wanted."

Red Roan slowly, very slowly, turned his eyes back to Sam. "What you've done is wrong," the chief's son said, "and you will pay."

SAM RODE INTO the village as he'd led Meadowlark away, his horse on a lead tied to another man's mount, hands lashed behind his back. He felt like Coy, who was slinking instead of trotting.

As Sam rode, he pondered something. Back there in Ruby Hawk Valley, he threw a lot of anger in Flat Dog's face. And his friend answered gently, as though he didn't notice the anger, or it flew by his face and didn't touch him.

Sam wanted to learn to do that.

On the ride back he found out what happened. They let him talk to Flat Dog, but not to Meadowlark, who was forced to ride in front next to Red Roan.

Flat Dog said they'd checked on one likely spot the first day, another the second, and on the late afternoon of the third, they saw the travel lodge in Ruby Hawk Valley. Flat Dog had told them places that were probable, areas he and Sam had hunted and Sam liked. Actually, this wide spot on Black Creek had been his first guess, but he misled them. They crept close in the middle of the night. Coy had gone into a barking fit, Sam remembered, but he assumed whatever noises the coyote heard were animals.

"I didn't lead the party there first because I hoped to give you enough time to be gone."

"Why did you come at all?" Sam knew the answer, but he wanted to hear it.

"I thought they'd kill you if I wasn't there."

Sam had never thought that warriors might come after him and Meadowlark. She hadn't either. He asked Flat Dog why they came.

"It's unusual," Flat Dog admitted.

"Who got it started? Never mind, I know. Was Yellow Horn or Red Roan the loudest?"

"Yellow Horn," said Flat Dog. "I think Red Roan would have let it go."

"What happens now?"

"She'll be Red Roan's wife."

Sam felt as though a lightning bolt cleaved him top to bottom. He'd meant, "What happens to me now?" But Flat Dog's answer told him that, too.

Part Seven

LOST

Chapter Twenty-Six

GIDEON HAD THE only sensible suggestion. "Let's find the brigade."

The four men looked at each other, Sam and Clyman the white men, Gideon the French-Canadian (which in his case meant Cree and Jew), and Flat Dog the Crow.

"Crazy," was Sam's immediate response.

"You no talk about crazy," said Gideon, "considering."

It was the very evening Sam had been brought back in shame and separated forever from Meadowlark. They were sitting around their fire.

"I don't think it's crazy," said Clyman. "We sure got cause to get with 'em."

The reason was that Clyman had six traps, and no other man had any. You couldn't make a spring hunt without traps. Also, four men might make a risky hunt, even if they stuck to the creeks here in Crow country. Being with a brigade would be safer, in any country.

Sam didn't feel a bit like talking about what they were going to do. His mind was strictly on how he'd been brought down. *What an idiot I was, thinking I'd "finally" done the right thing. I made the biggest mess of my messy life.*

Gray Hawk had made that absolutely clear. First he and Needle went to Meadowlark and talked quietly with her. Then Needle led Meadowlark away. Gray Hawk walked up to Sam as he was leading his horses back to the lean-to, his head hanging. In a soft, lashing voice Gray Hawk said, "Get out of here. Get out of this village. I will never let you near my daughter again."

Now Gideon and Clyman worked out how they would get a fall hunt. Probably the brigade would be along the Siskadee somewhere. "The sign, she will be easy to pick up," said Gideon.

"If they're not on the Siskadee," said Clyman, "we know where else they hunt."

The conversation batted back and forth considerably. Flat Dog paid sharp attention, Sam none.

The conclusion was that Gideon and Clyman intended to look for the brigade. "I have no possibles," said Gideon. "I need a fine spring hunt."

"What you gonna do when you can't find the brigade?" challenged Sam.

"Meet up with all the coons at rendezvous," said Clyman.

It was set for the Bear River this summer, north of Salt Lake.

"At ze worst," Gideon said, "we will come together wit' zem at rendezvous."

"Can't miss rendezvous—see everybody, trade. Ashley will bring lots of whiskey, he promised."

"Diah and Fitzpatrick, they're inviting lots of Indians. Come and trade, they'll tell the Indians." The bear man gave a huge grin. "Whiskey and Indian women . . ."

"Count me out," said Sam.

"I want to go," said Flat Dog.

Gideon and Clyman jerked their heads toward each other, taken by surprise. Then they nodded. "Welcome," said Clyman

"I don't give a damn what any of you do," said Sam.

THE THREE HUNTERS spent the next morning packing up. They asked if they could trade Sam something for his travel lodge. He said he didn't care what they took.

Coy trotted from the departing group to Sam, and back, and back and forth, confused about what was going on.

In late morning they were packed and ready. The three looked at Sam.

"You sure you don't want something for this travel lodge?"

He didn't answer. He didn't want one thing on earth but what he couldn't have.

"You sure you want to stay here?"

No answer.

"You coming to rendezvous?"

No answer.

Flat Dog handed his reins to Clyman and walked over and sat down by Sam. He blew out a couple of big breaths. "You want me to talk to Meadowlark?"

Sam snapped his head toward Flat Dog.

"You want me to ask what she wants you to do?"

"I . . ." Sam stopped his foolish answer.

"I'll tell you exactly what she says, whatever it is."

Sam thought. He had a feeling like a fish jumping in his heart. "Yes."

Flat Dog stood up and spoke to Gideon and Clyman. "You mind waiting a while?"

"We're easy," said Clyman.

Flat Dog disappeared for half an hour. He came back pursing his lips.

"Meadowlark says to tell you this. 'I love you.' She said it in English. 'If you stay here, you're throwing your life away. Someone will kill you. Then I couldn't live. Go, please go. I love you. Go.'"

Flat Dog stood up. The three swung up onto their horses, and Clyman took the pack horse lead.

Coy looked from Sam to the mounted men, back to Sam and back to the three, and gave one loud bark. He barked again.

"Go ahead," said Sam. He took hold of Coy.

They went.

Before they rounded the first bend in the river, Flat Dog turned in the saddle and looked back. He could see the boulder where Sam sat and the trees behind. He wished he could see a rider coming their way.

Sam and Coy didn't catch up with them until they were ten miles downstream.

Chapter Twenty-Seven

SAM WOKE UP when Paladin flabbered her lips. It wasn't just the sound, but the spray that came with it. When it was a fine night and he slept outside, she woke him like this. The other horses, including Pinto, were moved out of camp at first light and put on grass until the company was ready to get going. Not Paladin, though. Sam kept her staked right by his bedroll, wherever it was. She woke him because she got jealous of the other horses, or she wanted her treat, Sam didn't know which.

Coy raised his head and shook it. He'd caught the spray too.

Sam reached beneath his buffalo robe and got some bark of the sweet cottonwood, which he kept close at hand for these occasions. Paladin gulped it down greedily and flabbered her lips again.

Sam sat up and found Gideon sitting up too. "Time, I guess," said the big man.

Sam looked around the camp. It was sizable, about thirty men. He, Gideon, Flat Dog, and Clyman had found this outfit easily. They came over the Southern Pass and trapped south along the Siskadee and then up Ham's Fork. They met these trappers, led by David Jackson, working their way down Ham's Fork after wintering in Cache Valley of the Bear River.

And with them, a friend. Jim Beckwourth, the strapping mulatto, was in the outfit. He'd gone clear to St. Louis with Jedediah Smith, and come back with Jedediah too. He was full of stories. As usual, Sam cut them down by half before he believed them.

Jackson, though, seemed like a man who considered the facts before he spoke. He spoke of one place so sweetly that Sam made up his mind he had to go see it.

"There's glorious country," Jackson told Sam, "north of the Siskadee. At the top, where it bends back, you go on over the divide and come on the Hoback River, the one the Astorians followed. Go down that to where it joins the Lewis Fork and up that river, you come to the finest hole you'll ever see. Mountains on all four sides, on the west high ones that are always snowy. Creeks full of beaver rolling down from all four sides. Too high to winter, and needs a sharp eye when you're getting in and out, but a heaven of a place to trap." He added with a reluctant smile, for David Jackson was a shy man, "The boys call it Jackson's Hole."

Jackson's Hole. And the good news was, Jackson was headed back there right now.

Sam and his companions went up the Siskadee with the Jackson brigade. Tonight they'd camped on the river bank, right where it started a shepherd's-crook turn back into the Wind River Mountains.

As usual with a big party, they made a square camp right on the river, divided into four messes. At night they staked the horses about ten steps apart, between their bedrolls and the river. Every morning the horse guard close-herded them out onto some grass.

Now Sam could see horses grazing on the top of a nearby hill, further away than usual.

The mess's fire was dead out.

"I have to put Paladin out to graze," said Sam unnecessarily.

"I'll start the coffee," said Gideon.

The other men of the mess, including Flat Dog and Beckwourth, were beginning to stir.

Sam restaked Paladin no more than twenty or thirty steps from camp. He didn't want her loose, and he didn't want her clear up on that hill. Some of the men thought he was peculiar, keeping a horse and a coyote right next to him at night, but they didn't know how special this horse and coyote were.

He wanted to check Pinto's hooves. Sam thought she was walking a little gingerly when they came into camp last night.

Sam started up the long hill, Coy at his heels. A dozen steps away they stopped. Sam realized he wasn't carrying The Celt. "It's all right," he told Coy. The horses were guarded, and not far off.

He was huffing and puffing when he came up to Pinto. Coy ran ahead to the little mare. She was pulling up grass at the left edge of the herd, highest on the summit ridge. She had a way of snatching bunch grass hard out of the ground, throwing her head a little, like a kid taking a toy from a sibling.

Pinto grazed right where the ridge rose into its summit and the timber of the north slope bunched nearly to the crest. Sam walked right up to Pinto and dropped the halter on her head. Pinto didn't have a lot of virtues, in Sam's opinion, but one was that she let herself be caught easily.

Coy barked at something.

Sam knelt to check the left front hoof.

As his head dipped downward, an arrow furrowed his scalp.

Sam took a split second to breathe. He held tight to the reins and jumped toward Pinto's back.

Pinto crow-hopped and Sam missed. Coy yapped like hell.

The guard, where the hell is the guard?

He tried again to get on, but now Pinto was shying in every direction, way out of control. An arrow waved jauntily from her left hip.

Keeping Pinto between him and the timber, Sam ran.

"Yi-ii-yii!" An Indian hollered, and charged toward them.

Damn. Sam couldn't run flat out leading Pinto, especially not with her acting up. He dived behind a bush.

Coy charged the Indian, and got kicked away for his trouble. Coy huddled behind the bush with Sam and Pinto.

The Indian started walking—sauntering, actually—and stopped about twenty steps away. He was grinning arrogantly.

Yeah, you caught me without a gun. Sam felt of his scalp. Lots of blood. He stuck his long white hair to the bleeding spot.

The Indian squatted and eyed Sam like an animal he'd trapped.

Sam looked desperately toward the camp. Men were stirring. He yelled at the top of his lungs, "HE-E-ELP!"

No reaction. Too far.

The Indian made some signs. He looked Blackfeet, from his clothes. That language Sam didn't know a word of. 'Give yourself up,' he signed, 'and I won't hurt you.'

Sam's answer was to get out his belt knife, a good weapon, but not against arrows. Blackfeet were the worst.

'I won't even eat your dog,' the Blackfeet signed.

The Indian waited. After a while he signed, 'If you lay down your knife, I will lay down my bow and arrow. Then we can meet and talk and be friends.'

Sam tucked the reins under his arm and signed, 'How many of you?'

The guards must be dead. Just like the Blackfeet not to stop at stealing the horses, but to want to kill some people too. Maybe all the people, and steal the furs, utensils, guns, the whole kit and caboodle.

The Blackfeet took a few steps closer. 'Notice,' he signed, 'I have already laid down my bow and arrow. Come out.'

The bastard sure wasn't aware of the way he walked or stood, like he was ready to pounce and drink blood.

Sam ran his brain hard to figure the situation. His summary was— worse than desperate. He couldn't run and expose his back. He couldn't attack. Eventually, the Blackfeet would tire of this game or his friends would come up.

On the hill the horses were gone, no doubt gathered up by Blackfeet.

Sam's knife hand felt wet and sticky. His blood had run all the way down the arm of his shirt. Thinking he ought to stanch that bleeding with a rifle patch, he reached for his hunting pouch.

Whack! An arrow broke a limb in front of Sam's face and glanced off.

Coy yipped and ran at the Blackfeet.

Instinctively, Sam jumped and ran after Coy.

The damn Indian got another arrow nocked and shot just as Sam came onto him bellowing.

Pain! Sam's ribs screamed.

Sam screamed louder and drowned out the pain.

He embraced the Blackfeet. The man swung a tomahawk, and Sam felt its bite on his back.

Once Sam knifed the Blackfeet—twice!—and got solid flesh.

Cries rose from the hilltop like angry calls of a thousand geese.

Blackfeet charged down the hill, and a musket cracked the dawn silence.

Sam ignored Pinto and ran down hill pell-mell.

Maybe catching Pinto will distract them.

Pinto gave a loud whinny of protest. Sam pictured her kicking Blackfeet, fighting for her freedom, and maybe saving Sam's life.

Sam ran like a blue whistle.

Arrows shimmered through the air.

Sam nearly stepped on Coy, and almost lost his balance avoiding the coyote.

No more musket blasts. They must have had only one.

Sam sprinted across a spot that was nearly level and plunged onto steeper ground. It was tricky, getting sure footing on such a steep slope. Sam bounded, trying to make each foot placement exact, but . . .

He tumbled headlong and rolled, and rolled, and rolled . . .

Snap to! He wondered if he'd lost consciousness for a moment. The Blackfeet were too damn close.

Musket shots! A bunch!

No, rifle shots!

Gideon was charging up the hill on Paladin, Beckwourth and three or four men running hard behind him. Several others had stopped to reload.

The Blackfeet flocked back up the hill, two men helping their wounded comrade.

"Here's a chance at a fair fight, you bastards!" screamed Sam.

As though that was all the energy he had, his mind whirled and grayed out.

"THIS IS GONNA hurt."

It did. Sam's ribs barked at him again.

Flat Dog held up an arrow. "In your ribs. It was just hanging in the skin, almost clear of the ribs."

Coy sniffed the arrow, wanting the blood. Flat Dog grinned and pushed him away.

"Almost . . . ," said Sam through gritted teeth. *Why couldn't the damn arrow have almost hit me?*

"You've lost a lot of blood. I'll help you onto Paladin. We'll go back to camp, but we're taking it slow."

Sam pigeon-toed his way down the hill to his horse. He felt a gush of relief at seeing her unhurt.

Then he saw Gideon rolling around on the ground behind her. He was cussing and fooling with his foot. Suddenly, he held up an arrow triumphantly. "I got the devil, zis child did." The arrow was bloody.

Beckwourth and another trapper helped Gideon to his feet.

"We gotta get back before they decide to attack," said Beckwourth. But he walked and led Paladin. The two men supported Gideon, one-footing it slowly behind.

THEY BUILT A breastwork. Brush, limbs, saddles, pack saddles, furs, kegs, blankets and other trade goods—everything went into their fort. It was three-sided, the river forming the fourth side. "If they want to charge across the Siskadee," said Jackson, "they're welcome to it."

The river was running full in spring flood.

All the men, nearly thirty, fit inside. What normally would have been seventy horses was one—Paladin. The Blackfeet had all the others.

Flat Dog said he was going to scout. Before Sam could say, "Hey, that's risky!" he disappeared.

Clyman poulticed Sam's scalp, back, and ribs as best he could. Sam lay resting on his bedroll, under orders to stay put. Coy crouched like a stone lion beside Sam's head. The back wounds were shallow cuts. The arrow didn't get inside the ribs, hadn't done any internal damage.

James seemed more concerned about Gideon's foot. "Lots of little bones in a foot," he said. "You may not walk so good again."

His hip had healed, only to give way to a bad foot.

Gideon rasped, "Next time I get hit in the leg. Then, if hits big artery, I die fast. If miss artery, am fine. But not a cripple." He sighed. "Not a cripple."

"My guess is," Jackson said to the men's unspoken question, "they're a horse-stealing outfit meaning to go against the Snakes. Them Snakes have good horseflesh. If I'm right, there might be twenty or twenty-five Blackfeet."

"I *seen* that many," someone said.

"Flat Dog will tell us how many there are," said Sam.

A voice came from behind where Sam lay—"If he don't sit down and eat breakfast with 'em."

Sam was glad he couldn't see who said that.

"They won't want to attack us beavers with rifles behind a breastwork," said Jackson.

"Not a chance," someone chipped in, reassuring himself.

"Besides," said Gideon, pain coppering his voice, "now they got our horses."

The men laughed uneasily.

There was nothing to do but wait.

FLAT DOG SAID they were gone. "Cleared out."

"Skedaddled," a Kentuck said from behind Sam.

All the men gathered close. Sam and Gideon lay on their bedrolls at the front. Coy curled around Sam's feet.

"Got our horseflesh instead of the Snakes'," Jackson said.

"They stuck us good," Beckwourth said.

"I want to go after them." This was Flat Dog.

"What you gonna go after 'em with?" said Jackson sharply.

"I run," said Flat Dog soberly. "I run and catch up with them."

From the rear came laughs and raspberries.

Flat Dog's expression never changed.

"It ain't funny," said Beckwourth loudly. "A man can run down a horse if he's good and has a lot of stick-to-it."

Flat Dog gave Jim a look like, "You understand."

Jim said, "Maybe I'll just go along with Flat Dog."

"It ain't safe," said Jackson. Seemed like he wanted more to measure them than keep them back.

"I'm going," said Beckwourth.

Flat Dog gave him a small nod.

Silence. Coy snuggled closer to Sam's feet.

Jackson squatted down by Sam. Coy gave him a suspicious look, but Davey ignored it. "Morgan, I'm going to ask you for something. It's big, real big to you." He looked Sam hard in the eyes. "Let them take Paladin."

Beckwourth spoke up. "We don't need the horse. Sam loves that horse."

Flat Dog watched Sam curiously.

"You're a member of my outfit. We take care of our own when they're hurt. I could order you. The safety of the whole outfit depends on them horses. But I'm asking you."

"Flat Dog?" asked Sam.

"Would help. We take turns riding and walking, stay fresher."

"Jim?"

For once speechless, Beckwourth shrugged.

Flat Dog squatted and spoke softly to Sam. "I won't kid you, she may not come back. But if I come back, Paladin will."

Sam knew a solemn pledge when he heard it.

It was a matter of how you treat a friend. He took a deep breath and let it out. "All right," he said. He struggled to his feet, minced over to where Paladin was staked, and rubbed her muzzle. Coy whined.

Flat Dog and Beckwourth had a quick conversation with Jackson about where to meet. They were gone in hardly more time than it took to reload a rifle. Flat Dog rode, and didn't look back at Sam. Trails get cold fast.

THE BRIGADE DUG a big cache for their belongings—plews (packs and packs of these), saddles, trade goods, kegs for water, kegs of whiskey—everything except their rifles and what they carried around their necks, over their shoulders, stuck in their belts, and the like.

They worked in silence, not speaking of the hopes that remained. The best hope, they believed, was that they would run into some friendly Snakes. The Snakes had apparently decided that having fur men in their country was a benefit. If the Snakes believed their story, they might come back to the cache with the whites. Then Jackson would barter his Indian trade goods for enough horses to carry the men and their furs to rendezvous.

Another hope, fainter: That Flat Dog and Beckwourth would steal the horses back, or enough horses to carry the belongings, even if the men had to walk. Catching up on foot, or the same as on foot, as Beckwourth and Flat Dog were attempting to do, then getting those horses back—most men thought it was ridiculous.

What they didn't want to think about was walking the whole way to rendezvous, having no furs to trade, and being forced to come back later to raise the cache. Rendezvous this summer was on the Bear River. A long walk—you went back down the Siskadee, cut over to Ham's Fork, crossed a divide over the Salt River Range, descended to Bear River, and followed that around its big bend to Cache Valley, several days' ride above the big Salt Lake. Nobody wanted to a walk couple of hundred miles, but they would if they had to.

That day, for sure, they couldn't start walking. Gideon's foot gave him too much pain, and Sam was half dizzy.

The next day Sam was much better, but Gideon's pain was sharp. "Why so much hurt in such a little hole?" complained the bear-sized man.

Jackson had the men construct a litter from poles and a blanket. They dragged Gideon along, with the big man grousing loudly.

That night the puncture wound looked red, and Clyman thought it might be infected. Puncture wounds, they knew, were the most likely to fester. The next day it was red, oozed puss, and was even more painful. "Infected," James said soberly.

Now every man was thinking of gangrene. Gideon squeezed his eyes closed and said nothing.

One morning Gideon sang canoeing songs as he bumped along. During the afternoon he acted tired, but he told occasional cripple jokes. The brigade walked quietly downriver, trying not to jounce him too much.

One night the swelling and redness seemed no better. The next, the wound looked green around the edges. Clyman sniffed. "It's beginning to stink."

Except for Sam and Clyman, men stopped talking to Gideon. No one wanted to cozy up to mortality.

The next day Gideon sang songs again. And either he forgot his English or his mind was weakening. He didn't speak, and sang only in French.

Sam slunk along beside the litter all day, and Coy slunk behind Sam.

Late one afternoon they made camp along the river with a good grove of cottonwoods at their backs. Clyman checked the foot. The green around the wound had turned to black. Red streaks ran up the calf. "Blood poisoning," said James loud, like an announcement.

The men looked at each other. Everyone knew.

Suddenly, they heard a kind of a roar. *What is that? Horses!*

Men ran for the best cover available, trees, bushes, boulders. They primed their muzzleloaders.

Horses for sure. The roar was becoming *rat-a-tat-tats*.

They couldn't see beyond the cottonwoods. Friends? Enemies? They squirmed. They looked along their sights.

"Some niggers, coming on us in the broad open," whined a nasal voice near Sam.

A voice came through the trees, or voices.

Men heaved big breaths in and out. Hammers snapped back. Powder was poured into pans, ready for the flint spark.

The voice made melody.

Sam lowered The Celt. "It's Beckwourth," he said happily.

"How does you know?" whined the voice.

"He's singing, 'My Lord, What a Morning.'"

"Yi-ii-ay!" So it was Flat Dog too. And Paladin. Sam grinned big. He gave the long, loud whistle he used to call Paladin to him.

About a score of horses *rat-a-tat-tatted* into the grove on the trot. Sam saw his big white mare come galloping around them, looking for the source of the whistle.

Sam laughed. Flat Dog slid off the mare and the friends grinned at each other.

Sam set to stroking Paladin's fine head, sliding up onto her bare back (which made his injured side hurt), checking out her hooves, and the like. Beckwourth and Flat Dog headed for fires and meat fresher than the jerked stuff they'd been eating. The men gathered around, curious.

In the end it was left to Beckwourth to tell the story of how they got the horses back. Well, some horses—twenty-one to be exact.

Jim was big with the story. The tale of their trek over the pass to the north and down the Hoback River was epic. The episode of sneaking up on the Blackfeet camp was nerve-tingling. The attack on the guards was hair-raising and bloody, and Jim himself was as mighty as Joshua at the walls of Jericho. Someone said he seemed to have killed, by his own hand, more Blackfeet than there were in the party. When he got to the part about running the horses off—*all* the horses—someone called out, "Jim, if you run off all the horses, where's the other forty-nine?" Guffaws all around.

Jackson asked some hard questions. Were the Indians on their tails? Was the camp in danger of attack right now?

"I don't think so," said Jim. "They had all the lead they'll be wanting."

Flat Dog confirmed that he had doubled back at first light this morning and found no one on their back trail.

Jackson pulled at his chin and allowed that the Blackfeet might be satisfied with getting away with fifty horses, particularly if they lost a couple of men. Blackfeet took dead comrades hard. Their idea of winning was strictly to go home unscratched.

Jim and Flat Dog felt damn lucky, Jim said, to find the outfit not many sleeps from where they left it.

That brought out some grousing noises.

"But any coon can see why, that's sure," said Jim. He kept himself from looking at Gideon.

"Matter of fact, we're acting like we don't know the true business of this evening," said Clyman.

Men peered at him like they didn't know what he was talking about.

Clyman asked softly, "What do you say, Gideon?"

"Do it," Gideon roared in English. Everyone recoiled from the violence of his tone. "For sake of *le bon dieu,* do it."

He shook himself wildly on the litter. "I am coward. A man, *vraiment,* he choose death over cripple. I am no longer such big man. I am afraid to die. Do it."

Chapter Twenty-Eight

S AM KNEW THAT he and Clyman were somehow elected.

Jackson broke out whiskey, enough for Gideon only. Gideon got drunk enough to pass in and out of consciousness. Sam, Clyman, and several other men whetted their knives as sharp as they could. Sharp blades would make it easier. They thought of themselves. In Gideon's place, they would insist on sharp blades.

Flat Dog looked at his friend's wound and ran his eyes from it to

Sam to Clyman to Jackson and back to the wound. He couldn't feature what on earth they were about to do.

"I've never done anything like this," said Clyman. It sounded like a statement of fact, not an excuse.

"Me neither," said Sam.

The long May evening would give a lot of light, probably enough. A fire was built within reach of the surgeon. They put a log under Gideon's knee.

Flat Dog sat down bewildered, but no one noticed.

Though no man there had performed an amputation, or even seen one done, frontier people had heard about how such things were performed. "At the knee," Clyman. "We don't have a saw to cut through the shin bones, and they say the joint is best anyhow."

Jackson tied a tourniquet around the thigh and cranked it tight, using a stick for a lever. Sam felt sheepish that he hadn't thought of the tourniquet. *What other ghastly mistake are we making? Are we doctors or killers?*

A half dozen knives gleamed on a slab of sandstone next to Gideon.

"I'll hold his leg," said Sam.

Gideon lifted his head for a moment. "I want Sam to do the job," he said.

Everybody stared. They thought he was gone. Jackson poured more whiskey down his throat. "Sam," Gideon choked out. "He's my man."

Clyman looked at Sam and nodded. James went to the foot, squatted, and clamped the foot between his knees.

"I want Flat Dog hold leg," said Gideon harshly. "You watch careful," he said to Clyman.

Flat Dog took the leg. His mind was whirling. *Surely these white men weren't about to* . . .

Clyman regarded Flat Dog carefully, then duck-waddled up beside the knee.

Sam picked up his own butcher knife, held the blade in flames for several moments and studied the knee carefully.

After consideration he made his first cut.

Gideon screamed.

IT TURNED OUT that Clyman thought of things Sam didn't. For instance, you leave skin a couple of inches below the joint, so you'll have enough to fold back over the wound.

Sam worked in a sort of trance. Gideon bellowed sometimes— loud, wordless, howling roars with no apparent relationship to what Sam was doing. Sam heard, but they were remote and unreal to him. Even Gideon himself was remote, in a way. Sam saw only the flesh, the ligaments, the tendons, the cartilage, the bones. And the blood, too much blood. Part of his mind wondered whether Gideon would survive the blood loss. Most of Sam's mind was focused, with a dream-like intensity, on the joint itself.

Every frontiersman, every rural cook, had seen lots of joints of animals, and had some basic idea of how they worked. Sam went forward with this knowledge and common sense—that was all he had, and hard necessity.

He switched knives often. Other men whetted them again.

Flat Dog held on grimly, his face pale, his mind numb.

No one spoke, except that Clyman occasionally pointed and said, "There," or "Like that."

Gideon's hollering occurred in another world.

Then Sam was to the bones. He had to go between the knobby bone ends and pull the leg apart, not cut it apart.

Soon the joint no longer joined anything. Sam let out a big breath of relief. From here he more or less knew his way.

After another eternity, or passage through a surreal world, Clyman eased Gideon's lower leg away. It was done. For better or worse, done. Forever done.

Flat Dog dropped the half leg. Then he flopped onto the ground on his back.

Clyman handed Sam an axe whose head glowed lurid red. Sam

nodded to himself. He understood. He pushed the flat side of the head firmly against Gideon's stump. Sizzle, steam, stink.

Gideon, unconscious, uttered no sound.

Sam looked at his work, turned the axe head over, and applied the other side to another part of the stump.

Gideon writhed and uttered soft, mewling sounds.

Flat Dog sat up and stared at what was happening. He didn't know human beings did such . . .

Jackson handed Sam needle and thread. Sam took the flaps of flesh that had once covered the upper part of Gideon's calf and folded them over each other. The bloody wound was completely covered. Patiently, with a coppery feeling of revulsion in his mouth, Sam sewed the pieces of flap together.

He sat back on his heels. He put down needle and thread. He let his head drop. Done.

"Well done," said Clyman.

"Damn well done," said Jackson.

Flat Dog couldn't decide whether it was well done, or insane.

Sam felt . . . He could not have said, so many strange, winding, blowing feelings, wisps of gauze in a breeze of consciousness.

The men, who had watched with rapt attention, began to drift away. Time for coffee, time for a bite to eat.

Jackson said, "I think we ought to loose that tourniquet, see how bad it bleeds, and tighten it again. Keep doing that until the bleeding stops."

The brigade leader looked inquiringly at Sam, as though he now had some authority.

Clyman set the calf and foot in Sam's lap. "Seems like you oughta be the one decides what to do with this." Then he took over at the tourniquet.

Sam cradled the severed leg in silence and wept gently.

He sat by himself for half an hour or so, rubbing Coy's head.

In the very last of the evening light, he carried Gideon's leg upstream into the densest part of the cottonwoods. A melancholy memory walked with him—how he had done the same for Third Wing in this same valley. He climbed into the biggest cottonwood he could find and carefully set the half leg in a fork. Then he took thought, pulled the tail of his shirt out of his trousers, and cut a long, wide strip of hide off the bottom. He wrapped the leg in that. It seemed respectful.

He slid down the tree and stumbled back to camp, wanting and not wanting to see his maimed friend.

Gideon was sleeping. Not sleeping forever, from what Sam could see.

Clyman had taken the tourniquet off.

As far as Sam could tell by the firelight, the wound wasn't bleeding.

He took Gideon's hand, held it for a moment, squeezed, and put it on the bear-man's belly.

Though he stretched out near Flat Dog, he didn't sleep all night. He scratched Coy's ears and watched the stars. They wheeled very, very slowly across the sky, dancers beyond the reach of time. Somewhere, somehow the world turned. Time tick-tocked, somewhere.

Sam looked but didn't think. In the first light he closed his eyes and eased off.

THE NEXT MORNING Flat Dog got breakfast for two and took one bowl to Sam, who was just waking up. Gideon lay nearby on his litter, half-conscious.

"Let's see if we can get Gideon to eat something," Flat Dog said.

Sam sat up, wiggled his eyebrows to wake up, and eyeballed Gideon. "Probably not," he said, and accepted his own bowl.

"If we can," said Flat Dog.

James Clyman joined them. The other men stayed at their mess fires. Flat Dog noticed how most of the men didn't want to associate with a badly injured man. Were they embarrassed by his wound? By his . . . half-human state? Or was it just an aversion to being so close to injury and death, like it might be catching?

A man without a leg. Flat Dog had seen dogs without legs, but never a man. A man *deliberately* made legless.

"Lot of sitting to be done today," said Clyman.

And for a few days, thought Flat Dog. *If we want him to live. If he wants to live with one leg.*

Sam's head was hanging. He looked exhausted from the ordeal.

Clyman seemed even-keeled. Not much excited Old James, as he called himself.

Flat Dog still felt like somebody'd whacked him in the head with something heavy and made him silly. He kept looking at Gideon's face, down at the missing leg, back at the face, and across at Sam, and then repeating the whole cycle.

Clyman spooned a little broth onto Gideon's closed lips. The lips opened and the tongue accepted. Clyman spooned more. The eyes opened, and the head lifted a little.

Coy went up to Gideon's leg, sniffing. The one-legged bear man cuffed at the coyote irritably, missing by a wide margin, but Coy skittered off. Gideon lay back down and closed his eyes. "I'll eat a little," he said softly. "Though, *le bon dieu,* maybe I should starve until I die."

Clyman spooned it to him.

"I'm going to hunt today," Flat Dog told Sam.

"I'm too tired," said Sam.

Flat Dog nodded, smiled with his eyes at his friend, and headed off.

White people had always been strange. The men traveled without their families. For years, amazingly, they went without their families. They earned lots of *things,* but seemed to have no reason for owning them, except to do more traveling without their families and get still more things. They liked adventure. Flat Dog now understood the adventure part, and enjoyed it himself.

But Gideon. Gideon, and what Sam had done to Gideon, that slapped Flat Dog in the face. It brought up questions that stunned him.

Flat Dog rode out to find elk or deer, but his mind was elsewhere. He was learning something tremendous, maybe, something that knocked his idea of the white man cockeyed. He hefted this new bit of understanding, rubbed it with his fingers, prodded it, checked it from every side to learn its true nature.

*   *   *

SAM AND FLAT Dog inspected the wound. Coy wanted to sniff it, but Sam pushed him away. Sam said the wound seemed to be healing fine. No bleeding. Jackson had already said the outfit would travel tomorrow, Gideon on a litter. They were in luck—now the litter would be pulled by horses, not men. But all this only half-mattered to Flat Dog.

When they had poured coffee from the pot on the mess fire, Flat Dog said, "I don't understand cutting off a man's leg. It's wrong. This is not life, a man should not be like this. It's . . . wrong."

Sam said a bunch of something.

Flat Dog heard the words but he didn't regard them. At the end he asked one question. "So Gideon will use a crutch for . . . however long he lives?"

"No, he'll wear a peg."

Flat Dog made a gesture of complete bewilderment. Sam got a piece of driftwood, held his own foot to his butt, and mimicked walking on a peg. "He'll strap it to his leg with a leather belt."

Flat Dog understood, but . . .

They drank coffee for a while. Coy lay with his head on his front paws and made pathetic eyes at them. Finally, Flat Dog said, "My uncle told me something. Life is a butterfly, delicate and beautiful. You cup it in your hand gently, but it is always ready to fly. Your life is an opportunity to dance with it. If you grab it, though, you'll kill it. When it wants to fly, you must watch it wing away and love its beauty."

Sam studied Flat Dog for a moment. "Say that another way."

Flat Dog shrugged. "It is a good day to die."

WHEN HE WOKE up the next morning, Sam realized he was wondering if Flat Dog was still there. Two or three times during the night he'd dreamed that he woke up and his friend was gone forever.

Flat Dog sat up in his blankets.

Sam grinned crookedly at him. Coy went to him to get his head petted.

Jackson called the men together. The stolen horses belonged, he said, most of them, to the Ashley-Smith company. The twenty-one that came back, fourteen belonged to the firm. Sam would get Paladin back, and because of his job on the surgery, a horse to replace Pinto. Beckwourth and Flat Dog would get back the two horses they started with, plus one each for their good work in recovering the mounts. The rest belonged to Ashley-Smith.

"Now you, Morgan, Beckwourth, Flat Dog, I have to ask you. We need all the horses for the moment, to carry the equipment."

"And carry Gideon," Sam put in.

Jackson acknowledged that with a nod.

Gideon still kept his head down, as though he didn't see or hear a thing.

"Is that all right?"

Sam spoke up. "I'm not easy with Paladin being used as a pack horse."

Jackson thought on that. Then he said, "How about if she's the one drags Gideon? With you beside her?"

Sam pondered, then nodded yes.

The rest of the day was given to sending men back to the cache, opening it, loading up the furs and as much other gear as the horses could carry, and getting back to the camp where they started. A lot of equipment got left in the cache, since they were short of horses.

The next morning they headed downriver toward rendezvous, slowly, like a one-legged bear. Sam thought, *Now we'll find out if Gideon can stand the travel, or withers away.*

WHERE THE BIG Sandy flowed into the Siskadee, below the Southern Pass, they came onto a huge and recent trail—two or three hundred horses, most of them shod. They knew it for what it was, Ashley's supply train, headed for rendezvous.

They camped that night at the river's mouth, where the general and his men had camped. The evening air was bright with possibility. A recent trail—maybe they could send ahead and get help from Ashley.

They were worn out. Their moccasins were in tatters from walking. Catch the Ashley crew in two or three days maybe, and in five days have horses back here. A chance to ride. This country wasn't for walking, and mountain men were critters that belonged on horseback. Let's *ride* into rendezvous.

Within the hour, before the coffee pots were empty, Jackson called them together and said what every man hoped to hear. He and Clyman would leave the next morning, catch up with Ashley, and get whatever mounts they could. At the very least the brigade would get a rest for a few days, and the horses too. Men exclaimed "Wagh!" and "Hoorah!"

Late that evening Sam and James Clyman were walking Gideon. For three or four days they'd exercised the bear man morning and evening, supporting him on both sides while he clomped along one-legged. "That big body has to have some exercise," Clyman had said. Coy pounced at the bottom of a sagebrush, maybe at a small critter the men didn't see.

Flat Dog and Beckwourth walked up. "We got a present for you," Jim told Gideon. Flat Dog took one hand out from behind his back and stuck whatever it was toward Gideon. For a moment Sam didn't realize . . . A crutch.

Sam grinned. Gideon groaned.

"Maybe not today," Beckwourth said, "and maybe not tomorrow, but soon."

Gideon groaned again.

Beckwourth flashed his toothy grin at Sam. "You two are going to have to coach our friend through his healing."

Sam looked at them, puzzled.

"We're going to meet my village on the Big Horn," said Flat Dog.

"Him and this child both," said Beckwourth.

"Do the big buffalo hunt. See my family."

Sam felt betrayed.

"We'll be back for rendezvous."

"Late, maybe, but we'll be there," said Jim. "We got six weeks before it's supposed to start."

They smiled like they were keeping secrets. It pissed Sam off.

Noting the forlorn expression on Sam's face, Beckwourth said, "Six weeks isn't long."

When dark fell, Sam lay in his blankets rubbing Coy's belly and wondering if it was the amputation. For sure Flat Dog had a hard time with Sam's cutting off a limb, the idea of Gideon being a cripple.

Or maybe Flat Dog had just seen enough of white men.

The red man and the black man were gone the next morning before anyone else woke up.

Part Eight

RENDEZVOUS

Chapter Twenty-Nine

THE FIRST COUPLE of days Sam wandered around the rendezvous site half-addled, missing Flat Dog, and brooding about his situation.

A year ago he'd left rendezvous to go on a raid to get the horses he needed to win his woman. Since then, he'd gotten the horses, and lost them. Gained the woman he loved, and lost her. He'd gotten his best friend killed, Blue Medicine Horse. He'd lost another friend, Third Wing. He'd lost everything he owned, even his clothes, every stitch and every single possession except the knife he kept hidden in his hair.

He'd gone through a powerful ceremony, the sun dance, which at the time made him feel like a Crow forever. Now he was banished from the Crows.

"Pup, I'm still broke." The spring hunt he'd counted on had gone bust when the Blackfeet got the horses. He had very few plews to trade to Ashley-Smith here at rendezvous. If he wanted to trap on his own in the coming season, he'd need to use those plews to get powder and lead, and trade goods for the Indians. He couldn't afford a pack mule or two, a pistol, a capote, a keg to carry water, a tomahawk, a throwing knife . . . Hell, he couldn't even dream up a list of all the things he needed and couldn't afford.

"I don't want to hire back on with the company. Feels like a comedown." True, they provided you an outfit, and offered the safety of numbers. The price was, you trapped where they decided to trap, you took orders, you wintered where the brigade leader chose, and at the end of the year you paid Ashley half your catch for the privilege.

"But we need an outfit. It's safety. That sticks in my craw."

He rubbed Coy's ears and murmured again, "Safety." Sam was glad, sometimes, to think that if he lost his hair, Coy would still be fine.

"Here it is, even bigger. I'm not white and not Indian, not any longer." The beaver hunters he ran with, well, he fit in well enough with that motley crew. If you sat down to trade stories with a dozen of them, like as not four would be American backwoodsmen, three French-Canadians who were more than half Indian themselves, two Spanyards from Taos who were also half Indian, two Iroquois or Delawares, and maybe one mulatto. What man of any color could be left out of a rainbow battalion like that?

"I'm changed." Changed beyond the braid he wore his white hair in, his breechcloth, his moccasins. He had the Indian's soft way of walking now, the careless but proud stance, the ever-watchful, ever-moving eyes. He would feel more at home at a Crow dance than a Christian church. To him the sacred pipe wafting its smoke up to Father Sky had as much power as the Bible, or more. "And my heart belongs to a Crow woman."

He pulled on his chin. "I am a cast-out."

He jolted himself out of his mood. "Hey, we're here to relax."

The general had brought them into rendezvous a month early. In the mountains you never knew. Early, late—it depended on whether the plains decided to rain on you, or hail, or fill every gully with swift water and flood every river out of its banks, so you could find no ford and had to wait. It depended on whether the mountains decided to bring another snow or two, and block the passes. It depended on whether the Indians ran your horses off and left you no way to haul the treasured supplies to the men who craved them.

Since few mountain men were in camp, Sam decided to spend most of each day working with Paladin. He wanted to learn that trick Hannibal did, jump off one side of the horse, hit the ground, and bound up and over to the ground on the other side, then repeat until you wanted back into the saddle. Now that might impress some Indians, who were the best horsemen in the world.

He also set his mind on teaching the mare a little circle dance. He would have her go forward in a curvet, a leap where the hind legs left the ground just before the forelegs hit; then she would sidle sideways, curtsey, rear, turn, and prance back to him, flashing her forelegs high. She would go sun-wise, what white folks called clockwise, because that was the way everything should go. He could awe Indians with this trick, he thought. The Medicine Horse dance, he would call it, in honor of his friend.

He also decided to try to teach Coy a somersault. If Coy learned that, he might be able to learn to do it on Paladin's back. Hey, a fellow had to have some fun.

Sam talked Gideon into crutching over to the training ring with him. As Sam circled Paladin around the ring, Gideon yelled out encouragement, orders, or curses, depending on his mood. Coy watched, envious of the attention. Which meant he would give good attention to learning his own tricks.

After about a week Sam, Gideon, and Paladin wearied of the training, and Cache Valley began to fill with friends.

Two long hunting seasons since the 1825 rendezvous, two long hunts on the remote creeks with only a few companions and the wily beaver for company. These fur hunters were hungry for human faces and lots of talk. Rendezvous meant gossip, stories, and news. It meant a chance to hand over plews for needed supplies. It meant the raw taste of whiskey (Ashley had kept his promise), the sharp-sweet taste of coffee with sugar (lusted after almost as much). It meant a chance to buy new flints, powder, and lead. It meant tobacco, for chewing, smoking, and trading to the Indians. It meant everything else a coon needed to make himself welcome in an Indian village, especially the foofuraw the squaws loved.

This second rendezvous also offered something new, two circles of lodges of Snake Indians, or Shoshones, as they called themselves. Sam shook his head. Twice he'd had trouble with these Indians, and he'd lost a friend to them, Third Wing. But other trappers had made peace with them, and the Snakes had apparently decided to be friends. So be it.

Sam recognized a trapper sitting on a big slab of sandstone. This man was carrying on activity seldom seen among the mountain men, writing.

Sam clapped him on the shoulder and sat down. Coy tried to lick the man's paper, and he jerked it away.

"Potts. Glad to see you've got your hair." They'd spent a winter together in Rides Twice's village, the winter of '24, Sam in Jedediah's camp, Potts with Captain Weber's outfit.

Daniel Potts looked Sam in the face. "I've heard you lost yours a couple of times."

Sam laughed. The story of his walking seven hundred miles down the Platte River, and other stories, weren't going to get smaller over time. The added story of Third Wing demanding Sam's white hair in turn for releasing him—that tickled the men.

He eyed the pen, ink, and paper enviously. "You write down stories like that?"

"I'm writing my brother Robert," said Potts. "I make the life out here sound good."

"It is good," said Sam.

"A mite more dangerous than I make out," said Potts, and they shared a chuckle. "I can get poetic. Listen to this. I'm telling about Cache Valley:

"This valley has been our chief place of rendezvous and wintering ground. Numerous streams fall in through this valley, which, like the others, is surrounded by stupendous mountains, which are unrivalled for beauty and serenity of scenery."

Sam couldn't resist. "Well, here at the first of June, it is full of waters. Come August, that will be a different story." They laughed. Every man had seen the sere grasses that covered most of plains and valleys of the West during the summer and fall. Each plop of a horse's foot threw dust up to where you had to breathe it.

Potts gave Sam a merry eye and read on: "You here have a view of all the varieties, plenty of ripe fruit, an abundance of grass just springing up, and buds beginning to shoot, while the higher parts of the mountains are covered with snow, all within 12 or 15 miles of this valley."

This time Potts corrected himself, grinning. "That fruit, well, the berries will be ripe in August. The grass is coming on strong, that's the truth, and the snow will last on the mountains another couple of weeks yet."

He read. "The river passes through a small range of mountains and enters the valley that borders on the Great Salt Lake."

He raised both eyebrows comically at Sam. "Which is a lake so salty that nothing grows in it or around it, you couldn't irrigate with it, and it will kill you if you drink it."

Sam had heard all about the Salt Lake—everybody had—from Jim Bridger and Etienne Provost at the last rendezvous. Dared to go down the Bear River, Bridger went alone and found a body of water that tasted like pure salt. Everybody decided lucky Jim had come on the Pacific Ocean. Only when Provost saw the far shore, later, did the word spread of a huge, salt, inland lake.

"You been there?"

Sam shook his head no. Coy whined at the very thought.

"It's one crazy piece of lake, hoss. You can roll yourself up in a ball and bob up and down in the waves like a cork. You stand up and hold out your arms like Jesus on the Cross, and the water props you up. You can make any design with your body and hold it—you'll never sink."

"Jedediah said he wants to circle in a boat and find the outlet."

"Yeah, the outlet, that's the thing. That river probably leads right to California. That's what the maps say—Ashley calls it the Buenaventura. How'd you like that, coon?"

Something flickered in Sam's mind. California . . . Coy squealed, *Mmnn, mmnn, mmnn.*

Sam regarded Potts. "So how come, when you write your brother, you just don't tell him the way this place is?"

"Don't you see, hoss? This ain't like no other place. It's bigger, uglier, more beautiful, higher, drier, more dangerous, more of a kick in the ass . . . Wagh! We got grizzly bears bigger and meaner than ten of their panthers back home. We got mountains make theirs look like pillows. We got deserts even the A-rabs can't imagine. And you know what? The books say Californy's got trees a thousand years old, as tall as the clouds, and wide enough at the bottom to build a whole town in.

"Not to mention we got boiling springs where the Old Gentleman hisself lives just under the surface, and hot water fountains that shoot two hundred feet high.

"Hell, you can't tell the plain truth about this place—no one would believe it."

SMALL PARTIES OF men continued to wander in, about half of them Ashley men, half free trappers. The date set for rendezvous was July 1, but most men arrived early.

Sam and Gideon spent the days catching up with friends. Sam accompanied Gideon wherever the big man was willing to walk on his crutch. Mostly they walked from mess fire to mess fire, and there were plenty. Ashley and Jedediah had combined their outward-bound parties, about a hundred of them and twice as many horses and mules carrying thousands of dollars worth of goods—$30,000 Ashley claimed, as much as half a dozen ordinary office clerks, for instance, would earn in a lifetime.

Of the fur hunters, fifty were into rendezvous already, both Ashley men and free trappers. Ashley said half of his men were still out, and was willing to bet a cup of whiskey they'd end up with a hundred trappers and two or three times that many Indians. As he spoke, his eyes turned into gold coins.

Hundreds of animals, both American horses and Snake ponies, meant the camps were well spread out along the river, and the horses and mules herded even further out.

As Gideon hobbled from mess fire to mess fire, Sam and Coy kept him company. The big man ate and ate and ate—buffalo was plenty. With good food and old friends he seemed to be regaining his zest for life.

The trouble was, Sam was losing his. He didn't know why. Rendezvous wasn't fun. Or not yet.

Catching up with the news was the good part. Who had gone where, discovered what river flowing which direction, who'd come on Indians and fought 'em and made 'em come. Who'd lost his hair, who'd rode up a cold, winding creek and was never seen again. Who took a squaw. Who got a squaw, bought her all the foorfuraw she could wear, and had her run off. Who'd got how many packs of beaver, and where.

Beyond the news and the tales of what happened where, a new kind of story reared its head, the yarn, what some might call stretchers. Though these yarns might not be strictly accurate, they were something bigger and handsomer and more captivating—they went beyond the facts to truth.

Jim Bridger seemed to be the best storyteller. In fact, Sam saw the young Jim, who bore a bad reputation after the Hugh Glass incident, had developed considerable regard among his fellow trappers. Sam liked the fellow himself. He had a slow way of walking and a slow way of talking, an easy geniality, a serious face that hid a love of fun, and a world of pull-your-leg humor.

Bridger told one story, for instance, about a place he called Echo Canyon. Big canyon it was, so it had a big echo. Why, it took eight hours for a shout on this side to make the trip across and bounce back. So the booshway used the canyon as an alarm clock. At night when the men rolled up in their blankets, he walked the edge and hollered, "Wake up! It's time! Time to get up!"

Eight hours later, sure enough, here come the echo back—"Wake up! It's time! Time to get up!" And the boys rolled out slick.

Everybody's favorite, though, was Bridger's grizzly bear tale. "One evenin' I come back into camp soaking wet, clothes scratched and torn, no pants nor breechclout on my hind end.

" 'What happened, Gabe?' the boys asked, worried there might be Indians around.

"I was down along the river, and maybe I got between a sow and her cubs. Anyhow, all of a sudden, here comes a monster silvertip roarin' out of the willows right at me, a geyser of plenty pissed off.

"I dropped my rifle and scooted up a tree. But this old griz, she walks up, gives that tree a true *bear* hug, and tears 'er plumb out by the roots.

"Whooee. I got throwed and didn't know where I'd come to earth. Lucky, it was right in river. Quick I takes off downstream, swimming fast as a fish. That silvertip, though, she was *some*. She jumps in after me, and right quick, hell, I see she's catchin' up fast.

"Now I begin to hear a big roar—the falls is coming. I got to get out! Drop my pistol, off with my leggings, and splash hard toward the far bank. There I flop out on the shore and am catchin' my breath when what do I smell? Griz breath. She's clambering right up next to me.

"I dive back in. No hope but one, I decide, and that the same as none. It's either Old Ephraim's teeth and claws or—the falls!

"Swoosh! Out over the edge I sail, all mixed up in water and sky at once, and breathin' both.

"Smack! I hit that pool at the bottom, and underwater I go, held down on slimy rocks in the pounding falls by a current that's stronger'n any bear in this world. How I got up to the surface I'll never know, and when I did, I still couldn't breathe. The smack skedaddled my breath far, far away.

"Then finally comes one breath, and while this child is just a gulpin' air, he looks up and sees, and sees . . . I couldn't believe my eyes. There was Madam Silvertip soaring over the edge of them falls, heading straight down on top of me.

"I made lickety-split for the bank. Things was looking bad, though. If that griz wanted me bad enough to come over them falls . . ."

He shook his head in hopelessness.

"On the bank I decided to make my stand once and for all. I took out my butcher knife" (here he set himself in a knife-fighting stance) "and faced my tormentor.

"Straight at me she comes, fast and fierce. Boys, I . . ."

He shook his head and shivered, like the memory still haunted him.

"What happened, Jim?" some eager soul would usually say. "What happened?"

"That bear, she killed me and et me."

NEW OUTFITS CAME in, led by Provost, Weber, Sublette, and Fitzpatrick. Sam greeted old friends, and one man who seemed to be both friend and foe: Micajah. Sam shook his hand with a wary smile. Micajah pretended like he was about to use the grip to throw Sam over, but then he laughed and walked away.

As everyone got into camp, times got better. Ashley took the bungs out of more whiskey kegs. Trading got furious. Snake women got friendly. And the games got riotous. Every kind of physical competition, running, jumping, racing, wrestling, target shooting, and several kinds of card games. Anything one man could best another in and win a dollar.

Gideon started having fun at the shooting competitions. He couldn't hold a rifle—one hand was required for his crutch—but he was a first-rate shot with a pistol. Several times he challenged men with rifles to one-on-one shoots and beat them. Though Sam was worried that Gideon didn't have enough plews to get much more powder, he said nothing. These shoots were the first spark of life in his friend.

The evenings grew spirited, too. Fiddles came out, including Gideon's. Every kind of tune sashayed through the long twilights, and mountain men and Indian women stepped lively to the tunes. They drank many a toast to lift the merriment, and often as not headed for the willows to top it off with a little sport.

Sam noticed uneasily that Micajah got drunk every night. The giant knew that he was steady when sober, crazy when drunk. But he took a notion: In the mountains, he said, there wasn't enough whiskey for a man to be a drunk, so when the chance came, he might as well indulge freely. Twirling a slight Snake girl, Micajah saw Sam staring at him. "Oh, take it back to the States, Morgan," he shouted. "You're worse'n a preacher."

Later, spinning another girl, Micajah called, "Come on, Sam, kick up your heels. Get out here and have some fun." He even brought the girl over and joined her hand to Sam's. But Sam felt a spasm of self-disgust. The hand wasn't Meadowlark's.

Sam wasn't ready for fun. He was stuck in what he couldn't forget. Sometimes he mulled on Blue Medicine Horse's death. Sometimes Third Wing's. Sometimes he couldn't help staring at Gideon, crippled, a fiddler who would never dance again. Every night, in the wee hours when the dark world hovered near, he thought bitterly of Meadowlark.

Meadowlark, wife of Red Roan.

He recalled, deliberately, movement by movement, what he and Meadowlark had done during their honeymoon in his tipi. Then he recounted the same movements, postures, caresses, smiles, joinings, and in place of himself he inserted the form of Red Roan.

He didn't like himself for that.

As he often did when he didn't like himself, he took Coy for a walk. Sometimes they talked, too. This time Sam didn't feel the need to say anything. By the brittle moonlight they walked up a hill overlooking the camp. The hill was steep and the climb a breath-stealer—somehow it felt right to do something hard.

From the top Sam looked out over rendezvous. The dark blobs were people, or bushes, depending on size, or trees. The shiny threads were creeks. The red-gold glows were campfires, probably with men sitting around them, sipping coffee and trading stories. Off to the left rose the tipis of the Shoshone camp. The low fires inside made the lodge covers glow, cones of light in the wilderness. It seemed a grand sight.

Sam sat and rubbed Coy's head for a long time. Men, women, and children were in those tipis. Families.

THE TALK ACROSS the fires in the mornings was that General Ashley was leaving the business. He was selling out to a new firm, Smith, Jackson, and Sublette, made up of three top brigade leaders. In four years, Ashley had gone from deeply in debt to owner of a bonanza in furs, 12,000 pounds of peltries worth five dollars a pound, if he could get them safely to St. Louis. Now the General intended to spend some time in Missouri enjoying his wealth. He would bring supplies to rendezvous, but no more. Some men said he intended to run for governor. It was left to Jedediah Smith, David Jackson, and William Sublette to explore, trap, venture, struggle, and make or lose the next fortune in beaver pelts.

"Sam?" Gideon's voice. Sam was training Paladin, which took full concentration. "The cap'n requires your attention." Diah was standing there waiting. An anarchist in spirit, Gideon always spoke titles like they were silly.

Sam put the mare on a lead and walked over to talk to his friend. Jedediah was all business. "I'm going out to the southwest, to look for beaver. You want to come?"

Sam considered his poverty. *But damn it, I like to be on my own.* Since he had only half an outfit, though, he might have to sign on with the new firm.

"We'll be a score of men. You're a good trapper." Jedediah didn't use phrases like, "You know what way the stick floats." He also didn't often say much that was personal, about himself or others. Sam supposed Diah's few words were a high compliment.

The offer had a lot behind it. Sam knew Jedediah had traveled northwest, clear to Flathead Post and back. He'd been straight west across the Snake River Plains, a starving country. Now southwest, searching for beaver, or maybe trying to fill in the blanks on his maps, or maybe just giving in to the urge to see new country, any new country, anywhere.

"I'll think on it."

Jedediah turned, accepting that as answer enough for right now.

"What about the cripple?" said Gideon. "You have any job, it's a very humdinger for a cripple?"

Jedediah looked at Gideon, perched on a block of sandstone. "Poor Boy, my prayers are that you'll be fine. You'll ride into the next rendezvous. Maybe you'll even be wading into cold creeks again."

"You Americans, you are sentimental," said Gideon. But his tone was soft.

Sam led Paladin back into the training ring, musing. Diah's invitation was a surprise. Sam would listen to the camp talk. What did Diah really have in mind? It really might be new territory for the new firm to trap. To the northwest, Oregon was jointly held with the British, and the Hudson's Bay Company was doing all it could to keep the American fur hunters out. To the southwest a few miles was Mexican territory, and few beaver men hunted there.

But, then, Jedediah might be thinking of California. If he was, he wouldn't say so.

The world had heard report of the golden clime from the British and American sailors who visited those shores. The tales were glowing. Flowers bloomed and crops grew twelve months a year. The Indian and Mexican women were alluring. The country was beautiful, the mountains magnificent, the rivers mighty. Maybe a young, disenchanted, lonely American could start fresh in California.

ON A DAY just beyond the solstice, it is long twilight of summer evening. The sun drops behind western mountains, but its light lingers in the world, gentle as a lover's fingers stroking long hair. Snake women ghost through the camp. Some of them wear the finery their husbands have traded for, or they themselves have accepted graciously from trappers for their love.

Sam sits on a rock braiding a quirt from deer hide thongs. Paladin wouldn't take to a quirt, but Sam can trade it to some trappers for something he needs, like a patch knife. A fetching young woman walks past, smiles at Sam with a hint of coquetry, and hesitates. It's modest enough behavior, but for a Shoshone woman provocative.

Coy eyes her suspiciously. Sam strokes his head and watches the young woman walk on toward the circle where the fiddler is tuning up for the evening's fun. She's young enough to be unmarried, but old enough to have a husband. He'll probably never know. Since she's all dolled up, though, he knows how the evening will end for her. Not with him. He's not interested. He wishes he were.

Her scent wafts back to him on the evening breeze, and makes him miss Meadowlark even more.

Paladin whickers. Maybe Paladin wants to mate. If her time comes while they're at rendezvous, Sam will pick out the best stallion he sees and breed her.

This is his family, a horse and a coyote, missing a woman. Missing *the* woman.

The evening air seems special. The world pauses in a moment of perfection and holds its breath, forgetful of tomorrow. A mouth harp lifts a tune into this lucent tranquility. A moment later a fiddle joins it. The men will soon abandon their meals or games for dancing.

Gideon's voice clamors loud and jangly over the music.

Sam stands up and looks. A hundred yards away Gideon is pivoting around on his crutch and yelling at some irritant. Sam peers hard, and sees who the irritant seems to be—Micajah.

Quickly, Sam leads Paladin that way. Gideon's half crazy these days, and. . . . Yes, Gideon and Micajah swore eternal friendship at the last rendezvous, and they even included Sam—three-way eternal amity. Gideon and Micajah did it with the traditional rite of shooting the cups off each other's head. But Sam feels uneasy. Has Micajah really forgotten the fight at the Crow village, two falls out of three, when Gideon outwitted him? Has Micajah really forgotten the time in Evansville when he and his brother Elijah tried to rob Abby, Grumble, and Sam, and Elijah ended up dead?

When Sam gets there, maybe the shouting is over. Sam restakes Paladin. In front of a group of men, Micajah is circling Gideon, who pivots on his crutch. "You are right, I admit," says Gideon in a placating tone. He holds a pistol out to Micajah. "You are right. You beat me."

Micajah stops, looking at Gideon. His eyes are . . . calming down. He nods. He walks up and takes the offered pistol, then sticks it in Gideon's belt. "You done an honest mistake," he says, and offers his hand. Gideon shakes it.

"Besides," said Micajah, "I never forget." He steps to one of the on-lookers and takes a whiskey jug. He takes a swig. "You, me, and Morgan—we are friends forever. I drink to it—the three of us, comrades." He takes another swig.

Then he strides over to Gideon and offers the jug. "Come on out here, Sam," calls Micajah, "and drink with us."

Gideon swigs. Sam goes out, Coy following reluctantly. Handed the jug, Sam swigs.

"Sir Samuel Morgan," Micajah cries, "it is time that you made the pledge of friendship yourself. This time *you* will shoot with me. Off my head you will shoot the cup of whiskey."

Sam can't tell if Micajah is half-drunk or just acting that way. *Probably drunk by decision rather than inebriation,* he thinks. He looks at Gideon and shakes his head no.

"No," shouts Gideon, "Sam is not that kind of man. Sir Samuel does not stoop to vulgar games."

"Friendship," cries Micajah. "We must renew our pledges of friendship."

"We will, pledges of friendship. You and I will shoot, and Sam is included by . . . tradition." Gideon grins crookedly at Sam. Sam thinks maybe he suspects trouble. But right now maybe Gideon welcomes trouble. Will he accept, with a Gallic shrug, a quick death?

"We will," exults Micajah. "Friendship."

Micajah struts off and takes a mock shooting position.

Sam mind screams at him, *You're only guessing.* Nevertheless, he says quietly to Gideon, "Don't do it."

"It is well," says the big Frenchy, and winks at him.

"Gideon . . ."

But Gideon walks away. *You crazy bastard . . .*

"I show my complete trust in you," cried Micajah, "by giving you the first shot. I insist that you, my friend, shoot first." He takes a tin cup from one man, a whiskey jug from another, and fills the cup. Delicately, he sets it on his head. "Shoot the cup," he says pointing. Then he puts his finger in the middle of his forehead and chuckles madly. "Not the flesh."

Coy trots to the group of men near Micajah. *That's odd,* thinks Sam, but he follows.

Gideon pours powder into his pan. With an extravagantly careless gesture, he brings his pistol level and fires, Wham! The sound slaps Sam in the face.

The cup flies off Micajah's head. He licks whiskey off his face with mock lust.

Now Gideon puts a cup on his own head and takes a jaunty pose.

"No," Sam mouths futilely.

Micajah wheels, plants his rifle butt between his feet, leans on the muzzle, and launches into oratory. "I first saw this feat performed," he says, "by the mountaineer's only competitor as the greatest frontiersman, the keelboaters of the Ohio. Half-horse, half-alligators they call themselves, and by God they are. Those men eat ten Injuns for breakfast and use their bones for toothpicks. They shoot the cup to bond together, a way of saying, 'We are brothers.'

"I first performed it with my older brother, Elijah." Micajah puts his head down, maybe remembering. Sam wonders . . . But all Micajah says is, "I miss him still. I have broken many of the commandments," he goes on, "but one commandment I hold sacred, the eleventh. A man shall be true to his friend. In that spirit I shoot."

Coy howls something to the skies.

Micajah primes his pan, lifts his rifle, and makes elaborate gestures of getting comfortable. At last, as he settles the barrel into position, Sam sees what he fears. A look of low cunning, peppered with blood lust, warps Micajah's face. It is unmistakable. Micajah cocks. His finger pressures the trigger.

Sam leaps forward. His hand knocks Micajah's barrel upwards.

At the same instant, Blam! The muzzle spits death.

Sam twists his neck toward Gideon, heart hollering that he has been too late.

The bear man stands, and the cup rests undisturbed on his head.

Slap! The open-handed blow knocks Sam to the ground.

Coy rushes Micajah, growling and barking. The big man kicks Coy in the belly, and the coyote goes tumbling.

Sam uses the moment to get to his feet. "I saw what you were going to do . . ."

"Bastard," shouts Micajah.

"You were going to . . ."

Gideon is crutching toward them. A dozen men crowd close.

Micajah roars and lunges at Sam. A dozen hands restrain him.

Sam appeals to the crowd. "You all saw it, that look on Micajah's face. He was going to . . ."

"Reading a man's heart in his face, that's pretty tricky." The voice is a soft drawl, Jim Bridger's.

Sam appeals to Gideon. "Didn't you see it?"

Gideon shrugs.

"I am INSULTED!" Micajah roars to the skies.

Bridger looks around. "What do y'all think?"

Some say the insult was bad, damned bad. Others say young Morgan was sincere. No one says he saw what Micajah was about to do.

"Morgan," says Bridger, "maybe you ought to apologize."

"Never on this earth," says Sam. "He was about to kill my friend."

Micajah roars again, and then with words shouts, "I'll beat an apology out of you."

"Let 'em fight," someone says.

"Yeah, let 'em fight."

"May the honest man win."

One hand keeping Micajah back, Bridger holds Sam's eyes. "Maybe you should."

"It's not a fair fight," says Gideon. When he had two legs, Gideon was probably the only man in camp who might whip Micajah bare-handed.

"The man who's right will win," says a voice.

"True, that's the way of it," someone else says.

Bridger still looks at Sam. Sam nods.

"No weapons," says Bridger.

With preening movements, Micajah hands his rifle to another man, puts his pistol beside it, flings down his butcher knife, and sets down his hunting pouch, which probably has a patch knife in it.

"Morgan?"

"You see I have no weapons," says Sam, holding his arms out. That's almost true.

"There will be no killing here tonight," says Bridger. "This is a fight of honor, to see who is telling the truth. No gouging of eyes. Everything else goes. When one man can't go on, the fight is over."

Grunts and nods indicate that satisfies most onlookers.

"Break 'ees arm, ze interferer, zat will show him," cries someone.

Arm? Sam wonders if he'll escape with his life.

He gets onto the balls of his feet, ready. *Right now his mind, heart, feet, sinew—all of me must be a war.*

The last of the light has dwindled. A gibbous moon is enough to cast shadows. Blackness infiltrates everywhere, including men's minds.

FIRST COMES A bull charge. Sam waits until the last moment, side-steps, and flicks a kick at Micajah's head. His foot feels bone, and he smiles.

Micajah gets up rubbing his shoulder. The charge wasn't serious, the kick maybe more than Micajah expected.

Micajah belts out a war cry, sprints at Sam, leaps into the air, and kicks with both feet.

Sam rolls sideways. One of the heavy boots clips his head. For a moment he's dizzy.

Micajah, having caught his fall with one arm, is on his feet and launches himself in a huge flop toward Sam. Sam rolls. One of his arms gets caught.

But Micajah bounces a little, and Sam snatches the arm away.

Quick as can be, Sam jumps on Micajah's back, gets a forearm on his neck, and cranks it tight with the other hand.

Micajah's neck muscles are so strong that Sam is not getting a choke. Micajah lumbers to his feet, pauses mightily, and hurls himself onto his back.

Sam barely pushes himself clear, rolls, and comes up on his feet.

Avoiding is not enough. Attack.

Voices cry encouragement, mostly to Micajah. Despite one voice, Gideon's, Sam feels the blood lust of the mob. Coy is howling piteously.

Sam decides to try something wildly unexpected. He charges Micajah, head lowered, intending to leap at the last moment and head-bash Micajah's face.

The giant lithely drops onto his back, raises his legs, catches Sam on his feet and hurls him straight the way he's going.

Sailing over, Sam thinks he sees Micajah's hand go to his boot, but he's not sure.

Sam rolls through the weeds, rages back, and launches a head kick.

Micajah's hand flicks, the kick is deflected, and Sam lands on his back. Oddly, Sam's calf is cut.

"A knife!" Gideon hollers. "He has a knife!"

"Don't see that," says Bridger.

Sam can't see one either.

Micajah hurls himself through the air at the prone Sam. In the moonlight something in Micajah's hand flashes.

Sam rolls. Something slashes his ribs.

Quickly, Sam rolls straight back into Micajah. *Inside the knife,* he screams at himself. *Stay inside the knife.*

He gets a wild idea.

Micajah rolls on top of Sam, and Sam lets it happen.

Sam blocks the knife arm with one hand. The bodies are too close. Micajah drops the knife and goes for the choke with both hands.

The choke is terrible. Sam will never get breath again. *Be quick or die.*

He jerks the small, sharp blade out of his hair ornament and stabs Micajah's throat.

The choke still holds.

Sam rams the blade deep into the throat and slams it home with the palm of his hand. It almost disappears, even the handle, into the thick flesh.

Micajah gouts blood into Sam's face.

Bridger and another man roll Micajah off Sam.

Sam breathes. He breathes again. The second time he inhales blood and blows it back out.

He rolls over and vomits into the dust. He breathes. He vomits, and does both again.

Bridger picks up the knife Micajah dropped and inspects it. He waits for Sam to come back to this world. Gideon squats beside them with the help of the crutch.

Sam looks up into their faces.

"I'm sorry. My fault," Bridger says. "You are *some*."

Jim stands up. He calls to everyone, "Sam Morgan has won in a fair fight. Does any man say otherwise?"

Silence.

"Micajah drew the knife first. Everyone see it the same?"

Three or four yesses trot out.

"Then I say, by the rule of the mountains, Sam gets ever'thing Micajah owns. Rifle, pistol, horses, ever'thing."

Bridger walks off. The dancing has started, and the other men head for that. In the mountains, blood doesn't stop the fun.

Sam props up on his elbows and looks into Micajah's horrible face. He tells Gideon, "I'll bury him in the morning."

"Zat will be taken care of," says Gideon.

Sam sits up.

"We should get to the river," says Gideon.

Two half-wrecked men, one on a crutch, support each other in painful steps to the water. One coyote skitters along behind. Sam splashes into the shallows and lies face down. After a moment he looks into Gideon's face and says, "Who the hell am I?"

"A good man," says Gideon.

But Sam doesn't seem to hear. "Who the hell am I?"

Coy howls, maybe asking the same question.

Chapter Thirty

SAM SHOOK HIMSELF awake. He was lying face down, near his blankets but not on them. He sat up and brushed the dust off his face. He looked across at Gideon, lying tidily on his blankets, eyes taking Sam in. "I have blood and dust caked on my face?"

"Just dust."

"I better get to the water and wash off."

"I am been dreaming of last night."

"Me too." All night Sam had dreamt slivers and slashes of the fight. It gave him the chills.

He grimaced. Some sort of low, lower than Sam Morgan ever intended to get. A life where you fight with your fellow trapper, he tries to kill you, and you do kill him. Self-disgust flared up in Sam's belly like bile.

"Sam," came the voice. Horses' hooves thumped.

Sam realized now that this was what had woken him up, this thumping. He saw movement behind a nearby sagebrush. Several horses and . . .

Beckwourth came out from behind the bush. "Good to see you, hoss."

Sam stood slowly, looked gladly into the face of his black friend, and clapped him on the shoulders. He nearly felt teary. Beckwourth laughed.

"I got a present for Gideon."

He brought his hand out from behind his back.

It was a peg leg. A wooden peg a couple of feet long, glowing with oil. A wooden bowl on top of the peg. Attached to that, a thick rawhide strap about half a foot high, long enough to wrap around twice, and with thongs to tie it.

Gideon crawled toward it. "You made this?"

"We did," said Flat Dog, stepping out from behind the horses. "A man who can make an arrow shaft smooth and straight can make a peg smooth and straight."

Sam clapped Flat Dog on both shoulders, and Flat Dog clapped Sam back. He felt dizzy—dizzy with pleasure, with change, with the whirl of the world . . .

"I got a present for Sam," said Flat Dog, holding an arm out.

Out from behind the horses stepped Meadowlark, beaming.

SAM WANTED TO borrow a tent instantly. She insisted on walking with him to the river and cleaning him up. They didn't talk. Words wouldn't carry what needed to be said. Stories could fill in the gaps later.

She insisted on putting up the small lodge she'd brought.

Sam and Meadowlark disappeared into the lodge and stayed all day. They discovered themselves again as lovers. As friends. As husband and wife.

After an hour or two, words overflowed like streams in the spring. Every tale of every struggle over three months of separation got told, at least in part. Still, the silences said more than the talk. Then words would bubble forth again, froth and spray down the mountain of their feeling, and fall once more into deep, still pools.

She had one essential statement for him:

"I am your woman."

She saw the uncertainty in his face. "No man but you has ever touched me," she said.

He wept. They both wept. They held each other. They rolled all over the ground holding each other.

She also made sure that Sam understood that coming to rendezvous was her idea. "Flat Dog, he not so sure. I already decided, and was ready."

"I want to get married," said Sam.

Then he had to translate for her the white notion of marriage into the Crow language and the Crow way of seeing.

In the end she said, "A ceremony," and accepted gladly.

"A pledge to each other," said Sam.

They smiled deep into each other's eyes, both knowing that the real pledges had already been made. Sam's when he took Meadowlark to Ruby Hawk Valley. Meadowlark's when she fled her village to come to rendezvous.

Nevertheless, Meadowlark now said in English, "I will marry you."

Sam laughed. "Your English is way better."

In English she replied, "I live no with my family, live with Bell Rock two moons. He and Flat Dog teach me English."

Sam hugged her.

They didn't come out of the lodge until evening, and then they were famished.

Their last of feast of that day was hump ribs and friends.

GENERAL ASHLEY CAME to Sam and Meadowlark's fire the next evening when he got word, and accepted coffee.

It was quickly done. Yes, the General would perform the marriage ceremony.

"Congratulations to you both," he said.

Gideon pitched in. "Congratulations!" The big man's spirits had bounced upward since he got his peg leg. He'd stuffed the bowl with padding, wore it constantly, and had leaned a little weight on it. His friends encouraged him to try a few steps, but Gideon said the pain was still too great.

Then Sam took a chance. "Diah," he began tentatively, "may be offended that we don't ask him to do it. With the Bible."

Ashley nodded. "You don't want the solemnization of your vows to be over-solemn."

Sam was tickled. General Ashley had a way of putting things. "We want it to be a party."

"Day after tomorrow will be July the Fourth, Independence Day. Jedediah has decided to spend the day going to the cache and raising it. He's taking two others who don't like drunkenness." The General looked at the couple benevolently. "And I've already announced that the whiskey will be free that day."

Sam grinned. "That will make a party." Then he frowned. "I've never been in church, but my two sisters were married by the traveling preacher when he came around. They gave him five dollars. I'm going to have to owe you that."

"Your good work has given it to me a dozen times over."

"Day after tomorrow's good with you?" Sam asked Meadowlark in the Crow language.

"What does Independence Day mean?"

Sam explained briefly why it was a huge ceremony day for Americans.

She risked speaking in English. "It is good. By this ceremony, I no more depend on my father, mother." She said directly to Sam, "You tell me *all* about this ceremony."

Sam agreed.

"And it is two days from now," Meadowlark continued in her English. "Good. I need time to look my best."

THE NEXT MORNING, long after the usual hour for breakfast, they had a surprise visitor. Jedediah squatted in front of the coals. "May I have some coffee?"

Sam's heart sank. *Now we're going to get a lecture about the Good Book and how to be united in holy matrimony.* But he reached for the coffee pot, poured a round for everyone, and waited.

Diah threw Sam for a loop by addressing himself to Meadowlark.

"I want to say something to you in the strictest confidence. Strict for all of you," he added quickly to Flat Dog and Gideon. Again he addressed himself especially to Meadowlark. "Have you ever seen the Pacific Ocean?" Flat Dog translated it as big-water-everywhere-to-the-west.

Sam felt a flicker of irritation. Diah knew the answer to that one.

But Meadowlark gasped. "No."

"Would you like to?"

"I'd love to."

Sam was drop-jawed.

Jedediah ran his eyes around the circle. "How about the rest of you?"

They all said they would, even Gideon.

Diah turned back to Sam. "Then I want you to come with my brigade. We're going to California. But we're not telling anyone that. Not *anyone*."

Meadowlark gushed out, "Yes." Then she gave her husband a look that meant, I'll explain later.

Sam chimed in with another yes.

Flat Dog started to speak and stopped.

"I want you, too," said Diah.

"Yes." Flat Dog grinned.

"What about Beckwourth?" Sam put in.

The captain shook his head. "Captain Sublette has asked him to go with an outfit toward Blackfeet country. They expect it to be lively."

Jedediah plunged on. "I don't know how long we'll be gone. We may not find beaver in the dry country to the southwest. I'm told we'll find plenty in California." Sam wondered if Diah had learned that from the Britishers when he went to Flathead Post. "We don't know whether the Mexicans will make us welcome."

Sam reflected that dangers always seem an enticement to Jedediah.

"It's settled then?"

Sam couldn't believe it. Marriage and an adventure to California. His head spun. "It is," he said.

Flat Dog nodded.

Gideon said, "I want to go."

Jedediah looked at his peg leg.

Gideon hopped up on it. He caught his balance carefully and took his first steps, straight to Jedediah.

The obvious pain made even Jedediah flinch.

"I'll be able to ride," he said, "and you know this child can shoot."

Jedediah looked at the French-Canadian with a face drenched in sympathy.

"Poor Boy," he said, "we leave in one moon. If you can ride a horse then, you're hired."

The moment they were alone, Sam asked, "What did you want to tell me about the ocean?"

Meadowlark hesitated. "I dream about the water-everywhere-to-the-west. Often. In the dreams I dip myself into it, and the descend far, far down. I see strange and wonderful creatures . . ."

Sam grinned to bring them back into the light of day. "I'm wanting to jump into that thing myself. But not descend."

*   *   *

GENERAL ASHLEY HOLDS Diah's worn Bible open at his waist.

Sam waits in front of the General, looking back through the aisle created by the trappers. Behind him in the first row of onlookers is Jedediah Smith. Diah has hurried back from the cache to attend the wedding of his friend Sam. Next to Sam is his best man, Jim Beckwourth, also looking back.

At the end of the aisle stands Flat Dog, and on Flat Dog's arm is the love of Sam's life. The brother and sister have been persuaded that marching arm in arm is really the proper thing to do.

She is radiant. Sure of what she wanted, she spent weeks preparing to look splendid when she came to her husband. Her dress is made of two deer hides tanned very white, ornamented with bright beadwork on the cape and down the arms. The bodice sports a four winds wheel in the colors of the directions, red for east, yellow for south, black for west, and white for north, plus green for the earth and blue for the sky. The hem is fringed with bells that tinkle when she walks and will jingle-jangle when she dances. Her waist is girded by a wide belt woven of bright-colored yarns, the kind brought out from Taos, a special gift from Bell Rock and his wife. Ermine tails are wrapped around her braids, velvety white against glossy black, and her part is defined with a streak of vermilion. She has rouged her lips scarlet, and she wears a perfume she made herself from grasses, herbs, flower petals, and wild mint.

Gideon sits on a cottonwood log, peg sticking out jauntily, fiddle and bow in hand. Now he begins the entrance music he has asked to play. It is a traditional song of the Jewish people, based on a scripture from the *Song of Songs* and taught to him by his father. He puts the bow to the strings and lifts it into the air.

Flat Dog leads Meadowlark toward his friend, her husband. They do not walk but dance in the stately Crow ceremonial step, toe-heel, toe-heel.

Only Gideon knows the words to his song, and he sings them in his head.

You have ravished my heart, my bride,
Awake, north wind, and come, thou south!

Blow upon my garden that the spices thereof may flow out,
Let my beloved come into his garden and eat its pleasant fruits.

As he fiddles, he weeps.

Meadowlark arrives in front of the General. Jedediah nudges Sam and gives him a surprise, a small gold ring for her finger. "A gift from Ashley-Smith," he whispers.

Smiling tipsily, Ashley begins, "Dearly beloved, we are gazzered here together . . ."

Fitzpatrick and Clyman, standing close to this master of the ceremony, grin at each other and echo, "Gazzered."

Sam smiles merrily at Flat Dog.

Soon Ashley is saying something about "not by any to be entered into . . ."

"Entered into," says Fitz, "that's the thing."

". . . lightly, but reverently, discreetly, advisedly, soberly . . ."

"We're past that point," says Clyman.

"Wagh!" cry half a dozen drunken voices. "*Well* past."

The General cannot suppress a smile. ". . . Now speak or forever hold his peace . . ."

"I'll speak, by God. I want her for my own self." This is Beckwourth, the best man.

Ashley pushes forward, perhaps skipping sanctioned and esteemed passages. ". . . Forsaking all others, keep thee only unto her, so long as ye both shall live?"

Sam turns and looks fiercely into the eyes of his beloved. "I will," he roars.

Following Fitzpatrick's signal of a raised fist, fifty men holler, "Me, too!"

The General is blubbering with laughter.

Mercifully soon, he arrives at the point where he instructs Sam to say his crucial words.

First Sam holds up the ring for all to see. Then he shouts to the mountain tops, "With this ring I thee wed."

Meadowlark lets him put it on.

She says, "And I wed you."

Then she permits a kiss that is probably the most conspicuous public display of affection ever permitted by a Crow woman.

"What God hath joined together," announces Ashley, "let no man put asunder."

"Joins with Buffalo!" shouts Beckwourth. "Meadowlark!"

A dozen voices echo his cry. "Joins with Buffalo! Meadowlark!"

Gideon strikes up a another tune. This time it's "Mairi's Wedding." The newlyweds lead out and the whole company, whites, Frenchies, Spanyards, Delawares, Iroquois, and even some watching Shoshones dance behind them. The whites and Frenchies do jigs. The newlyweds and Indians dance with restraint, toe-heel, toe-heel. Some of the white men sing.

Step we gaily one we go, heel for heel and toe for toe,
Arm in arm and on we go, all for Mairi's wedding.
Cheeks are bright as rowans are, brighter far than any star,
Fairest of them all by far is my darling Mairi.

Around the fire they dance, across the buffalo grass, between the shrubs of sage, and on to Sam and Meadowlark's lodge.

Quick as a flash, the couple dashes in.

Beckwourth hollers, "I wonder what will happen in there."

He backs up, takes a run at the lodge, and scrambles right up the buffalo skins. Just as he starts slipping, he lunges and grabs a lodgepole sticking out of the smoke hole. He pulls himself up. He pretends to peer down inside, where the lodge fire is nearly out, and the fleshly fire is not yet lit.

He throws a mock leer at the crowd.

A hundred men laugh, propose toasts, stumble over bushes, and collapse onto the ground. Some head for the Shoshone tipis, seeking their own fun.

Inside, Sam and Meadowlark undress each other slowly. They look at each other with wonder. Sam takes her left hand, raises it to his lips, and kisses the gold ring. Then he tumbles her onto the buffalo robes.

Author's Note

BEAUTY FOR ASHES is the second novel of the Rendezvous Series, which tells the story of the fur trade in the American West during its glory years, from the early 1820s to the late 1830s. It is an adventure tale and a love story told against a background that is scrupulously re-searched.

Most of the characters around Sam Morgan are historical. William Ashley, Jedediah Smith, Jim Beckwourth, Tom Fitzpatrick, James Clyman, and many others are characterized as the record shows them.

Aside from Sam, the main fictional characters are the Crow characters, Gideon, Third Wing, and Micajah.

The fur trade, its conditions and circumstances, the landscape, the Indian peoples, and so on are also drawn carefully from the record. The struggles and subsequent success of the Ashley firm were just as suggested here. I have described the first and second rendezvous from accounts of men who were there. Ashley's instructions on how to find the meeting place (complete with "pealed trees"), for instance, is as he wrote it; Daniel Potts's letter telling his brother about the second rendezvous is what he actually penned.

My hope is to create, over the entire series, an authentic picture of a particularly splendid time in America, even more full of danger, conflict, wild possibility, villainy, cowardice, heroism, tragedy, and joy than most eras in American history.

A final note: Money was very different in the 1820s. A profit of $50,000 then may be the equivalent of a couple of million dollars now. The $1.50 a trapper paid for a pound of coffee was wages for a day or two back in the States.

Most of the unfamiliar words the mountain men use here are defined in the glossary in the first novel in the series, *So Wild a Dream*.

Acknowledgments

FOR THE MATERIAL on the Crow people, thanks to my friends among the Crows, especially the men of medicine, Larsen and Tyler Medicine Horse. I also relied on the bible about Crow culture, Robert Lowie's *The Crow Indians*. I have relied for the doings of the mountain men particularly on two fine books, Dale L. Morgan's *Jedediah Smith and the Opening of the West* and Fred R. Gowans's *Rocky Mountain Rendezvous*.

Thanks to Jan Blevins, Richard Hoyt, and others who provided crucial information.

My editor, Dale Walker, is a rock.

The Honorable Clyde Hall, man of medicine of the Shoshone people, has acted as my mentor for twenty years. Thank you, Clyde.